Bound for Canaan

STANDING ON THE PROMISES

A Trilogy of Historical Novels about Black Mormon Pioneers

BOOK TWO

Bound for Canaan

MARGARET BLAIR YOUNG
AND DARIUS AIDAN GRAY

BOOKCRAFT
SALT LAKE CITY, UTAH

Library of Congress Cataloging-in-Publication Data

Young, Margaret Blair
    Bound for Canaan / Margaret Blair Young and Darius Aidan Gray.
    p.   cm.   — (Standing on the promises ; v. 2)
    ISBN 1-57008-791-1 (hbk.)
    1. African American Pioneers—Fiction.   2. African American Mormons—Fiction.   3. Mormons—Fiction   4. Utah—Fiction.
I. Gray, Darius Aidan   II. Title

PS3575.O825 B68 2002
813'.54—dc21   2001006370

Printed in the United States of America   72082-6928
Publishers Press, Salt Lake City, UT

10 9 8 7 6 5 4 3 2

To the memory
of our friend and sister
Susie Mae Young Thomas
and to our friend and teacher
Eugene England
May their legacies of peace
and compassion live on
and continue to bless
and inspire

Standing on the promises of Christ my King,
Through eternal ages let His praises ring!
Glory in the highest I will shout and sing—
Standing on the promises of God,
Standing on the promises of God!

—R. KELSO CARTER, "STANDING ON THE PROMISES"

ACKNOWLEDGMENTS

We have received great help and much information from Ron Coleman, Joel A. Flake Jr., Joe Fretwell, William Hartley, Armand Mauss, Margery Taylor, and Henry Wolfinger, for which we are grateful. We are also indebted to Bruce W. Young for his careful attention to the details of documentation.

Authors' Note

The reader will notice different dialects in this book. We have used a deeper "black vernacular" for the speech of the Mississippi slaves and a more standardized vernacular for Elijah Abel and Jane Manning James. We have also included a few uses of the offensive epithet *nigger*, though (frankly) fewer than would have been used in the time these people lived. We have used that particular word with great care, usually in actual quotations.

The title of the book and all of the chapter titles are from traditional Negro spirituals. *Canaan* refers to the promised land.

PROLOGUE

I don't recommend you start reading this book until you've finished the first one. Otherwise, how will you know who Jane and
Isaac James were? Or Elijah Abel? I should warn you, this book gets
hard in parts. When we get to the hard parts, how will you understand the faith of these folks unless you've read about their trials?
How will you know how dear and difficult her religion was to Jane
Manning James unless you remember her eight-hundred-mile, barefoot walk from Connecticut to Nauvoo, not to mention her migration from Winter Quarters to the Salt Lake Valley? How will you
realize how much a Mormon temple meant to Elijah Abel unless
you know what he felt at Kirtland and how he loved Joseph Smith?
So I don't suggest you even turn the page until you know who you're
reading about.

But can't nobody control you from here, so I'll tell the easy facts:
Jane and Isaac James were free blacks, hoping they'd find Zion in
the Rocky Mountains, where the Latter-day Saints were settling.
Jane's brother Isaac Lewis (called "Lew" in these books, mostly to
avoid confusion) didn't make the westward trek from Nauvoo but
holed up in Missouri for a time—which was not the friendliest place
to be during the Civil War. Elijah Abel was one of the first converts

1

of color, a member of the Third Quorum of the Seventy in the Melchizedek Priesthood, ordained by Joseph Smith himself.

This book tells how all these Negro pioneers got along while this nation was bustling about, North hovering over South, South bucking like a mad mule, both sides forging guns and cannonballs, arguing over slavery, setting up for war, and then fighting until the Mason-Dixon Line got blotted out by blood.

Liz and Green Flake: Wedding Gifts

1

I WANT TO GO HOME

*For where your treasure is,
there will your heart be also.*
MATTHEW 6:21

She had another name once but couldn't recall it. It was a sweet name only her mama used. Mama had said it like a sad song, braiding her hair, whispering, "Massa say he goin' put you in his pocket. That pocket like to hold every one of us before long, and all we be doin' is jingle." Mama pulled hard to get the braids tight. "He actin' crazy. Why he want to sell off my baby for? What might you do, so young? Fetch and carry?" Mama finished the last braid. "If you was mine, I'd have you pluckin' flowers for the table. Nothin' but pluckin' flowers."

"I *is* yours!"

Mama turned her around and nodded. "Today you is." Tears made gold streaks down Mama's cheeks. "Some folk put young 'uns in the field where the cotton be taller'n they is. What they want with a baby anyhow?" The tears glistened. "I cain't recollect my mama's face, and I don't reckon you goin' recollect mine."

5

She did recollect it, though, even after she forgot her sweet name. She recollected her mama's weeping face, her mama's stretched-out arms, her mama's legs running to beat the band when the horses pulled the cart away.

As you know, that was the way the world worked for us colored folk back then. We had no choice in much of nothing and no lawful right to cling to our own kin.

Inside the cart, all she could do was cry herself to sleep atop the turnips and rutabagas. She and all these vegetables were being taken to Mizz Agnes Love's daddy, Massa William.

She recognized Massa William Love straight off. He was a tall, sharp-faced man with a plump belly, who had paid a visit to the old massa only a few days before.

At the Loves' big house, she got a new dress and a permanent name. The dress was stiff gingham, and the name was Elizabeth.

Of course, she was dressed so fancy not to pleasure her but because she was a gift for Mizz Agnes, whose wedding celebration was upcoming. The place was Anson, North Carolina, and the marriage date was October 2, 1838.

There sat Elizabeth, on a stair landing next to a black boy called Green. Her hair had been pomaded and combed into a knot at the back of her head. She was dressed in a yellow frock that matched the roses she was supposed to carry. Green was wearing a yellow shirt and brown suspenders, hitched to new pantaloons. The pants fit him tight. Seemed someone wanted to show off how big Green was. It appeared to Liz that he might bust out of those pants with one big step and stand embarrassed in front of all the white folks.

Looking like a matched set, these children could see everything from where they'd been told to wait.

Mizz Agnes's face was round and pale as a full moon. Her smile never quit her and appeared pained after a time. Her chestnut hair was styled in a whirl of side curls, and she was wearing white silk over a lace petticoat. The hem swayed whenever she took a step.

James Madison Flake was dandied up like he was a present too. He was bony and darker of skin and hair than his bride, though both of them were skinny as cornstalks. And they both appeared stiff, stunned, and scared to shed their smiles.

The table was decked out with full-lit candelabras, engraved pitchers, platters, and filigreed lantern bases. All the silver glinted. Chattering women in big skirts leaned to admire the display—and there was much to admire. That table was a sight! On one end were china plates and blue goblets so thin they'd fall over in a breeze. At the other end were patchwork quilts, Bible verses stitched in needlepoint, tatted doilies, lamps, and a portrait of an old man. Filling the spaces between these gifts were white persimmon blooms, sending out so much perfume the Negro gifts could smell it from the landing.

In the parlor, three women played violins. But their music quit when William Love took his place by the table and raised a hand to shush the crowd and the music. He began his speech: "We appreciate all y'all taking time to celebrate this day with Madison and Agnes, and we do thank you for starting off their married life with such generosity." Then he listed each gift and which family had given it. Whenever he named a gift as "From my good wife and myself," his voice got loud and happy.

Finally, after all the other presents had been acknowledged, Green was led to the table. Massa William put his hand on Green's shoulder. "From the plantation of Mr. and Mrs. Jordan Flake, a well-built Negro boy called Green."

Then Elizabeth was brought into the room and set beside Green. Mizz Agnes's daddy said in his deepest, proudest voice: "And finally from our family—from the Loves—a mannerable, healthy colored girl, named Elizabeth." The human gifts, who had been greased down for their presentation, shone in the candlelight almost as fine as the silver did.

Elizabeth Flake stood straight and looked pleasant as she had been instructed. Since leaving her mama, she had cried every day, but Mizzus Love had warned her that if she spilled so much as one tear to spoil this celebration, she would understand the limits of kindness. So Elizabeth had not dropped a single tear this evening, though she tore a mess of petals from her yellow bouquet. You understand, she had to keep her hands and mind occupied and hardly realized she had disrobed these blossoms until she saw the results: A few of the flowers were only spidery heads with no skirts at all.

Mizz Agnes was still wearing that tight smile, though she clearly noticed the naked blooms, for her eyes narrowed.

Elizabeth braced herself for whatever would happen, expecting no less than a slap. But no slap came. Massa William called out: "Y'all just enjoy this little party now. We thank you again for this fine beginning to our children's new life," and the guests applauded.

Agnes's brothers and sisters were all at the wedding. Three of them would die within five years, when cholera spread down river. Augustus Love would survive it. He was a copper-haired child and the first one to call her "Liz."

Massa Madison and Mizz Agnes started their family straight off. William Jordan Flake was born in 1839, followed the very next year by a brother, Charles Love Flake.

Soon after Charlie's birth, the Flakes moved from North Carolina to the wilds of Kemper County, Mississippi. There, Massa Madison bought prime bottomland suitable to cotton. He bought more slaves too. A woman named Edie was the first and came with four babies of her own. (Back then, Southern men thought themselves saintly if they purchased a slave woman's children with her. They got a bargain, too, right alongside their halo.)

Allen was the next slave Massa Madison purchased. He was a sullen, "griff" Negro who didn't care for conversation about anything. He wasn't even given to song. There was something about Allen always half-hid. He liked shade and sheds and wouldn't even carry a lantern when he went to the outback house at night. Such was his way. He didn't speak to the other slaves unless they spoke to him first, and he kept to himself after doing his fieldwork. He was a fit laborer, but his eyes showed numb grief.

Of course, it was many a slave who wore such eyes.

Before long, though, the white folks of this family would also show grief in every movement of eye or finger.

NOTES

The title of this chapter is from a traditional Negro spiritual cited in Higginson, "Negro Spirituals," 687.

The expression "Massa put you in his pocket" was used during slave times, as recalled by William Johnson, a former slave, who remembered, "Master used to say that if we didn't suit him he would put us in his pocket quick—meaning that he would sell us" (Johnson, *Soul by Soul*, 19).

That Liz Flake was given as a wedding gift to Agnes Love and James Madison Flake is documented in a variety of sources, though there is some difference of opinion about her age at the time. Osmer Flake claims Liz was about ten years old (*William J. Flake*, 2); Kate Carter (*Negro Pioneer*, 19) and Joel A. Flake Jr. ("Green Flake," 3) both set her age at five. The 1860 San Bernardino census (as cited in Fretwell, Miscellaneous Family Papers, 13) lists her as age twenty-six, which would mean she had been born in 1834. If that date is accurate, she might not have reached even her fifth birthday when she was sold away from her first home and given as a wedding gift.

Green was most likely ten years old when he was given to the young Flake couple, though he still legally belonged to James Madison Flake's father, Jordan, who deeded Green to his son in his will (Flake, "Green Flake," 4). Though Carol Read Flake claims Liz was a gift from the Flakes (*Of Pioneers and Prophets*, 48), Joel A. Flake Jr. suggests that the Loves had made her their present to Agnes ("Green Flake," 3).

That James Madison Flake was likely referred to as "Madison" is suggested by Osmer Flake's biography of his father, William J. Flake, which recalls Osmer's personal interview with one of his grandfather's old slaves: "After looking me over and over, with her hand up over her eyes, she said to me, 'Is you really a grand-son of Madison Flake what joined de Mormons and went to de Debel?'" (*William J. Flake*, 4). Fretwell's interview with Green Flake's descendant Bertha Udell, however, records that Green Flake referred to his master as "James" (Miscellaneous Family Papers, 9). We have chosen to use

"Madison" to avoid confusion with all the "Jameses" (Isaac and Jane) in this novel.

Mississippi had become the nation's biggest cotton producer by 1840. As Oshinsky states: "Mississippi experienced an explosive population growth . . . as white farmers from Georgia and the Carolinas left their worn-out plots for the fertile lands and deep river highways of the 'Old Southwest.' . . . Black slaves compris[ed] more than half of its 375,000 people. The great bulk of whites were rough back country folk, well armed, fiercely democratic, deeply sensitive to insults and signs of disrespect" (*Worse than Slavery*, 3).

Griff denotes a brownish black color. The term was used in the nineteenth century to describe the "offspring of a 'Negro' and a 'mulatto'" (Johnson, *Soul by Soul*, 139, 256 n. 10).

2

JESUS WITH US

*Jesus answered and said, . . . Are ye able to drink
of the cup that I shall drink of, and to be baptized
with the baptism that I am baptized with?*
MATTHEW 20:22

Life changed direction for all the Flakes—Negroes and whites
alike—in the winter of 1843. That was when a stranger stopped by,
a Bible in his hands.

By this time, Liz was almost a teenager. She knew the ways of
the household better than Mizz Agnes did. Liz tended the children
and performed every chore assigned her, getting slapped only occasionally for being "lazy." She kept herself clean, combed, and
aproned and looked the part of a well-maintained household slave
when she answered the door on a particular rainy evening.

Before her stood a tall fellow with a dimpled chin and blue-
blood fingers. He was wearing a top hat, but it hadn't done much
good on this day. The weather had found its way to his hair just fine.
Water was dripping down his temples and past his ears.

"Is your massa or mizzus in?" He removed the hat and shook it.

A good amount of water spritzed the porch plants, and Liz had to step back to avoid getting hit in the eye with his raindrops.

"You have business with 'em, sir?"

"My name is Elder Benjamin Clapp. I'm a preacher."

"Is my massa 'spectin' you?"

"I'm sure he'll welcome me in."

"I hate to make you wait in this rain, sir."

"It's only a drizzle now. Your massa's name is—"

"Mister James Madison Flake. I hope you won't object to waitin' just a moment whilst I fetch him."

Massa Madison came to the door directly. After a brief conversation, he invited the visitor inside, calling for Green (in the slave quarters) to attend to the man's horse. Southern hospitality did not leave gentlemen or their horses alone to cope with rainy evenings.

Madison Flake led Benjamin Clapp to the fireplace, asking Liz to bring them coffee and a second lamp. She could hear them talking about the weather and general news of the day. But it was clear Elder Clapp had another focus. The moment Liz returned with the coffee service and lamp, Clapp was opening his saddlebag and bringing out a book. He called it the Book of Mormon and said—easy as a comment on the weather—that one of God's angels had conveyed it into a modern prophet's hands.

"Coffee, sir?" Liz offered the guest.

"Just set it on the table if you would," he answered.

Massa's posture showed polite resistance to this man. The Flakes were Methodists. Though they were open to discussions of religion, the idea of angels handing books over to everyday folks was not something Madison Flake would include in serious conversation. At least not the Madison Flake Liz knew. He said, "I'll have a cup, Liz. This is a cold night, and I'm sure the coffee will warm me. Mister Clapp, from the looks of things, you could use a sip. Why don't we delay this discussion until you're warm and dry?"

Benjamin Clapp answered fast. "As you might imagine, I would

not venture out on such a night if I didn't have something of impor-
tance to share. I appreciate a good cup as much as the next man, but
my purpose here is not to find a drink."

The massa glanced up at Liz. "I think you have just made the
perfect cup, girl. Hot enough to surprise the mouth but not to
scorch it."

"And it sho' is a cold night," she offered.

The two-Bible man was not about to surrender his subject. "The
message of this book—"

"Try your coffee, Mister Clapp," interrupted Madison. "It would
be a pity to let it cool when this girl has found its perfect temperature. Would you care for sugar?"

"No sugar, thank you, and I do appreciate your hospitality." He
drank a swallow and acknowledged, "Indeed, the girl has made a
fine cup."

Madison smiled. "What more can I offer? You must be hungry.
How long have you been on that horse?"

"I don't eat after sundown. And my horse is not a bad ride. I am
quite accustomed."

"Perhaps you aren't accustomed to the way Mississippi brews her
storms. Mississippi skies take no time at all to open their clouds and
rain pitchforks on a man's head."

Benjamin Clapp palmed his wet hair from his face. "The storm
did startle me. God heard my prayers, though. I saw your boy carrying a lantern past your window."

"Green?"

"No, he was a black boy. The one who hitched my animal to
your post."

Now Madison laughed full. "That's Green. And you possess a
fine sense of humor, sir."

Elder Clapp did not smile. There was unbending purpose in his
eyes and voice. "Now if I may continue what I was saying—"

Massa Madison stood. The preacher stood too, set to leave if that's what was to be. But Madison did not show him the door. He faced the fire and then faced Clapp. "Tell me why God should have need of a book other than the Bible."

The preacher clasped his hands behind his back, pleased and ready to answer questions all night long. "Don't we need God speaking to us today?"

Madison made the thoughtful frown Liz knew well. This was the frown that could mean Green was going to get a kick in the pants or it could mean Madison had just discovered an idea worth announcing. Or it could mean both—that Madison had just discovered the idea that Green required a kick in the pants. "Doesn't the Bible speak to us?" he asked. "Has its message lost its savor?"

This Clapp fellow was an earnest one. His words came urgent: "The Bible is as full and rich as ever it was. But it isn't the only word God has given to man. This other book," he said, holding it up, "contains the records of a people who were in the New World. Now, we know God is no respecter of persons—that's in the Bible. We know he cares about all of his creations."

"The Lord knows about the fall of every sparrow," Massa Madison said. "And about the lilies of the field."

"I see you are a Bible-reading man."

Massa squinted at his visitor. Of course he was a Bible-reading man! What Southern gentleman wasn't? "But angels bringing books? Sir, you appear to be an educated person!"

"I have had adequate book learning, yes."

"From books God's angels have delivered?" Massa was pushing now. Liz had seen him do this on occasion. He tended to get the best of his opponent too.

"Only one of those books, sir," answered Benjamin Clapp in a church-fit voice. "The one I'm holding now."

Massa raised his brows. This was part of the push. "And you believe angels fly to earth with books in their wings?"

"Sir, I frankly do not believe angels have wings."

Massa sat down with his legs loosely sprawled. He laughed hearty. "Many artists will be disappointed to hear you say so. Some of their best work must be relegated to the cellar, I'm afraid."

Elder Clapp sat too, his legs together and his hands folded around the book on his lap. Without even the hint of a smile, he said, "I have always thought our cellars neglected."

"Oh? So you approve of putting winged angels next to a store of potatoes and carrots?"

"I have always approved of gold wings. Why, none of us knows what Jesus Christ looked like. Artists depict the Lord according to their own visions."

"That is true." Massa Madison drew his legs into a more dignified pose. This conversation was about to take a serious turn, that was plain. Both men were leaning towards each other, Benjamin Clapp holding the angel's Bible.

"I do believe angels exist," Clapp said, "just as I believe the Lord lived—and lives yet. I more than believe it. I bear witness of it."

Massa fidgeted, but when he spoke, there was no mocking in his tone. He was not pushing now. "Have you ever seen an angel?"

Standing ready to offer more coffee, Liz bent forward to hear the reply. It didn't come for a moment.

"No sir, I have not."

Liz had hoped for some stories—true or not—about how angels worked and how they dressed. Did they wear clouds? Or were they so bright it wouldn't matter if their bodies were naked? Did they even have bodies? Like most of us, Liz loved a good tale.

Massa shrugged. "In that case, I must say I have you, Mister Clapp. For I've seen an angel—without wings."

Liz bent forward again—too far, for the pitcher spilled three drops of coffee on the pine floor. Massa glanced at the drops but continued, "Indeed I have seen a wingless angel. In fact, I married her." He turned to Liz. "Why don't you fetch that particular angel, girl? This conversation might be of some interest to her. And I believe you are in need of a cloth just now, aren't you? That coffee will stain the wood."

Mizz Agnes had been listening at the door and was ready to be presented.

Soon Elder Clapp was a regular guest at mealtimes, and Massa Madison was asking questions and reading both Bibles. Then he and Mizz Agnes up and joined the religion Elder Clapp was peddling. They walked down the path toward the pond one chilly afternoon and came back soaked to the bone. Liz squealed, "You'll both catch yo' deaths!" and ran for blankets.

Massa answered, "We have just been baptized Latter-day Saints. We have no intention of catching anything but what God sends our way. And that we'll catch with joy."

Not long after the Flakes joined the Latter-day Saints, a fellow named John Brown accompanied Ben Clapp to the plantation. Brown was a wide-mouthed, blue-eyed man with hair just past his ears, wearing a homespun suit he had long outgrown. When he spoke, though, nobody paid mind to how bad his suit fit. There was weight in his words, and even the slaves were invited to listen.

John Brown taught that everybody, including Green Flake, was a member of a family, and one day Green would meet his mother, his brothers and sisters, and all his family members. "In our Father's house are many mansions," Brown told them—and there was a place for colored folks too. There was a Heavenly Father who would accept Green Flake and all the rest of the Flakes' Negroes into his kingdom.

I don't know if you can imagine what such good news meant to a slave. As a child, Green had been kept away from his mama and told he was an orphan. He wasn't sure if he believed his mama had really died, though. Another slave said she knew his mama. She told him that she and another woman nursed him, but so did his own mother. Green was sure he had brothers and sisters too, for he recollected growing up with other colored children. He remembered being cared for by different women in the Negro quarters before he got gifted to the Flakes. He thought maybe he was kept from knowing about his mama, because if they loved each other too much, then when one got sold off, they both might pine and worry and maybe run away. So the idea that he could know his mama in a heavenly house, and know his brothers and sisters too, came as the sweetest tidings he had heard in his life.

Both Allen and Green decided to get baptized.

Green was fifteen at that time but big as a buck deer. Allen was a skinny one, though strong in the arms from his fieldwork. They went under the waters at Mormon Springs (that's what Benjamin Clapp had renamed the pond) with no fight at all. Allen had no comment, but Green said he liked his new believings.

The same day Green and Allen got baptized, John Brown put his hands on Massa Madison's head and made him an elder in the Latter-day Saints' church. He said, "You hold the priesthood now, brother."

Green Flake wouldn't have minded holding a bit of priesthood himself, he told Liz. A man with priesthood could heal the sick, command fig trees to wither, and direct devils into the fat bodies of pigs. At least, that's what John Brown had given him to understand.

Liz hadn't got herself baptized and didn't care to hold such dangerous magic, even if it was real. But she sure did think that if Green Flake got the priesthood and it worked like he said, he'd change her into a slug just out of mischief. So she was relieved when John Brown announced that the priesthood wasn't for slaves.

But who could guess what the Almighty had in store?

Notes

The chapter title is from a traditional Negro spiritual cited in Higginson, "Negro Spirituals," 689.

The record of the Flakes' conversion to The Church of Jesus Christ of Latter-day Saints is recorded in various Flake family histories, including Osmer Flake's *William J. Flake*, 3–5, and Carol Read Flake's *Of Pioneers and Prophets*, 45.

In the early days of the Church, Latter-day Saints drank tea and coffee. The Word of Wisdom, which forbids the use of "hot drinks" (D&C 89:9), interpreted as black tea and coffee, was originally given "not by commandment or constraint" (v. 2) and was not strictly enforced for many years.

The description of Green's longing for family is from Fretwell's interview with Green's descendant Bertha Udell (Miscellaneous Family Papers, 9): "Green said that the reason why they kept him from his mother or family was because if they love one another too much, if one was sold they could pine and worry so much . . . they could run away and search for each other. The masters didn't want to lose a valuable slave, so he would set mean dogs after them and whipped [them] when they were caught. That is why Green Flake was kept away from his mother and told he was an orphan." On page 5 of the Fretwell interview, Udell says: "It was the masters and slave owners who said [Green's] mother had died. . . . As a child, he grew up with other colored children about his own age and he was cared for by different women in the Negro Quarters. They were given plenty to eat, did their assigned chores, and learned to fear and respect all white folks. He remembers getting his first whipping for [not] acting quickly enough when the White Man spoke. He learned early that he was a slave."

The description of John Brown as "tall and thin with a wide mouth . . . wearing a homespun suit, which he had definitely outgrown" is from Carter, *Treasures of Pioneer History*, 5:214–15.

John Brown's journal records that he baptized "two black men, Allen and Green, belonging to Brother Flake" and ordained James Madison Flake (and Washington Cook) elders on April 7, 1844 (Brown, *Autobiography*, 46).

3

DEEP RIVER

In me ye might have peace.
In the world ye shall have tribulation:
but be of good cheer; I have overcome the world.
JOHN 16:33

What the Almighty seemed to have in store for the Flakes first off was tribulation. Mizz Agnes's and Massa Madison's relations—the Loves and the Flakes and all the aunts, uncles, and cousins in between—shunned them after they took on this new religion. When three of Agnes's brothers died from cholera that same year, the Loves declared God had sent the Death Angel to punish their daughter's disgrace. They were not about to speak to Agnes again—not while Charles, Richmond, and Thomas Love were sleeping in their graves. The Loves would not receive Agnes's messages, so they never knew how many days and nights she wept over her brothers, wailing their names and asking her husband, "Why would God take them?"

Madison couldn't answer any better than the rest of us would, using words like, "God's ways are mysteries."

During these fits of grief, Agnes took to her bed. Liz cared for her, wiping her brow with a damp cloth and fetching her cups of water and the chamber pot when it was called for. Agnes's skin grew so pale it looked almost blue, and her cheeks were brick-red. She was a woman given to blushing, but this fiery blush refused to cool.

Throughout these ugly-sick days, Agnes spoke to Liz in ways she never had before. She asked in a soft, needy voice: "What do you think of our new faith?"

Liz knew to answer with comfort. "You cain't feel bad about gettin' 'ligion."

"We've always had religion," whispered Agnes. "You didn't want to get baptized. Why not?"

"I jus' have a fear of water, ma'am."

"I know you believe in Jesus."

"Oh my, yes! Where would I be without the Lord?"

"Do you feel the Lord's Spirit in this household—since we joined the Latter-day Saints?"

Liz considered this a moment and then spoke the truth: "Ma'am, I do."

"Have I ever treated you unkindly?"

Now, Liz could have recited a number of incidents that sure had felt unkind—sudden slaps or sharp words her mizzus had given. But she didn't feel inclined to mention such, not at this moment. "You always be a good woman, Mizz Agnes."

"My mama says my brothers died because of—"

"I knows what she say. But Mizz Agnes, I cain't believe God work schemes like that. Yo' brothers—they passed to they reward because it was time! And I think they was happy to go. That cholera be so wicked—oh, I seen it work!—I reckon they was grateful when the Lord finally called 'em. Ma'am, you got to believe in the Lord even when it be hard goin'."

Agnes clasped Liz's hand. "I do believe." But Liz could tell there was something more the mizzus wanted, so she waited until the words came: "Liz, would you do something for me? It may sound

strange. I want you to pray. On your knees. I've seen you pray over
dirty clothes and sick dogs. You talk to the Lord like he was right
here all the time. I've heard you."

"I didn't 'spect I was so loud."

"Madison and I pray more on a schedule. Before we retire at
night. Before we eat our meals."

"And you make fine prayers too."

"You talk to the Lord as if he's beside you all the time."

"I don't know how I learnt such. From my mama, I reckon."

"Have you ever talked to the Lord about me?"

Liz didn't want to reply to that question in full, for she sure had
talked to Jesus about Mizz Agnes Love Flake, asking the good Lord
to work his ways into the mizzus's heart so it wouldn't get so fussy
and mad when all Liz was doing was her best. She answered soft and
safe, "I prays for you all the time."

"Say one I can hear, then."

"Right now?"

"Please. Now."

So Liz got down on her knees, and she prayed. "Lord, you know
what it be to lose someone you love. And you know Mizz Agnes's
pain at this time. She done lose three of her brothers, and every one
was like her own baby. Especially little Tommy. Remember, Lord,
how Tommy was runnin' all over the place when Mizz Agnes and
Massa Madison got theyself married? My, my, I remember it like yesterday! And when Mizz Agnes and the massa leave North Carolina
for this here place in Mississippi, poor Tommy cry him a river, and
Mizz Agnes cry so much herself, seemed her eyes spent all they
water. Now ain't it enough pain to have Tommy underground without havin' Mizz Agnes's people blamin' her for it? You knows, Lord,
how it be to have someone you love turn against you. Jesus, you got
sold, Lord, by one who say he love you. You got sold and lifted up
and nailed on that cross. Now Mizz Agnes, she bearin' her own cross
at this time, and even the ones she love, they turnin' they backs on

her. So she need yo' comfort, Lord Jesus. Let her know it ain't her brought about the passin' of them boys. Let her know she ain't committed no crime for believin' in you and in them Bibles. Let her repose in the bosom of your mercy. We ask it in your name, Lord Jesus. Amen."

"Amen." Agnes tapped Liz's hand and said, "You must finish your work now."

Of course, Liz wasn't the only one who prayed for the mizzus. The poor massa was scared his wife might not survive her fever, so he blessed her by the power of this priesthood he held, setting his hands on her head and whispering words of consolation, as well as a few scriptures. Sometimes, a blessing was the only way Agnes could find any respite from tears.

But the Love family up North Carolina did not receive such blessings or much ease. They reported to their own slaves that Madison and Agnes Flake—with all their Negroes too—were going straight to the devil.

Where they decided on going, though, was Nauvoo, Illinois, the gathering place of the Latter-day Saints. They made this decision when Mizz Agnes finally felt up to another move.

Madison journeyed just with Green at first, riding muleback through Tennessee and then taking a steamboat to St. Louis and finally to Joseph Smith's city.

Though Nauvoo had started out looking like a marshland a pack of devils might enjoy, by the time Madison and Green got there, it was a fine place. Its inhabitants were poor but all made of sturdy stock. It seemed not a one of them was half-tugged in this Mormon faith. They had drained the swamps around Nauvoo, built up their industries and houses—some large brick structures and some simple cabins—and were constructing a grand temple in honor of the Lord. Steamboats blasted their horns down the Mississippi River, and most roads led to water full of lily pads, cattails, and wet grass. It was a city smelling of smoke, brine, hot metal, and rich mud. Both massa and slave liked what they found. Madison even met Joseph and Hyrum Smith and got himself a patriarchal blessing under Hyrum's hands—just three weeks before the Smith brothers took the killing bullets at Carthage Jail.

Green stayed in Nauvoo to build the Flakes a house, while Madison returned to Mississippi for his family. He aimed to move them all, black and white, to the gathering place. Allen didn't join them, but Liz did. Mormon or not, Liz was attached to the family— to Mizz Agnes in particular—and somewhat afraid that with them gone, she might have to start a less good life. Maybe she'd get claimed by a mean and wily massa. Now that she was near woman, she would surely be required to do more than care for babies and polish silver. Under another massa, she might find herself bent over short cotton for the rest of her days. Or worse. A trek to what James Madison Flake called "The City Beautiful" did sound more favorable. Besides, Liz loved the new baby girl Mizz Agnes had birthed— little Sarah.

Edie started towards Nauvoo, having been convinced to leave her own children behind with the Flakes' property, which was to be sold complete with its Negroes. But within two days, mother-love overtook her. She could not go on without her babies. Massa accompanied her back to Mississippi and bought him more supplies at St. Louis.

Well, the house Green built was solid, but it couldn't keep death and danger out. Two more Flake babies, Thomas and Richmond, were born and then passed on. It fell to Liz to wash and dress those little bodies. It was the saddest thing she'd done since leaving her own mama.

Baby Samuel Flake was born in Nauvoo too, and he didn't seem strong. Sammy's body looked like the product of dismal days—gray in the flesh and unable to make much cry. Liz knew this child wouldn't last, though she didn't share her knowings with the mizzus.

In June 1846, the Flake family and their slaves left Nauvoo with a good many Mormons fleeing mob persecution. I can say where they went and how long it took to get there, but you just imagine the shock of their sudden poverty; the toil required of all hands and arms, not just the colored ones; the knee-deep mud; the constant repair of wagon wheels and tarps; the chopping up of trees for fuel and bridge making; the smelly blacksmiths' fires with aproned men pounding out horseshoes and sometimes melting lead for bullets.

At last they crossed the Missouri, went to Cold Spring Camp, and then to Cutler's Park. By October 1846, they began settling in dugouts at Winter Quarters.

Such poor shelter did little to fend off icy winds. Sammy got weaker.

Mizz Agnes could not prepare herself to lose another child. She kept saying he was looking better, like if she said it enough, it'd turn true. He was smiling more, she claimed, and even making some laughs.

Liz agreed with her to keep the peace, but she was not surprised to find him sleeping the long sleep one frosty morning. She woke Mizz Agnes with the words, "Ma'am, little Sammy got called back to Jesus."

Agnes would not believe it until she saw the body herself. Then she took to her bed again, where she lay for two weeks, moaning and fevered once more.

Liz laid Sammy out, and Madison bought a windowed coffin where the baby's face could show until the first dirt was cast.

The next child Mizz Agnes birthed—Frederick—died too, directly after he was born. Mizz Agnes was so weak, she just couldn't bring out a strong child. For a time, it seemed sure she was headed to Jesus herself.

Liz carried her soup and tea and sometimes sang to her. Agnes enjoyed the Mormon hymns, but she especially liked the songs Liz remembered from her sweet-name days, and most especially one that went—

And I couldn't hear nobody pray.
O way down yonder by myself,
I couldn't hear nobody pray.
In de valley
I couldn't hear nobody pray.
On my knees,
I couldn't hear nobody pray.
With my burden
I couldn't hear nobody pray.
O way down yonder by myself
I couldn't hear nobody pray.

Mizz Agnes tried to sing with her, but her voice wasn't much beyond a warble even on a good day.

Oh, these were mournful times indeed, times that might have made other folk turn their backs on this new religion and settle for something easy. The Flakes were not ones to turn tail on their promises, though. Agnes got out of bed four weeks after Frederick died. In the moonlight, wearing her long, white nightdress, her hair falling unbound to her hips and her feet bare, she looked like an angel set to take a starry walk to heaven. Liz leapt up from the wagon box and ran to her, saying, "Ma'am, what you doin' out here?"

Agnes had her eyes fixed on a particular group of stars. The sky was all aglitter. She lifted both arms and said, "Lord, I am ready to walk where you tell me."

Well, Liz wouldn't have been surprised if clouds had unfolded that moment and made a chariot for this white sufferer. The night was that magical and the mizzus that close to the other side of glory.

No chariots appeared, though, and no invitations came from on high. All they could see earthwards of the stars were many campfires blazing. All they could hear were folks mending their wagon wheels and forging tools.

It wasn't until later that Liz realized what she had seen in her mizzus that night—the change that had come on her. Frail and pale though she was, Mizz Agnes Love Flake had found some fire in her soul, some mettle in her bones.

NOTES

The chapter title is from a traditional Negro spiritual found in Burleigh, *Spirituals*, 74.

The James Madison Flake family was disowned by both the Loves and the Flakes upon their conversion (Flake, *William J. Flake*, 4). Insight into that event may be found in the death dates of Agnes Love Flake's brothers, which were very near the time of the James Madison Flake family's conversion. Charles, born in 1823, died in 1844, as did Thomas, born in 1827. Richmond Love, born in 1821 (just two years after Agnes), died in 1845. It is likely that a common disease of the day claimed these three lives, but the timing of their deaths may suggest why the Love family might have been particularly bitter towards Agnes for her conversion. (Information on the deaths of Agnes's brothers is from Family Search File.)

Osmer Flake's biography of William J. Flake records the dates of the Flakes' departure from Nauvoo: "They crossed the Missouri in February 1846" and at Winter Quarters "lived in a dug-out during the winter of 1846 and 1847" (*William J. Flake*, 7–8). Historian William Hartley suggests different dates, which we have chosen as the more reliable: "Saints reached the Missouri in June [1846], and began crossing July 1st, went to Cold Spring Camp, then Cutler's Park, and finally began settling in Winter Quarters only in October 1846" (personal communication, August 1, 2001). Hartley also cites Patty Session's diary notation of November 3, 1846, which records payment to the midwife of two dollars, "no doubt for helping with delivery of a baby" (personal communication, August 1, 2001). It is certainly possible that this baby was Frederick Flake. Both Osmer Flake and William Hartley would place the Flakes at Winter Quarters during the winter of 1846. Other sources place them there the winter of 1847 as well.

Though some Flake biographies claim the Flakes freed all their slaves upon joining the Church, we consider this unlikely, because Green and Liz were certainly considered slaves and treated as such (see notes to chapter 7, page 68).

Carol Read Flake records the deaths of the Flake babies: "Thomas passed away sometime during that year of 1844. . . . A second little brother, Richmond, died [in Nauvoo], and another brother, Samuel, was born. . . . [In

Winter Quarters] little Frederick Flake was born—and died, the same day" (*Of Pioneers and Prophets*, 48–49). Samuel's death is recorded in Family Search File.

The traditional Negro spiritual "Couldn't Hear Nobody Pray" is found in Burleigh, *Spirituals*, 83.

4

LET US CHEER THE WEARY TRAVELER

*Henceforth I call you not servants . . . but I have
called you friends; for all things that I have heard of
my Father I have made known unto you.*
JOHN 15:15

There would soon be other colored folks at Winter Quarters, as the pioneers knew it. Green Flake prepared the dugout the family would live in, with straw for a roof, cloth for a door, and a willow fence surrounding it. Meanwhile, Jane and Isaac James with their sons, Sylvester and Silas, were making their way toward this temporary dwelling place of the Saints. They arrived in October too, though somewhat later than the Flakes.

Jane was outside the George Dykes family's wagon. She had given birth to Silas four months before and was holding him in one arm, stirring a pot of thin soup with the other. Liz approached and started conversating straight off: "Good evenin'. How's ever'body?"

Jane James turned to the voice. The question on her face moved into a smile. "Lord be praised! For a second, I thought you was my sister Sarah. Only you're too young. Been awhile since I seen one of us. I'm Jane James." It wasn't just a handshake Jane offered but a big hug.

"My name's Lizzy Flake, and I be happy to stand in for yo' sister. She nearby?"

"I wish she was." Jane gave her a quick kiss on the cheek. "No, she stayed put. In Illinois."

"I guess you miss her."

"Especially when I see somebody remindin' me of her, such as yourself."

Liz took a whiff of what Jane was cooking. "Anything I can help with? I'd be pleased to hold yo' baby and free up that arm."

"Mind you, keep the blanket 'round his neck." Jane passed Silas to her. "It's powerful chilly since the sun dropped."

Liz held the child close and commenced bounce-rocking him. "My mizzus had a good many chil'ren. Only three be left now. I cared for ever' one."

Jane raised her brows. "Three left of how many?"

"Four little babies done pass. I loved ever' one like they was my own."

"I see motherin' comes natural to you. You bounce my baby just the way I do. Next thing you know, he'll be sleepin'.'"

"He halfway there already. He sho' is pretty. Remind me of Samuel. That's one of Mizz Agnes' boys what passed on."

"You care to join us for supper?" Jane asked.

Liz smiled and sighed. "Wish I could, but I gots to do cookin' of my own. I belongs to the Flakes. We been here awhile."

"What you cookin' tonight? It might be better than what I got here. The meat in this soup's so tough, you got to chew it ten times to swallow it once."

Liz laughed. "So who you with?"

"Oh, I'm freeborn. From Connecticut. But we travelin' to Zion with the George Dykes family. They white."

Liz gasped at the news that this black woman was free. "You the first free coloreds I ever done met," she said. "Is they other folk with you, besides yo' baby? I don't mean to get personal, but you got a man?"

"My husband's Isaac. I have another son too, name of Sylvester."

Silas was gone to slumber now, breathing happy. "Is your family Mormons?"

"Oh yes."

"I wonder if they be other free coloreds with the Mormons."

"I heard of one," said Jane. "Elijah Abel. You know him?"

"The name don't bring nothin' to mind."

"Him and my husband got acquainted back in Nauvoo. Elder Abel was a friend of Brother Joseph Smith's. Ordained in the priesthood by the prophet hisself."

Now Liz was truly stunned. "What you say? A Negro got the priesthood? And you and yo' family free? My, this Mormon religion more than I thought! Wish I had the time to talk to you 'bout it, but I gots to get my own cookin' started. Oh, I could hold yo' baby forever." She handed Silas to his mother. "Maybe we can talk this evenin' after I get my chores did," Liz suggested.

"I'll be lookin' for you later tonight, then," said Jane.

Well, Liz did her chores as fast as she could, but Mizz Agnes wasn't ready to dismiss her after the work was done and didn't take kindly to Liz holding conversation with free Negroes. Such talk might give her ideas. So it was several days before Liz could return to the Jameses. Agnes gave her leave for just a few minutes away from the wagon—and only after supper was done and all the children sleeping.

When Liz approached, Isaac James was beside his wife, looking up at the stars. They were both about the same height, though Isaac was rounder in the jaw and flatter in the nose.

Liz called out, "How y'all? Pretty night, ain't it?"

Jane hugged her. "Isaac, meet my friend I tol' you about. This is Lizzy Flake."

"Hello, Lizzy," he said.

"Sorry I couldn't get back till tonight," Liz said. "The mizzus keep thinkin' up new work for me."

Isaac knew all about how that happened and assured her no apology was called for. "Pleased to make your acquaintance," he said. "We just gazin' at the glories of God."

"Ain't them stars somethin'?" Liz said. "A whole sea o' sparkle."

"Trail for the angels," Isaac said. "That's what it be. Shows where they been a-walkin'. Every time a angel take a step, some of his shine fall to the ground. That's what make the stars. The biggest angels drops the biggest shines. From the looks of things, I'd say some giants been walkin' that sky."

"I never knowed they was giant angels," Liz said.

"Oh yes," Isaac said. "Sometimes their halos falls off too. That's when you sees a string of light. They usually grabs it quick, so the string don't last long."

"I never heard such," said Liz. "Does all Mormons believe it?"

"Only the best ones," Isaac said. "The mos' faithful ones."

Jane hit her husband's arm. "You forgive my man, Lizzy. He makin' up stories all the time. He got stories in his blood."

"Oh." Liz nodded like she understood, though she didn't. She still wondered about angels dropping starlight and how a person could get stories in their blood but asked another question instead: "You freeborn too, Mister James?"

"Free now."

"And you holds the Mormon power?"

"Priesthood? No," he laughed, "not me. My friend, Elijah Abel, he hold it fine."

"Well, why don't you hold it too?"

He shrugged. "I just never asked for it, I guess. I was hopin' Elijah'd be here already."

"Ain't heard tale o' his comin'," Liz said. "First I hear of him be what yo' wife say—that this Elder Abel be a friend to that Mormon prophet."

"She tol' you that?"

"Ain't it true?"

"Hah! And she say I got stories in *my* blood! Let me tell you, if my Janey get cut, her blood starts in babblin' all over the place. You never seen or heard the like."

"Talkin' blood?" Liz's whole face was amazed.

Jane tried not to bust out laughing. "Isaac, don't you go makin' this girl a fool. 'Tain't right, especially since you jus' met her."

Isaac patted Liz's head like a daddy would. "Maybe that's enough for one evenin'. Yes, Elijah Abel and Joseph Smith was friends. More like they was brothers. Prophet had him other colored folks too, you know—and not for slaves. Prophet hated slavery. He had colored folks for friends. Janey likely ain't told you I myself was Brother Joseph's good friend. One of his best, if I do say it. I knowed him even longer than Elijah did. Why, I can't count the times Brother Joseph would clap my shoulder and say some compliment about me."

"Now I ain't full sure what to believe," Liz said.

"Or did Jane mention she lived right there in the Mansion House alongside Brother Joseph? Smiths wanted to adopt her as their own child in their own family."

"Now that can't be so."

Jane gave the sweetest, truest smile Liz could imagine. "It is so."

"Lord have mercy!" It was a good thing Liz had nothing in her arms, for she would have dropped it right then.

Jane testified strong, so there could be no doubt. "I lived in his place, washed all his clothes. He always treated me like I was his own child. And yes, him and Emma both wanted to adopt me, but I said no."

"Ain't that somethin'! How about them other white folk? They treat you good?"

Jane put her hands on her hips and arched her back, looking content but weary. "Ain't none of us Mormon folk been treated all that good, though I'd guess the colored ones catch the most heat— and sometimes comin' from all directions."

"These be ticklish times," said Liz.

"Worse than ticklish. Worse'n mean," Isaac added.

"But you got the spirit and the faith—both of you. You keep on steppin' forwards, no matter what."

Jane shrugged. "We just coax the Lord to keep us sweet till the trump of doom. Ain't that so, Isaac?"

"Exactly so," he said.

"Seem to me the Lord done answer yo' prayer." Liz lifted her eyes to the stars once more. She wanted to believe that story about the angels, for this night spread a show of glitter such as we rarely behold. An occasional star leapt from its place and peeled away a strip of night. She wanted to believe it was a halo rolling down heaven's street and some angel child was chasing after it. Like I said, Lizzy always enjoyed a good story.

All three of these colored pioneers gazed at the heavens a long while, until Liz knew it was time to return to the Flakes.

Before long, a few other Negroes joined them at Winter Quarters. She imagined all the coloreds would become fast friends, being in the same fix and of the same hue. But everybody got so busy with their own folk that there was no time to visit.

Winter came early and fierce. It was a cold that crawled through blankets, through skin, and straight to the bone. There was about as much burying as praying and so much to do that the Negroes hardly had a moment to weep together, even when some of their own died from the cold. Liz waved to Jane from a distance, but they never had much chance to pursue their first conversations or really learn about each other.

NOTES

The chapter title is from a traditional Negro spiritual found in Burleigh, *Spirituals*, 176.

The James family arrived in Winter Quarters in October 1846 and departed in June 1847 (being there at the same time as the Flakes, who were also there from 1846 to 1847), so we may conjecture the likelihood of their becoming acquainted with other camp members of color. Jane's life story says: "When Brother Brigham left Nauvoo I went to live at Brother Cahoon's. In the spring of 1846 I left Nauvoo to come to this great and glorious valley. We traveled as far as Winter Quarters [and] there we stayed until spring" (Wolfinger, "Test of Faith," in *Social Accommodation*, 151–57).

The description of a typical dugout "with straw over the top for a roof, a cloth door, no windows and a willow fence around the dugout" is from Sarah Doney Hatch's reminiscences, quoted in Hanks, *Blossom*, 36.

The
Mississippi
Saints

5

SHIP OF ZION

I trust I shall shortly see thee, and we shall
speak face to face. Peace be to thee.
Our friends salute thee.
3 JOHN 1:14

In April 1847, Green Flake went on ahead as a trailblazer and
one of three "colored servants" with the very first Mormon pioneers
to open a settlement in the Rocky Mountains.

Liz never imagined she'd feel so lonesome without him. There
was no romance between them, but they had known each other
since that day when they stood shoulder to shoulder amidst all the
other wedding gifts. After Green departed, she was one lonely child.
Besides that, several of Green's chores fell to her, and there were
only a few other Negroes to keep her company.

Shortly thereafter—mid-June, to be specific—Jane and Isaac
James with their sons joined the Ira Eldridge Company in heading
towards the Rockies. So Liz was pretty much alone to represent our
race at Winter Quarters.

That's why May 27, 1848, was a day of gladness. Eleven wagons
arrived, led by that same blue-eyed John Brown who had baptized

Green and Allen, conferred the priesthood on Massa Madison, and arranged for the Jameses to keep under the Dykeses' shelter.

Brown had already done much exploring in the west. (A ridiculous amount, if you want my opinion.) He and a few others had made their way to Pueblo, Colorado, before any other Mormon cast an eye on a single peak of the Rockies. After that adventure, he went all the way back to Winter Quarters and then even farther back to Mississippi, where he picked a few men (including several Negroes) to join the advance company headed west. Two of the Negroes died before they got far, but two others—Oscar Crosby and Hark Lay—joined Green Flake in that historic trek. They were among the first Mormon pioneers to view for real the valley Brigham Young had seen in vision.

Believe it or not, John Brown returned South yet again after that journey to fetch the rest of his folks and bring them along. On April 16, 1848, he met up with other Mississippi Saints, who had gotten as far as St. Louis, Missouri. Of course, he guided them all westward like there was nothing to it. By the time they reached Winter Quarters in May, the Mississippi Company of Saints of 1848 had traveled some seven hundred miles by land and another two hundred by water—though their leader had gone many times that distance.

With the Mississippians' arrival, the population of Winter Quarters increased by fifty-six white persons, thirty-four colored persons, twenty-eight wagons, forty-one yoke of oxen, twenty-two horses, thirty-two mules, forty-eight cows, one hundred sheep, and two pigs.

Now, it may seem to you that John Brown went to a lot of trouble and travel to lead these folks, but you must understand that many of the Mississippi Saints were his wife's people. You see, John Brown had converted a widow named Elizabeth Crosby to the Latter-day Saint church and then married her daughter Betsy. When Mizz Elizabeth became Mormon, her son and most of her daughters entered the waters after her example—as did a good number of their slaves. First baptized was Elizabeth's son William, who owned Oscar and Grief. (Oscar, you recall, went in the lead company alongside Green Flake.) Also converted were Elizabeth's daughters and their husbands: Sytha and Billy Lay with their slaves, Hark (who likewise journeyed with Oscar and Green), Henderson, and Knelt; Nancy and John Bankhead with their eleven slaves, including Nate and Nancy Banks and George and Sam Bankhead; and Ann and Daniel Thomas, with their slave Toby.

Widow Crosby brought three women slaves who knew midwifing better than most whites. Vilate was her personal maid and helped birth children, both black and white. She was the mother of Hark Lay, as well as of Rose and Martha Crosby. Vilate was a strong woman, though she had a withered arm from her early slave days when one of her massas plunged it in boiling water to teach her a lesson.

In that same company were Robert and Rebecca Smith with ten slaves, three of whom would become Liz Flake's best friends in this world: Hannah, Biddy, and Biddy's daughter Ellen.

When the white folks took to visiting amongst themselves, the slaves got acquainted too. Before long, they had some news to chew on: A man called Mr. Cook had accidentally shot hisself dead. He had leaned over to pick something up when his pistol fell out of his pocket and fired. He took the ball in his neck and then ran to the campfire, where he fell down, crying, "Oh, Lord!" Death claimed him fast.

Biddy Smith and Liz Flake talked of it as they gathered greens for supper, making bowls of their aprons.

Liz opened the conversation: "Wasn't it a shame about Mr. Cook?"

"I heard enough of that last night," said Biddy. "Henderson couldn't talk of nothin' else."

"Sad way to die," said Liz.

"Stupid way," Biddy said.

"At least he didn't leave no wife to mourn him." Liz glanced at Biddy, who was old enough to be her mama. "You belong to the Smiths all your life?"

"I be the best wedding gift they ever got. Every other thing they was give is broke or lost by now. I's all what be left." Biddy had hefty arms and fleshy cheeks. She was a sturdy-built woman. It was no surprise she'd survived past all the other presents.

"Ain't that somethin'?" said Liz. "I was a weddin' gift too. I was a gift from the Loves. Don't that sound nice—bein' a gift from the Loves?"

"If that's what you want to think." Biddy's voice didn't care one whit.

A pond spread out before them. The ripples had caught the sunset and shimmered gold. It was a beautiful sight, and Liz was taking it all in when a good-sized toad leapt from nowhere to a mossy rock. Biddy said, "Hold my greens whilst I nab that critter."

"There was a family of freeborn coloreds in this camp, you know that? You heard of Jane James?" Liz set the greens in her apron dish.

"Onlyest folks I met is from Miss'ippi."

"Jane got her two sons. Prettiest babies you ever seed. They set out for the new place last summer."

"Mizz Sytha Lay set to birth her a child any day now. Boiled toad help a woman's bosom commence its milk," Biddy said, and straightway she chased and caught that toad.

"I ain't never heard that one," Liz murmured. The toad's throat pulsed in Biddy's hand, and its legs kicked.

"Time you learned. You may need it someday. Secrets to healin' got passed on to me straight from Africa."

"All the way from Africa?"

"Down the slave line. I got healin' gifts. Now, I give you the recipe, so open your ears: You boils down four toads and keep the water. You adds you a slab of butter and some arnica tincture. That concoction help everything from bad blood to caked milk."

"Sound like it sure would have some effect."

"Mighty healin' effect. I use it myself." Biddy had three daughters: Ellen, Ann, and Harriet. Harriet was still a suckling babe, so Liz wondered if Biddy might be eating toad soup herself that night.

"I learns new ways by the hour," Liz said. "And I sees new sights. The James folks, they the first freeborn coloreds I seen since all my days. Like I say, they be headed west. Probably arrived already. I reckon we won't be makin' that journey ourself for some while."

"I reckon you right."

"So how old you be, Biddy?"

Biddy made a quick motion with her hands to kill the toad. "How old you thinks?" She dropped the dead critter into her dress pocket.

"My mama say my old massa was goin' put me in his pocket, same you did that toad."

"You was never in no danger, girl. A dead toad got some use, but a dead nigger can't work."

"You remember yo' mama?"

"Some." Biddy had spied another toad, a smaller one, and was ready to snatch it up too.

"I remember my mama a little. She call me by a pretty name, but I cain't recollect it."

"Name don' matter."

"All the same, I wish I might remember."

"Honey, it don' matter." Biddy squatted down and leapt forward, like a toad herself. Liz had not expected such a motion and yelled out, "What!"

"Now why you scream for?" Biddy stood and set her fists on her hips. "You near scare that toad outta my reach!"

"I didn't intend no harm. I cause you to lose that critter, didn't I!"

Grinning, Biddy opened her hand to show the little toad. "When I sets my mind to something, I never comes up short. Even if some girl be screamin'." Biddy bit the toad's neck, snapping it clean.

"Hope that taste better than it look," said Liz.

"Ain't about taste or looks. Jus' somethin' need doin'. You awful tender-minded, ain't ya?"

"Maybe."

"Well, I is too, at times. Sometimes I sees poor, starvin' folk— even some of them Indians—and I want with all my heart to give them better than they got."

"You ain't likely to get means for such as that. No slave gettin' any kind of means."

"Not without the hand o' God, that fo' sho'."

They started back to the wagons. This was a marshy place, though they had camped on the dry parts.

"The Smiths, they treat you good?" Liz asked.

"Depend on what you calls 'good.' I got me a child by Robert Smith. He got two children by Hannah besides."

Liz drew in a breath and let out the word "Oh." She asked if Ellen was Massa Robert's too.

"We all his property," Biddy answered. "Bought and paid for. Do Ellen come from him, you askin'? No. But Smith do visit on occasion. His mizzus don't like it, but she jus' keep her eyes closed."

What amazed Liz was how easy Biddy was walking. Biddy's steps were cat-quiet, while Liz's every step sounded like the earth was trying to suck out her soul. Seemed Liz always found the wet places where her bare feet would sink and the mud squish up between her toes. Biddy's feet found every dry spot there was.

"Sure a shame about Mr. Cook," Liz said.

"Honey, it's always a shame to die stupid. If you goin' die, you'd best die for somethin' good."

The next Wednesday, Mizz Sytha Lay birthed a son. Biddy

Smith had the toad potion all ready, but Sytha would have nothing to do with it. And though Biddy had been efficient and cold in killing toads, she was gentle as could be with Mizz Sytha. There was powerful tenderness in her, and she couldn't hide it.

NOTES

The chapter title is from a traditional Negro spiritual cited in Higginson, "Negro Spirituals," 691.

Osmer Flake suggests that Green was included in the advance pioneer company headed for the Salt Lake Valley because "[Brigham Young] needed the very best teams and outfits to be had. James M. Flake, who had put his all upon the altar, sent his slave, Green, with the mules and mountain carriage, to help the company to their destination" (*William J. Flake*, 9).

That John Brown had something to do with the Jameses' stay with the George Parker Dykes family seems likely, because Brown had much to do with the "colored" pioneers and Dykes had taught and baptized him (Brown, *Autobiography*, 17).

John Brown's journal records that the Mississippi Saints were reunited in late May 1848 (a number of them had gone to Utah and Colorado during 1846 and 1847) and that the Flakes, Browns, and Crosbys had a good visit on Sunday, May 28, near Winter Quarters (Brown, *Autobiography*, 97). Elizabeth Crosby's daughter Susan remained in Mississippi until her old age, when she joined the Church and journeyed to Utah.

The Mississippi company, which joined the Flakes in May, included the following: John Powell, Moses Powell, Robert Smith with ten slaves, John Lockhart, George Bankhead, John Bankhead with five slaves, John D. Holladay, Frances McKown with two slaves, William H. Lay with two slaves, Elizabeth Crosby with three slaves, John Brown with one slave (his other slave, Henry, having died at Winter Quarters during Brown's previous journey, as mentioned in *One More River to Cross*, 289; Carter, *Negro Pioneer*, 8), William Crosby, and Ekles Truly (Brown, *Autobiography*, 96). The numbers of white and black persons and the various animals are also from Brown, *Autobiography*, 88.

Arrington's "Mississippi Mormons" gives some sense of John Brown's extensive travels.

Most of the names and relationships of the Crosby slaves (including those with Lay, Bankhead, and Brown surnames) are from Kohler, *Southern Grace*, 63.

Vilate Crosby, mother of Rose Crosby, Hark Lay, Oscar Crosby, and Martha Vilate Crosby, was, according to Fretwell's interview with Udell (Miscellaneous Family Papers, 9), "one of the women chosen to be in the 'Crosby's Breeding Farm.' The Crosby Master practiced selective breeding on his plantation so that healthy and strong slaves could be produced, so he could sell them for profit. A strong, healthy slave fetched a good price."

That Vilate Crosby had a withered arm from a master's abuse (immersing it in boiling water) is from Taylor's research (personal interview).

According to Hayden, "Biddy's daughter, Ellen, was born Oct. 15, 1838, when Biddy was twenty; her second, Ann, about six years later; and her third, Harriet, four years later" ("Biddy Mason's Los Angeles," 88).

The details of John Cook's accidental suicide are recorded in Brown, *Autobiography*, 97.

The toad-juice cure for caked breasts is midwife folklore noted in Arrington, "Pioneer Midwives," 47.

That Biddy Smith had at least one child and possibly three by her master, Robert M. Smith, is suggested by Hayden, "Biddy Mason's Los Angeles," 90. Indeed, several sources indicate that Robert Smith had children by both Biddy and Hannah. According to Mills, an expert on the California Mormon pioneers of color, however, Biddy's descendants state that Smith fathered children only by Hannah, not Biddy (personal interview, July 19, 2001). The claim that he used at least one of his slaves in such a way is consistent in all sources.

Biddy's training in healing arts from Africa is commented on by Hayden, who states: "Biddy Mason's medical knowledge was no doubt the result of training by older midwives and slave doctors on the plantation where she grew up. . . . Many slave doctors knew African, Caribbean, and American southern herbal medicines" ("Biddy Mason's Los Angeles," 92–93).

Elijah and
Mary Ann Abel
1848

6

WE'LL SOON BE FREE

*Though I have the gift of prophecy, and understand all
mysteries, . . . and though I have all faith, . . .
and have not charity, I am nothing.*
1 CORINTHIANS 13:2

While the Southern Saints endured the chill of Winter
Quarters and celebrated the first blade of spring grass, Elijah and
Mary Ann Abel were meeting their own challenges and finding
their own joys in Cincinnati. They were a family now, with their
new baby, Moroni. Elijah had built them a fine house and found
more work than he could do alone. Tolerable pay too. There was a
good-size community of free Negroes there, and social life was full.
Elijah felt blessed, though he was aware that some Mormons were
wary of them, in part because of the sayings of that half-Indian, half-
Negro fellow, Pete McCary.

Black Pete had come to town and set up his own religion, which
he claimed was nothing more nor less than what Joseph Smith had
preached.

Unfortunately, McCary was crazy to the bone.

Well, Elijah knew from the get-go that Black Pete was no

prophet. Elijah had been in the presence of a real prophet and felt the power of God breathing under all that prophet's sayings. The power of God was so warm and so joyful, it woke you full up, from your tallest hair to your longest toenail.

Black Pete didn't bring any such power with him. Elijah visited McCary once, but halfway through the conversation, Pete insisted on speaking in tongues. All Elijah heard was gibberish and bluster, and he doubted the Lord ever had been this man's teacher. Black Pete appeared to get revelation from his own stomach rumblings.

McCary finally left Cincinnati, but the damage was done. Another ex-Mormon, a white fellow named Charles Thompson, started in preaching. Somewhere along the line, Black Pete and Thompson must have had a fight, for Thompson was soon saying more than gospel words; he was spouting hateful things about Negro people in general. He said we wasn't even human but a race apart, called the Nachash, whose forefather seduced Eve into eating that forbidden fruit.

Mary Ann claimed the white folks at Church stared at them more than usual after Charles Thompson came on the scene. "You may have stature," she said to her husband, "but they turn they eyes away the instant they sees me."

Elijah answered, "From what I observe, you turn away first. You hide yourself like a groundhog in its hole! Folks are probably concerned you'll run away if they cast an eye your direction. You powerful shy, and you know it."

"Maybe so, but I can make out what these folks be feelin' toward me."

It didn't take long for Elijah to suggest that since they were not going to change religion, they'd likely find better welcome among the Saints out west. Folks in Deseret knew him. They knew how respected he had been in Kirtland and Nauvoo and how loved by the Prophet. Cincinnati was a fine place, but Elijah thought they should journey west—unless the Lord instructed otherwise. He was thinking that very thought one June night, even making plans, when a knock interrupted.

A slump-shouldered colored man stood staring at him when Elijah answered the door. "You 'Lijah?" he asked.

"I am." He held the lamp up. "Do I know you?"

"Friend of a friend—Mister Levi Coffin send me yo' way."

At those words, Elijah pulled him inside, telling Mary Ann to check the curtains.

That cabin had but one window—and it wasn't even what you might call a window. There was no glass, just thin animal skin oiled down so you could see light through it. Mary Ann's curtains were two flour sacks strung on twine which was wrapped around two pegs. With little Moroni in her arms, she moved quick and made sure the curtains overlapped.

Elijah set this runaway in the fireplace chair. Mary Ann lit another lamp.

Mary Ann had seen slaves but never one in such a state. Thorns and twigs poked from his outgrown hair. His face was sweaty; his clothes were damp and tattered. And by the light of this second lamp and the low fire, the Abels could see the wounds around the man's ankles.

"You been shackled," Elijah stated. "Those irons done damage."

"Mister Coffin work with my ankles some, but they get worse over the past day, and catchers be circlin' the Coffins' place like buzzards." His ankle bone showed through a veil of grey flesh. The stink was bad. Some of the wounds on his left ankle had gone to green death.

"Get a charcoal poultice together," Elijah instructed his wife. "He need the poison pulled out. And fetch me that shallow wash pail too."

Mary Ann went outside, Moroni in one arm, a lamp in the other, an empty bucket hanging from her wrist. She returned shortly with the bucket full but tarried only long enough to make the poultice and give it to her husband. Then she toted their baby back to the open. She needed air.

Elijah wet two rags in the kettle water. "We have to do some doctorin', and it might hurt some. Maybe I should know what you called before we start."

"Amos Luther."

"Amos, you got a bad infection. Needs to be dug out. Poultice alone won't do. We got to give the herbs some live flesh. I can't say how painful it'll be, but I'm willin' to tend to it.

"I'd be grateful."

Elijah took his knife to the wound. "You holler if this hurts too much—only it'd be best if you holler soft."

"I cain't feel nothin'."

"Where you from, Amos?" Elijah was slicing into the dead flesh now, though from the easy tone of his voice, you might've thought he was slicing bread at a meal.

"Kentuck, outside o' Falmouth—on the Tenney farm. I been on the run four or five days. Got slowed down with the fetters. Mister Coffin was my last stop 'fore you."

"Where was Mister Coffin? I ain't seen him in months."

"Outside a place called Covington, down the Lickin' River. He give me how to find you. Sent a message."

"You doin' all right, Amos? Ain't my intent to cause you pain."

"You doin' what needs doin'."

"You say Coffin sent me a message?"

"Mister Coffin say time come for you to help."

Elijah stopped picking with the knife. He gave a solemn nod. "Brother, I am ready to do what I can." He started digging again and deeper, still talking calm. "This your first try on escape?"

"My second. Massa was set to sell me. Chained me up for the block."

"So you been on the run near a week."

"I been hidin' in every bush or bog I come across. Country pretty flat here. Sleepin' by day, runnin' by night."

"I know. I remember."

"You a runaway too?"

"Ran with my mama and brothers out of Maryland. Went to the Lion's Paw."

Amos grabbed Elijah's wrist. "You done that?"

"Yes I did. Now, you got to leave off my wrist so's I can work. This painin' you yet?"

"No sir." He released his grip. "Cain't feel nothin' below my knees."

"Ain't that a blessin'! You know I got no choice but to grub into this infection."

"I so sorry for the smell. Such foul smell."

Elijah burrowed. The mushy flesh sluffed off easy. He wiped the wounds with his cloth, putting the dead skin into the washpail of water, where it floated. It was the color and texture of grits gone bad. "No need to apologize, Amos."

"Foul smell. Foul!"

"I can't object to doin' something the Lord himself would do, or smellin' something the Lord would smell." Finally, Elijah set down his knife. Pressing the poultice into the cavity he had dug, he tied it to Amos's ankle. "That tolerable?"

"Like I say, I cain't feel."

Elijah gave a dim smile. "You eat today, Amos? There's some leftover stew with corncakes from supper."

"I 'preciate it. Right hungry."

Elijah dished him the last of the stew with three corn cakes and a cup of water. "After you eat," he said, "you needs to be restin'. You take the bed. My wife and me can sleep fine on the floor."

"No sir, I cain't take yo' bed." Mister Luther spoke strong. But not as strong as Elder Abel, who announced, "We ain't discussin' it.

Those legs of yours needs to be put up, and that'd best be done on the bed."

"I hate to—"

"I know your feet ain't workin' good, but I think your ears work fine. You'll be sleepin' on the bed. That's all there is to it, Amos."

Elijah dumped the pail out back, where Mary Ann was walking Moroni.

"You done in there?" she asked.

He nodded. "Moroni sleepin'?"

"Yes. Honey, you mind washin' your hands before you touch either one of us?"

"I plan on washin' before I touch my own self, Mrs. Abel." He took the soap from the laundry bucket to prove his intent and cleaned up thorough.

Mary Ann whispered, "'Lijah, we don't know this man."

"We know enough. He one of us. A runaway like I was." He glanced over his shoulder at her.

"He look all wild."

"He been runnin'."

"I can't guess what kind of past he got."

"Ain't ours to guess. Just ours to help."

"Could be wanted by the law."

"Woman," said Elijah, "he *is* wanted by the law."

Amos Luther slept on the rope bed that night. Moroni was in the cradle his daddy had crafted from walnut. Elijah and Mary Ann took their slumber on the floor.

Some hours after Amos's breathing got heavy, Mary Ann jerked her head towards the door. "Listen," she hissed.

Inside a yawn, Elijah asked her, "Why ain't you sleepin'?"

"Listen! Can't you hear 'em?"

"Who?"

"Them dogs!"

He lay still a long moment. "Them be the dogs we hear ever' night. You just lettin' worry get hold of you."

"What if we gets caught?"

He sat up. He was always one to take command of a situation and preach a sentence or two if possible. "Quakers risked their lives for me and my family."

"It's one thing if a white man gets caught. It's another for colored. 'Lijah, I love your neck unbroke."

He ran his fingers over his Adam's apple. "I like it unbroke myself. But I need you to understand one thing, now: I can't turn my back on a runaway. I know what it's like to be alone. Fearful, runnin' for freedom. I can't—and I won't—turn my back."

"So this ain't likely the last time."

Elijah lifted his eyes to Amos. "I hate slavery. I hate the laws that nurse it. No, I reckon this won't be the last time."

"Thought we was movin' west."

"The good Lord sent me a messenger to say time ain't come as yet. And the good Lord will send another to say when."

Elijah lay back down. Since he was in charge of this family, the conversation had just ended.

It was a full week before Amos was healed enough for Elijah to direct him north, taking him in a skiff up the river. By this time, Elijah had razor-cut Amos's hair and given him good clothes. The two could've passed for brothers, both of them lean, their cheeks shiny brown globes, their eyebrows thick.

Mary Ann had been a fine caregiver, though she hadn't spoke much to Mister Luther. But she came to understand the need and wouldn't complain at the prospect of other hungry guests dropping by or of having a lit lantern in their window to identify this safe haven.

Walking Amos to the skiff, Elijah told him something of his religion. They had talked about the Lord and how Jesus surely wanted all his children free. They had talked about slavery, and

Elijah had told the tale of his own escape. But he had not mentioned his Mormon religion at much length. He did now. He said, "Amos, you must know you be named for a prophet."

Amos scratched his head. "Ain't never heard that."

"Ain't you? Why, Amos is right there in the Bible. Fine, fine prophet."

"Is that a fact?"

"Fact indeed. And I believe in prophets. I believe God talks to his servants on this earth."

"Well, I believe that too."

"I been fortunate in my life, for I knowed a real prophet. Not just a name in the Bible but a flesh and blood prophet."

Amos stopped in his tracks. "How you knowed a prophet?"

"Name of Joseph Smith. He's passed on now. Got murdered, actually. But before he departed this life, he gifted me a great blessing. Maybe it weren't so much a gift as a door he opened. Brother Joseph had power direct from Lord Jesus himself. And Brother Joseph laid his hands on my head and gave me some of that power. Priesthood power. I got it in my hands now."

Amos's gaze lingered on Elijah's fingers. "I don' see nothin'."

"Ain't nothin' to see. It be *inside* my hands."

"How's that work? You can start fires with yo' fingers? Somethin' like that?"

Elijah chuckled. "Likely could, but I wouldn't unless it was called for. Priesthood ain't for showin', just for blessin'. See that river?"

"Sure does." The arm of the Ohio was still as a sheet, and moonlight danced on it.

"Priesthood be like a river from God to man—a river of power come down from heaven like a waterfall you can't see."

"Do it sound like a river too?"

"No, not usually. It be quiet power. When I use the priesthood,

I feels my head and hands get warm, like God's sending sun through my body. Then I speak whatever words God give me."

"God give you what words you say?"

"That's right. And I want to bless you before we get in that skiff. Now, I know this land is boggy, but I want you kneelin' on this grass. You jus' let me use the power of God to call angels from their places. I plan on directin' them angels to hover near you."

Amos knelt and Elijah laid his hands on this runaway's head and said in the name of Jesus, "I call down angels to surround you and guard your every step to freedom, just like they done mine."

Of course, the blessing was somewhat longer than that, but those were the words that most touched Amos Luther, and he was touched to tears when he rose up. He was wiping his eyes as they continued to the skiff.

Though this was considered safe country, both knew there could be catchers on the other side of the water, waiting with new shackles and old hounds. Neither spoke until they hit shoreline.

There Amos Luther said, "I cain't thank you, but if ever I gets the chance, you will find me grateful."

Elijah Abel nodded as his passenger stepped onto land. They both could see a lantern light in the distance. That was where the next conductor waited.

Elijah sure was right about Amos being the first of many runaway slaves the Abels would help. Mary Ann's fear flattened some as time wore on, so the sound of whistles or dogs didn't make her heart leap. But whenever she saw her husband come in the door after a "trip," she embraced him like a new bride.

The underground system was getting more sophisticated all the time. Before long, there were songs to help fugitive slaves north— songs you may have heard of, like "Follow the Drinking Gourd." That one in particular instructed runaways to keep an eye on the Big Dipper's handle. It pointed to the North Star. And they were to follow the trail of dead trees, where conductors had carved peg-legged figures. Soon there were secret handshakes and knocks as well. Elijah learned all he needed to.

Someday, the Abel family would go west and gather with the other Latter-day Saints, who were meeting their own trials and making their own paths.

But not just yet.

NOTES

The chapter title is from a traditional Negro spiritual cited in Higginson, "Negro Spirituals," 692.

There are various spellings of Elijah Abel (often *Able*) and of his son Moroni (usually *Maroni*) in the historical documents. The spellings we have used are simply our preference.

The 1860 census records Moroni Abel as being twelve during that year, thus having been born in 1848.

That "Black Pete" (William) McCary was in Cincinnati from 1846 to 1847 (before going to Winter Quarters, where he was rejected as a false prophet) is documented in Bringhurst, "Changing Status," 135. McCary's association with Charles B. Thompson, who had originally followed the Strangites, is documented in Bringhurst, "Charles B. Thompson and the Issues of Slavery and Race." According to Thompson's theories, the Lord "set a mark upon the seed of Cain, that they might be known in all generations. . . . Enoch the son of Cain [was] disinherited of the rights of priesthood by the sin of his father" (qtd. in Bringhurst, "Charles B. Thompson," 40). Thompson's reasoning included the idea that Cain "took a wife from the 'fugitive Nachash' or 'vagabond race'" (Bringhurst, "Charles B. Thompson," 41). Although we do not know if Elijah Abel had association with these two men, we do know that they were all in Cincinnati at the same time and all had some Mormon connection. It is not much of a stretch to imagine some interaction.

Saints to Zion

7

GO IN THE
WILDERNESS

Go ye therefore into the highways,
and as many as ye shall find,
bid to the marriage.
MATTHEW 22:9

After Green Flake finished his trailblazing job and built a cabin for the Flake family in the Valley of the Great Salt Lake, he returned to Winter Quarters—retraced all those steps—to guide his owners to it. It was dusk when Liz saw him fresh arrived, though he didn't smell fresh at all. She ran and leapt into his arms, crying, "Thank God, thank God. You made it safe. And my! You done filled out and growed to a proper man!"

Green swung her around in the air. "Well, little sister," he said, "the Lord ain't been so kind to you. You still a skinny child. How old is you now?"

"You know my age," she giggled. "And I knows you be dead tired."

"I won't lie to you. They ain't words for how tired I be."

"'Least you can rest up now. And there's a good cause for you to get some shut-eye. There be fine lookin' girls done join us. They ought to see yo' face when it be awake, not this half-dead man."

"What girls? You teasin' me?"

"I never would tease you, Green!"

"Then the times has changed indeed."

"You might trust me better. The Crosbys been here two months and brought all they slaves. Another Miss'ippi family come too with a whole mess of colored women. You got some pickin' and choosin' ahead o' you."

Green stretched his arms and yawned. "That sound like a good thought to wake me up after a night's slumber. You tryin' to marry me off?"

"I'd be so relieved to get you off my hands, I'd make your weddin' hat myself."

He sat himself down on a stump. "I jus' bet you would. And it'd fall down over my eyes."

Having Green back again made Liz jumpy with joy. She was bouncing on her toes all the time they were talking. "Like I say, you might trust me better."

"I might? Well, I be pleased to let you earn that trust by feedin' me a hearty supper. Right now, I'd best report to Massa Madison, let him know what's waitin' on the trail. You go on and spoon me up whatever you got cookin' while I talk to him. You know I be back fast and hungry." He stood and stretched himself again.

It wasn't a fancy supper—potatoes and salt pork—but it contented Green fine, and it contented Liz to watch him enjoy it.

The next morning, he saw Rose and Martha Crobsy. Sure enough, they were lookers, both of them, and he had to ask Liz more about them. He knew the Crosby families but hadn't had much chance to view their girls. And even if he had, times had changed them all by now. These was women.

"They belongs to Mizzus Crosby. They mama be Vilate," Liz told him.

"They both available?"

"All three 'vailable. If you takes a fancy to older woman, Vilate need her a man too."

He rubbed his head, which was gritty with trail dust. "Is that a fact? Maybe I'd best look over the whole countryside before settlin' on my acre."

"You want me to go plant some seeds on your behalf? Make yo' introductions?"

"I can plant them particular seeds myself, girl. Just decidin' on where."

Liz hitched her chin towards the Crosby women. "Tall one named Martha, 'cept white folks calls her whatever come to mind. I heard her called Louise, Liz, Hazel. Sometime I think they just can't keep us straight. You could probably say any name in yo' head and she'd look yo' direction."

"And the other one?"

"You likes her better? She ain't near so pretty as Martha. That be Rose."

"Jus' one name?"

"Jus' one."

Green rolled his shoulders, arched his back, and fanned his fingers like a preening turkey. He had him some dense muscles, worth showing off. "Well, I thinks a little walk around might be in order," he said.

Liz giggled. "I knowed you'd come to that."

"And I knows you knowed." He strolled his way to the Smiths and the Crosbys, making introductions and taking in the most agreeable sights.

It was another two weeks before these Southern Saints started their journey towards the Valley of the Great Salt Lake. Green was not quite ready for the toil of this upcoming trek, but he knew what lay ahead—which was more than the other pioneers could say, except for John Brown. But this walk would be different. By now, Green knew all about the company he'd be keeping.

The Mississippi Saints got divided into three groups, headed by Amasa Lyman, Willard Richards, and John Brown. All together, there were five hundred and two white folk, twenty-four of us colored, one hundred and sixty-nine wagons, fifty horses, twenty mules, five hundred and fifteen oxen—and many other animals. If you think about it, the journey was like Old Noah's, only with wagons instead of a boat. These folks herded their flocks over dry land as well as water. Biddy Smith and Liz Flake were two of the herders and gave chase to mules and horses, ducks and turkeys, and whatever wild critter scampered onto the path.

Green Flake, along with the other men, was called upon to do every needful thing, including fashioning bridges and fixing wagon wheels. He got to fix more than a few wheels on that journey, and at least one of them was a prayed-for break. You see, Betsy Crosby Brown, set to birth a child, prayed for some kind of miracle so's she could labor in a place that didn't roll and bounce every minute of the day. The good Lord answered her prayer, and the wagon wheel broke directly.

Now Green didn't much care for the white folks praying toil on him, but he understood Mizz Betsy's need. The womenfolk were all grateful to the Lord for having mercy on Betsy, while the menfolk were grumbling about their own labor. Betsy finally birthed a son, and the journey continued.

Many companies had gone ahead and seen the sights awaiting these travelers: waves of bearded buffalo, occasional Indian scouts, endless prairie with tufts of yellow grass or scorched stubble, jutting rocks of many shapes and hues, and then ranges of steep-cliffed mountains. Green was proud to announce what sort of landscape lay ahead and what trials waited between the travelers and morning. He derived pleasure in describing the first buffalo calf he ever laid eyes on, which resembled something between a goat and a big,

ugly dog. He told his tales to a number of the Saints, black and white, though before long, he chose one particular audience: Mizz Martha Crosby.

By the time he took serious note of her, Green was nineteen years old and near two hundred pounds. He was strong in every way and strong-willed enough that William Crosby accused him of being saucy to his owner.

He may well have been saucy in Crosby's mind. In those times, we was considered saucy if we so much as paused before answering a white man's order. But even though Green could get bought and sold like an ox, he saw himself as a man. He had helped to clear the path for these pioneers and held the reins of the very wagon wherein Brigham Young lay sick with fever, when the Saints first entered the Valley. Probably Green Flake's ears had been among the first to hear Brother Brigham declare, "This is the right place. Drive on."

He reported all this to Martha, and she relished hearing it. She considered that when a white man called a Negro "saucy," it really meant "bold." Green was bold, for sure, and brave too. And he was the strongest man Martha—or just about anyone else—had ever seen.

The white pioneers' accomplishments were already becoming legends, but the contributions of coloreds were seldom acknowledged. Well, Martha's heart acknowledged every good thing Green had ever done, even if she didn't know about it yet.

Martha's sister, Rose, esteemed Green like he was half god. Who knows why women get so competitive over men, but it sure does happen. Rose was likely the chief reason Martha told Green before they held much conversation at all that she'd be willing to marry him, should he feel so inclined.

Green said he'd think on it, as it wasn't every day a woman proposed marriage.

Martha was pretty, no question of that. She was the color of rich bottomland after rainfall. Seemed she had brought the best of Mississippi with her. Her hair was braided neat, and her lashes were so long, Green was afraid they'd blind her if she blinked too much. Hers was a proud face too. She kept her chin high. Green admired the way she carried herself.

When the wagon train stopped and moved into its evening circle by the Platte, he suggested they both carry themselves towards the bluffs, searching out grass where the cattle might graze. They might also find game to make a meal, so he took his gun—an old flintlock—with him.

Now, it may surprise you that the Mormons let a slave carry a gun, but it says something about how much Green was trusted. Nobody distrusted a slave who would travel two months and then come back to guide his owners to their destination.

The country was rocks and hills now, with an occasional cliff. It was near a place called Deer Creek, a spot bears might enjoy. No surprise that Martha was nervous about what size meal they could encounter. As far as any bear might be concerned, Martha would make a sizeable meal herself.

In the timbers, they saw another pioneer—laid out cold under a tree. Green knew him as Homer Duncan and shook him awake.

When Homer sat up, he demanded the gun, so Green gave it, not knowing that Duncan had smacked into a tree only moments ago while trying to get clear of a grizzly. As Green and Martha watched, Duncan ran back to where his dog had distracted the grizzly by nipping it in the ham. There was that huge, hump-backed animal. The little dog that wouldn't even make a mouth-ful for a grizzly was pestering it still, darting in and out like a horsefly.

Martha yelled "Bear!" the instant Duncan leveled the gun and fired. The grizzly leapt seven feet into the air and then ran in circles before falling over dead.

Homer Duncan returned the weapon, nodded once, and made his way back to camp.

"Oh my," Martha managed. She stood staring at the grizzly. "You might think I's strange, but I pity that bear." Her eyes filled with tears that moved Green's whole soul. There was something awful pretty in a tender woman's tears.

"Better see it like that than standin' on the hind legs growlin'."

"I hates to see it suffer. I hates to see most anything suffer."

"That's because you got a softhearted nature. But girl, a grizzly's bad. Wily as a snake in the grass. You follow grizzly tracks, and you thinks you just about to find him. Then you looks over yo' shoulder and there he be, claws set to rip off yo' face."

"Green, don' you be scarin' me now."

"Hush," he said. "You hear that?"

"What?" she breathed.

"Behind you!" he yelled, loud as he could. "A big one!"

Just as that mischievous rascal had known she would, Martha screamed and jumped. If he'd been ten inches closer, she would've jumped straight into his arms. He wished he had planned his joke ten inches better.

Green Flake was given to laughs, belly shakers every one, and he let loose a laugh so hard he had to sit down.

Martha warned Green not to do that again or she might run away.

He answered true—he'd been hoping she'd jump into his arms, and he wasn't sure he could resist a joke if such might be the result. Besides which, he told her, he was fast on his feet. Should she attempt running, he'd catch her no problem.

She smiled love's sweet, silly smile as they started back towards camp. He had her heart, and she didn't want it back.

"Wasn't nothin' behind you 'cept a big tree," Green said. "If it had been a grizzly—well. Such a pretty face as you got, I sure don' want it tore off by no bear. I'd have to kill that bear first, no matter how big it be. Kill it with my hands, if I had to."

"I think you would at that. Mighty gen'rous of you."

"Because I don' want your face tore off?"

"Because you thinks it be pretty." At this moment, she was setting her face on display best she could.

"Oh, I can't lie about somethin' so important. And you sure got fine eyes for weepin'."

"Does I?" She stopped walking and stepped towards him.

Now Green Flake wasn't stupid. He knew an invitation when he saw one, so he stopped walking too. She tilted her chin up, and he kissed her long. Seemed he didn't need to scare her into a thing.

"You like the name 'Martha Flake'?" he said afterwards, his mouth still puckered.

"You aimin' to make yo'self permanent with me?"

"Ain't said nothin' about permanent makin's. I only ask how you like the name."

"Might take some gettin' used to." Her eyes were the size and color of old pennies and so soft and dreamy, Green had to gaze.

"Start gettin' used to it," he said.

"Why?" They started walking again, slower now, their hands touching.

"Why you think? Because you might put it to use."

"Who come up with your name—Green? I ain't never hear such a name in all my days."

"Whoever birthed me. My color wasn't full cooked when I come into this world. They says I arrived green as moss on a river rock. 'Course, my color be full-cooked now."

"Oh yes."

"On my first trek west, a bunch of Injuns came 'round us, faces all war-painted. They look at me like I be somethin' special. I think they took interest in my hair and my color. They figured I mus' be the one in charge, and I never say nothin' different."

"I likes yo' name," she said. "And I likes yo' color too. I likes it jus' fine."

"How about that other name?"

"Martha Flake?" she said. "I likes it mighty much."

The company arrived in the Salt Lake Valley in October 1848, a year after Jane and Isaac James had settled there. The log house and lean-to barn Green had built for the Flakes were part of the Amasa Survey, in Cottonwood.

During the first night in their new place, the weather was calm enough that the children and slaves slept out-of-doors in the wagon boxes. Sarah Flake was near four years old and slept with Liz.

The second night of this arrangement, little Sarah got startled awake and called for Liz to quit pinching her. Liz sat up to defend herself. "Sarah, baby, I never pinch you!"

Sarah went back to slumber, only to wake up a few minutes later with the same accusation.

Liz was rubbing her eyes, whispering, "You been dreamin', baby."

The child was making ready to call "Mama!" when Green, who had been resting on the ground nearby, sat up. He said, "Sarah, I tell you what. I goin' lay myself close to this wagon box. If Lizzy pinch you again, I will learn her a lesson. Now how's that sound?"

"All right," she said.

They all ventured back to sleep but not for long. No more than ten minutes passed before Green himself was yelling: "You rascal! Would you bite a nigger?" There stood Green Flake. A coyote was scampering away from him.

Come dawn, that coyote was on its haunches, half-hid in the brush, watching the cabin with the kind of hunger only a wild animal can show. Massa Madison took his gun and taught that creature how much faster a musket ball is than a coyote.

There'd be no more pinching.

But there would be a wedding.

Green Flake and Martha Crosby got married on October 11, 1848—both of them still slaves of different masters, though they settled down as a family.

Most all the pioneers were ready to settle down now. But for several of these Southerners, including colored ones, Utah was not their destiny.

NOTES

The chapter title is from a traditional Negro spiritual cited in Higginson, "Negro Spirituals," 690.

Though some of the Flake family histories suggest that Green was freed by James Madison and Agnes Flake before they all went to Nauvoo, the facts suggest otherwise. As Joel A. Flake Jr. points out, that Green's labor and ultimately Green himself were used as tithing indicates he was still considered property even after the arrival in Salt Lake City ("Green Flake," 16). Historian Coleman writes that both Green Flake and Martha Flake worked for the Crosby family until Martha's master decided they had paid "a fair price for a colored girl"; neither was granted freedom until the mid-1850s ("History of Blacks in Utah," 39). According to Green's descendant Bertha Udell, "Green and Martha gave the Crosbys produce from their garden and farm. Brigham Young was upset with the Crosbys and said that the debt had already been paid in full" (qtd. in Flake, "Green Flake," 20).

Though some believe that Green remained in Salt Lake after his first trek there from Winter Quarters, many historians concur that Green accompanied Brigham Young and John Brown back to Winter Quarters to help the other Saints travel to their new home. Flake quotes historian Coleman as saying, "Green Flake was a part of the group that left with Brigham Young on August 16, 1847" ("Green Flake," 15). This certainly seems likely, because Green and Martha were married in October 1848, when the Mississippi company of 1848 arrived in the Salt Lake Valley. It's hard to imagine they would marry so quickly after the company's arrival unless they had gotten better acquainted on the trek. We have taken liberties in placing the time of Green's return to Winter Quarters after the arrival of the Mississippi Saints. Though we cannot be certain when he returned, if he was with John Brown, his return would have been in October 1847, before Brown set off to gather the Mississippians. If, however, he was given extra work to do in Salt Lake or on the trail, his return would have been later—and possibly where we have placed it in this story. No available records indicate with certainty that Green returned to Winter Quarters or when.

Savage suggests that Martha Crosby Flake had been acquired by "Herbert Kimball" (almost certainly Heber C. Kimball), who subsequently "made arrangements for James Flake to take possession" of her before her marriage to Green (*Blacks in the West*, 28). It is of interest that Martha is sometimes listed in family records as Martha Morris Flake rather than Martha Crosby Flake. Although we do not know the origin of that discrepancy, we do know that after the Civil War, many slaves rejected the names of masters they had not liked. It could well be that Martha chose a new name for herself when she was free to do so.

Martha Crosby Flake's various nicknames are recorded in Joel A. Flake Jr., "Green Flake," 20. Predictably, some confusion has arisen over Martha's nickname of "Liz," which was also the name of Agnes Flake's slave.

The descriptions of Green's personality are from Johnson, "Utah's Negro Pioneers of 1847," and from Bankhead's reminiscences of her grandfather (as qtd. in Flake, "Green Flake," 15, 10). Flake records Bankhead saying that Green Flake "was much of a man. He did not allow anybody to touch him or argue with him. He would do his work real well, but he was not going to be whipped. . . . They said he was a strong man and a kind man, but he did not tolerate whippings" ("Green Flake," 10).

That William Crosby regarded Flake as "saucy" is also from Flake, "Green Flake," 18, quoting a letter from William Crosby to Brigham Young, March 12, 1851.

Green's first view of a buffalo calf impressed him so greatly that it was one of two experiences he recalled fifty years later, the second being a band of war-painted Indians who surrounded the company and demanded payment (Flake, "Green Flake," 12).

The baby who was born in the wagon after a wheel broke in answer to Betsy's prayer, as she interpreted it (Carter, *Treasures*, 5:215), died of whooping cough soon after they reached the Valley (Brown, *Autobiography*, 102). Betsy Crosby Brown's first three children died in their infancy, but she eventually became the mother of ten.

The incident of the coyote "pinching" Sarah Flake and being chased off the property by Green is from Flake, *William J. Flake*, 13. The words "You rascal, would you bite a nigger?" are reported to have been Green's.

The origin of Green's name is cited in Flake, "Green Flake," though it is likely folklore, because Green was not a unique name by any means in that day.

Gold
Missionaries

8

O ROCKS, DON'T FALL ON ME!

My fruit is better than gold, yea, than fine gold;
and my revenue than choice silver.
PROVERBS 8:19

There was hardly any settling time before Brigham Young called a number of men—including Madison Flake, Amasa Lyman, Charles Rich, George Q. Cannon, and Porter Rockwell—to uproot once more and head towards California. There was gold there, which might be useful to improve Zion.

In 1849, these men with two slaves, Hark Lay and Oscar Crosby, said goodbye to their families again and directed themselves south in a pack train. Amasa Lyman and Porter Rockwell left first, in April. Charles Rich followed in October. Three weeks later, Madison Flake with his Negroes and a mess of twenty "gold missionaries" caught up with Rich's men.

Amasa Lyman was a round-faced, green-eyed fellow who loved to hunt and eat hearty, though he could get tired enough to quit the most promising chase. Back at Winter Quarters, he and Madison had hunted antelope and lost their horses. They pursued their mounts all day and didn't catch them till dusk. After that, Amasa said, "No more hunting for me. Too much walk."

But he would walk where Brother Brigham told him to, even if it meant California. Amasa was a Church apostle, ordained by Joseph Smith. He would go where God's prophet said.

Charles Rich was a six-foot-four Tennessee man. He had fought in Missouri's Battle of Crooked River and defended the Saints time and again when mobs came howling after blood. The Mormons called him General Rich because he was a major general of the Nauvoo Legion. He was also a new apostle.

Port Rockwell was big as a bull, but he wasn't no apostle. Some folks couldn't even decide if he was a human being, for he did resemble a renegade, his face unshaved and hair so long and tangled it could pass for brambles. He had been Joseph Smith's bodyguard, and everyone knew he'd protect any Latter-day Saint from gentile threats—might even shoot first, ask questions later. A few folks thought he preferred shooting to talking, because his voice was so high-pitched and his hands so womanly that a gun gave him some extra manhood. (Nobody would ever voice such thoughts to Rockwell, though.) Besides, he wasn't just a gunslinger; he was a slick businessman too. Once he got to California, Port did more than missionary work. He set up three taverns for the gold miners and made good money too.

George Cannon was a short, stocky fellow with a wide forehead and thick, dark brows, who had once stood guard for Brother Joseph. Cannon said straight out that there was no place he would rather *not* go than California. But, as with Amasa Lyman, he'd go where Brigham Young told him. Even so, he wasn't shy about speaking his mind. One evening at campfire, he blurted out, "I despise the prospect of digging gold. It's a poor business indeed when men are running all over the country for metal."

Madison Flake was of like mind.

Hark Lay and Oscar Crosby, on the other hand, were not at all opposed to this new mission. They had shoveled and seeded enough dirt in their lifetimes that pay dirt sounded like a right reward. They were more than willing to spoon it out of mountain veins, or pan it out of streams, or fish it out of deer droppings or any other nasty place it might hide. They loved to hear Henry Bigler tell about the prospects and the prospectors.

Bigler, dressed in buckskin from head to foot, was also a gold missionary, but he'd had more experience than the rest. He had already been to California with the Mormon Battalion. In fact, he had been present when James Marshall discovered the first hint of treasure at Sutter's Mill. That was January 24th of 1848.

Hark and Oscar listened close as Bigler recalled the day at Sutter's Mill when Mister Marshall announced, "Boys, I believe I've found a gold mine," and then set his hat on a work bench, pulling yellow metal from the hat crown, testing it with his teeth, and declaring, "It is the pure stuff." Bigler's own eyes had seen that gold burning like cold fire in Marshall's hat, and he quick became an expert on the yellow stuff. He was in position to teach these gold missionaries all about the forms gold can take: "The finest grains are dust. Flattened grains are scale. Grains larger than a pea are lump, and pieces bigger than a walnut are nuggets."

Funny thing was, though he knew more than anyone else about California's possibilities, though he had seen and handled its treasures, Henry Bigler had had enough of gold fever. Like others, he was on the expedition only because Brigham Young told him to go. Truth is, Henry Bigler thought he had seen enough adventure for one life. He had seen Indians beat back from land they owned and seen them in war paint wielding hatchets. He had even seen the remains of the Donner party at Prosser Creek: dead, dried, former humans. He didn't care to see more trouble. But Brigham Young had asked, so Bigler was on the trail—and as you'd surely guess, there were many more adventures awaiting him, not just in California but elsewhere. Anyone thinking they've seen enough adventure is probably verging on their biggest one yet, unless they decide to quit walking.

Well, this mess of brethren was not about to quit walking, though their path often led straight to trouble. The most constant trial was a sore lack of food and water. Besides that, each was carrying such weight as could test Sampson himself. Then the animals started dying off. George Cannon's horse, Croppy, drowned in a pool, and soon other pack animals expired too. Charles Rich let his mule loose, but it kept turning up at camp anyways, bones showing sharper every time it brayed.

Hark asked Oscar if these folks might forget to feed their Negroes too, should the animals keep dying off and the food keep getting scarcer.

Oscar shrugged.

"I done shoot prairie dog and elk for this people. I built them cabins and planted them taters, but cain't nobody make me give my own body for them to feed off," said Hark.

"Don't go livin' up to your bad reputation or we both goin' suffer," Oscar answered.

Now, you should know that Hark's "bad reputation" claimed he was "hard to manage." Of course, you have to remember who was most likely to get quoted. White men expected quick submission from us colored folk. We was their property, and they couldn't see otherwise. Truth told, Hark just preferred surviving to dying like George Cannon's horse. And he full intended to keep on surviving. He had been bred to survive, even to thrive, for he was a human buck, a stud for slave generation, raised up to that very purpose.

"Hark, you gettin' uppity and above yo'self more ever' day," Oscar said. "'Fore long, you ain't goin' be able to find yo' boots or yo' feets, because they be so high up in the clouds."

It's a sad occasion when a colored man calls his brother uppity, but it was out of love and protection Oscar said so. He knew what befell a proud Negro. "Best not walk around like you somethin' big," Oscar added, "'cause these folks can quick cut you down to size."

Hark didn't answer.

All this time, the explorers were in unmapped land. They headed up what we now call Shoal Creek and Beaver Dam and finally reached the open desert of Nevada. Then came hunger, like hunger was the air itself and they had no choice but to breathe in. They'd eat when and what they could: rabbits, rodents, an owl. And they'd be grateful for whatever food they found. At the bird feast, George Cannon said he never imagined owl would make good eating and felt pleased it did.

Madison answered, "This is manna from heaven. This particular manna happens to have pinfeathers."

Of course, slaves was accustomed to eating whatever made itself available: pigs' ears, chicken heads—you name it. This was not the first time Oscar Crosby and Hark Lay had tasted owl. The whites would likely be surprised at what all a black man's palate could accept if it meant one more day of living.

On December 22, 1849, the Madison Flake group reached Rancho del Chino. It was winter, but the season's chill didn't reach far south. This was a balmy land of palm trees and cactus, grape vineyards and giant redwoods. It was a hard-packed land which the sun loved and snow hardly chanced on. But Rancho del Chino was not their destination. They would know their destination when the Lord said they'd found it. In the meantime, they would learn what lessons God had in store. There would be good news, and there would be bad.

It was bad news first: Even some good Latter-day Saint boys were getting greedy and refusing to pay their tithes. And the collection of tithes was part of this gold mission. Money-lust had taken hold of this land, and Mormons were at risk—though it sure wasn't just the Mormons looking for gold. California was getting crowded with folks from every state and territory of the Union. They'd all heard about the find at Sutter's sawmill.

The '49ers came so fast and so ravenous, they'd whip their horses through the desert until the animals just gave out and died. Madison Flake counted over a thousand dead animals—mostly horses and mules—on the roadside, with more scattered over the plain. And sometimes it wasn't just a dead horse drying up; sometimes it was a man. A fellow would expire and his companions wouldn't even bother with the burying of him. That's how desperate they were for pay dirt, how eager to make rocks bleed yellow.

Madison Flake, however, knew his purpose. He was a missionary, sent to explore this place for the Lord. This was God's country, and if there was gold in the streams or in crevices of rocks, it was God's gold, planted for a purpose.

Come spring, Madison and a few other Mormons—Jefferson Hunt and Henry Bigler, to name two of the whites; Hark Lay and Oscar Crosby, to name two of the blacks—set out to explore the territory by Sacramento. As usual, Madison rode his white mule.

When a member of the company couldn't manage his horse, Madison noticed the reason: The man had a broken cinch on his saddle. So Madison offered his own. It was a hospitable thing, as natural to him as providing a place by the fire for a cold missionary. But this particular courtesy cost him his life. Almost immediately his mule took a scare, jumped to one side, and threw Madison off. His shoulders struck ground first and doubled his head into his chest.

Oscar got close enough to hear Flake's last words: "Brethren, lay hands on me!"

Well, what could Oscar do? There was no priesthood in his fingers, and he couldn't even guess the right words. He said, "Breathe easy, sir," as Madison Flake took in his last air and let it go in a long, rattling sigh.

Bigler hollered for help, but no answer came. They were too far from any camp. He murmured a weak prayer, and then he got bold and laid hands on Madison's head, asking God to put the breath back into those unmoving nostrils.

The prayer did no good. Madison Flake wouldn't be moving or breathing again.

Finally, Bigler took the blanket off the mule and wrapped the body in it. Hark and Oscar dug the grave, though they wouldn't do burial until dawn. Bigler sat up with the corpse and in the morning reported that Brother Flake had come to him in a dream. The ghost had put his hand on his breast and said, "Something in here broke, and that's what killed me."

At dawnlight, the gold missionaries buried James Madison Flake by the roadside in the San Joaquin Valley. I suppose his bones are resting there to this day.

It would take a long while to get the word to Utah.

NOTES

The chapter title is from a traditional Negro spiritual found in Burleigh, *Spirituals*, 55.

Byrne, "James Marshall," reports that Henry Bigler was nineteen at the time gold was discovered at Sutter's Mill, though such is not consistent with the birthdate of August 28, 1851, Bigler gives in his diary (Diary, 1). Descriptions of the various sizes of gold grains discovered at the mill are found in Byrne, "James Marshall," 25.

Apparently, Bigler had quite a bit of experience in the discovery of gold, if the journal of James S. Brown (not the Captain James Brown of the Mormon Battalion) can be trusted. Brown claims that Bigler went out duck hunting one day and returned without any ducks. When asked where his ducks were, he answered, "Wait a while; I will show you; I have got them all right." He then retrieved from his pocket "at least half an ounce of gold tied up" (Brown, *Life of a Pioneer*, 102).

Bigler's involvement in the trek of the gold missionaries is described by Gudde in *Bigler's Chronicle of the West*, 130. Though Bigler had already been to California once, he was asked to return to "dig gold" for Father (Patriarch) John Smith, who was stake president in Salt Lake City. Bigler left Salt Lake City on October 12, 1849 (Gudde, *Bigler's Chronicle of the West*, 131). Two days later he joined the Flake-Rich packers. Arrington summarizes the arrangement between Patriarch John Smith and Henry Bigler: Smith would provide all the expense of fitting out Bigler for the gold mines. Upon arriving there, Bigler was to save and be "prudent" and, "after all the expenses" were paid, receive half the gold (*Great Basin Kingdom*, 73–74).

The description of Charles C. Rich is from Stegner, *Gathering of Zion*, 47.

That Porter Rockwell opened three taverns in California is from Cowan and Homer, *California Saints*, 133. Said Rockwell: "The most accessible money was not in the gold claims, but in the pockets of those who worked them" (Cowan and Homer, *California Saints*, 133).

The sequence of expeditions to California—the initial one (Amasa Lyman's) leaving in April and Charles Rich's leaving on October 8—is recorded in Flake, *Of Pioneers and Prophets*, which also documents that these missionaries were to "dig gold . . . for the use of the Church" (124). That the Flake company caught up with the Rich company three weeks after the Rich departure is documented in Cowan and Homer, *California Saints*, 138.

Oscar Crosby and Hark Lay were sons of Vilate Crosby, but each had a different master and used that master's last name as his own.

That Hark Lay was a stud (in the word's literal sense) is documented in Kohler, *Southern Grace*, 42, which records that Hark Lay and three other black men—Philliman, Osea, and Hardy—were "seed for a human crop. . . . [John Crosby] was able to charge high stud fees for their use. . . . They were top quality—tall, well-muscled, and intelligent." After John Crosby's death, Hark was given to Crosby's daughter Sytha and her husband, Billy Lay, as a wedding gift.

The account of Croppy's drowning is from Bitton, *George Q. Cannon*, 62. Bitton also records the story of Charles Rich's returning mule, Cannon's reaction to a dinner of owl meat, and an outline of the path the California-bound pioneers took (*George Q. Cannon*, 64–65).

Hark Lay's reputation of being "hard to manage" is according to Amasa Lyman Jr., who is quoted in Brown, *Autobiography*, 73, as follows: "I knew all three of those negro servants who were members of President Brigham Young's pioneer company of 1847. Hark Lay . . . was always hard to manage. He died in California. William Crosby also went to California and took his servant, Oscar Crosby, along with him, where the latter died."

The details of the abandoned animal and human carcasses along the trail to California during the gold rush are from Lyman, *Amasa Mason Lyman*, 203.

Arrington says that "from 40,000 to 50,000 persons journeyed overland to California in 1849, and an equal number in 1850, of which an estimated ten to fifteen thousand went by way of the Salt Lake valley each year" (*Great Basin Kingdom*, 68).

The details of James Madison Flake's death are from Flake, *Of Pioneers and Prophets*, 129. Henry Bigler's dream of Flake's postmortal explanation of how he died is from Bigler's diary (qtd. in Gudde, *Bigler's Chronicle of the West*, 161).

It is important to recognize the tremendous role of the gold missionaries in funding the building of Zion. As Davies points out, "By the spring of 1851, a total of over $80,000 (mostly gold) had been funneled into the Mormon mint" (*Mormon Gold*, 391). "'Good' Mormons," says Davies, "were substantially involved between 1848 and 1857 in the discovery and exploitation of California gold. It was the first successful export industry for the staggering Mormon economy, providing both a domestic money and a 'foreign' exchange which could be used for the much needed capital improvements of Deseret" (*Mormon Gold*, 394).

9

THE BLIND MAN
STOOD ON THE ROAD
AND CRIED

*He that leadeth into captivity shall go into captivity: he that
killeth with the sword must be killed with the sword.
Here is the patience and the faith of the saints.*
REVELATION 13:10

Back in Salt Lake, Mizz Agnes and Liz were carrying on with life in blissful ignorance. Agnes Flake did not learn she had become a widow for several months. When she did, she moaned, fainted, and took to her bed. There she lay for weeks, as she had done every other time when heartache overwhelmed her. She couldn't eat but a morsel of what Liz offered. This family had passed through tribulation, but losing Madison brought the saddest time yet.

Though Green felt bad Massa Madison had died, he wasn't entirely mournful. With his massa dead, wasn't Green a free man? He had always thought he belonged to Madison rather than Agnes, for it was always Madison who gave him work and sometimes a whupping or a kick. Now Madison was gone, so wasn't that Green's freedom papers delivered by the almighty hand of God?

When Agnes Flake declared Green her property now that she was widowed, he was surprised to his marrow. He couldn't even speak and feared of what he might say when his voice did return. Here he had thought *freedom* and then it got stole away. Oh, slavery was bitter to him then—more bitter than ever, because he had seen himself free. He had felt liberty turn the key of his bondage.

His memories were a torment. He recalled how some of his fellow slaves would catch and hold him while he got his whuppings. He tried to ignore what came into his head now, the recollections that beat at him. He tried to tell himself the whuppings were only to remind him of his place and teach him out of belligerent doings. But with Madison gone and Agnes laying claim on him, the memories were whooshing inside him in mean, nasty flurries. He wasn't set to bare his back for any whip. He swore he would never submit to such a thing again and asked Liz what she'd do if the mizzus should order him beat. Liz said she'd hide so as not to see it.

"How about if you hides me?" he suggested.

She laughed, but he didn't laugh with her. He just sat on a barrel, holding his head like it might burst.

He whispered, "You can't know how hard I work to help clear the trail to this place, Liz. And no one even say a thank-you or mutter one kind word. I made this house for the Flakes. Then soon as they arrive, they moves me out to live in a dugout and a shed. I gather and cut firewood, and then I scrounge wood for myself."

"You ain't alone in that." She was feeding the chickens at the moment, spreading grain on the yard.

"My clothes and my shoes is passed down from white men. I have to mend all my stuff they give me, or set Martha doin' it. And she got enough work from her own people. Liz, I hates wore out clothes. Look at me. Look how raggedy I be!"

"You ever see any of us lookin' fine? I don' look no better, and neither do Martha."

"That's my meanin'. I wants better. I feeds and milks the cows. Then the white folks get the whole milk and the cream, and we gets the skim and curds."

"Sometimes they gives us better." She clucked at a hen and its chicks.

"If the cow give more milk, they gives us better. That's the only when. I cares for the chickens, and I gathers the eggs."

Liz murmured, "I know," though she wasn't really a part of this conversation. Green was having it mostly with himself.

"You recollect how the mizzus thought I done keep a few eggs for myself?" he asked. "You recall how she set the massa on me? Or how she slap yo' face when she think you be takin' somethin' before they gets their first choosin's?"

"Ain't never been nothin' different."

"And now, Mizz Agnes layin' claim on me—even though Massa Madison done found his reward with God. My massa be dead, so why can't I be free? Feels to me, down deep in my heart, like I got fresh punished when I didn't even do nothin' wrong."

"Massa Madison the one got fresh punished. You think maybe God set that mule to kicking massa because of all the kicks massa give you?"

Green shook his head slow. "Aw Liz, don't talk such a thing. I hate to think it. Let it pass. No good can come from such sayin's." He clenched his mouth and set about the work Mizz Agnes had given him: chopping more wood for the fire.

Others were suffering too, of course. When the gold missionaries set out for California, many of their women were left with no food at all.

By this time, polygamy was being practiced by most all the Mormon leaders, though it wouldn't get officially announced for a few more years. Apostle Amasa Lyman had taken on several wives himself. One was Eliza Partridge, a widow of Brother Joseph. Though Eliza considered herself eternally sealed to the Prophet, she married Amasa so's he could protect her on this side of glory.

It was a good thought, but truth be known, protection was in scarce supply, and Amasa was in California. Eliza had no food in the house nor any way to get it. All she had was her faith.

I've often thought it's a shame you can't eat faith. Faith will save a soul and fill a heart, but it won't do a thing for the stomach.

Or maybe that's not true. For in this instance, Jane Manning James came to Eliza's rescue like an angel from God. Maybe Eliza's faith had something to do with Jane showing up at her door.

Or maybe it was Jane's faith sent her there.

Notes

The chapter title is from a traditional Negro spiritual found in Burleigh, *Spirituals*, 99.

That Green Flake expected he'd be free after James Madison Flake's death is documented in Fretwell's interview with Udell (Miscellaneous Family Papers, 11). Details of Green's view of slave life are also from that interview: "[Green]'s temper was well known, and a few times in his life he refused to do the bidding of the master. It wasn't proper for a slave to be belligerent and out of control. In his early days, some slaves would catch him and hold him when he got his whipping. Green later stated that he got out of control and he needed a whipping to teach him his place. A good kick in the pants was needed now and then, to keep Green in control. When James Flake was kicked and killed by a friendly mule on a trip to California, some thought it was only providence in kind being returned for the kicks he had given to Green. . . . Green has told his family: 'Let it pass! No good can come from it! Let it pass!'"

Another description of slave life is apparently transcribed from Green's words at the "Pioneer Appreciation Day" in Mill Creek, Idaho: "Sometimes I would work long and hard on a difficult job and no one would even say thanks or tell me and say a few kind words. Sometimes a colored person would be given a kick or a cuff because he may have taken more time than was necessary to do a task. I drove a team and wagon to the Salt Lake valley for my master, James Flake, and helped build him a home and a fit place to live. They moved into the home and I was moved out most of the time to live in a dugout and a shed. I would gather and cut firewood for another person's fire and then I would have to scrounge wood for myself. Other things that made me sore and angry: All the clothes and shoes I wore were usually first worn by some white man. I would have to patch and mend a lot of the stuff they gave me. Once in awhile, I was given better clothing and I liked that, but I did not care for worn out things. Then I fed and milked the cows and they would get the whole milk and the cream and I was given the skim milk and the curds. If the cows gave more milk, I was given more. I cared for the chickens and gathered the eggs and sometimes the Mrs. thought I had kept a few eggs for myself. Liz would take something and Mrs. Agnes would catch her and she would get a whipping. When the grasshoppers, crickets and jackrabbits came and it was hard to find anything to eat, we would dig for wild onions and sego bulbs and we had to share what we found" (Fretwell, interview with Udell, Miscellaneous Family Papers, 7).

10

PLEASE DON'T LET THIS HARVEST PASS

And now abideth faith, hope, charity, these three;
but the greatest of these is charity.
1 CORINTHIANS 13:13

Isaac James had built his family a cabin not far from Temple Block. There was little leisure. Most every moment had to be spent in work, with every other moment spent preparing for more work. Jane spun and dyed all the cloth for her family, most of it good wool.

For a few months, things were splendid. The Jameses either bought or were gifted horses, cows, oxen, sheep, a bunch of chickens, and a rooster so primed and energetic they didn't need but one. Life was sweet and brimming with promise for a while. But the promise withered, and good times turned the corner.

The first crop of wheat they planted came under attack soon as the green shoots appeared. Hoards of bulgy-eyed grasshoppers and black-armored crickets leapt onto the sprouts that were to have become fall's harvest. If you ask me, I'd say the devil himself took over the bugs. The Saints had long since noticed great numbers of crickets in the foothills. Now it seemed Satan was coaching these ugly pests straight into green Zion to chew up the Saints' hopes. Even the trees were stripped of their leaves.

When Jane went out to combat the little armies, they jumped at her hair and apron like she was free food. She slapped the air, grabbed as many bugs as she could, and dashed them to the ground. That didn't do much of nothing. She knew the just-starting wheat couldn't thrash like she could. The just-starting wheat was set to be wasted to stubble.

Sylvester James, now ten years old, made a game of killing the crickets, toeing their crackly bodies into the dirt. The whole James family dug holes and drove the bugs to their burial. Isaac plowed a ditch around the garden, filled it with water and corralled the crickets into death by drowning. They even tried burning a portion of their infested crop.

But the crickets had come in thousands. By morning, all the dead bugs were replaced by lively swarms. You'd step on one, and fifteen more would jump from the grass.

Seagulls rescued the wheat that year, gliding down on the hoards and swallowing the bugs whole. Like angels of mercy and vengeance, these gulls let the Saints keep at least a portion of their crop, which brought prayers of thanks from every Mormon mouth, including Jane's and Isaac's, though they'd lost near every plant they'd sowed.

And the miracles weren't steady. Insects multiplied from one season to the next.

For Jane, the beatingest part of losing their crop came in the cries of her children. After selling off her goods, she had nothing to offer her babies but what she begged for. And how Jane Manning James hated to beg! She did it, of course, just as you would in her place. She often begged milk off Elizabeth Chase, who had a good cow and a mill and could afford to share something.

And when Jane could, though, she shared too. Like I said, when

Eliza Partridge Lyman was starving, it was Black Jane who came ready to provide.

These two had known each other since Nauvoo days, when Eliza and four other women told the secret of plural marriage to her, which was not something you'd be casual about. That kind of secret took trust, and Jane felt honored to be trusted. They had been at Winter Quarters together too, when Eliza fell sick with childbed fever and lost all her hair—and then lost her baby son. Jane felt she and Eliza were friends, as much as white and colored could be in those days. Though Eliza called her "Jane," not "sister," they had history together. And now Eliza had need of flour. Any friend would try to meet that need.

Spring had arrived on a chilled breeze the day Jane wrapped herself in a shawl and headed for the Lyman cabin.

Eliza opened the door, looking skinny and haggard as a stray puppy. But at least her hair had grown back, brown and glossy as ever. It was looped under her ears in the fashion of the day, though it appeared she hadn't combed it in awhile. Eliza raked her fingers fast through it, as though that might make a difference—which it did, but not for the better. Now tendrils dangled over her forehead. Her skin was so white, her embarrassment showed like fever.

"Jane," she said, "hello. I've been carding candlewick."

The moldy smell of the cabin drifted outside when Eliza opened the door wider. This was a poor dwelling indeed, even poorer than the Jameses'. The roof and floor were dirt. Since the past week had been rainy, this was more a mud cabin than a log cabin, and its only light was a blue haze coming down that chimney. This cabin looked and smelled like a good place for whooping cough to grow—and whooping cough had carried off a number of folks that winter.

A throng of people were living in the Lymans' log room. Jane felt all of them watching her. She didn't speak but held out the bowl to her friend. In it were two pounds of flour, half of what Jane herself possessed.

Eliza put her hands on the bowl. "Oh, Jane," she said. "You know, there is some good in this poverty."

Jane pushed the gift into her friend's arms. There they stood, both of them holding onto that bowl. When Jane dropped her arms, Eliza came out of the cabin, blinking at the light. She looked around as though she hadn't seen the outdoors since the first snows of winter. There wasn't much to see—mostly other poor cabins and some sprigs of wild grass stretching for light.

"A fine day," Eliza pronounced. "Hardly even cold."

"You'd do well to use a wrap, Sister Eliza."

"Why, the cabin is colder than the outside. It appears the sun might show its face."

"There's a hint of spring," Jane said. "Yes indeed."

"A hint. Still, I do not think our enemies need envy us this locality. Do you?"

"Oh no, ma'am!" Jane laughed.

"I do not think they'll come here to disturb us."

"Not unless they stupid."

"Like us?" She brought her eyes to Jane's. Eliza had such kind brown eyes.

"Ma'am, we ain't stupid. We just devoted. We see past the uglies to the possibilities of this place."

Eliza smiled at this in a weary way. "And so do the crickets."

"With them buggly eyes, I 'spect so." Jane couldn't help but think how far they had come from the comforts of Nauvoo.

Eliza looked into the bowl. "This flour might save our lives," she said.

"We couldn't ask for better than that." Jane backed up a step.

"Jane?" Eliza stood rocking on her feet. "I never imagined this."

"How poor we be?"

"That a colored woman would be bringing me her own flour to keep me from starving. That's twice I've been helped out by Negroes."

There was a simple bench in front of the cabin. Eliza sat down, holding the bowl in her lap, and beckoned Jane to sit beside her. "I don't believe I've told you," Eliza said. "I was not raised poor."

This was no news. Everything about Eliza—the way she spoke and the way she walked—said she was highborn. Though her hair could've used some help, poverty did not sit right on Eliza Partridge Smith Lyman. Poverty fit her like someone else's dusty old coat.

"My father, Bishop Partridge, was not a poor man."

"I never met him, but I've heard tale."

"When I was born—his first child—I suppose he imagined me dancing at balls and living in a mansion." She glanced at the cabin. "Then he joined the Church. He left his business—left every-thing—for the gospel's sake."

"And he died for it too."

"A martyr's death. All he suffered when we were driven out of Missouri!"

"A martyr's death sure as if he'd got killed 'longside Brother Joseph."

"When we were leaving Missouri, we stayed with a Negro family. We were in one room, and the Negroes were in another. We couldn't get outside without going through the Negroes' room." Eliza's face was vacant, her words steady, straight, and numb.

Jane didn't know exactly how to respond. It took her a moment to come up with a polite question: "They treat you good?"

"I remember myself as a young girl. My mother always dressed me in fancy clothes. I never imagined I would be poor. How could I have imagined that? I'm like a servant myself."

"A servant of God," Jane offered. "Ain't nothing bad in that."

"That's a fine thought indeed. So many things I never would have imagined in my child days."

"I'm like you in that."

"How could I have imagined a Negro family would give me

shelter when I needed it? That a Negro woman would bring me sustenance when I was starving?"

Again, Jane was not sure how to answer. She finally said, "Ain't that what the good Lord expect? For us to help one another?"

Eliza rose, stiff as her bones. "How can I thank you for this dear gift?"

Jane rose too. "You just enjoy that flour, ma'am. You make you some good bread. You keep that baby from cryin'. That's all the thanks I want."

"May the Lord bless you, Jane."

When Eliza opened the door, the moldy scent escaped again.

Jane wasn't sure just how long the remains of her flour would keep her own babies from crying, but she felt fine sharing what she had.

Indeed, before long, most supplies were used up. It came clear that farming would not sustain the James family. So Isaac asked Brigham Young for employment as his coachman. And Brother Brigham gave him the job. It came with some prestige, too, since many Mormon folk thought it exotic to ride in a carriage driven by the only Negro coachman in all of Utah. And there were occasional adventures.

One time, years after Isaac got his job, a child decided to hitch a ride on the back of Brigham Young's sleigh for awhile. But Isaac drove a team fast. That poor child knew he couldn't slide off the sleigh without getting half skinned, and he was shivering with cold. When Isaac got set to cross a stream, President Young finally saw the boy and yelled, "Brother Isaac! Brother Isaac! Stop! Pick up that child. He's almost frozen!" Brigham Young himself wrapped the boy in a warm lap robe and then asked his name.

"Heber," came the reply.

"Heber what?"

"Heber Jeddy Grant."

Brother Brigham went on and on then about how he loved Heber's father, Jedediah, and told the child to visit him at his office sometime.

Of course, no one back then would have guessed that young Heber J. Grant would someday lead the Church himself. Back then, no one could guess who or what anyone might become.

NOTES

The chapter title is from a traditional Negro spiritual found in Burleigh, *Spirituals*, 189.

Many pioneer journals recount the cricket infestation and the miracle of the seagulls. Jane James's own history (qtd. in Wolfinger, "Test of Faith," in *Social Accommodation*, 155) records the following:

"My husband Isaac James worked for Brother Brigham, and we got along splendid accumulating horses, cows, oxen, sheep, and chickens in abundance. I spun all the cloth for my family clothing for a year or two, and we were in a prosperous condition, until the grasshoppers and crickets came along carrying destruction wherever they went, laying our crops to the ground, stripping the trees of all their leaves and fruit, bringing poverty and desolation throughout this beautiful valley. It was not then as it is now, there were no trains running bringing fruits and vegetables from California or any other place. All our importing and exporting was done by the slow process of ox teams.

Oh how I suffered of cold and hunger and the keenest of all was to hear my little ones crying for bread, and I had none to give them; but in all the Lord was with us and gave us grace and faith to stand it all."

Jane's journal seems to suggest that the crickets in Utah weren't a problem for the James family for several years, though the Jameses had arrived in the Salt Lake Valley in September 1847, early enough to experience the best known cricket war and seagull miracle in the spring of 1848. But if her memory is accurate and they did not have difficulty with crickets for a few years after their arrival, she could be referring to one of two other infestations—in 1849 and 1850.

The James family poverty is documented in Wolfinger, who cites the Works Progress Administration (WPA) biographical sketches at the Utah State Historical Society: "[Jane] used to go down to get milk off Isaac Chase's wife, Elizabeth. When she had not one thing in the house to eat and felt very bad at having to beg milk but had to do so for the sake of her little child. The mill was built by Isaac Chase and called the Chase Mill" ("Test of Faith," in *Social Accommodation*, 159 n. 13).

Jane's generosity is recorded in Eliza Partridge Lyman's journal: "April 8, 1849, we baked the last of our flour today, and have no prospect of getting more till after harvest. April 13th, Brother Lyman started on a mission to California with O. P. Rockwell and others. May the Lord bless and prosper them and return them in safety. He left us—that is, Paulina, Caroline, and I— without anything to make bread, it not being in his power to get any. April 25: Jane James, a colored woman, let me have two pounds of flour, it being about half she had" (holographic journal, 45).

Eliza's account of the Partridge family sharing a cabin with a Negro family is also recorded in her journal, as quoted in Carter, *Treasures*, 2:215: "We children were five in number and the weather was so cold that we were obliged to leave the Missouri river . . . and wait for Father to come with wagons to meet us. We procured a small, dark room from a family of Negroes, our only light being what came down the chimney and no way to get in or out of the room except to go through the room occupied by the negroes. We occupied this doleful place about a week. . . ."

Eliza's description of her living circumstances are recorded in her journal: "Moved into a log room. There are seven of us to live in this room this winter. . . . We are glad to get this much of a shelter, but it is no shelter when it rains, for the dirt roof lets water through and the dirt floor gets muddy which makes it anything but pleasant." She records on April 8 that her baby and her brother had both suffered bouts of whooping cough and that "many children around us died with it" (holographic journal, 44).

Eliza Lyman's words "I do not think our enemies need envy us this locality or ever come here to disturb us" are from her journal and are quoted by Arrington and Bitton (*Mormon Experience*, 224).

That Isaac James likely served as Brigham Young's coachman is historical (Wolfinger, "Jane Manning James," 19), but we do not know the length of his employment. Carter identifies one coachman named Isaac (though she gives a mistaken account of his origins, if that Isaac was Isaac James) from Clarissa Young Spenser's records, in which Clarissa recalls sitting "in front with great dignity with Black Isaac" (*Negro Pioneer*, 14). Heber J. Grant's recollection of skating behind Brigham Young's coach, driven by Isaac, when Heber was about six years old indicates that Isaac was the coachman in 1861, when Heber, born in 1856, would have been five or six. He recalled: "We came to a stream a mile or two south from my home. As the driver was about to cross the stream, President Young saw me for the first time and he called out, 'Brother Isaac [his Negro coachman], Brother Isaac, stop. Pick up that child. He is almost frozen.' I was tucked under a warm laprobe and when we had gone a little distance he said, 'Are you warm, my boy?' I answered, 'Yes'" (qtd. in Carter, *Negro Pioneer*, 14–15).

11

OH, DIDN'T IT RAIN!

As cold waters to a thirsty soul,
so is good news from a far country.
PROVERBS 25:25

Isaac got to know the new president of the Church not through direct talk but from what he heard from inside the coach when Brother Brigham was accompanied.

Brigham Young stood near six feet tall. His shoulders slouched some, so he didn't appear his full height. His hair had been auburn but was more sandy-colored now, with gingerish lights. It was cut just past his ears, parted on the left. His eyes were bright blue and every bit as piercing as his speech—which was not loud but always direct and sure. He often dressed in the style of the day—black vest and black overcoat with swallow tails—though he didn't object to wearing homespun and a straw hat. He was not a man of much pretension; he was a get-it-done leader, a potatoes-and-buttermilk fellow, whose clothes showed more sense than style.

But even if he was not stylish or high educated, Brother Brigham was comfortable as the new president of the Mormon

Church. How could the Mormons have tamed and settled a desert without a leader who was forceful as the mightiest wind? Such a man was Brother Brigham. He had some race attitudes, but back then, it was the rare man in these United States—Mormon or Gentile—who didn't. If you read what Brigham Young said about our people, it's pretty much like reading what most everybody was saying at the time. Just because the gospel got restored didn't mean everyone got his heart cleaned. Even the most honorable men had to contend with the slyest enemy the devil can muster: traditions. Same as always.

As far as other controversies of the day were concerned, well, Isaac James pretended not to notice the different women who accompanied President Young in his carriage. Time soon would reveal to the world that Mormons were polygamists. For now, folks in Utah were just finding out that all those rumors about plural marriage weren't rumors. Even Isaac was surprised, though Jane had told him she knew about plural marriage since Nauvoo.

After a long day of driving President Young and one of those women, Isaac greeted Jane with the words: "I guess you right about some folks havin' more than one wife. I been listenin' to Brother Brigham talkin' today."

Jane was outside washing clothes. "You ain't notice nothin' until this moment? Sure took you long enough." She lathered a shirt on the washboard.

"I been busy—gettin' the wheat planted, killing off bugs, gettin' the wheat planted again, killin' more bugs."

"'Course there's plural marriage, Isaac! Open your eyes! Has been since Brother Joseph's time. Jus' like Solomon and Abraham, I guess."

Isaac pursed his lips. "Well," he said. "What good news that is— ain' it? I guess I better be openin' my eyes, like you say. Lookin' for my number two wife!"

Jane smiled up at him—but it was her wicked smile. "Not unless you ready to see Jesus real soon."

He bellowed. Oh, he did enjoy teasing Jane. "Truth is, honey, you more than I can handle already," he said. "One more like you, and I'd lose my mind clean off."

"And don' you go forgettin' it!" She splashed him with a handful of water from the wash bin.

That same year, a familiar face showed up in Utah: Dr. John Bernhisel, one of the first Mormons Jane had laid eyes on in Nauvoo. He came with the news that Emma Hale Smith had married Major Lewis C. Bidamon—a non-Mormon. A Methodist preacher had done the ceremony. Bidamon, said Dr. Bernhisel, had fallen in love with the Prophet's widow because of the comely darns in her stockings.

Dr. Bernhisel appeared surprised to see Jane and Isaac at church. He thought all free colored Saints had stayed behind and told them he'd met another free Negro Mormon, a Mister Elijah Abel.

"Why, Brother Elijah one of my bestest friends in the world," said Isaac. "He down Nauvoo?"

"Ohio, I believe," said the doctor. "He was visiting Nauvoo. Stayed for supper at the Mansion House when I was there."

"He comin' out west, sir?" Isaac asked.

"Anything is possible." Dr. Bernhisel tipped his tall hat to let them know the conversation had ended and moved on to some white folks, answering their questions about Sister Emma and her Gentile husband. Most Mormons back then figured Sister Emma would be shoveling coal for the devil before long. Truth is, she was just trying to find some joy and purpose, like all us are.

Dr. Bernhisel himself was soon to be finding more purpose than carting gossip from Nauvoo. The Mormon people wanted recognition as a proper state called Deseret. Brigham Young was to be governor. Dr. Bernhisel was chosen to make the petition for statehood in the nation's capital.

The politicians in Washington paid hardly any attention, though. Their efforts were involved in trying to prevent a war between the states. Finally, in what they called the Compromise of 1850, the United States of America admitted California as a free state and designated Utah (the name Stephen Douglas chose instead of "Deseret") and New Mexico as territories.

There was one difference between the two new territories: Utah chose to be slave-holding.

Washington might have forgot all about Utah, except that the Church decided to announce plural marriage. Then all the outrage of the northern press fell on "the twin relics of barbarism": slavery and polygamy.

The first "relic" was threatening to tear the nation asunder. The second would soon bring federal troops to Utah and threaten to repeat all the tragedies of Haun's Mill and Carthage Jail.

NOTES

The chapter title is from a traditional Negro spiritual found in Burleigh, *Spirituals*, 26.

Dr. Bernhisel and Almon W. Babbitt were Latter-day Saint representatives to Congress. Babbit portrayed himself as "pro-slavery," but "Bernhisel was bothered by the presence in Utah of 60 to 70 slaves belonging to twelve Mormon masters. . . . He wrote Brigham Young of this fact and requested that 'no person of African descent be reported as a slave. I make this suggestion because a large majority of the members of both branches of Congress, and a vast majority of the jurists in the United States entertain the conviction that slavery does not, and cannot exist in the Territory of Deseret without the sanction of positive law, yet to be enacted'" (Bringhurst, *Saints, Slaves, and Blacks*, 66). Nonetheless, though there were superficial signs of an antislavery status for Utah, "Bernhisel's efforts to cover up Utah's black slavery failed" (Bringhurst, *Saints, Slaves, and Blacks*, 67). Allen and Leonard document: "After a heated debate that almost tore the nation apart, the dispute ended with the famous Compromise of 1850. California became a state, with a constitution prohibiting slavery, and the territories of New Mexico and Utah were organized with the understanding that they could decide the issue of slavery for themselves. . . . [The general assembly of Deseret] . . . resolved in March

1851 to 'cheerfully and cordially' accept territorial status" (*Story of the Latter-day Saints*, 258). In 1852, slavery was officially permitted in the territory of Utah. As Brigham Young put it in an 1852 speech, Bringhurst writes, "'many [brethren] in the South' . . . with 'a great amount' invested 'in slaves' who might migrate to the Great Basin if their slave property were protected by law" (Bringhurst, *Saints, Slaves, and Blacks*, 68).

1850 to 1855

12

HARD TRIALS

God has delivered me . . . from bonds,
and from death; yea, and I do put my trust in him,
and he will still deliver me.
ALMA 36:27

The Fugitive Slave Law of 1850 wasn't big news in Utah, though Brigham Young discussed slavery on several occasions. If Isaac had had more religion or more nerve, he might have asked God a question or two about Brother Brigham's sayings. But he didn't.

Jane, on the other hand, was bold as brass. She never hesitated to ask God about anything, including slavery. She remembered all that Joseph Smith had said about it, remembered his words: "Take off the shackles from the poor black man!" She didn't ask the Lord if slavery was his will; she asked him why he kept allowing it, why he didn't strike the masters down with one swoop of his mighty arm or one great bolt of lightning that would shock the Carolinas like Sodom and Gomorrah. It didn't bother her if a thousand of the best Mormons said slavery was God's will and justified by the scriptures. A thousand good people could be wrong. A thousand people crucified the Lord, and they was dead wrong. Anyone who believed slavery was the will of Jesus was wrong too, and she didn't care what colored person heard her say it, though she tended to be less vocal around white folks.

She didn't hesitate to take any request or opinion to the Lord, though. She asked God to set the captives free, howsoever he chose. She knew he would, for she knew God heard her prayers. Jane was certain it was an answer to prayer, for example, when Sister Annie Thomas, a Southern woman she had met at Winter Quarters, came to use her service as a laundress. That employment, coupled with Isaac's, kept hunger outside the Jameses' fence.

Jane would pick up the Thomas laundry at the back porch, and the two would talk at some length. Sister Annie enjoyed seeing Jane's "pickaninnies" and asked that she bring "every single one of them" with her on laundry day.

Annie was a Southern belle with dark, wavy hair, green eyes, and pale, shimmery skin. She had owned a slave child before coming west and enjoyed crying pitifully as she told how much she had loved that "precious little niggerchild." It was no slim regret she harbored now for leaving it behind. Jane never knew if the child was a boy or a girl, for Annie never used a name, just "my pickaninny," "my little niggerchild," or "it."

Though Annie seemed leery of Sylvester (him being older), she treated Silas, Mary Ann, and Baby Miriam grand, offering them honey taffy while Jane was piling up dirty clothes. Sister Annie would check the children's heads for lice (which she never found) before allowing them to climb onto her lap, but she enjoyed holding them and often rubbed their heads for good luck. And Annie kept Jane abreast of all the current happenings, which was another blessing from God, since the newspaper words were too hard for Jane to read.

"Brother Brigham said Utah should pass a slave code," Annie mentioned one day, trading the laundry for Baby Miriam.

Jane perked up, wondering if God was answering her prayer right then. "What would that do?"

"Why, it would protect the Injun babies," Annie said. "The slave code would make Injun slavery illegal."

Jane waited, sure there must be more. "And what about the other slavery?"

"Negro slavery?" Annie laughed as she stepped outside the door. "Now, Jane, I know you're freeborn—which must be the will of God. It must mean you were especially polite in the pre-earth life, which I don't doubt, since I know you. But you understand good as I do that the others of your race are set precisely where God meant. Why, the end of Negro slavery would mock the Bible, wouldn't it?"

This was one of those occasions when Jane guarded her tongue.

Annie carried on about Indian slavery then—how awful it was when Indian chiefs raided other tribes and threatened to kill those stolen "papooses" to force Latter-day Saints into trading guns for them.

Then, all of a sudden, Annie started weeping.

"Mizz Annie, you sheddin' tears about the papooses?" Jane asked.

"I suppose holding your pickaninny makes me miss my own all the more." She patted her eyes with a handkerchief.

"Maybe you should go back inside your house and rest," Jane offered. She herself was set to go home now and start toiling over this laundry. Annie's easy words about Negro slavery had made her a little sick.

"Oh, I'll rest later. It's too pretty out here." Annie walked down the porch stairs, bouncing Miriam in her arms. Jane followed after. "I've been keeping myself busy," Annie said. "I'm finishing a quilt, changing all the furnishings. My whole life is changing." Her tears swelled again.

"You been cryin' more than usual these days, Mizz Annie."

"I don't wish to appear foolish. Mister Thomas thinks me so dramatic."

"Mizz Annie, more cryin' than usual—that could mean somethin'. I know some women, when they gets in a family way, if you pardon me, the tears come more easy. Always happen that way for me."

"You think I'm in a family way?"

"Ain't my business to ask. I can be headin' for home now. I need to soak this wash."

"Jane, I'll tell you. My family is getting larger, but I'm not 'in the family way.' I don't seem able to be in the family way. And I must not deny Tom a posterity."

That was all that needed saying. Jane understood. Tom was taking a plural wife.

Annie looked away. "I think your baby's hungry. She's nibbling on my button."

"Your husband got him a second wife?" Jane asked softly, setting the laundry basket on the porch and taking Miriam into her arms.

"Yes." The tears came hard.

"Oh, that must be a trial. You know you can tell me all about it, but you're right about my baby bein' hungry. I'd best feed her while we talk." Jane commenced nursing Miriam.

"She makes the sweetest noises when she's eating. Most contented sounds in this world," Annie said.

"I always think so too."

"I've prayed to God to have a baby making that noise." Annie sat on the top step and lowered her head into the crooks of her elbows. "I understand the principle, plural marriage and all. But I just didn't expect—I don't feel ready."

"Is she a nice woman?"

Annie lifted her head. "She's a pretty woman. A young one. Younger than me. I was seventeen years old when I married Mister Thomas. Did I ever tell you that?"

"Not that I recollect."

Annie's whole body drooped. "I'm barely into my twenties now. Am I doing something wrong?" It sounded more like a plea than a question.

"Because you ain't had children yet?" Silas and Syl, in the yard, were kicking dirt at each other. Jane warned them to stop.

"I always considered myself—I don't intend to sound haughty—but folks told me, young men told me—I was somewhat of a beauty. I came into my womanhood early. I never thought Tom would even have eyes for anyone else."

Jane instructed her boys to go on ahead and feed the goat some grass while she held conversation with Sister Thomas.

"You more than a 'somewhat beauty,' Mizz Annie," Jane said. "You a full beauty. All the world can see that."

Annie dabbed at her eyes and cheeks and then smoothed her hair with her palms. "Do you think God punishes us for sins from our past?"

Jane tried not to appear surprised. "Our past before this life?"

Annie frowned. "Why should God punish us for sins we don't even recall committing?"

"Good question, ma'am."

"I mean, he does punish us for sins of our recent past, doesn't he?"

"I don't know as I can answer that, Mizz Annie. I think whatever steps we take sets us on one path or another. You got a memory troublin' your mind?"

Annie lowered her head into her elbows again. "I was cruel to my mother when I joined the Church and eloped with Mister Thomas. Broke my parents' hearts. Do you think God would punish me for that?"

"Now why would God punish you for following his prophet on this earth?" Jane asked.

"You do believe he was a prophet, don't you?"

"Oh, I better than believe it. I know it. I seen him in vision before I ever beheld him in person. I was his household servant until the day he died. I guess I did know him. That lovely hand! He used to put it out to me. Never passed me without shaking hands with me wherever he was. Oh, he was the finest man I ever saw on earth."

"And a good man?"

"The best man! I didn't get much of a chance to talk with him—I was so busy, and so was he. But he'd always smile, always just like he did to his children. He used to be just like I was his child."

"You knew about plural marriage even in Nauvoo?"

"Oh yes. Four of Brother Joseph's own wives told me. Now plural marriage be a test of your faith, Mizz Annie. You'll pass it fine. Just like you passed all your other tests in gettin' here to Zion."

"You believe in the principle?"

"Plural marriage is fine by me, but it ain't been my trial and ain't likely to be. I think colored folk don't be included in this test. But I seen some plural wives who love the principle much as they love the Lord. Eliza Lyman and her own sister be sharin' one husband—Brother Amasa—and they get along splendid."

"You believe we get punished for sins we forgot?"

Jane did not answer for a moment. Then she said softly, "I think you believe it."

Annie regained herself. "I thank you for listening, but we'd best get on with our chores, both of us. Now, I do want my husband's collars starched in the usual way, but you know I don't like my underskirts stiff. Last time you did the work, I felt like I was wearing wood. I like my clothes to flow when I move."

Jane chose not to mention that Annie herself had requested more starch for her petticoats last laundry day. "I'm sorry about that starch, ma'am. I'll make sure it won't happen this time. Well, looks like Miriam had enough feedin' for now. Time for me to get home and start all this work. I do appreciate you using my service, Mizz Annie." She buttoned herself up.

"It was only that one time my underskirts came back over-starched. Other than that—. I don't wish to arouse your pride, Jane, but it is my opinion you are the best laundress in the territory of Utah." Annie forced a fine smile.

"Thank you kindly, ma'am. I be on my way now."

"The clothes will be ready on Thursday?"

"I ain't never failed you yet."

Jane beckoned to her boys, who abandoned the goat with happy shrieks. Syl took Miriam, and Jane showed herself out the front gate, the laundry basket on her head, her children making a line before her.

"My, my," Jane said. "You never know what some folks be suf-ferin'. Mizz Annie have such pain right now. She look at you chil-dren and take to weepin' over every single body she left behind. Family and slaves both."

Her thoughts went to her own family then—the family she had left behind. She was as separate from her brothers and sisters as if she had got sold down the river. She hoped her brother Lew's mis-chief had found some control. She prayed for him specifically most every day of her life.

NOTES

The chapter title is from a traditional Negro spiritual found in Burleigh, *Spirituals*, 157.

The slave code referred to was set in 1852, when Brigham Young observed, referring to Indian slavery: "Human flesh to be dealt in as property, is not consistent or compatible with the principles of government. My own feelings are, that no property can or should be recognized as existing in slaves, whether Indian or African." There was a distinction between Indian and Negro slavery, however. The Indians were to be "purchas[ed] into freedom, instead of slavery" ("Governor's Message to the Legislative Assembly of Utah," qtd. in Bush, "Mormonism's Negro Doctrine", 68). By contrast, Negro slavery was, according to the thought of the day, divinely instituted. Brigham Young stated: "Treat the slaves kindly and let them live, for Ham must be the servant of servants until the curse is removed. Can you destroy the decrees of the Almighty? You cannot" (*Journal of Discourses*, 10:250).

Jane's words describing Joseph Smith and his care for her are from her interview with the *Young Woman's Journal* (551): "Yes indeed, I guess I did know the Prophet Joseph. That lovely hand! He used to put it out to me. Never passed me without shaking hands with me wherever he was. Oh, he was the finest man I ever saw on earth. I did not get much a chance to talk with him. He'd always smile just like he did to his children. He used to be just like I was his child."

The idea, implied by Annie, that blacks were being punished for pre-mortal sins was not uncommon in early Mormonism. Although the Prophet Joseph Smith and Brigham Young taught that there were no neutral spirits in heaven (see Journal History of the Church, December 25, 1869), other early Latter-day Saint leaders taught that blacks and others were punished on earth for premortal behavior. Through repetition, these teachings gained some acceptance, even though numerous scriptures emphasize that one's standing before God is ultimately a matter of individual responsibility (see D&C 93:38; Article of Faith 2; Alma 3:19; 17:15). On June 8, 1978, a revelation received by President Spencer W. Kimball extended the priesthood to all worthy male members of the Church. Current Church doctrine states simply that we do not know why certain restrictions had earlier been placed on the African race (see "Blacks," *Encyclopedia of Mormonism*, 1:125).

By 1852, the Latter-day Saints were taking public initiative in regard to plural marriage. An August 1852 missionary conference "was something of a watershed in Mormon history" wherein Orson Pratt "argued that its practice was the result of modern revelation and protected by the American constitution" (Whittaker, "Polygamy," 44). That the principle was difficult for many Mormon women is not at issue, for numerous pioneer journals attest that it was.

Lewis Manning
and Louis Gray
1851

13

Many Thousands Go

For ye suffer, if a man bring you into bondage, . . .
if a man take of you, if a man exalt himself,
if a man smite you on the face.
2 CORINTHIANS 11:20

Jane had no way of knowing it, for none of her family could write, but Lewis Manning was alive and kicking and living on the water. Their sisters, Angeline, Lucinda, and Sarah, were still in Illinois. Their brother, Peter, had started off for Iowa. Lew was working as a cook on a steamboat and also had duties of loading and unloading cargo. His boss lived in St. Louis, which is where Lewis Manning met Louis Gray.

Manning was wearing wool trousers and a cotton shirt. Gray was in overalls and a worn, floppy hat. At the moment, alongside the steamboat, Louis Gray was unloading a barrel of salt pork onto the dock. He and his owner had spent eight days in traveling to St. Louis to sell their wares and look over the slave market. The massa, in a top hat and travel clothes, stood a good distance away from the Negroes.

Gray told Manning there were more barrels in the wagon and

then lifted his hat and took a rag from his pocket, mopping the sweat from his forehead and eyes.

"I can help for a spell," said Manning, "but I got other things to unload besides yo' wagon today."

"I ain't used to the mugginess in the air 'round this river," Gray said. "Don' know how you stand it."

"Where you from, you don' know muggy?"

"Marshall. It ain't dry there, but it sho' ain't as drippin' as here."

"Marshall, Missouri? I ain't heard of it."

"It ain't much to hear. So where you from?"

"Nauvoo, Illinois," Lew Manning said proudly. "And it used to be mighty much."

Louis went for another barrel, calling over his shoulder, "I heard o' Nauvoo. That be where the Mormons set up."

"That's right."

"That be where they moved to, once General Lucky run 'em outta Missouri."

"That's right. Was set to be Zion, till some mob men up and kill our prophet. Now it's just a busted dream." They heaved the barrel to their shoulders and toted it to the ship.

"Nauvoo," repeated Louis Gray as they passed the load to the cargo men. "Yes indeed, I sho' hear 'bout it."

"Some folks call it 'The City Beautiful.' I stayed there until I see the mobs spoil our temple," Manning said.

"*Our* temple?" Louis Gray dropped his jaw. "You ain't Mormon, is you?"

Lew grinned. "Tried and true and tried again." They headed back to the wagon for the next barrel.

"Well, if this ain't somethin'! I done met what must be the only two colored Mormons in the whole world!"

Now it was Lew Manning dropping his jaw. "Who else you know?"

"Can't recall the name. Met him years ago. A missionary man. Preacher, so he say."

"Gotta be Mr. Elijah Abel. That name sound familiar?" Lew himself had never met Elijah Abel, though he certainly had heard of him. Every colored in Nauvoo had heard of him, and a good many whites had too.

"Could be." Gray lifted the next barrel, and they shouldered it. "Can't say for sure. Whatever his name, he tell me God was goin' free that leader man of yours outta jail."

"He was mos' likely referrin' to Joseph Smith, the prophet. Well, like I say, Brother Joseph got killed."

"Seems yo' lively colored preacher was flat-out wrong, then."

Lew sighed. "Not exactly wrong. God got Joseph outta Missouri jails all right. God held him free from harm for near six years. Then the devil whipped up some meanness, churned up some blood, and the mobs killed Brother Joseph dead. I dug his grave myself."

"Ever'where you look, they's good folk and they's folk what got the devil. Mos' time, feel like the devil claim the larger pack."

Louis Gray's massa hollered at him that this trip was about work, not conversation. "We off to the auction," Gray whispered, after they unloaded the last barrel. His massa was already waiting in the wagon seat.

"Sorry t' hear that," Lew Manning murmured, not sure if this slave was about to be sold or if he was driving his owner to buy a coffle of field hands.

Gray and his massa, Mortimer Gaines, had come especially for this sale, where rice hands and hog handlers were being offered at decent prices. Gaines had read the ad in the paper. *For Sale: Rice Negroes, farmhands, and servants will be sold on the fourth and fifth of March.*

Louis had never been to a slave auction, and he was anything but prepared for what he would see that day.

The auction would get conducted in a dank and shadowy place which used to be a prison. Happenings in this large room were not displayed in open light, for there were many, especially among St. Louis's German population, who deplored slavery.

Nearly one hundred Negroes had come by rail, wagon, and steamer to meet their fate at this dungeon. They had been kept in sheds built for horses. Now they needed to appear healthy and eager to please.

Outside the auction room, Massa Gaines put on his frock coat and cravat so he could show his station. He did appear well-bred, with his combed dark hair, light skin, and pink cheeks. From the looks of him, he had never done more work than lifting a teacup or an eyebrow.

While Louis was waiting on the massa's final preparations, he heard one of the slave drivers say: "You can manage ordinary niggers by lickin' 'em, givin' 'em a taste of the hot iron once in awhile when they're extra ugly. But if a nigger really sets himself up against me, I can't never have any patience with him. I just get my pistol and shoot him down. That's the best way."

The driver meant him to hear that, Louis knew for certain.

"Look sharp, boy," said the massa. "I don't want you mistaken for the ones getting sold. Where's my top hat?"

"In the wagon, sir." He had already taken two steps before calling back, "I'll get it."

But the moment Louis bent to pick up the hat, an eery silence fell like fog around him. He could sense something gloomy and important. Doors were opening. People were moving. He heard the shuffle of many feet, the clinking of many chains, the crack of a whip, moaning.

The slaves were coming.

Louis sat up. Then he couldn't move. He kept repeating the words, "Lord, Lord, my Lord!"

The slaves, every one looking beat, were led to a trough of green water and given rags to wash themselves. The same driver Louis had overheard was yelling, "Get that dress off, gal. Don' be thinking you got anything to hide. You clean up and get yourself presentable!"

Beside the trough was a bucket of lard, which the slaves were to smear over their bodies. Oh, they would be polished by the time they entered the big room.

Louis had forgotten why he had gone to the wagon. He returned to his massa without the hat, making a stunned apology when Gaines asked where it was. He didn't try to explain how the sight of these poor, bound souls had stopped his mind and made him forget everything he ever knew. The top hat was still in the wagon.

"I'll do without it. There's no time now. Come on," ordered Mortimer Gaines.

Louis obeyed, trailing him down the long, ever darker stairs.

The slaves were already inside and on display. Louis had to blink away the sun before he could take in the scene.

There they were, the whole mess of them. Most stared at the ground, waiting to be called to the block, which was actually a table. Children clung to their mothers' skirts. The mothers knew, even if the children did not, that this could be their last day together for the rest of their lives. That knowledge showed in every mother's face.

At first, there was little crying. But when a boychild—no older than five—got sold out of his mama's handclasp, there was crying indeed. The boy wailed and the woman went to her knees, begging the heavy-bearded buyer, "Mister, he the bes' boy when I can help him. He can be whatever you want. Let me train him. In the name of Jesus, buy me too."

Seemed her words fell straight to the floor. Nobody paid her mind. The buyer picked the child up and swung him over his shoulders like a bag of grain. The mother's words grew louder and more desperate. Louis heard a slap but didn't look towards it. The mother was sobbing—full-voiced at first, with cries so sharp they could've clawed the air. Then it became a sob song and finally a long, muffled moan. Louis's eyes insisted on finding her.

Whoever had sent this woman to auction had gone to some trouble making her look good. Her hair was braided down both sides and tied in colorful ribbons. Her blue dress and muslin apron were not new, but they were clean. He wondered why anyone would sell her off. Well, sometimes folks just needed money. He understood that and knew that if his own massa should find himself in straits, the slaves would likely get sold before the furniture would. (Of course, the massa would never sell off *all* his slaves. That household couldn't run itself, and nobody but the colored help knew how to keep it running. If some slaves got sold, the remaining ones would simply get more work.) He thanked God his massa was living well off, with hogs to process and meat to sell. Louis Gray had known his mama, Maria Gaines, all his born days, and he had never seen an auction until now.

"That's a healthy woman," said Massa Mortimer. "We might be able to get her for a better price right this moment. She's not showing herself to advantage, acting up that way."

Louis could not speak the words that were filling him, so he stayed silent.

Massa stroked his cravat. "I personally couldn't do that to a mother, but not everyone is like me."

"No sir," Louis murmured.

"Ripe hips on her, though she's trim built. From the size of the boy, seems her milk is good. I heard once of a man stuffed rags down a slave woman's dress so the buyer wouldn't realize she had no chest, only consumption. Slave died two weeks after her sale."

"Is that a fact, sir?"

"You have to beware. Even a white man will cheat you blind if he thinks he can do it. At an auction, you check the item's joints. Stiff joints can't pick. You check a female's dugs, so you don't find yourself paying for something death has already bought. And you check the back for whip marks. No use trading good money for a slave who can't keep his feet where they belong. Isn't that the truth?"

"Yessir." But Louis had not heard. There were too many sounds—the auctioneer, bidders, buyers asking questions, slaves answering in all the varied voices of defeat.

"Well, that woman's not wearing rags down her dress, is she? What do you think?"

"Sir?"

"Take a good look."

Louis obeyed. "She sad but not sick."

"How about her arms?"

"They fine, massa."

"Tolerable strong, from what I can see. Legs?"

"Can't say cause I can't see."

"She'll need to walk for us. I won't have a cripple. What else do we need to look at, Louis?"

It was then, in a cold sweep of realization, that Louis understood why the massa had brought him on this trip and to this auction.

"Massa, this my first time. You knows your way around."

"I want to view the teeth. No need to buy a mouthful of trouble. You pay enough for a slave, and you'd better get your money's worth. I paid considerable for your mama. Found her at a fine auction over in Kentucky. And she's been worth my investment. I won't settle for less than the best. I'll need to check the teeth on that woman before I turn over a penny."

Louis watched his massa examine the woman's teeth. Her face was vacant as she opened her mouth. All the while Louis could hear the auctioneer telling a teenaged girl on the block, "Turn. Bend over. Smile." The girl did everything she was told to do with no words or questions. A big, burly man bought her. Next, an old couple was led to the table, and the bidding began all over again, though with less interest than the girl's sale brought.

Massa decided the woman's teeth were in good condition. When she went to the block, the auctioneer introduced her as a well-cared for household servant who had done both cooking and field work, though she would be best placed in the kitchen or the home.

"Have her hold out her hands," Mortimer Gaines called.

She heard and obliged.

"Have her bend her fingers."

She bent them.

"Have her walk a few steps and then turn."

She stiffened her back and took a step. Despite this indignity, there was a presence, a substance to this woman.

"Hold your head up, girl," the auctioneer said.

When she did, her eyes closed. Seemed her whole face closed, shut down. Seemed the spirit in her retreated to some unknowable distance.

"She'll do," the massa said.

The bidding commenced, and he purchased her. He also bought a male field hand, whose growth was just coming on him and looked to be promising. This young man was handcuffed and shackled as soon as his price was paid.

On the way to the wagon, Massa Gaines instructed Louis to stay with the two new slaves. He was in the mood to drive, he said, and he wanted Louis to put them at ease, let them know they were lucky to be going to the Gaines residence. They had been bought by civilized, God-fearing people. It would be well for them to recognize that another, evil sort could've had them.

The field hand was kept in his chains. Up close, Louis could see that this was a child. His body may have started its bloom, but he wasn't no more than twelve years old. He seemed resigned but curious too, watching the scenes change around him: hills, woods, great pine forests, small farms, an occasional lake. When Louis smiled at him, he smiled back.

"We get the shackles from off you soon as we arrives. Massa don't keep us chained. He got a couple of sons just older than you— Wilbur and Ben. You got a name?" Louis asked.

"Adam."

"My name Louis."

The woman was huddled in the wagon corner, staring straight ahead with a face so empty and eyes so glazed she appeared dead. She did not answer when Louis asked her name. He didn't try talking to her again until they stopped at a little town to feed the horses and themselves. Massa spoke to a farmer while Louis took care of the animals and unpacked the ashcakes his mama had sent.

When he offered the woman some food, she shook her head. He dropped the ashcake into her lap anyway and suggested she might be hungry later. "I ain't never seed a auction," he whispered to her. "It's a ugly thing. I seen them take yo' boy."

She met his gaze briefly. There was no life in her, except the quick movement of her eyes away from his.

It wasn't until a week later, after they were back in Marshall at the Gaines slave quarters, that the woman told her name—not to Louis but to his mama, Maria.

"My name Gracie," she said.

Gracie was a good worker and soon showed some personality in her face. She even smiled a time or two over the next month. The days were healing her, though Louis was careful not to ask certain questions. There was private pain in her. He would not violate that pain by asking her to show it to him.

It was the massa who decided Louis and Gracie should marry— and not in a broom jump but with papers showing that the law recognized their union.

Truth was, though, even in the "legal" union of two slaves, no words were used like "What God hath joined together, let not man put asunder." In a slave wedding, the bride and groom belonged to somebody besides each other, and if that somebody took a mind to put the match asunder so he could make a profit, he'd do it. Nobody would even notice. A slave marriage could last forever, or it could last until dawn.

But this was a settled household; nobody was getting sold off unless they ran. And they wouldn't run. Especially not now, not since that new law got passed. A slave's running now was more dangerous and more deadly than it ever had been before, and they all knew it.

On their wedding night, Louis told his bride, "I know this ain't something you picked. But I will work hard at being a good husband, and I ask you to meet me bein' a good wife."

"Yes," said Gracie Gray.

NOTES

The chapter title is from a traditional Negro spiritual cited in Higginson, "Negro Spirituals," 692.

Through Darius Gray's personal family history research (ably assisted by Margery Taylor), it appears that the name of Louis and Gracie Gray's owner was either Mortimer or Thomas Gaines. We have chosen Mortimer.

Though Carter lists Isaac Lewis Mannning's birth date as May 31, 1815 (*Negro Pioneer*, 12), he clearly was born after that. Inasmuch as we have placed his sister Jane's birth year at 1822 and Isaac was younger than she, we estimate his birth year as 1825, thus making him a close contemporary of Louis Gray, whose birth year is estimated between 1823 and 1826. Louis Gray is the ancestor of Darius Gray. Information about him is from Gray family records extracted from Family Search File.

We do not know the particulars of how Louis and Gracie met, or if she was purchased at auction or in some other way. We know that her name before marriage was Gracie Montgomery. She was born somewhere in Missouri and lived from 1833 to 1875 (Gray family records). We know that Louis and Gracie Gray's marriage was not a "broom jumping" because we have a record of the certificate of their marriage.

The words of the slave driver about "managing niggers" are from Johnson et al., *Africans in America*. These words are purported to be a direct quotation from a slave driver at an auction, overheard by Mortimer Neal Thomson, "who disguised himself as a slave speculator to write an exhaustive chronicle of the sale for the *New York Tribune*" (432–33).

Cincinnati
1850 to 1853

14

I WANT TO BE READY

The nation to whom they shall be in bondage
will I judge, said God: and after that shall they
come forth, and serve me in this place.
ACTS 7:7

When the Fugitive Slave Act got passed in 1850—the harshest law ever to corral our people, letting masters chase their slaves to kingdom come or straight to hell—the abolitionists got inspired. They had to, for there was many a money-grubbing, stonehearted gunslinger who tried to make his fortune pursuing slaves who dared step towards liberty.

Abolitionists met often and angry, and Elijah Abel told several that if Joseph Smith had got made president instead of made dead, slavery would've been done away.

Elijah was in the hall when Sojourner Truth addressed an abolitionist assembly at Cincinnati. He had rarely been more impressed by any mortal, male or female.

She was a tall, coffee-brown woman, big-boned, a ways past middle age, wearing a gown of simple serge and heavy shoes. When she approached the pulpit, power came right alongside her. This was a woman indeed.

Sojourner Truth told about the breakup of slave families, told of herself pleading years ago with her mizzus, "Have you been an' sent my son away down Alabama?" and the answer coming back, "What a fuss you make about a little nigger! Got more of 'em now than you know what to do with!"

To Elijah, Sojourner Truth's voice changed as he listened. He was hearing his own mama, Delilah Abel. He was remembering her wakeup call that one great morning.

It's time!

He was wondering how planned their escape had really been.

Wake up your brothers, 'Lijah!

How could it have been planned? Was Delilah Abel another Sojourner Truth just hoping God would light up a path, then stepping into the night with nothing more than prayer for protection? He hoped his mama knew what all he was doing in Cincinnati to free the captives. He knew she would be proud.

"I kneeled down," said Sojourner Truth, "and says I, 'Well, Lord, you've started me out, and now please to show me where to go.' Then the Lord made a house appear to me, and he said to me that I was to walk on till I saw that house, and then go in an' ask the people to take me. I went in, and I told the folks that the Lord sent me, and they was Quakers."

Elijah was reliving it all. After all this time working on the freedom side of the underground, he knew how brave and faithful his mama had been. He wished he had given her his cloak first thing instead of wearing it himself. Wished he had protected her better. Wished he had at least built her a prettier coffin. It pained him to think of her bones freezing under Canada's ice in that flimsy box he had cut from scrap wood.

Sojourner was talking now about a vision she had had of Jesus "like the sun shinin' in a pail o' water." Her voice got deeper, dropped into reverent tones. "And finally somethin' spoke out in me and said, 'This is Jesus. *This is Jesus!*'"

Elijah was weeping. He had never seen Jesus, but he had heard the voice of his own dead mother, back when the Kirtland Temple got dedicated. And he had imagined Joseph of the Rainbow Coat talking about the heavenly shine, that core of love. But Elijah was far from such love right now. His glittering robes seemed so distant when he thought of slavery, of Amos Luther's wounds, and of the whip marks on many a slave he had helped.

Surely it was one thing for a man to offer his service to God. It was another thing entire for one man to kidnap another and claim him as property, proclaim him servant of servants, chain his feet, and then hoist the sails of a ship and carry that man across the ocean to a life that would spend him up. That kidnapper would whup and bloody the black man's hide and sell off the black man's woman and child without a second thought.

At all these abolitionist meetings, Elijah Abel felt his insides swell with bitterness so strong he could taste it like acid in the back of his mouth. It could put out a Southern massa's eye should Elijah spit just right. And here was Sojourner Truth testifying that because of Jesus, she could love "even de white folk."

Yes, certainly Elijah could love Brother Joseph, and station-master Levi Coffin, and a number of his fellow carpenters in the Nauvoo Guild, and several of the brethren, and these good abolitionists around him—certainly, Lord. But the slave holders, the massas, the whip-snapping overseers and drivers, the auctioneers who sold off his people like lamps, and some of his fellow Saints—Church members who either owned slaves or hated black flesh—no, he could not imagine how in this world God might peel away his anger towards them. Elijah's was a frosty rage, layered like a frozen onion. Nothing but the blaze of God could melt its skins away. And God wasn't boiling his blood at this moment, just pricking him, bidding him to continue doing his part to deliver the slaves.

Everyone in this room was called to usher in the glory of the Lord and lead the slaves to Canaan—the promised land. Everyone at this meeting was called to be Moses. Surely the walls of Jericho would come tumbling down.

By now, he was accustomed to hiding runaway slaves in his root cellar, just as he himself had been hidden all those years ago. Mary Ann was accustomed to thinning the soup to provide for "company." Elijah was used to steering a skiff of fugitives across that last arm of the Ohio River and pointing them north. Mary Ann was used to watching them depart, though she always prayed, "Lord, take mercy on my man, the father of my child."

He'd often start his work with questions to identify the slaves as true runaways, not paid spies.

"How does he expect to get deliverance?"

"By his own efforts," would come the response.

"Has he faith?"

"He has hope."

Elijah helped a group of colored minstrels once, who had performed their way from South Carolina to Cincinnati.

As far back as the 1820s, white men had mocked Negroes in these minstrel shows. White actors would black their faces with burned cork, circle their lips in white, and proceed to act like the most wretched and ignorant Negroes who ever walked the earth. White folks enjoyed such shows, and it didn't take long for blacks to figure they could mock themselves as well as any white man could.

The minstrels sang and acted like giddy plantation slaves. One of the songs might sound familiar to you:

> *There is beauty all around*
> *When there's love at home;*
> *There is joy in ev'ry sound*
> *When there's love at home.*

Of course, when the minstrels sang it in the 1850s, it suggested a picture of happy slaves callusing their hands on cotton bolls so their massas could build big barns and more slave quarters.

Many white folks, seeing the minstrels sing so pretty and act so foolish, took comfort in believing that all the slaves wanted was for their massas to pet them some, so's they could make their huge, toothless smiles and say "Thank you, massa" a hundred times on their way to the fields.

The particular minstrels Elijah Abel met up with weren't looking for their plantations or their massas, though. They were looking for liberty. Their owner had put the group together, thinking it great sport, and of course he kept the money they made.

Elijah asked them what they planned on doing once they reached the Lion's Paw (the only safe place now). They said they aimed to mine or farm. No more burned cork for their faces. No more mindless grins for their mouths. They were set to be better than the jokes they made of themselves for their massa's pocketbook.

"You think you might miss your fame?" Elijah asked.

"No," they said together.

The shortest, stockiest one thrust a banjo into Elijah's arms as payment and told him to learn to pick it good.

On the shore, the band sang a new song softly: "*O Freedom, O Freedom, O Freedom after awhile . . .*"

It was a song that most blacks would soon learn, though its words would change as freedom got closer. Some would sing, "O freedom, Lord, for me," and others would hear that as "O freedom over me." But after much tribulation and anguish of soul, the last verse would be the triumph of all freed men:

> *And before I'll be a slave,*
> *I'll be buried in my grave,*
> *And go home to my Lord*
> *And be free.*

Elijah strummed his new banjo when he entered his house. He experimented with his fingers, trying one chord and then another, not making much music, though. With his untaught voice, he sang a piece the minstrels had taught him: "Polly wolly doodle all day."

"I might need some practice," he said.

Mary Ann tried not to laugh. "You might," she agreed.

So he took to practicing, which Mary Ann endured with admirable humor. Most every night, Elijah sang songs with his banjo—except when a knock came at his door. Then songs got replaced by prayers.

There was one night especially worthy of prayer, when he helped a round-faced woman lead two families out of bondage. The dogs were barking fierce, and he knew these weren't the dogs he heard every night. Their howls were not distant, and they were not harmless. The runaways—four adults and five children—had come from the Deep South to Cincinnati, crossing the Ohio once in thrashing attempts at a downriver swim. After a day's rest, they were set to cross the bend in Elijah's skiff.

He got them safely across, quiet as could be. Years later, he wondered if their leader might've been Harriet Tubman, though he never knew for sure. There were certainly many conductors risking their lives for liberty. Maybe the names didn't matter. History would choose which names to wreathe, but the Lord knew them all.

On several nights he helped women who resembled Nancy, but each denied that name. One stared at him with familiar eyes, and he was certain it was Nancy, except she was older than he'd expected.

"How you called?" he asked her.

"Molly."

"You remind me of another woman. Name of Nancy."

Molly had a man, who put both his arms around her. A child was with them too. Molly squeezed that child and covered his mouth so he wouldn't cry out.

"What be that sound?" she asked as Elijah started rowing.

Elijah's oar swished the water aside. Sticks cracked from the woods.

"What sound?" he said.

"Like somethin' waitin'."

"Could be a deer. Or could be a friend of mine set to guide you to your next station. Ain't nothin' to arouse your fear."

A lantern flickered from the shore. Elijah said, "It's a friend. Just like one who helped me years ago, when I escaped outta Maryland. You ever been to Maryland?"

"No sir," said the woman.

"You sure?"

The man answered for her: "She know where she been."

When they reached land, a tiny old Quaker woman was waiting, her lantern low.

Molly looked up as Elijah took her hand to help her out of the skiff, but her man had his arm tight around her shoulders. They started down the damp swath towards that hoop of freedom's light, and Elijah returned to the boat.

Even if she was Nancy, she did not belong to him. Not even in his dreams. Her voice and look may have been Nancy's, but she did not belong to him. Mary Ann Adams Abel belonged to him, and he belonged to Mary Ann.

In his lonely years, it used to be that Elijah would imagine companions from the Bible so's he could talk with someone. Joseph of the Rainbow Coat was his most favorite. Since his son's birth, though, he hadn't made up companions. He didn't have the need. Mary Ann filled all the spaces in his days and exchanged understandings with him even when she wasn't talking. That was a good thing, for she didn't talk all that much.

Four years after Moroni's arrival, Enoch Abel was born. The Abels had been helping with the Underground Railroad all that time. But their work in Cincinnati was about to end.

Elijah watched Mary Ann suckle their son and knew that the day had come to move west. Mary Ann's head was lowered, and the baby was nursing. Simple as that. But the sight of such a simple thing jolted Elijah. Maybe it was even a warning from the Lord. Elijah understood he was in sore danger and catchers were ready to wreck his world.

Maybe Elijah was just being seized by fearful memory, but every part of his soul was telling him what he already knew: Any Negro anywhere could be tagged a runaway and sold to cotton country. You wouldn't think such would happen in Ohio, but it could happen anywhere.

As Elijah watched his wife stroking their baby's cheek, the worst memory of his life throbbed down his chest: Nancy and his firstborn daughter, getting carted away to auction.

He had not lost his devotion to the cause, but he could not bear to lose his woman and baby. Not again. And something told him danger was too near.

Harriet Beecher Stowe had just published *Uncle Tom's Cabin*, and Northerners were becoming more aware of the horrors of bondage. Many whites on the north side of the Ohio—and some on the south side too—were becoming stationmasters in the Underground Railroad. And with Utah deciding to be slave holding instead of free, Elijah thought his particular skills might be called for out west, where peril wouldn't lurk so close at hand.

That very evening, he announced to Mary Ann that their job was done. The call had come to make their way towards Zion and gather with the Saints.

"We finished helpin' runaways?" Mary Ann was a tiny woman, small of bone, small of feature, and small of voice. She always spoke soft, even when she was sitting on a three-legged stool plucking a chicken, as she was now.

"Others here to do the work."

"You give up on findin' Nancy?" She turned the chicken over and went on plucking.

He wanted her to hear the truth he had never really told and asked that she stop her work and listen. "Honey," he said, "can't no woman—past or present—ever take your place or be to me what you are. Memories is ghosts, and you is flesh and blood."

"Well, if you found her, she'd be flesh and blood too."

"She wouldn't be you."

"But you been lookin' for her—in your heart—for so long."

"I know who I want." He frowned. "You ain't never talked like this before. How long you been thinkin' on it?"

She wiped her brow but didn't meet his eyes. "It cross my mind on occasion."

"If you'd asked me, I coulda comforted your soul."

"What would you tol' me?"

He knelt. If he'd been wearing a hat, he'd have swept it off his head. "Mary Ann, I am bowin' on my benders to tell you this: You are the wife of my heart, the joy of my life, the part of me I never knowed was missin' until I found you. I want to be with you longer than life. I aim to partake of everything with you. The Brethren, they say the Church got ceremonies now to seal up a wife and her husband for all eternity. That's what I desire. I want you forever."

"I wants the same," she said in that sweet, soft voice. She returned to plucking before tears could take her. "This journey to the Rockies—for how long we goin' be on the plains?"

"Plain and prairie both. A few months." Still kneeling, Elijah put his arms around her, nestling his head in her belly. "Mary Ann, remember you married a man takes angels with him wheresoever he travel. I been ferryin' fugitives across the waters all this long time, and the Lord ain't forgot me yet. You got no cause for fears."

She didn't need to speak any words out loud. Her face was speaking for her: *'Lijah, I believe in you since the first day I laid eyes on you. You jus' tell me when to be ready, and I will be. I always follow you.*

It took a month to prepare the wagon and resolve business in Cincinnati. Then they headed out, a team of mules hauling their tarp-covered, rolling house. Elijah's old horse—the very horse he had ridden from Nauvoo to Kirtland and then to Cincinnati—walked behind. The wood wheels creaked as the Abels stepped towards their future, making their journey in the heavy heat of summer.

Elijah walked alongside the team. Mary Ann drove from the buckboard, with Moroni next to her and Enoch on her lap. They traveled with some white folks who were headed for California but kept mostly to themselves.

It's hard to imagine all these journeys I can describe so easy. For those who walked the distance, there were long, long days when it felt they were in a bottle of sun with the lid screwed down. There were days when rain lashed the wagon and days when cool winds rustled the grasses and the air was clean and fragrant. There were days when wind tore over the low hills, swirling sand and turning the air grainy for miles, and there were days with no breeze at all. Many nights, coyotes yipped in the distance, and sometimes wolves bayed. Sometimes they heard rattlesnakes' warnings like dry beans.

Still, Elijah identified miracles almost by the hour. They never ran out of food, for one thing. If they had nothing to eat, seemed a quail or a rabbit would skitter up to their camp and pretty much offer itself. And Elijah was never one to refuse the offer. There were times the Platte was so murky, Mary Ann had to sweep her hand through green scum before she could fill their jugs with water, but somehow they didn't thirst—at least not much. And never once did Indians or sharp-toothed animals come near enough to threaten.

Now maybe these were miracles, or maybe the Abels stayed blessed because Elijah took out his banjo at the close of every day. Sitting apart from the whites, the Abel family would sing. Truth be told, their singing was enough to keep most any animal or Indian far away. Elijah and Moroni belted out songs, and Mary Ann held a timid tune, though sometimes she enjoyed the music so much she giggled. Once or twice, she even danced an embarrassed jig with her husband.

Their favorite song went like this:

> 'Tis sad to leave our tater land
> And all we there loved well
> Yet hard as am this loss to bear,
> And deep all stomachs smart
> 'Tis worse to be no longer near
> The regions of our heart.

Of course, they sang gospel songs too, and Mary Ann remembered her church life from before she met Elijah. She couldn't help responding to familiar hymns with "amen!" or "yes Lord!"

Elijah didn't strum the banjo during these spirituals but tapped or pounded or knocked on it like a drum. He wasn't sure where that drum impulse came from, but he thought probably Africa.

"Glory! Hallelujah! Let the halleluian roll," he sang as Mary Ann murmured, "I praise my Lord!"

> I'll sing my Savior's praises,
> Sing them far and wide.

Elijah knew this song and many others from his childhood, though he didn't know he remembered them until they poured from his mouth. He recalled his mama shouting, "Glory be to God! Bless His holy name!" from way back, when they had attended the slave church in Maryland. If he closed his eyes, he could see her so clear and so young, stamping her feet, clapping her hands, and yelling straight to heaven, near overcome with joy. Even working, she often hymned thank-you's to Jesus.

"I've opened up to Heaven all the windows of my soul," Elijah sang, happy as his mama had been. Mary Ann chimed in, "Yes Lord, yes!"

"And I'm livin' on the halleluian side!"

"Oh yes I am!" that shy woman said. She never shouted her praises but seemed to be truly praying and reverent as a rose.

After the nighttime singing, Elijah hauled his family down the paths and designs of his own life, telling them stories from his slave years and from the scriptures. Moroni was old enough to appreciate tales about the angel whose name he bore and asked for the "angel one" many a starry night. Elijah didn't tell him only the angel parts but made mention of Ancient Moroni's life on this earth too, when he was a hunted man just as Elijah himself had been, a fugitive running from enemies who would take his life for one cause only: his skin was different than theirs. He told how Ancient Moroni kept thinking he'd die, but then he wouldn't die, and he'd have time to carve more good thoughts into the gold pages of his book.

"Moroni," said Elijah Abel, "he keep on livin'. Trials and tribulations, woes and worries surround him like you can't imagine, but he keep on livin'. Same will happen to you and me, and we keep on livin'. Fiends and devils come a-callin', and he keep on livin'. Same fiends is like to beset you and me, and we keep on livin'."

"That's right. We do," whispered Mary Ann—who was just now learning these stories herself. Elijah had taught her some letters and shared Bible tales with her but not much from the Book of Mormon until now.

"I know how it be. Moroni thought his enemies was about to hang him high, but he keep on," said Elijah with rhythm under his words.

"Keep on," Mary Ann would echo. "Keep on. Keep on."

Sometimes, after a story, Mary Ann would rise to testify, being moved by the Spirit. "My Lord be guidin' us," she'd breathe. "We headed towards the Promise Place. His mercy bless us, yes it do. His love bring light to our darkest times, as we press on through this land." Her voice was softer than Delilah Abel's had ever been, but Elijah could imagine his mama saying exactly those words.

Their devotionals always ended with prayer, which Elijah

offered—and he could pray powerful: "Oh, Lord," he'd say, though the words changed nightly, "we come before you tonight to glorify your name and thank you for another day of safe journey. We know you is our strength and power. Your light shines brighter than the sun, and it give us life and hope. You holds us in your hands, and we know we safe. Now we ask that you send your guardians to watch over us whilst we sleep beside this wagon. Look after our trails and keep danger far away from us and from the others who share this path. We ask you, Lord, to set your mighty eyes on them we left behind. My brothers be somewhere north, and I ask you watch after them. All those we help when they lit out from the fetters of bondage, we ask you guide their steps. Look down on them, Lord, wherever they be. And while you doin' your lookin' down, we ask you keep a strong eye on our brothers and sisters who be in the chains of captivity still. Look down on the slave in Kentucky and in the Carolinas. Look down on the slave in Mississip and Tennessee. Look down on the slave wherever a overseer or massa hold a whip. And bless the feets and hands of them who help the slave, of them who visit the hopeless ones in prison. Make us all be free, Lord, and forgive the ones who don't know what they do. We all need your mercy, for you be our shelter in the storm and the rock of our salvation."

The Abels arrived in the Valley of the Great Salt Lake near the time when the Latter-day Saints were set to build another temple—this one greater than any before it.

Elijah was ready to help.

NOTES

The chapter title is from a traditional Negro spiritual found in Burleigh, *Spirituals*, 195.

Sojourner Truth, born Isabella Bonefree, was bought by her master, John Dumont, the year Elijah Abel was born—1810. The same year Abel converted to Mormonism, Isabella "left Zion African Church to join self-appointed messengers of God. . . . In 1832, she followed the Prophet Matthias

[Robert Matthews], one of the independent holy men inspired by the Second Great Awakening" (Painter, Introduction to *Narrative of Sojourner Truth*, ix). Coincidentally, this "prophet" visited Joseph Smith in Kirtland, which visit is recounted in some detail in *History of the Church*, 2:306–8. It is likely that Elijah Abel would have at least glimpsed "Matthias," as many of the Saints were curious about the man and visited the Smith place to meet him.

The *Narrative of Sojourner Truth* was published in 1850, and in 1851 she "set out to lecture and sell her book to audiences of reformers" (Painter, Introduction to *Narrative of Sojourner Truth*, x). It is not much of a stretch to imagine her lecturing at an abolitionist meeting in Cincinnati, one of the true hotbeds of the Underground Railroad because we know that she spoke on women's rights in Akron, Ohio, in 1851 (Painter, *Narrative of Sojourner Truth*, x). The excerpts from her speeches are from Stowe, "Sojourner Truth," 103–6.

Beginning with the early slavers, this passage from Genesis was used to justify Negro slavery: "Cursed be Canaan; a servant of servants shall he be unto his brethren" (Genesis 9:25).

The questions a fugitive slave might be asked to identify him are found in Katz, *Black West*, 100. There were also "arranged passwords and grips, and a ritual" (Katz, *Black West*, 100).

Black minstrelsy, begun in the 1820s, is attributed to T. D. Rice, a white man who blacked his face with burned cork, borrowed the tattered clothes from a crippled African-American man, and created the character "Jim Crow," a caricature of the "Sambo" slave, submissive and happy-go-lucky. At the time, Rice was called an "Ethiopian delineator." The name "Jim Crow" took its beginning from a song whose chorus went, "Reel about and turn about and jump just so/ Every time I wheel about, I jump Jim Crow." Eventually, blacks themselves became minstrels. The *New York Times* bought into the Jim Crow myth: "Absurd as may seem negro minstrelsy to the refined musician, it is nevertheless beyond doubt that it expresses the peculiar characteristics of the negro as truly as the great masters of Italy represent their more spiritual and profound nationality" (Johnson et al., *Africans in America*, 302).

The lyrics "'Tis sad to leave our tater land" are from T. W. Strong, published around 1850.

Hicks suggests that John Hugh McNaughton's song "There Is Beauty All Around" was in fact "popularized by Christy's Minstrels in the late 1850's. [It] depicted the tender feelings of plantation servants bound together by family ties" ("Ministering Minstrels," 52).

15

DON'T LEAVE
ME BEHIND

*For a friend of mine in his journey is come to me,
and I have nothing to set before him?*
LUKE 11:6

Isaac James was one of the first to learn that Elijah Abel had
arrived at last. He made his way running to the Abels' wagon. Janey
walked fast behind him, though she refused to run. She held her
dress up so the hem wouldn't get dirty, for Jane James disliked
dirt something powerful. She did everything she could to present
herself, her children, and her home as better than tolerable clean.
She tried keeping her husband bathed, though he generally
resisted. Sometimes he would not surrender his clothes for days at a
time. Unfortunately, on this important day, Isaac was so ripe, flies
wouldn't light. He wasn't one to notice his own smell or care about
it, though, and leapt into Elijah's arms.

"Elijah Abel, I been waitin' day by day for you to arrive!
Welcome to the new place!"

Elijah eyed him blankly. He wasn't at all sure who this
affectionate man was. "You ain't no happier to see us than we happy

139

to be here. Now, brother, you'll have to pardon me, but as spent as I be, I can't seem to recall your name."

"Why, I'm Isaac! Isaac James, from back in Nauvoo. And here's my mizzus. Meet Jane."

Elijah tried not to look surprised at the toll the years had taken on Isaac. Brother James had wore himself out since Nauvoo times. For one thing, he had lost his dog teeth, which Elijah chose not to mention. He beckoned to Mary Ann. "Honey, come on over here and get acquainted with some folks," he said.

She shot him a nervous glance. Baby Enoch clung to her skirt as she walked forward to meet these other Negro Mormons.

"Hello." Mary Ann offered a stiff hand to Jane. "Been journeyin'. I must look a sight."

Jane took Mary Ann full in her arms. Jane Manning James was not one to greet another colored woman with only a handshake. "Sister Mary Ann," she said. "I can't tell you how glad it make me to see you arrived. Now you join us for supper."

Elijah said, "We brought our two little boys across the plains from Cincinnati. Been a back-breakin' trip."

Isaac waved that news away like it was a trite little bug. "Everybody here know about that. Fact is, we brung two little boys across the plain ourselves. And Jane was in a family way too. Had us a little girl. And guess what we named her?" When Isaac grinned, Elijah couldn't help seeing that not only his dog teeth were missing but some back teeth too. "We named her Mary Ann! Same name as you, Sister Abel!"

"Ain't that somethin'!" Elijah said. "You gave my wife a namesake before you even met her!"

"We live close," Jane said. "I got potatoes cookin', and I know the rigors of the trip you just done." She took Mary Ann by the elbow. "Why don't we let these men do what needs doin'—settlin' the animals and all. You come meet the child we named for you.

You bring that baby too. And that little boy standing by the wagon—looks like the big brother. How he called?"

"That one be Moroni." Mary Ann's eyes were fixed on her feet. "And this baby be Enoch." She picked him up.

"My! What fine names!"

Jane was already leading her away when Mary Ann looked over her shoulder, calling, "Elijah?"

"Go on now, Mary Ann. Make friends," he answered as Jane led her to the cabin.

While they unhitched the mules, Elijah asked Isaac if there were many colored folk in the Valley.

Isaac showed off his missing teeth again in a big grin. "There was a passel of us, but some gone on to California."

"How many left?"

"I 'spect a dozen or more." Isaac helped lead the animals to the watering trough at the staging area. "After they drink they fill," he said, "we'll walk 'em over to the lines. Plenty of feed there. Folks got things organized for newcomers, being as there's such a steady stream. Then we can join the womenfolk for supper."

Supper sounded mighty good to Elijah, but he wasn't sure he should leave his family's belongings unattended. Isaac assured him the Saints had patrols around the area day and night. There was no cause for concern. So they settled the animals and then headed to their own meal.

"You got yourself a fine lookin' wife," Elijah said as they walked. "What else you done in the ten years since Nauvoo?"

"Let me think. Been awhile, hasn't it? We was in Winter Quarters like so many. Was there a year 'fore comin' west. Been here near five. Put us up a good home. Jane takin' in laundry, and I been workin' for Brother Brigham. I's his coachman."

"Is that a fact? How's workin' for Brigham Young? He treat you right?"

"Right enough."

"Last I saw Brother Young, he was passin' through Cincinnati. We spoke some, but he wasn't overly familiar."

"President of the Church now. Governor too. He ain't a man to be trifled with. The Indians calls him 'the red-headed chief.'"

Elijah laughed at that. "Is he as good at keepin' peace among his women?"

Isaac stopped walking. "You heard about that?"

"Whole country heard about that."

"Well," he said, resuming the walk, "he got him a good many to keep peace with. And to spread his reputation."

"Any of us coloreds got more than one wife?"

"No, and I don't advise you raise the subject to yo' woman." Isaac shuffled his feet and stopped again. "Elijah, I gots to tell you—lots of things been changin' since Brother Joseph die. But—well, I think everything be lookin' up, now you arrived. You was always the link between us and them. You and Brother Joseph was such good friends."

"That is a fact," said Elijah. "But I knew Joseph. I don't know Brigham Young all that good. And he sure don't know me."

Isaac gestured to an adobe-chinked cabin. "See that house there? What you think of it?"

"Looks fine enough."

"That be my fine enough house."

"Mighty fine indeed," Elijah said.

Inside, Jane had supper laid out. Mary Ann was nursing baby Enoch and covered herself quick when Isaac called from outside, "Woman! We home and ready to be fed!"

Jane answered back, "You know better than to yell at me like that, Mister James. Just you be sure to clean your feet off before comin' into my house. Brother Abel, the wash pail's out back, and you'll see the convenience down the way."

Isaac ushered his guest in one door and out another.

The Jameses did not have company often and were not situated to receive a large group. They usually sat at a table with tree stumps for stools. But tonight, new arrangements were called for. They had a split-log bench outside, which the men brought in. The children sat on the bench while the adults sat at the table. Isaac offered thanks. Conversation was casual until after supper, when Elijah and Isaac returned the bench outside and sat for talk.

"You been blessed," Elijah said.

Isaac shrugged. "Well, we all somewhat poor. Things still gettin' started here in Zion. Some doin' better than others."

"Does 'some' include coloreds?"

"'Tain't nothin' much equal in this world."

Elijah picked up a bit of wood and started whittling with his penknife. He had cut away a sizeable portion before asking, "What you know about the new ordinances, the most sacred ones? I read a little down Cincinnati."

Isaac had figured that'd be coming and was ready with an answer. "You the only colored here with priesthood. Lotsa folks be waitin' on you so's you might speak to the Brethren about all us."

Elijah whittled some more. "What needs sayin'? Church things or city things?"

"Church things. Us colored show up at church, even pay tithing. But they don' seem to see us with the same eyes they use on each other. Same story as in most places. They sayin' we cursed, same as other folk in this country keep sayin'. Lots of us sure would like to get them ordinances you askin' about."

"You're Brigham Young's coachman. Have you tried talkin' to him about it?"

"'Lijah, ain't none of us got the standin' you got. They respect you."

"Could you get me in to see him, Isaac?"

"I could tell him you arrived. Maybe he might ask to see you before you ask to see him."

Elijah whittled some more. "Might be so. Now, I ain't entirely sure how I should address Brother Brigham, him bein' governor and such. If I gets in, what do call him?"

"I heard some call him 'Your Excellency.' Others call him 'The old boss.' Or 'Boss Brigham.' But not to his face."

Jane and Mary Ann joined them at that moment. They'd been listening, and Jane didn't pretend otherwise. She spoke right up. "Well, what'd you call him in Nauvoo? Brother Brigham, wasn't it?"

"It was."

"I called him that too."

Isaac explained, "She lived with him for a time, doin' his house-keepin'. We was married in his house. Right there in his very house."

"Then call him by the same name," Jane said. "Time passed, but he the same man. No need bein' fearful."

Elijah stiffened as though she was accusing him of something. "Fearful how?"

"In askin' for what you need. I know he believe all us humans, black or white, is one blood. He said it hisself, back at Winter Quarters. You ask for everything your heart desires. I think he might answer you in a way he won't answer the rest of us, bein' as you is who you is."

"I told her all 'bout you," Isaac said. "You famous!"

Elijah returned to his whittling and pondered. "Ain't seen Brigham Young in a while," he said after a moment. "All right. I'll call him 'Brother Brigham.'" He made one last cut in the wood and then led his family back to their wagon.

NOTES

The chapter title is from a traditional Negro spiritual cited in Cone, *Spirituals and the Blues*, 35.

Bringhurst documents the Abel family's migration from Cincinnati to Utah in the early 1850s in "Changing Status," 137.

The reference to Brigham Young's declaring that "of one blood has God made all flesh" is in Bush, "Mormonism's Negro Doctrine," 215.

16

By and By

How long will ye vex my soul,
and break me in pieces with words?
JOB 19:2

It took several weeks for Isaac to arrange a meeting between Elijah Abel and President Young, for whenever he brought it up, Brother Brigham expressed weariness or talked on how little time he had to meet with everyone who arrived in the Valley. Isaac gave Elijah the news that Brigham Young was "puttin' him off."

"Tell him I want to work on the temple, when they undertake constructin' it," Elijah urged. "He seen my work."

And that was how an appointment got made between the black elder and the governor of Utah Territory.

At this time, Brigham Young was living in the White House, a sun-dried adobe dwelling covered with white plaster. His wives were living in a row of cabins called Harmony House. Sister Zina met Elijah at the White House door late in the afternoon.

He knew Mizz Zina from Nauvoo, from when her mother died. He had heard Brother Joseph comforting her and remembered the words even now. She was Zina Huntington then. Now she was Zina Young, one of those good women testing the mettle of Brother Brigham.

Many things had changed since Nauvoo, including Zina's face. The desert sun and many kinds of journeys had aged her. Stark lines frowned between her eyebrows and made small fans at her eye corners. Her hair was folded into a net just beneath her ears, a style typical for the women back then. It emphasized Zina's sharp cheekbones. She was too thin.

Elijah had worn his stovepipe hat for this occasion. He took it off as Zina stepped back. "Elijah Abel?" Her voice had grown coarse, but it was still lively.

"Here to pay my respects to the governor. His Excellency knows I was comin'."

"Yes. He is expecting you."

"I wanted to offer my services on the temple, give him to understand I'm willin' to work."

"Step in," she said.

He did, and thought it a fine place for a prophet to occupy, though it wasn't much compared to Joseph's Mansion House.

Besides being prophet, president, and governor, Brigham Young was a glazier and a carpenter. The White House showed off his work to advantage. The windows weren't oiled paper like so many of the pioneers' (including the Jameses'), nor thin animal hide, like what the Abels had left in Cincinnati. These were good glass windows with a bluish tint and only a few bubbles. The sitting room had two lamps, a soft red couch, and four wingback chairs, all set on a braided rug.

Zina led him to an inside door and knocked. Brigham Young's familiar voice answered, "Yes?" It still had that New England accent and fluty twang.

She opened the door a crack. "You have a visitor. It's Elijah Abel."

Brother Brigham was sitting behind his desk, wearing a vest and shirt, a dark wool jacket, and a black collar tie knotted at his throat. His hair had a natural curl to it, and every wave found some light from the window behind to show off that auburn shimmer. Brigham wore it somewhat longer than he had at their last meeting, near a decade ago in Cincinnati. His eyes were the same, though: kind, confident, and wise, though there was more determination and protectiveness in them now. Looking into those eyes, observing that firm jaw, firm lips, and shiny mane, Elijah didn't wonder why folks referred to Brigham Young as the Lion of the Lord. He had a mighty presence in and around him. It showed in his every feature and movement and saturated the room.

The new prophet didn't smile as easy as Brother Joseph had. That wasn't his nature. He had become a man to rule a people, to see them from one land to another, just like Moses. He hadn't aged much but was thicker in the neck and shoulders. It made sense he had grown that way, for his neck and shoulders carried quite a burden.

Elijah's grip tightened on his hat. He wasn't sure if he should extend his hand to the governor or wait for the governor to offer his.

Brigham Young stood. "Come on in. It's been a long time," he said, taking Elijah's hand from across the desk and gripping it. His voice was friendly, but it had a suitable undertone of strength. "Good to see you again. How long have you been in Utah?" He gestured to a chair, and Elijah sat down.

"Good seein' you too. Me and my family been here 'bout six weeks, President Young." It felt natural to call him that.

"I hear you want to work on the temple, when we begin it."

"Yessir, I do, with all my heart."

"We'll use your arms more than your heart," the prophet chuckled. "I know you're up to it. I remember when we worked on the Nauvoo Temple."

"Yessir, and I remember you bein' more than a fair carpenter."

Brigham Young took up his pen and tapped the desk with it. "Those were long days ago."

"Yessir, but 'pears you ain't lost your skill. You make these furnishings?" He motioned to the ladderback chair in the corner and the pine desk, painted to look like oak. Elijah knew wood.

"I did for a fact, and I thank you for the compliment."

Elijah laid his hat sideways on his lap, fiddling with the brim. "Brother Brigham, there's somethin' else besides workin' on the temple I want to talk to you about." He turned the hat over and glanced down before meeting Brigham's eyes. Those eyes looked more protective than kind at the moment. "You know I been washed and anointed. Them holy doin's got done at Kirtland, right in the temple."

Brigham's eyebrows raised. "I didn't know that. Who authorized it?"

"Joseph Smith himself."

"Brother Joseph? When did that take place?"

Elijah was feeling defensive, though he couldn't explain why. "Oh, 'bout seven or eight years 'fore the Prophet got killed, I 'spect. It's all on the record, sir. And I got made a seventy in the Melchizedek Priesthood."

"A seventy? And who performed that ordinance?"

"That'd be Zebedee Coltrin. And I remember that bein' 'bout 1836."

Brigham tapped his pen again and pressed his lips together. "But wasn't your priesthood limited?"

"Limited how, sir? Wasn't no limit on it. I served two missions. You seen me in Cincinnati. All I'm wantin' is a continuation of what I already been give. I hear tale about new doin's. Endowments. Sealin's. You see, sir, I'm a married man, and my wife and me—"

"So you got married," Brigham interrupted.

"Yessir, and more than anything, my wife and me wants—"

Brigham leaned back in his chair. "Tell me about your family. I'd love to hear. You have children?"

"Two sons, and we wants so much—"

"That's a fine beginning. What are their names?"

"My boys? Moroni and Enoch." Elijah scooted his chair forward. He knew his purpose, and it wasn't a conversation about his children's names. "President Young, I don't mean to presume a thing, but I gots to know when my wife and me can get sealed up."

Brigham's expression sobered. He sighed long and deep. "Brother Abel, I have no ill will toward you or the Negro people. But God has set limits on each of us on this earth, and there are limits on what you can do. Negroes are more blessed here in Zion than in most parts of this nation. We give every man his due. Why, my children loved to hear Hark Lay sing. He's in California now, but what a voice that boy has! I miss it. He'd put meadowlarks to shame. He was at our home on several occasions. Are you acquainted with Hark Lay?"

"No sir. I maybe heard the name but never met the man."

"Hark Lay, Green Flake, Oscar Crosby—all colored servants who came with me in the first company. My heart holds the deepest fondness for each one of them. I am pained when they or any Negroes are treated without humanity. I suspect you've known ill treatment yourself."

"Yessir."

Brigham sat straighter and spoke loud. "I regret that most of your race have known ill treatment. Shame on those who have rendered it. They will be judged by a just God." His voice became softer. "But, Elijah," he said, leaning across his desk, "you know the burden your race carries by divine decree. That burden is the very sin of Cain. I cannot undo the mandates or the curses of the Eternal I Am. You understand that, don't you? You always understood that the Negro has his separate place on this earth."

Elijah was not about to give up on this. "I know it be separate on this earth, but we talkin' about heaven things."

"I appreciate your feelings. Surely all of mankind would like God's blessing. You understand that better than most. And you must understand that it is not mine to give."

Elijah answered reverently, "God saw me fit for the priesthood. Why would he take me halfway and not the whole way?"

Once more, Brigham sighed. "I cannot answer that, and we may not be able to settle the matter to your satisfaction this afternoon, as my time is short."

Elijah was not finished, though, and would not be put out easy. He placed his hands on the edge of the desk. "Sir, you talk about my people gettin' treated without humanity. President, I seen such sights! Seen a eight-year-old girl dyin' because she got whupped and tied to a tree for two days and nights. Her back was cut so bad it— sir, you could see to the bone." His eyes teared up at the memory, and he could barely speak. "Clear down to the bone! I think God gotta weep over that child."

Brigham looked up. "I weep over her myself," he said, and indeed his eyes were moist. "Elijah, that time will come when your people will have the privileges of all we have, and more. But, in the kingdom of God on the earth, the Africans cannot hold one particle of priesthood power."

"Brother Joseph weren't bothered by the color of my skin. He said I'm entitled to the priesthood. And you know Brother Joseph's feelings on slavery, sir."

In a calm, straight voice, the governor replied, "Now you need to comprehend what I'm about to say. I am as much opposed to the principle of slavery as any man. It is abused. I am opposed to abusing that which God has decreed a blessing. Elijah, I recognize God's blessings to my people, and I believe it a great blessing to the seed of Adam to have the seed of Cain for servants. But those they serve must use them with all the heart and feeling as they would use their own children."

"Use children, sir?"

"The masters' compassion should reach over them and round about them. Masters should treat their Negroes kindly and with humane feeling." Brigham Young rose up and stepped from behind his desk.

"The principle of slavery I understand," said the governor. "At least I have self-confidence enough to believe I do. We're all slaves of one sort or another, aren't we?"

"You ain't knowed it the way I knows it," Elijah murmured.

"Long ago, Mother Eve partook of forbidden fruit. That made a slave of her. Well, Adam hated to have her taken out of the garden of Eden. So he says, 'I believe I will eat of the fruit and become a slave too.' That was the first introduction of slavery upon this earth, and there has not been a son or daughter of Adam from that day to this but what were slaves in the true sense of the word."

"Sir," Elijah said softly, "some of us more slave than others."

"And that has its own history. Adam and Eve had two sons, Cain and Abel. Cain became jealous of Abel, didn't he? Cain laid a plan to obtain all his flocks, and he took it into his heart to put Abel out of this mortal existence. And after the deed was done, the Lord inquired of Cain, 'Where's your brother?'"

"'Am I my brother's keeper?'" Elijah knew these words well, for he had repeated them many a night as he helped a runaway find freedom. And he had answered that question on all such nights: "Yes, Lord Jesus! I am!"

"'Now,' says the Father, 'Cain, I will not kill you, nor suffer any one to kill you, but I will put a mark upon you.' What is that mark, Elijah?"

"Scriptures don't say specific, sir. I read and read, and I don't find it."

Brigham lowered his chin into his neck. "Maybe you need more information, then." He pulled a pamphlet from his desk. "This is something our missionaries in England are using. Brother Joseph's translation of ancient Egyptian records. We call it *The Pearl of Great Price*."

"I've heard of it."

"Can you read?"

"Yessir, I can."

"Then I'll give this to you. You take it home and read it. You'll find your answer there—but you must already know the answer. You've heard it from your boyhood days, just as I have. There's nobody in this country doesn't understand this fact: You will note the mark of Cain's curse on the countenance of every African you ever did see—including in your looking glass."

"President—"

Brigham held up his hand. "Elijah, I cannot change your race. And the Lord told Cain he should not receive the blessings of the priesthood—nor his seed—until the last of the posterity of Abel had received it. That is the only answer I am authorized to give you."

"But sir, I was Negro before and Negro now, and God gave me the priesthood. Brother Brigham, I know what bondage is. I know what freedom is. I know God want all us free. I feel that down every white bone of my black body."

Brigham's tone was polite. "There's no need to argue. It's been good to see you again, and I pray God's kindest blessings be showered upon you and yours."

Elijah was being dismissed and knew it. No doubt the governor of the territory and the president of the Church had much to do.

"It's been good to see you too," Elijah said.

"I am happy to accept your service on the temple," Brigham added, solemn as an axe, "but I cannot give you hope that you will enter it after the dedication. That is a privilege I cannot grant." President Young stood and extended his hand for a quick, firm, final shake. "I do appreciate your visit and your offer."

So that's how it was. Elijah asked the Lord in silent prayer why the black man was yet to suffer and keep apart from the whites. Were colored folks cursed? He could hear no answer from the skies.

That night, he read the whole of the pamphlet Brigham had given him. He thought he saw the verses the prophet had in mind, but the reading raised more questions for him than it answered. The next night, after supper, he and Mary Ann read from the Bible.

In the six weeks since arriving, Elijah had built them a little cabin and crafted a table, though the children still slept in the wagon box. Now he and Mary Ann read at that table, a set of candles between them. Elijah was particularly interested in having his wife see some Bible verses about God being no respecter of persons. She struggled some with the hard words but managed to sound out every one. Elijah was satisfied over how well he had taught her letters.

"What does it mean," he asked, "that God is no respecter of persons?"

Mary Ann thought on it. When she was uncertain, her voice was always breathy. You had to stretch your neck to hear a thing. He came so close to the candles in trying to listen, he near got his hair singed. "Maybe," she said, "because God be so high up, he can't respect us folks on this dusty ol' earth."

"No," Elijah answered. "It mean God don't put one person above another. He don't respect one man more than any other."

Well, Mary Ann may not have been much for understanding scriptures, but she understood her man. She knew what was under his words. "You set high expectation on Brother Brigham," she said.

"God set high expectation on him."

"Last time I look, you wasn't the Lord."

He was not accustomed to her getting saucy with him. "What you meanin' by that?"

Now she stood and commenced sweeping the floor with her

feather broom. She did that often when she didn't wish to answer a question.

"Put down the broom," he said. "Now tell me what you be meanin' by that."

"'Lijah," she sighed, "I don' want to start hard conversation."

"You already started it."

She stared at the feathers. "I remember when I met you. I call you 'Reverend Abel.' I seen you do a sad miracle for my daddy, and I thought you was next best thing to the Lord hisself. Well, I knows you better now."

"You disappointed in me? Is that what you sayin'?" He waited. When no reply came but a small shrug, he demanded, "Mary Ann, why can't you answer me?"

"I'm sorry. Honey, I knows you be a good man. Nothin' you done ever sway me different, and nothin' ever will."

"Stop dodgin' and have the nerve to say what you mean."

"You know more than I ever can. What I do know is that you are a good man, 'Lijah. Even when it seem you don't understand me."

He let out a mocking laugh. "Ain't no man on God's green earth understand a woman."

"Well, don't be thinkin' no white man goin' understand us colored folk, 'Lijah. You settin' yo'self up to get disappointed time and time again."

He met her eyes and then looked beyond her like he could see through the walls to the Valley. "Here we are in Zion, and there's slaves gettin' bought and sold. You know, their work and their bodies can get paid as tithing." He shook his head in lamentation. "I feel it a sorry shame."

"You mind I finish up with this sweepin'? The floor get awful bad."

"Go on and sweep," he said. "Let these feathers catch the dust. Lotta dust needs catchin' 'round here. Ain't nothin' more to say."

Maybe there wasn't more to say on that occasion, but soon Elijah got information that comforted his soul. Jane James told him the Saints had used Ensign Peak for their "natural temple," before ever setting up an endowment house.

That was all he needed to hear. If priesthood had dedicated Ensign Peak for the sacred rites, it hadn't likely got undedicated. And couldn't nobody stop him from praying there.

Ensign Peak was a grassy hill. Sagebrush and scrub oak flourished on it. The summit held slabs of rock and provided a view of the entire valley. Elijah climbed that hill week after week, taking his troubles to the Lord and begging for whatever blessings the Lord was willing to shed upon him, hoping there would be no limit.

NOTES

The chapter title is from a traditional Negro spiritual from Burleigh, *Spirituals*, 103.

The descriptions of Brigham Young at this time (1852–53) are from Holzapfel and Shupe, *Brigham Young*, 22, which quotes Huber Howe Bancroft's portrayal of him as "a little above medium height; in frame well-knit and compact . . . face clean shaven . . . features all good, regular, well formed, sharp, and smiling, and wearing an expression of self-sufficiency."

The fact that "when Abel 'applied to President Young for his endowments . . . to have his wife and children sealed to him,' the Mormon president 'put him off' because, according to one account, participation in these ordinances was 'a privilege' that the Mormon president 'could not grant'" is from Council Minute Meetings, January 2, 1902, George Albert Smith Papers, University of Utah Library, qtd. in Bringhurst, "Changing Status," 137.

Elijah Abel's status as a seventy is verified in the Nauvoo Seventies List located in the LDS Church Archives. His name is number 4 on page 1: "Able [Abel], E. [Elijah]. Ordained into 3rd quorum: 20 Dec. 1836, Kirtland, Ohio, by President Z [Zebedee] Coltrin. Joseph Young Home Contribution, 9 April, 1845: 1.00. Source: 70's Rec. Bk A, LDS Arc; 3 Qrm, pg. 76."

Several of the quotations from Brigham Young in this chapter are drawn from his speech on slavery delivered to the Utah territorial legislature on February 5, 1852.

Although the idea that blacks were cursed as the descendants of Cain and Ham was prevalent in the nineteenth century and taught by many religions, that tradition is not accepted today by The Church of Jesus Christ of Latter-day Saints. (Volume 3 of this series will describe the extension of priesthood to all worthy male Latter-day Saints.) Church doctrine teaches that "men will be punished for their own sins, and not for Adam's transgression" (Article of Faith 2) and that "every man that is cursed [doth] bring upon himself his own condemnation" (Alma 3:19). The Book of Mormon indicates that a "curse" (the separation of man from God) can be transmitted through lineage by teaching and continuation of incorrect traditions: "And it came to pass that they brought many to the knowledge of the truth; yea, they did convince many of their sins, and of the traditions of their fathers, which were not correct" (Alma 21:17). As the *Encyclopedia of Mormonism* ("Blacks," 1:125) states, "The reasons for [earlier] restrictions" on individuals of African descent "have not been revealed." That priesthood is now available to all worthy male members of the Church suggests that a curse upon the African lineage, if indeed there ever was one, did not mean what some early Church leaders assumed.

Hark Lay had been in Brigham Young's home and was a favorite of the Young children because of his musical talents (Kohler, *Southern Grace*, 65).

According to Bringhurst, Elijah Abel was denied sealing privileges when he appealed to Brigham Young ("Changing Status," 137). Brother Abel's claim that Joseph Smith had told him he was entitled to the priesthood is also from Bringhurst, "Changing Status," 139.

Ensign Peak was used briefly as a "natural temple." Tingen states that "Addison Pratt received his ordinances there on July 21, 1849, and the hill was dedicated that day for endowments" ("Endowment House," 2). The Council House was later used for endowments, and sealings were often performed in President Young's office. The Endowment House was ready for use on Saturday, May 5, 1855.

Saints to
California

17

HE'S JUST THE
SAME TODAY

*Thou knowest the greatness of God; and he shall
consecrate thine afflictions for thy gain.*
2 NEPHI 2:2

Green Flake's work had been used as tithing more than once. In
Nauvoo, Madison and Agnes found no shame in letting Green haul
rocks or mortar bricks and then counting his labor as their own
offering. After all, the way folks thought back then, we was nothing more than the muscled, moving part of their real estate. The last
time Green had got used in such a way was in March of 1851, when
Agnes Flake and her family set out to finish Madison's mission in
California. They left Green with Brigham Young, as human tithing.

William Crosby told the Church president not to free Green,
for Green would surely abandon Martha and get him a white
woman. (Of course, that's what most whites suspected their slaves
would do, given the chance.)

So "Nigger Green," as he was called, stayed in the Salt Lake
Valley with his wife. After Green had worked for a couple of years,

Brother Brigham gifted him not only freedom but some land in the Cottonwood area.

Truth is, Brigham Young thought kindly of Green Flake. Up till the time of Madison's death, Green was in the habit of answering any assignment from the Church president the moment it came and not telling Madison about it until later. His massa would never punish him when he learned Green had been filling a Church call. And after Green and Martha had their babies—a son and a daughter, named Abraham and Lucinda—Brother Brigham would dandle the babies on his knee and let them play with his own children. The way Green told it, Brigham Young would ask him a question and honor what he had to say. Many times the Church president found a seat for Green and other colored folks at general conference— right up front and sometimes on the very front row. Maybe most important, Brother Brigham had given Green a bottle of consecrated olive oil, to be used in the healing of the sick. Green would rub that oil over any hurt and pray. He saw many a healing too.

With Green staying behind in Salt Lake City, it was Liz who drove the Flake wagon. That was a good thing, for Mizz Agnes sure didn't have the vigor to do it. Heaven only knows how Agnes Flake summoned strength to make this move, for she had been in poor health a long, long while. Tragedy had overwhelmed her, and now consumption was plundering the very air in her lungs. Her whole body had been harrowed by a hard life since the day she married Madison, and nobody expected she'd last long.

Fortunately, the Flakes weren't the only ones in the wagon train. By the time they got to Payson, Utah, there were five hundred families set to move to gold country, even though not all of them had been called to do so. Amasa Lyman headed one company, and Charles Rich another. Robert and Rebecca Smith and their slaves went too, which meant Liz Flake and Biddy Smith would have more time to get acquainted.

The trail to California was the meanest wilderness you might conjure in a nightmare. Narrow-ridged passes snaked between the rough earth and orchards of prickly pear. Sometimes, these California-bound folk had to lower their wagons by rope down a cliff. Roads was rocky, water scarce, and the journey meant thudding across four deserts. It was probably a pure dee wonder that the human travelers made their way without much sickness. The Lord wasn't so merciful to their animals, though. A good many cows and mules had to be abandoned on the sand, parched and dying.

At Sycamore Grove, the Saints pitched camp and even set up a school. Come fall, they moved on to San Bernardino, having lived in the open for eight months with only their wagons for cover.

Nowadays, we think of Southern California as a thriving place, but it was nothing like that when the Mormons arrived. There was a small adobe pueblo at Los Angeles and a collection of adobes at San Diego, with Catholic missions in other spots.

When the Saints got to San Bernardino, they saw where they would be living: adobe shanties once occupied by Mexican laborers. The idea was to transform this scraggy piece of nothing to a community for farming and trading.

Sitting up in the wagon, Agnes groaned. It was as fair a reaction as any.

Of course, it took some time to build a more solid structure than what the Mexicans had left, but when it was finished, the San Bernardino fort was the sturdiest place west of Utah. It was a huge rectangle, with enough room for a hundred families. And water was easy to find, since a creek ran through the enclosure itself. It gave protection should Indians or Mexicans make a ruckus, or if miners decided to claim more than gold.

All in all, though, San Bernardino was a poor place. Before long, Amasa Lyman wrote back to Utah about the poverty, which was especially hard on a widow such as Agnes Flake. He asked Brigham Young if help could come "by way of the Negro man."

What he meant was, couldn't Green get sold and the money sent to Mizz Agnes?

Brigham Young might've told a small lie when he answered that request, but it was a sweet and blessed lie. He wasn't about to sell Green. He answered, "Green Flake worked for me about a year sometime ago, and when he went to Cottonwood his health was quite feeble, and from all I can learn he is still unable even to support himself and family entirely. Should he regain his health so as to be able to be of any benefit to Sister Flake, I will inform you."

Truth told, Green sure would've been sick if he had got sold one more time—especially away from his family. Brother Brigham knew that.

So Liz remained the lone slave left to the Flakes. She was the one who answered the door when a surprise came calling.

The surprise was named Augustus.

By now, gold fever was burning in many parts of these United States. From as far away as North Carolina, folks rushed to California. One of these was Mizz Agnes's little brother, Augustus Love. Liz hadn't seen him in more than ten years and wasn't prepared to recognize him now.

In this part of the country, though, you didn't admit a stranger into your house without some questions first. Southern hospitality quit somewhere around the Arkansas border.

Augustus said, "Elizabeth?"

She answered, "Do I know you, sir?"

"I'm Augustus Love. Aren't you Elizabeth—Liz? I know you remember me. I remember you from when you were a present for my sister. You cried a week and a creek before that wedding."

"Mister Augustus? It is you! My, you all growed up! You done filled out like yo' daddy."

Indeed, Augustus was a man now—twenty-six years old and as tall and strong as William Love stood in Liz's memory. Of course, there were differences. Massa William had always been careful about his hair, which was pomaded into stiff, dark bands. Augustus's hair was a mass of reddish curls. He wore a scraggly beard.

Augustus answered, "You've got bigger too, but your eyes are the same. I recall the very day my daddy brought you home from the Boones' place and set you before my sister and her damned husband."

Liz had been kindly disposed, but couldn't nobody call her deceased massa "damned" and stay on her good side. Her face turned stony, which didn't affect Augustus one whit. He strode past her with a casual, snooty walk.

"You and that boy, Green. You were the most costly gifts set before that big table. Where's Green?" he asked.

Liz drew her lips in tight. "Sir, don' nobody in this house want to hear disrespect towards Massa Madison. Mizz Agnes love him sore. His death near killed her."

Augustus turned. "Madison's dead?"

"Been two years now."

"Where is my sister?"

"I'll tell her you here, Mister Augustus, but I will not have you upsettin' her."

Frowning deep, she led him to the kitchen. Agnes spent hours there in her rocking chair, sometimes reading scriptures, more often sleeping. Though California days were pleasing this time of year, the evenings could be right chilly. The kitchen was the warmest spot of their place, being furnished with a wood-burning stove as well as a pinewood table and a hip-high cabinet for plates and cups. In the corner were a washbasin and a butter churn. One window allowed a slant of light to shine on the chair's armrests and the tip of Agnes Flake's nose.

Augustus was two steps ahead of Liz. She had to run in order to present him right: "It's Augustus, Mizz Agnes. Your brother."

When Liz saw the two together, there was no doubt they were related. Both had the same fair skin, the same dark eyes, the same chestnut hair (though his was redder). But it was a sad contrast, for

Augustus was robust, while Agnes's vitality had dimmed. Her hair was stark white at the temples and platted into two loose braids reaching her hips.

Agnes did not rise, but her tears did. "Gus? Oh my, your features are so like Daddy's, I might have thought you were he!" She held out her hand. Her fingers and nails were long and clean, for Liz scrubbed them daily. It was her duty to lengthen Mizz Agnes's time on this earth and help her feel good.

The visitor went to his knee and then burst into such tears that Liz had to fetch a handkerchief for everyone there, including herself.

"Do I appear so ugly you must cry?" Agnes asked. "Or did you never learn not to? You cried exactly like this the day we left North Carolina. You have a deeper voice now, but you cried just this way."

"You're much changed." His voice was hoarse and gravelly at the moment.

"And not for the better. Your expression doesn't hide a thing."

"Last time I saw you, you were plump as a partridge."

"Was I? I can hardly recall. Well, I am not so plump these days."

His lips sealed down. "I don't rightly know how you keep yourself from floating out of that chair."

"I might float out of it sooner than you think."

"Come, come, let's none of that," Augustus said. It was a phrase William Love had used. Augustus's voice was so like his daddy's that Liz was stunned by the memory.

"Let's move to family conversation," Agnes suggested. "We have much ground to cover, and I am eager for every detail. How's Mama?"

"She died," he answered quick. "I'm sorry to report it."

Agnes closed her eyes. "God bless her. How's Daddy managing without her?"

"He's passed too."

"Daddy's gone?"

"And your girl told me that Madison met with an accident."

Agnes let her head droop. "Got bucked off his mule. Neck broke."

"That's a bad death."

"It was a fast one. He didn't suffer." She looked away. "Did Mama and Daddy pass gentle?"

"Consumption for them both."

"I fear that is a hard death."

"Indeed." His eyes knew all about her condition.

"Did they speak of me—either of them?"

"Oh yes, Aggie, they did."

"Kindly?"

He breathed deep. "No." Then he took to weeping again and did not let up for some time. "Aggie, the old home is there waiting for you. Everyone in the family who's still alive has a plantation of their own. I've got one waiting for me, soon as I take a mind to return. Why don't you come back? I'll carry you home myself—in my arms, if I need to. I've had enough adventure, and I'd be glad to take you where you belong. You can have the land, the home we grew up in, all the Negroes you need or want. Everyone will welcome you, and you can live as God intended." He looked around. "Not like this," he said. "Oh, heaven, not like this! You are a Southern lady! I don't know if you've even heard the way Southern women dress these days—in crinolines?"

"I know what a crinoline is."

"It appears you're wearing homespun, no better dressed than your slave. Southern ladies—Aggie, they wear dresses like bells. Steel skirts that make their silk swish when they walk."

With a tolerant smile she said, "Dear Gus, I left that kind of vanity years ago. I don't need to resemble a bell when I walk. I have had seven children."

"So many?"

"I've lost more than I've kept. They're holding my place in heaven, alongside Madison. The ones I have left are William—"

"Named for Daddy. I remember Will's birth. I'm pleased he's thrived."

"Then there's Charles and Sarah."

"I believe I saw Sarah."

"I lost Richmond and Thomas."

He spoke with reverence: "Those were our brothers' names."

"Yes, I named my sons for them. Even after you all abandoned me, I grieved for my family." She sank into her chair. Liz could see she was trying not to cough, but such a battle couldn't be won. Mizz Agnes put the handkerchief to her mouth and coughed into it. Then she went on talking as though she weren't sick at all. "I lost my baby Samuel too. That was in Illinois. And I lost one more son, just after he came into this world. I called him Frederick."

The reality of what his sister had suffered weighed on him, and it showed in his whole body.

"Three children left," she said.

He leapt on her words. "Whom you could bring up as ladies and gentlemen. They'd be provided the best education. They would never want for food. You and I both know that's more than you can promise them here. They'd be far from danger. They'd have all they deserve as descendants of William Love."

Agnes leaned forward, finding more light with her face. Her cheeks glowed with sunset. "On what condition are you extending such a generous invitation, Gus?"

"No condition."

"We are yet Latter-day Saints. You must know that."

He cut his eyes away and spat. "Don't you see what that's brought you?"

Agnes fell back from the light, looking her brother over like she was smelling him with her eyes and didn't care for the scent. "I hope you are not purporting to be a gentleman, sir." She took as deep a breath as her lungs would permit, though her windpipes were clotted with disease.

"Aggie—"

"Not if you allow yourself to spit on your sister's floor and speak ill of her faith."

He rolled his eyes. Two more tears snailed down his cheeks. He swiped them with an angry, open hand. "Aggie, it's a dirt floor. I apologize for spitting on your dirt."

"It is my floor!" she said, but she had spent her strength. Her words just tickled the air. "Oh, Gus, I am glad to see you."

"You understand what's in my heart, don't you? It's—I didn't expect to find you like—"

"Am I so fearful a sight?" Agnes asked.

"No, you could never be anything but a beautiful sight. You remind me of Mama, that's all."

"In her decline."

He shrugged an apology.

"Well, I didn't expect you to come to my door the way you did, either. Looking like a gold seeker. It doesn't surprise me. No, you were always one to chase an adventure. But you talk to me of Southern gentility, and here you're wearing that ill-kept beard. Don't you know it looks like tobacco juice rusted on your chin? You spat on my floor. And your hair hasn't known a comb in some time, has it? Resembles cedar shavings more than hair. I remember the times in your childhood when you'd light off for some adventure and come back with your hair so mussed, I'd try to comb it myself before Mama could see it. Now if you were my boy—"

"You always hurt my head when you combed my hair. I haven't forgot that." He wagged his finger at her. "I wouldn't be surprised if I still have bruises. You treated my hair like weeds in a garden. You and that metal comb tugged at every tangle until I was half-scalped. I do recall that!"

"I see you do, and you still resist the comb. You probably wouldn't let the lowliest slave near those copper curls." She smiled. "But you are dressed tidy. That's an accomplishment in this place.

My, you resemble Daddy. Your cheekbones especially. He would be proud of you."

He glanced down. "I don't know if he would or not."

Again, she bent toward him, and the light found her chin and nose. "Are you a good man, Gus?"

"I try."

"I'm glad to hear that. It's a fine legacy you carry. A good man will pray morning and evening. Do you find time for prayer?"

"I forget it on occasion, but usually I manage at least a word or two for the Almighty."

"That doesn't mean just using his name like some of these gold-diggers. I've heard them drop the Lord's name into their conversations like cherry pits on the ground. It pains me."

"I don't take the Lord's name in vain."

"I'm glad. That makes you better than most. Now, Gus, a good man will be a Bible-reading man. You know that too. Daddy loved the Bible. I hope you love it as well."

"I do."

"And you have a copy where you're staying?"

"I confess I do not. I left it home down South. But whenever I get the chance, I read someone else's."

"You've holed up in California without the Good Book as company? Oh, Gus, Daddy would never approve! Now, I can't give you Madison's. His will be William's inheritance. But I can give you mine. It's on the table."

Augustus walked where she directed and picked up the book. "Is this a real Bible?" he asked with no small hint of suspicion.

"King James Version. We Latter-day Saints treasure the Book of Mormon, but we haven't abandoned the Bible. You take that with you, and you read it every night before you retire."

"I will do that. Thank you."

"A good man will respect another's choice of religion too. You must know that."

He grimaced. "Oh, Aggie, I'll lick your floor clean if you ask me, and I'll read this Bible night and morning too. But you cannot make me respect your religion. I apologize with my full heart, but my feelings will never change."

Agnes collapsed back into her chair, leaving the light between them.

"Aggie," he sighed, "come home for your reward."

She waved her hand weakly. "God will call me home to my reward soon enough."

"All I ask is that you give up this religion and resume the life you were meant for. I beg you to consider."

Agnes clasped her hands together. "You don't think you're asking much, do you?"

"Very little," he said. "Very, very little."

She called Liz, whispering, "Help me stand. I want my brother to hear this. And I want to be on my feet when I say it. I want to look at him direct, eye to eye."

Liz put both arms around her mizzus and lifted her. Didn't take much effort at all.

Agnes stood straight as a rail and peered down at her dress. Its wrinkles showed more now that she was upright. She swept both hands across the fabric and posed like Liz remembered her posing on her wedding day—as if she held a sprig of violets in each hand. "Augustus, what you are asking is more than my life's blood. I would rather wear my nails off over the washtub to support my children than to take them away from the church of my choice."

He shook his head. "A fine speech. You could speechify from your girlhood forward."

"You heard my answer."

"I guess I did. And Mama was right. You are stubborn. She said so on her dying day."

"I come from stubborn stock." She swayed, and Liz held her tight by the waist.

"I suppose that's right." Augustus turned and walked a few steps. Then, giving her a sidelong glance, he offered, "Aggie, if you ever change your mind, write me. I'm in Los Angeles, at the main fort. I will come for you the moment I have that answer in my hand."

She breathed to Liz, "Help me stay standing, girl. Don't you abandon me now." Then, in the loudest voice she had used since they left Salt Lake, she declared, "Brother, you will never get that letter."

Liz felt the mizzus lose strength as Augustus Love closed the door behind him.

NOTES

The chapter title is from a traditional Negro spiritual found in Burleigh, *Spirituals*, 106.

Green Flake's use as "human tithing" is documented in various sources, including Van Wagoner and Walker, *A Book of Mormons*, 86. Skinner, however, suggests that Agnes Flake did not get along with Green and asked Brigham Young for counsel. She was advised "that Green not be taken to San Bernardino, but given to William Lay" (*Black Origins in the Inland Empire*, 8).

Quoting Ida Blum, "History Explodes 'Negro Myth'" (*Nauvoo Independent*, 30 December 1965, 1), Joel A. Flake Jr. says, "James Flake . . . made arrangements for Green to help with many church projects, and LDS Church leaders willingly accepted Green's work as tithing on behalf of the Flake family" ("Green Flake," 9). Such use of "Africans" was not unusual. For example, John Brown (*Autobiography*, 144) records items he "consecrated and deeded to the church," including twelve sheep and two pistols ($72), sixty bushels of wheat ($120), and an African servant girl ($1000). According to Carter, *Negro Pioneer*, 32, this "African servant girl," named Betsy Crosby Brown, had been a servant of John Brown's wife. She served as a slave in the Crosby home "from 1848 until the slaves were freed during the war between the states. She later married a Mr. Flewellen, a colored man, a barber, in Salt Lake City . . . [and] became a domestic in the home of Governor Eli H. Murray."

The term "Nigger Green" is from information given to Darius Gray. He and his family live near where Green Flake lived, and there they were told that Green was so called.

The descriptions of San Bernardino, the fort, and the surrounding area (as well as the trek there) are extracted from Lyman, *Amasa Mason Lyman*, 288–89, and from Cowan and Homer, *California Saints*, 174. Skinner says that Liz was instrumental in constructing the fort and the Flakes' house within it and quotes Will Flake as saying, "She [Liz] was a worker" (*Black Origins in the Inland Empire*, 14).

That several of the rooms had only earthen floors is from Lyman, *Francis Marion Lyman*.

According to Carter, *Negro Pioneer*, 33, "The 1852 census of Los Angeles County names the following Negroes in San Bernardino: *Hannah*, 30 years; *Toby*, 50; *Lawrence*, 10; *Cato*, 9; *Toby*, 2; *Ann*, 16; *Ellen*, 18; *Ann*, 6; *Biddy*, 35; *Ann*, 10; *Harriet*, 8; *Grief*, 35; *Harriet*, 30; *Tennessee*, 18; *Dick*, 25; *Hark*, 27; *Phillip*, 26; one *child*, 2; one *child*, 3; one *child*, 6. Their birthplaces are given as the Southern States, with the exception of three children who were born in Utah, but all list Utah as their place of residence. No surnames are given."

The exchange of letters between Amasa Lyman and Brigham Young regarding Green Flake is quoted in Flake, "Green Flake," 16. Amasa Lyman's letter is number 185. The entire text reads: "Sister Agnes Flake wishes me to inquire of you if there is any chance for her to receive any help by way of the negro man she left when she came here. She has a family on her hands for which to provide. Her health is also very delicate and if she could realize something from this quarter it would be a benefit to her. Thomas I. Williams told me if he could, he would purchase the negro and pay for him. A word from you on this subject would be received a favor." Brigham Young's response, dated August 19, 1854, is listed as letter 1854 in Brigham Young's Letterbook on pages 635 and 636 of the first letterbook (second reel on the microfilm).

Information about Green Flake's relationship with Brigham Young is from Fretwell (Miscellaneous Family Papers, 7).

The details of the visit of Agnes Flake's brother (presumably Augustus, because all her other brothers but William had died in 1844 and 1845) are recorded in Flake, *William J. Flake*, 21–22.

18

EVERY TIME I FEEL THE SPIRIT

We see that God is mindful of every people,
whatsoever land they may be in.
ALMA 26:37

Liz had several colored friends in San Bernardino: Biddy, Hannah, and Ellen Smith being foremost. And there was another colored person in her life—a man. He was Charles Rowan, a free black who had come to the gold state without any family connections.

Charles was of high yellow complexion. Most folks thought him mulatto. His hair was somewhat long, just past his ears, and matted. His eyes were a little wild, with a hint of yellow around the rims. Truth is, he looked the part of a waylaid forty-niner, and some women might have found him frightening, what with his unwashed clothes and dusty brows. But Liz didn't scare easy. She had seen too much in her many travels. No man's rough looks could undo her. Besides, she liked his voice, which boomed even in saying something easy as "Good mornin'." Coming from his mouth, it was more command than greeting. He was telling the morning to behave itself.

Conversation between the two generally started like most California discourse—about gold. But one September afternoon, when Liz was standing in a peach tree picking fruit and the air was heavy with orange rinds and boiling corn, Charles Rowan undertook more pointed talk. Looking up at her in the branches, he said in that deep-thunder voice, "What you know good?"

Liz answered, "Not much today," then sat down quick. She had bunched up her dress to climb this tree, and she unbunched it fast. Now Liz had never considered herself a beauty, but at this moment, whether or not she knew it, she was beautiful. She appeared to be the tree's guardian sent from heaven's gates, her skin just a few shades lighter than the tree bark and her dress the color of the ripest fruit.

When a robin in another tree took flight, Charles said, "That be one good-lookin' critter. Why, that bird look good enough to eat."

"You enjoy robin soup, Mister Rowan?" She was barefoot, and her legs were swinging in the branches. Seemed the breeze was giving them rhythm.

He followed her feet with his eyes. Oh, you can tell when a man's eyes are scheming and when they mean good. Charles Rowan's eyes, to say the truth, were somewhere in between. He said, "A robin's underside make me think on sweet potato," but his tone suggested he was thinking other things too.

Liz slung her thumb towards the nearby birch. "Its nest be yonder. Prettiest blue eggs was in it all spring. I peeked inside every day 'til they hatch. That bird's the mama. The babies all found they wings by now."

"Lots of good lookin' birds in the trees around here," Charles said.

Liz started a smile and then snapped her mouth shut. "So what you be doin' here, Mister Rowan?"

"Come to see about you, what you think?" The sun flickered through the leaves and made patterns on his face. When a beam caught his eye, it made a pretty amber.

"I ain't much to look on today," Liz said.

"That's 'cause it ain't you doin' the lookin'. Now why don't you climb down that tree and let me take a closer gander? Or if you prefers, you can jump into my arms from there. I catch you. You can trust me."

She had to grin. "I be climbin' down real careful, thank you much. Finished with pickin' anyway. Would you take this basket please?" She passed it from the branches into Charles's arms. "Now if you be so kind and help me down," she said, letting him take her hand.

"The white women uses ladders if they wants to climb trees."

"I ain't climbin' trees for entertainment."

"I don' know. I thinks you just the right kind of entertainment. You the best fruit in that tree, Mizz Peach."

"And you the funniest man on this property, seein' as there ain't no other man around."

Charles Rowan let out the fullest sound of amusement Liz had heard from him—a knee-slapping, wet-eyed laugh she couldn't resist. They both were doubled over silly, until he put his arm around her. Then she pulled away and backed up against the tree.

Charles squinted, though the sun wasn't in his eyes now. "So what's that I smell cookin'?" That sure wasn't the question on his face, though.

"I don't suppose you be hungry." She offered him a peach and bit into one herself. "What you think be cookin'?"

He sniffed long. "I'd say tomatoes, green beans, corn."

"You got you a good nose."

"And me." He tasted his peach, licking it first and then chomping into the meat, letting the juice dribble down his chin and catch on his beard like crystals.

"You cookin', is you?"

"Burnin' set to boil. All around my heart." He got close enough to kiss her, so she turned her head.

"I ain't give you permission to take no bite of me," she said.

"Woman, you do look good enough to eat, but I don't bite."

"And you must like salty food if you think I'd be tasty, given all the sweat the sun done purge from my skin."

"Now you mention it, yes ma'am, I do enjoy salty food."

Liz looked up at him with baby eyes. "Ellen Smith better lookin' than me." She took another bite of peach.

"Ellen Smith got her a beau. Ain't you knowed that?"

"Then you agree she better lookin'? You just arrive too late to take advantage?"

Charles laughed hearty. "If I thought Mizz Ellen was better lookin', I'd be over there makin' time. So what's it say that I'm here with you?"

"It say, why don't you come on in and have a bite of supper? You already named what's cookin' straight down the line. Just as well get the satisfaction of swallowin' it too."

He toted the basket of peaches to the door for her and waited while she spoke with her mizzus.

Mizz Agnes was too weak even to sit these days. She was sleeping on her bed, and Liz chose not to wake her. She let Charles into the kitchen, dished him a bowl, and sat beside him at the table. Before he tasted the stew, he clasped his hands like he was fixing to pray, and Liz bowed her head. His next words weren't directed to God, though. His next words asked Elizabeth Flake for her hand in marriage.

This was the first time a man had proposed marriage to her. A woman don't take that particular question lightly. You ask any woman, no matter how old she is, about when a man proposed to her, and she will remember all the details. She might recall a name she's taught herself to forget and a feeling she can hardly admit she knew.

Liz was old enough to marry, and his words thrilled her like sudden dawn. But it wasn't time yet for dawn. The Flake family all was waiting on dusk right now, and she was responsible for the children and their ailing mama. Slave or free, these Flake folks had bonds to each other beyond what the law could settle. So her answer was not what Charles had hoped for, nor what she wished she could say: "You honor me. And to be honest, I got feelin's for you too, Charles." She couldn't even tell him how deep her affection went. "You must understand—and I pray you might—I got three children here with their mama sick."

"They ain't your family!"

"I promised my mizzus and the good Lord I'd take care of them. I knowed those children since the day each one got borned."

"Lizzy, this is a different world than Utah or Miss'ippi. California be free."

She gave him a look that asked, *Who you think you talkin' to?* "I ain't no fool, Mister Rowan," she said.

"So why you want to detain yo'self in slavin' when you livin' on free soil?"

She had to gather her feelings before she could answer, and it took a moment: "I loves this family like they my own. This the only family I have. Do you want to take me where I never see them again?"

He lifted the bowl to his mouth and took a long swallow.

"Well?" she demanded. "Would you take me away?"

He wiped his chin. "I wouldn't take you nowheres if I should strike gold nearby here."

"You been lookin' awhile and ain't discover much."

"I discover you," he said. "I call that a rich find. Lizzy, give me a kiss and see what your heart tell you." He set his palms on the table and leaned across till his mouth was a handspan away from hers. If you'd known Liz, it wouldn't surprise you that she hit that mouth— but with a gentle hand. This wasn't the time for trading kisses, though her mouth yearned to do it, and she had to fill it with talk so it wouldn't act on its own. "Keep to your seat, Charles. You know like I know. Some colored folk strike gold and a white man claim it first thing. Happen all the time. And around here, cain't no Negro man talk to a judge. Free or not, California law is what the white folk make it."

"I got my own law. And my own dreams. I ain't in danger of get- tin' took."

"And if you don' strike gold?"

"Ain't my custom to think on don'ts. Now Lizzy, you listen to me. Them Flake chil'ren ain't of your body. You gots to make your own babies."

She laughed. "What you mean is I gots to make *your* babies."

He smiled and lifted the bowl again.

"Too bad Ellen's got her a suitor already," Liz said. "I think she'd be willin' to get married."

"That is too bad," he murmured.

She stood. "I knew it!"

He stood too. "I didn't mean nothin' by that."

"Don' you be yellin' back and forth with me."

"Liz, it just hurt me when you wants to throw me to another woman and my mind is only on you."

She gave a wilted smile. "I cain't leave these children."

"Like I say, California be free, so that'd be for you to decide. But I ask you to consider my proposal. It ain't somethin' I trifle with. And you said yourself you got some feelin's for me stowed in your heart. So give it some thought. I be takin' my leave now." He opened the door, but she ducked under his arm and blocked his way, standing in the light. It made a halo for her whole self.

Charles Rowan cupped her elbows in his hands. He maybe

looked rough, but he could be gentle enough to tempt a determined woman. "You ought to trust me more, Liz. And you sure do look pretty, sun behind yo' head, and all yo' hairs a-shinin'."

"Don't try," she warned softly, for he was moving in to attempt another kiss.

"Thank you again for the food," Charles said. "I hope to partake of more someday."

NOTES

The chapter title is from a traditional Negro spiritual found in Burleigh, *Spirituals*, 5.

The 1880 census of San Bernardino reports Charles Rowan as "mulatto." Carter says he was in the original pioneer company traveling from Utah to San Bernardino (*Negro Pioneer*, 19).

That California law prohibited the testimony of black people is discussed in Katz, *Black West*, 133. According to Katz, "in 1852, the legislature of California passed a law prohibiting any black person from testifying in court. This prevented black men from supporting their land claims, black women from identifying assailants, and black businessmen from suing those who cheated or robbed them" (*Black West*, 135). Such a law is not surprising, given the passage of the Fugitive Slave Act of 1850.

19

THE BABY GONE HOME

*Have patience, and bear with those afflictions, with a firm
hope that ye shall one day rest from all your afflictions.*
ALMA 34:41

Legends of gold had long since reached Utah, and Isaac James—
who excelled at dreaming and pretending his dreams were real—
sometimes imagined striking it rich in that legendary country. Of
course, in Utah there wasn't much leisure time to tinker with. By
now, the James family was burgeoning with babies and all the toil
that came with them.

Syl was a husky fourteen, taller than Isaac by a brick-width, his
voice low as Hark Lay's and dramatic as the white preacher who had
fathered him. He and eight-year-old Silas had been joined by two
more sisters besides Mary Ann—Miriam and Ellen—and their
mama was set to birth another baby. Syl and Silas prayed out loud
it might be a boy, so the score could even itself up. It was a dangerous thing, Syl told his brother, for the women to outnumber the
men in a family. You had but to look at Brigham Young's brood to
see what that was like. Brother Brigham had himself—oh, two

dozen wives, Syl said. "You look at his house. 'Tain't nothin' but women, and every one of them carrying a soap rag." If their mama did her job, the score would get even: four men, counting Papa Isaac, and four women, counting Mama. Otherwise, Sylvester announced, life would be hell.

When Silas threatened to report him for saying *hell*, Sylvester insisted he was using the word in its Bible sense and then testified that if more women got born or married into their family, neither one of them would be allowed to say so much as *shucks* without feeling a hand across his cheek.

It was April 22, 1854, when Jane took the going-down pains. Vilate Crosby served as midwife.

The James children were ushered out of the cabin, Syl carrying Baby Ellen and Silas leading Mary Ann and little Miriam by the hand. Spring was breaking out at last. The snow was gone, and the trees were putting out buds. The children didn't even need sweaters. They would play leapfrog next to the corncrib while the newest James child came into the world.

Isaac sat on the tree bench outside the door. The bark was still on its underside, and Isaac rubbed his knuckles against it. Of course, that was one foolish way to show nervousness, and he kept reminding himself there was nothing to be afraid of. This was God's gift of childbirth. Happened every day in this valley. He and Jane had been through it four times already.

But he was nervous and got more nervous yet when "Black Tom" Colbourn dropped in on him. This was a bad omen, for Tom had been out of prison only a month or two, and his face showed every lick of the labor he had done in his prison year—the price of his shooting William Hooper's slave, Shep, in a senseless fight over women.

Here stood Tom, come to visit like the Grim Tyrant himself. His face was all bone and hanging black flesh, and he walked like death was eating his marrow. One leg dragged behind the other, the tendons spent. One shoulder sloped, and the arm hung useless as Vilate Crosby's. His eyes had more red than white. Seemed he would weep blood if he wept at all—though his eyes were not likely to drop tears. His were hard, cold eyes. A thick scar traced his left ear and pointed to his eyes. And his clothes looked and smelled like something a clutch of hens had used for nesting.

"Happy to see me?" Tom's voice was a rasp.

Isaac wondered if Colbourn had been limping through the Valley asking everyone this same question. They had never been friends, Tom and Isaac. Hardly even acquaintances.

"I see you survived." That was about the most polite comment Isaac could find in his head.

Tom got closer, gazing at him like he could see through his skin. "Happy to see me?" he repeated, like if Isaac didn't answer right, Tom would up and shoot him like he had Shep.

"I'm happy you survived through prison. That's gotta be hard on any man." Isaac moved his eyes to where his children were playing.

"You got older," Tom said. "You got you some silver in all that wool."

"So've you."

"Naw. My hair ain't turned."

"You got older. It show in other ways."

"I reckon it do," Tom sighed. "Some days, I thought I was done. I get whupped so much in there, ain't much skin on my body without a scar. Not much at all."

Isaac tried for a hum of pity.

"You been whupped?" Tom asked.

"Not even once."

Tom's lips folded in. "You plays like you one of them powerful white folk, but you ain't. I sees through you."

"Boy," Isaac said, facing him square, "is you doin' some job for your massa? Because if you is, I suggest you finish it."

"You sittin' there on that tree like you own the whole forest."

Isaac's whole body was rigid as he fixed his eyes on Tom's. "Don't nobody talk to me like that."

"This body do," said Tom through a toothless grin.

"The last time you started a fight with someone, it ain't turned pretty for either of you. I don' recommend you start one with me."

"No need for a fight."

"I'm waitin' on my nextborn. My wife's about to give birth, and it be a private thing. I prefer you to leave."

Jane groaned.

Tom looked toward her noise, wearing no expression. "Well, best I be goin' along anyhow. Leavin' you to yo' family business." He dragged his body a ways and then turned back. "For how long was you in bondage, Isaac?"

Isaac shot him a deadly stare. "I'm from New Jersey. Up north. New Jersey been free since before you could crawl."

"You maybe never been a slave, but you never been free neither. You black as me, and you goin' die black as me."

"You done talked long enough, Tom. Time for you to leave my property."

Tom obliged and dragged himself away. Then Jane groaned again, so loud it compelled Isaac to his feet.

All of Isaac's insides were on fire, and he couldn't cool himself no matter how he tried. He had always been a fun-loving, funny man, but something inside him—knowledge or age or raw fear—was burning up his fun. Maybe the fire had been brewing for a good while.

Vilate met him at the door, shaking her head in a long, sad no. Her withered arm hung at her side, reminding him of everything he wished to forget, including Tom's words. He knew how that arm had got withered. Dunked into boiling water by an angry massa. All the colored folks knew.

"Boy or girl?" Isaac said.

"Boy. But he never took air."

Isaac set his teeth and hissed like some creature that couldn't make words. His head fell. "How's Janey?"

"She goin' be fine. Give her a week. No sign of childbed fever."

The news of the stillbirth was so hard, Isaac felt dizzy. "That be my namesake in there. His name Isaac. Jane and me decide on that already. A boy would take Isaac; a girl would take Jane."

Vilate touched his hand. "Why don' you wait on a livin' child to carry your name?"

"The boy's name is Isaac. Can I see my wife?"

She nodded, and Isaac ventured inside, walking soft.

The baby's body was wrapped in a blanket atop the table. Isaac peeked at the tiny gray face and then turned to Jane. She appeared entirely sapped, lying on that bed.

"How you doin', honey?" he asked.

"You see him?" Her eyes were shut tight.

"Yes."

"I knew he'd be born dead," she moaned.

"You didn't say nothin' about knowin' that."

"Didn't want to worry you. You so busy these days trying to stay atop things."

"Jane, you should've said something once you knowed."

Though her eyes were shut, tears oozed down her cheeks and onto the pillow. "I tried my best to give you this boy, but I stopped feelin' life weeks ago. I jus' waited. Hoped. But I knew—deep down—this one wouldn't be born alive."

"That's hard knowledge to keep alone. You shoulda tol' me."

"You'd think the Lord would let the goin' down pains ease up when a baby won't even be movin'," she whimpered.

"They was bad pains, wasn't they. Aw, don' cry, Janey. I know you done the best you could, and I want our baby to carry my name, just like we talked about."

"Dear Lord," she prayed, "I am achin' everywhere down my soul!"

"We'll get through this, honey." But his words were hollow as a pipe.

It took a week before he said the words that had been dancing in his dreams for years but gnawing on him since he buried his baby. He told himself the words would help Janey, who still was weak abed and needed something to look forward to. Kneeling at her bedside, he asked her, "Ain't it time, Janey?"

His hands were clenched together. Jane put her own hands around his.

"California. You—our whole family—we all go together," Isaac said.

With all her strength, Jane pushed Isaac's hands off the bed. "A week after I birth a gone baby, you come at me with this?"

"Don't be no fool, Janey," he breathed. "Losin' the baby jus' the latest ripple in a whole river of sorry luck. Nothin' set to change here. Folks got their hearts set."

"I got my heart set too. And my feet. And my house. And now the first grave our property has knowed. Here! I told God I would let him guide me, plant my feet where he designed, and this is where!"

"Janey," he whispered, "calm down. Don't wear yo'self out. Honey, you gots to know by now, there is nothin' for me here—nothin'! Nor for you neither. There's opportunity in California—for gold, for business. Better place to be raisin' children. Janey, let's go to California."

Her head fell back to her pillow. "I thought we was sufficient to one another."

"That's so. Here or in California."

"This ain't been a bad place for us. We done better than a lot of folks."

"I admit things was good at first, but we barely inchin' out a livin' now."

She scoured him with her eyes, the way only Jane James could.

"What else you chasin' besides more work? You got somethin' else you want new?"

"What you sayin'?"

"Would you leave me if I don't go to California?"

He took this as a full accusation and felt abused. All he had been doing in talking up California was trying to make her feel better. At least that's what he told himself. "I ain't never said nothin' like that," he said. "I won't do that to you, Janey. But at some point, I got to get shed of this place. Ain't done me no good. No good at all." It wasn't until the words were out that he realized how strong he felt them.

"It ain't harmed you."

"Ain't done nothin' for me. That's the problem. Ain't done nothin' for none of us."

Jane gazed at her husband a long time before speaking. "I don't know what I'd ever do without you, Isaac, if you should take a mind to—"

He managed a quick laugh and forced a smile, trying for all the world to look like the man he'd always been, the man she thought he was. "Well, don't worry about it, then," he said. "I jus' thought if you could hope for somethin' like what I hear they findin' down there, you'd be able to get yourself out of bed."

"I can get out of bed right here in Utah." She made her point by standing. Her hair was a messy web of undone braids, and her nightdress was raggedy. But she was standing sure enough, strong and steady.

Isaac stood too and put his arm around her.

"It wasn't to get me out of bed you start talkin' on California," Jane said. "Don't pretend otherwise. You been holdin' imaginin's for that place a long while. I know your thoughts better than you 'spects. I know the imaginin's of your heart."

"If you livin' in a drab world, sometimes imaginin's is all you got," he murmured.

"Open the curtains," she said. "Let some light into this drab room."

"Open or shut, ain't much to see outside."

"Maybe not for you," she answered. "I sees the future."

"I guess that's the problem, Janey," he said. "I sees it too."

NOTES

The chapter title is from a traditional Negro spiritual cited in Higginson, "Negro Spirituals," 689.

Besides Isaac (stillborn on April 22, 1854), the James family consisted of Sylvester, born around 1841; Silas, born 1846; Mary Ann, 1848; Miriam, 1852; Ellen, 1853; Jesse J, 1856; and Vilate, 1859 (1860 First Ward census).

Though there is, to our knowledge, no record of who served as midwife when Isaac James Jr. was stillborn, we do know that Vilate Crosby (mother of Hark Lay and Oscar, Martha, and Rose Crosby) was a midwife and "presided at the births of both white and Negro children" (Carter, *Negro Pioneer*, 31).

The information on Tom Colbourn, who was convicted of manslaughter and sentenced to a year of hard labor in 1852 (and hence would have been released by the time of Isaac Jr.'s birth), is from Coleman, "History of Blacks in Utah," 52.

1855

20

SWING LOW,
SWEET CHARIOT

*For I pray continually . . . by day, and
mine eyes water my pillow by night.*
2 NEPHI 33:3

The Grim Reaper was busy. He was swinging his scythe not only through Utah but down the very place Isaac dreamed was all good: California. Agnes Flake was finally too feeble to resist Mister Death.

It was three years since Augustus Love's visit. Agnes had continued her decline steady as the pioneers were building up San Bernardino. Seemed the more they built, the sicker she got. Sometimes she'd rally, but such occasions were brief. The consumption which had already claimed her mama and daddy was working on her fierce.

Her last month of life, she spent in bed. Liz cared for her as though the mizzus were a baby. Finally, just as the sun was setting on January 4, 1855, Mizz Agnes told Liz to gather the children.

Liz started to ask a question. She was met with a stern "Don't argue. I won't have it. Do as you're told."

Liz made no more comment, just went to the cornfield after William and Charles and to the kitchen after Sarah.

Fifteen-year-old William entered the bedroom first. Charles and Sarah followed. Liz stayed in the doorway.

"Will, sit on the bed," said Agnes. She could draw nothing better than shallow, liquid breaths, but they were enough to hold up some talk. "You are the oldest, and I will hold you responsible for your every act. You must set an example worthy of your standing."

"Yes, Mama."

"Live to your father's memory."

"Yes." William was not a weeper, and his answers were stiff.

"And you children," she said to the others, "Sarah and Charles, you follow your brother. He'll lead you right. I know I can depend on him. Will, stay away from tobacco. It's a filthy habit, and I won't have you using a spittoon all your life."

"I'll stay clean of it, Mama."

She closed her eyes. "My, I'm tired. How can I be so tired?"

"Let me sit up with you," Will offered, but she shook her head.

"No. I want rest, and if you sit here I cannot sleep."

"But, Mama—"

"Do as you're told," Agnes said and instructed Liz to remove the children to another room. When she returned, her mizzus said that she wanted to look good on this particular night. So Liz brushed that long, pretty hair and coiled it around her head.

"You pretty as the day you married Massa Madison," she said.

"You remember that day? You were so young."

"I recollect everything about it."

"I'm glad," Mizz Agnes said. A cough took her. Liz held a bowl under the mizzus's mouth for the blood. When the spell was over, Agnes finished her thought: "I'm glad it was you they gave me. Glad it was you."

Just before dawn, Mizz Agnes called to Liz again. Her call didn't need to be loud, for Liz slept on the floor next to the bed. Agnes told her to fetch the children and to go after Lydia Jones and Maria Lyman. Liz knew something was brewing, for Mizz Agnes and Mizz Lydia had some trouble and hadn't spoke in years. Might be Mizz Agnes wished to make amends.

It didn't matter. There would be no time for amends. The moment Liz brought the children into their mother and went after the women, Agnes Love Flake passed on.

Liz wailed the second she returned to the house, the womenfolk at her side. She could see her mizzus from the outer door—stone dead—and could see the children weeping. Even Will.

Running to the bed, Liz cried, "No! Mizz Agnes!" Agnes Flake's face was peaceful. She had drifted off gentle and looked sweet as the day, her eyes full shut. Liz sobbed for a long time, until Mizz Lydia urged her to go to the well to draw water for washing Agnes's body. Liz insisted on warming it on the stove, though Lydia thought it silly to waste heat on a corpse. Lydia took pride in speaking her mind and didn't stop with the comment on the water's temperature.

"I understand the children crying," Lydia said, "but answer me true: Aren't you glad—in your heart of hearts—that your mistress can't whip you again? Agnes Flake could be a hard woman."

That was when Liz grabbed Mizz Lydia by the shoulders and shoved her out the door, shouting, "You cain't talk that way about my mizzus. She was the best woman ever lived. She was not mean to me. That is a lie! She never hit me when I didn't deserve it. I love her better than anyone in the whole world. You get out, and you keep from off this place!"

Mizz Lydia got out—she sure did—because she did not have a choice in the matter, Liz being the stronger of the two.

Mizz Maria Lyman set to work alone laying out the body, pretending not to hear any fight.

Agnes Love Flake was buried the next day, after a fitting funeral.

True to her word, Liz never spoke to Lydia Jones again, though you can be sure Lydia told anyone who would listen about Agnes Flake's saucy slave.

Amasa Lyman and his wives looked after the orphaned Flake children. Amasa's son Francis Marion (everybody called him "F. M."), was near the same age as Will Flake. The two were already best friends. They'd often swim in the pond on the San Bernardino River and dive off a ten-foot stump into that cool wet. With F. M.'s help, Will was able to play past his grief, and Sarah and Charles followed his example.

Lonely, Liz continued to care for them. She washed their clothes and often made their meals. She never spoke aloud about her pining for Charles Rowan. His wild eyes had sent their beams straight to her heart and scalded her blood. She was sure it would never cool.

Notes

The chapter title is from a traditional Negro spiritual found in Burleigh, *Spirituals*, 10.

The date of Agnes Flake's death is recorded as January 5, 1855 (Flake, *Of Pioneers and Prophets*, 131). The details of her death and Liz's reaction to it are recorded in Flake, *William J. Flake*, 23–24.

Though the incident is reported in a variety of sources, including Flake, *William J. Flake*, 23–24, and Carter, *Negro Pioneer*, 19, we do not know the identities of the women Liz brought to Agnes Flake's deathbed nor to whom Liz refused to speak after that woman demeaned Agnes (Liz's words in this scene are quoted from Flake, *William J. Flake*, 24). We do know that Maria Tanner Lyman, Amasa's first wife, was living nearby. According to Eliza Partridge Lyman's journal (Carter, *Treasures*, 2:240), on March 11, 1851, Amasa had taken all his wives, except Eliza and Paulina and their children, with him to settle in California.

21

O FREEDOM!

Praise him forever, for he is the Most High God,
and has loosed our brethren
from the chains of hell.
ALMA 26:14

A few months after Agnes's death, Biddy Smith showed up at the Flakes' door.

California had made her a round woman. In the past, all the walking had kept her legs slim, but California's lazy air let her whole body take on weight. Her cheeks were full and gleaming with a film of sweat, and right now, she was looking worried.

"Somethin' brewin'?" Liz asked.

Biddy shook her head, not comfortable entering conversation yet. She motioned towards the orchard, and they walked to tell their secrets. When they knew they were a distance beyond any white person's hearing, Biddy told it: "Massa say he takin' us to Texas."

"Texas? Ain't he figured you done walk enough by now?"

"White folks do as they pleases," said Biddy. "Us coloreds do as we can. Massa ride the pony, and I shovel what gets left behind."

On a normal day, Liz would've laughed at that. But this was not a normal day. This day had danger in it, looming like thunderheads. "Why Texas? What in Texas anyway?"

"I don't know. A slave-holdin' desert, I guess."

Liz didn't have to respond. If Texas was slave holding, then all of Robert Smith's slaves would become his property in a permanent way, and he could sell or trade them off if he happened to find himself needy.

Liz said what she thought and what Charles had planted in her head: "If you walkin' free soil, then yo' feets must be free. And if yo' feets be free, the rest of you must be free too."

"These feets was made to take care of this body," Biddy said. "I wouldn't put it past some folks to chop 'em off to keep me from runnin', if they thought I had a mind to."

"Do you have a mind to?"

Biddy was fussing with her apron, wringing a corner that wasn't even wet. "Ellen sweet on a fellow, and he courtin' her by the hour."

"I know."

"He tryin' to persuade all us to run."

"Run where?"

"Hush now. Don' let on. I ain't made no plans. Jus' thinkin' of puttin' some space between us and the Smiths so's we can stay here in California."

"I help you too, howsoever I can," promised Liz, feeling on the verge of a great and grave adventure.

The clouds above had stretched into a gauzy, lavender sheet.

"Ain't that pretty?" Biddy said.

"I don' know how you can think on sunset at such a moment as this," answered Liz.

"But ain't it pretty?"

"Yes, Biddy. God's painted us a good one tonight."

"It be a sign. That's what I thinks. And I will leave a sign too. If the massa start schemin' and packin' us for Texas, I will tie my headwrap—same color as them clouds—to the almond tree. If you see that sign, you get the message to Amasa Lyman, and you go quick."

"You got my word on it," promised Liz.

It took less than a week before Liz saw that headwrap signal. Sure enough, not a one of the Smiths was at home. Liz knocked on the door hard as she could and then pushed it open. It wasn't locked, and the house was empty. For all anyone could tell, the Smiths and their Negroes had disappeared off the face of the earth.

True to her word, Liz ran like a cat from a jackal, asking the Lord to guide her every panting step. She borrowed Will Flake's horse and galloped it to the Lymans' cabin.

Amasa answered the door himself, asking, "What's wrong, girl? Why are you riding so hard?"

She sat on the porch chair, holding her head and letting her breath settle.

"Is it one of the children?" Amasa's voice was so calm, seemed no danger could fluster him.

"No sir. The Smiths. They gone."

"Brother Robert?"

"Hotfootin' it for Texas, I figure."

Lyman had known Smith was considering this move. As an apostle of the Church, Amasa had counseled against it. He didn't think highly of how Robert Smith treated his Negroes, and he especially disapproved of the mulatto children that came from Smith's slaves. Amasa could get angry, and rage loosed his tongue now. If Lyman's words could accomplish it, Smith would have found himself heading direct to the devil that instant.

Liz told him there were Negroes in Los Angeles ready to help, and she named them.

Amasa bowed his head. When he lifted it, he announced that the Smiths and their Negroes would be found.

It appeared he had had a revelation, and Liz wasn't inclined to question.

Within the hour, Amasa had set out for Los Angeles. Charles Rowan went with him. Praying, Liz watched them leave. She knew she would never outlive her affection for Mister Rowan and begged God to bring him back safe with the Smiths' slaves.

For all those involved in pursuit, there was no time to spare. If the Smith Negroes were to be freed, then Smith had to be intercepted at once. The territories bordering California were uncertain, but once the border to Texas was crossed, nothing could be done or undone for the Smith Negroes.

Lyman and the rest went for the sheriff, a Mr. Frank DeWitt.

Now, if you had seen DeWitt from behind, you might've wondered how he could wear a star and impress anyone, for he was a short, stocky fellow. But when he turned, you saw the why. His mouth wore a natural snarl, and his face cautioned you to walk careful. He held his shoulders square, and you knew first sight not to make any comment on his stature. He may have been short, but his whole body was muscle and venom. His looks said he could spit you into the grave.

Amasa was a good foot taller than DeWitt, but he spoke in respectful tones as he provided details about Robert Smith, advising the sheriff that Smith was not a person most folks would want to tussle with. Smith was a big fellow and could wield a mighty whip on either horse or Negro.

The sheriff calmly responded he was neither.

Amasa knew and reported the situation precisely: Smith needed money. He had only five hundred dollars and some household belongings. Those living, breathing, black bodies were the greater part of his wealth and could easily be cashed in—but not in California. Smith clearly intended to keep his Negroes, at least until they got to Texas.

Seemed Robert and Rebecca had loaded their wagons in the

dead of night. Their overseer had likely corralled the slaves—including Biddy and pregnant Hannah—for the journey. Lyman suggested it might take several more men with firearms to dissuade Smith of his intentions. A confrontation was likely, and Lyman was certain he knew where it would take place. Some time ago, Smith had said if he ever had to conceal himself, he'd go to the Santa Monica mountains to a particular cave-pocked area.

That was all that needed saying. Amasa Lyman, Charles Rowan, Sheriff DeWitt, and a number of others, mostly Negroes, left at dusk.

Once in the mountains, the posse split up to investigate hiding spots. That first day brought no sign of their quarry, so they bedded down for the night, Amasa insisting on leading them in prayer (which was as much a preachment to the posse as it was a petition to the Lord). At dawn, they were up again. They broke bread, wet their mouths with creek water, and resumed the search.

It wasn't until noon that Charles Rowan spied the Smith wagons behind a bunch of scrub oak and signaled the others.

DeWitt instructed the men to fan out. "I want you to line up five abreast, three deep. Have your weapons out and ready. We're going to ride in hard, and I want them to know we mean business. No shooting unless I give the order. Is that understood? I'll fire three shots as we go in, to let 'em know we're here."

They did as he ordered. No more than a minute passed before he took his rifle from its scabbard and fired. The report echoed three times. He shot a second time and then a third. The echoes volleyed as DeWitt led them all into the Smith camp.

"Robert Smith?" the sheriff yelled.

Smith answered from behind the wagon. "I'm Robert Smith. Who are you?"

"I'm Sheriff Frank DeWitt. If you're carrying a weapon, I recommend you let it drop before showing your face."

"My hands are empty." Smith stepped clear of the wagon. "Now what do you want?"

"I have a writ of habeas corpus, and I mean to enforce it."

"A writ of what?" Smith's head was bare and bald, his arms muscled but nervous.

"A paper informing you that you have no right to remove free persons to a place where they cease being free."

"You referring to my slaves?"

"There are no slaves in California," said the sheriff.

"I misspoke," Smith answered. "These Negroes are as dear to me as my family."

Amasa Lyman muttered, "Some of them *are* your family."

"I'd as soon leave one of my children as one of my Negroes," Smith yelled. "And they're well disposed to go with me." Rebecca Smith joined her husband, looking pale as the clouds overhead and showing every ounce of her fear. Robert Smith instructed his over-seer to go untie the Negroes.

"You heading for Texas?" DeWitt asked.

"That's right," said Smith.

Amasa spoke up now. "Robert, you know I told you not to. I've warned you for years to bridle your passions and follow the gospel."

Smith glared at the Mormon apostle. "Is this your doing, Lyman?"

"It's the Lord's doing, and you should know it."

"I never thought in my life you'd turn against me. Never imag-ined you'd bring a brigade of Negroes to point rifles at me. Never thought you'd turn artificial black man. This is the same style of mob work that murdered Joseph and Hyrum."

Amasa's green eyes flared. "You compare yourself to Joseph Smith one time more, and I will show you justice. What you are doing is nothing like the Prophet's work. You never even knew him. I did, and I testify his work was of God. What you're working now is the devil's design. And what you've done to those girls—well, if your wife weren't here, I'd be explicit."

DeWitt approached, and Smith asked the overseer to bring out his "other family."

Once unbound, Ellen ran straight for her beau, who was in the posse. He swung himself down from his mount, offering her one hand, holding the reins in the other. Biddy and Hannah, who was near set to birth a child, watched from the wagon.

"Why are you going to Texas, Smith?" DeWitt was offering easy bait.

"Opportunity. California didn't work out for us."

"California seems to be working out for these Negroes," said DeWitt. "I am taking all them into protective custody as of now, until we know if they have a mind to accompany you. These men are authorized to shoot if you resist."

Robert Smith found Amasa Lyman's face again. "You would stand by and let one of them shoot me, Lyman?"

Amasa responded by taking his gun from its holster and aiming it at Smith's chest. "Would it make you feel better if I shot you myself? By heaven, I swear I'll do it if you resist in any way."

The trek back to Los Angeles was slow. For one thing, everybody knew Hannah was birth-ready, and no one wanted her pains to start.

Biddy rode with Amasa, thanking him over and over.

The Smith Negroes were lodged at the county jail and had no hesitation in letting the guard know how much they feared Robert Smith and what he might do. He had threatened them, and they hadn't felt free to say a thing. Liz visited her friends in the jail, but she had to wait until the case got tried before she could hear about it.

Of course, the Smith slaves were not allowed to speak in open court, for no colored person had such rights back then. But the jailkeeper told what he had heard. The judge invited Biddy and the others to tell their stories in his chambers. While two witnesses wrote her words, Biddy testified: "I have always done what I have been told to do. But I always feared this trip to Texas, since I first heard of it."

Robert Smith didn't help his case much when he bribed the lawyer representing the colored folks. Smith offered that man one hundred dollars to quit the case on the second morning of trial. Mind you, a hundred dollars was a lot of money back then, and sure enough, the lawyer went for it. He informed the judge that he was abandoning the case. Well, the judge asked a few questions, and it didn't take long for the bribe to come uncloaked.

Though the colored petitioners stayed silent in court, the judge had and gave his answer: "Appearing that Robert Smith intended to and is about to remove from the State of California where slavery does not exist, to the state of Texas, where slavery of Negroes and persons of color does exist, said persons of color are entitled to their freedom and are free and cannot be held in slavery or involuntary servitude; they are entitled to their freedom and are free forever."

Robert Smith was fined a handsome sum, but he left town rather than pay a penny.

So the case was over. Biddy Smith and all her family remained in California—free persons from then on. As the judge said, they were "to become settled and go to work for themselves—in peace and without fear."

Nobody was happier about that decision than Liz Flake. She and Biddy embraced like they both had found freedom—as indeed they had. Liz was so proud of herself and her friends and of one friend in particular: Charles Rowan.

By the time the case ended, though, Mister Rowan had left to pursue other adventures. Liz continued waiting on the Flake children, though not a day went by she didn't wrestle her mind. How could she have let Charles go? Did he ever think of her anymore? She promised herself and the good Lord too that if ever Charles should come back, she'd leap into his arms. She'd marry him the moment they found someone with marrying power.

Every knock on the door made her jump, and every dawn found her more lonesome and woeful.

NOTES

The chapter title is from a traditional Negro spiritual cited in Cone, *Spirituals and the Blues*, 40, which gives this variation on page 29:

> *Oh Freedom! Oh Freedom!*
> *Oh Freedom, I love thee!*
> *And before I'll be a slave,*
> *I'll be buried in my grave,*
> *And go home to my Lord and be free.*

The black "vaqueros" involved in rescuing the Smith Negroes included Robert Owen (a relatively wealthy livery owner); his son, Charles Owen (Ellen Smith's beau); Manuel Pepper (Ann Smith's beau), and eight to ten others. According to Layne ("Annals of Los Angeles," 333), "Uncle Bob Owen" was a freed slave, "who with his wife 'Aunt' Winnie and son Charles, had arrived in California from Texas in December, 1853." The first meeting of the African Medical Episcopal (A.M.E.) Church in California was held in the Owen house in 1854 and was attended by Biddy Smith, a nurse "at the home of Dr. Griffin" at the time.

Some of the information on Biddy Smith Mason is from Hull, *Story of Bridget "Biddy" Smith Mason.*

The phrase "artificial black men" denoted for Mormons "individuals who paint themselves and murder" (such as the mob who killed Joseph and Hyrum Smith), according to Bringhurst, *Saints, Slaves, and Blacks*, 93.

The likely possibility that Robert Smith intended to sell his slaves in Texas is discussed in Hayden, "Biddy Mason's Los Angeles," 91. The idea that Smith was poverty-stricken is challenged, however, by Lyman (*San Bernardino*, 291), who suggests that Smith "had prospered in California and planned to leave for Texas, allegedly to avoid paying tithing on his considerable earnings."

Details of the trial of Robert Smith, including his failure to appear on Monday, January 21, 1856, as well as the statements of Biddy, Hannah, and Ann Smith in Judge Benjamin Hayes's chambers and the judge's verdict are from Hayden, "Biddy Mason's Los Angeles," 90–91. Hayden says: "Smith could have appealed this local verdict to the California Supreme Court, where it is likely he would have won the support of conservative justices, such as Hugh C. Murray. However, presumably because of his bribery of the opposing counsel and [Smith's overseer, Hart] Cottrell's attempted kidnapping of the slave children, Smith left town. Biddy Smith Mason and her family were delivered from slavery, unlike other slaves in this decade who struggled with the courts and lost" ("Biddy Mason's Los Angeles," 91). Robert Smith was excommunicated from The Church of Jesus Christ of Latter-day Saints (Hull, *Story of Bridget "Biddy" Smith Mason*, 4).

The decision in the First Judicial District of the State of California, County of Los Angeles, regarding the Smith Negroes is quoted in Beasley, *Negro Trail Blazers of California*, 88: "It further appearing by satisfactory proof to the judge here, that all the said persons of color are entitled to their freedom and are free and cannot be held in slavery or involuntary servitude, it is therefore argued that they are entitled to their freedom and are free forever."

The Smith case resulted in a number of slaves of Mormon families pursuing their freedom. As Lyman documents, there were "considerable changes among the colony's black citizens in the months after [Robert] Smith's departure. Most of the adult African-Americans chose to abandon the community when given full opportunity to do so." Among those who left were Oscar Crosby, who took Harriet and Grief Embers with him. (Harriet had once belonged to Billy and Sytha Crosby Lay.) Eventually, however, Oscar, "married to a woman who had belonged to Robert Smith, returned to San Bernardino," as did Grief and Harriet. They, with Liz and Charles Rowan, "formed the nucleus of the permanent black community important in the Inland Empire from the beginnings of the settlement" (*San Bernardino*, 292–93).

Rumblings
of War
1857

22

THIS WORLD
ALMOST DONE

He denieth none that come unto him, black and
white, bond and free, male and female . . .
all are alike unto God.

2 NEPHI 26:33

During this time of tumult and turmoil, the makings of civil war were churning in the places these folks had left behind.

Jane James's brother Lewis Manning had quit his steamship job and settled in St. Louis, where a Negro named Dred Scott was about to make national headlines.

Lew had not heard about Dred Scott, but their paths had maybe crossed, for Dred Scott had traveled to Illinois just as the Mannings had—except that he had no freedom papers nor baptism certificate to present to anyone chasing runaway slaves. Scott tried to leave his master through the legal system. That got him exactly nowhere, but it did stir up a stew of feelings.

Scott claimed he must be free because he had lived in free states, on free soil. Then when his massa died and his mizzus remarried, Dred Scott was gifted to a man in St. Louis.

Most history books these days report how *Scott vs. Sanford* ended up in the very Supreme Court of this nation, for it was one of the last straws to break before war ripped this country through its middle. Chief Justice Taney, a man near eighty years old, announced the decision on March 6, 1857:

"Can a Negro, whose ancestors were imported into this country and sold as slaves, become a member of the political community formed and brought into existence by the Constitution of the United States?"

The answer, finally, was NO. Negroes were not even citizens of these United States, said the chief justice, for the Constitution made no distinction between slaves and other property. Taney said the Negroes were "beings of an inferior order, and altogether unfit to associate with the white race, either in social or political relations; and so far inferior that they had no rights which the white man was bound to respect."

It was a good thing for Biddy Smith that her case made the California courts before Dred Scott's took Washington, for the Dred Scott case would have sent Biddy Smith and all her family straight to Texas.

Lew Manning heard about the decision right in the center of St. Louis. An old shoeshine told him that Dred Scott got lost in the Supreme Court.

For a moment, Lew thought Dred had somehow locked himself in a closet and nobody could find him. But he understood quick enough: Dred Scott had got lost in the capital city of these United States when seven of nine robed men decided he had been lost from the moment of his birth. He wasn't even a full man, they said, only three-fifths of one.

"Supreme Court say no Negro is a citizen of this country," said the shine. "And he can't never be one. Sho' wish they'd decided that befo' I fought in that war of 1812!"

Lew was accompanied by his fiancée, Lucinda—a strong girl with skin shiny as molasses and lips the shade of plums. She had a double chin that quivered when she laughed, but there was no laughing now. Not on this sad day. No laughing, no dancing, no joking. Lucinda pulled her shawl tight across her shoulders.

"I knew it go that way," Lew said.

"I didn't think it would," said the shine. "So much goin's on, I thought they'd free the man to keep peace."

Lew answered that with a roll of his eyes. "What you expect? They free him, next thing you know the abolitionists will have us votin' and tryin' to be president. Them white men is scared of anything what ain't like them."

"But not even a citizen?" said the shine. "Not even a man?"

"It's a cryin' shame," Lucinda said.

"It's a weepin' and wailin' shame," Lew added.

He knew his sister Jane would have even harsher words for it. Jane Manning James could shake the sky with rage when it was right rage.

Well, Jane wouldn't hear of the Dred Scott decision for some time, since news made it slow to Utah and the telegraph system wouldn't be up for several years yet.

Anyways, Utah had its own scuffles with Washington. It seemed the federal government aimed to take care of at least one "relic of barbarism" before it had to deal with the other.

But when July 24th came around, Utah took time to celebrate. The Saints had arrived in the Valley of the Great Salt Lake ten years ago that day. The Jameses and other pioneers were gathered on a grassy field in Big Cottonwood Canyon, eating picnic lunches, listening to brass bands, joining in song, and dancing to fancy fiddling. They were having a grand time, until four horsemen galloped into the assembly. One of them hollered for everyone to hush up. Then he announced that a whole army of soldiers was on its way to install a non-Mormon governor and take over the territory.

Of course, the Mormons had experienced such interference

before. Many had buried loved ones when the government decided to have its way in Missouri and Illinois. There were new members now who hadn't experienced Governor Boggs's order to "exterminate the Mormons or drive them from the state" or Governor Ford's silent blessing on the mob that killed the Prophet Joseph. But all had heard tale. News of soldiers marching for Utah put a quick end to the anniversary party.

Come September, Brigham Young declared martial law and ordered the Saints in California home to Utah.

Amasa Lyman and his family—including the Flake children— answered that call. That's when Biddy Smith took Amasa Mason Lyman's middle name as her last one, in honor of all he had done to lead her to California and help her to freedom.

Liz Flake tried to convince herself to be happy about going back to Utah with the Lymans. For one thing, she'd be able to see Green again. She wondered if he and Martha had a bunch of babies by now and tried to care more about that reunion than the distance she'd be putting between herself and Charles Rowan.

She was packing her belongings when a familiar voice said, "Hello, Mizz Peach."

It was soft thunder. It was Charles.

Liz turned to see he had cleaned himself up something special for this meeting. His hair was close cropped, and he was sporting a fine, bushy mustache, though his chin and jaws were shaved. His clothes were so new looking, she figured he must've struck it rich indeed. But she didn't ask. She did what she had always imagined doing at this moment: she flung herself into his arms. And such loving and hugging you never did see! Liz kissed that man so much he had to tell her to slow down so's he could breathe.

The next morning, she told the Lymans and the Flake children that she wouldn't be journeying back to Utah after all. She understood she would never see Will or Charles or Sarah again, and she truly loved them. But her life was opening up in California, and she was fixed on living it to the fullest. She had accepted Charles's proposal, she told them, and begged the Flake children to remember her always and keep her in their prayers.

Though none of the Mormons were there to see it, Liz and Charles did get married. She made her own gown of fine cotton and thought it every bit as pretty as the one Mizz Agnes had worn all those years past, when two colored children waited on the stair landing to get gifted to a bride and groom, along with a table full of polished presents.

Well, Liz was her own gift now. Madison and Agnes were gone, and the Flake children were about to become part of a new adventure.

NOTES

The chapter title is from a traditional Negro spiritual cited in Higginson, "Negro Spirituals," 687.

The marriage year of Liz Flake and Charles Rowan (1858) is from Family Group Record 129 (Fretwell, Miscellaneous Family Papers, 3). The 1860 census in San Bernardino (cited in Fretwell, Miscellaneous Family Papers, 13) lists the Rowan family as follows:

> Flake, Elizabeth, age 26, female, Negro. Born: North Carolina. Occupation: Laundress
> Flake, James W., age 1, male, mulatto

According to Fretwell, Charles Rowan was in Utah during 1860.

Twenty years later, the 1880 census for San Bernardino lists the Rowan family as follows. Liz is not listed because she had died in 1868.

> Rowan, Charles, Mulatto, male, age 38. Born: Maryland. Occupation: Barber
> Rowan, Walter James, age 21. Mulatto. Born: California. Laborer.
> Rowan, Bryan, age 18. Mulatto. Born: California. Laborer.
> Rowan, Alice Ann. Age 12. Mulatto. Born: California
> Rowan, Charles. Age 6. Mulatto. Born: California

According to Skinner, Liz actually wanted to return to Utah with the Flakes, but Will Flake persuaded her that "she had earned her freedom many times over, and she should get married and raise a family of her own" (*Black Origins in the Inland Empire*, 19).

Justice Taney's words are quoted in Johnson et al., *Africans in America*, 418.

The strong possibility that Biddy Smith Mason adopted her last name in tribute to Amasa Mason Lyman is from Hayden, who quotes Barbara Jackson as saying that Biddy "may have chosen [the name] in homage to the trail-finder, Amasa Mason Lyman, who had led the Mormon wagons to Deseret and to San Bernardino" ("Biddy Mason's Los Angeles," 91).

23

WALK 'EM EASY

*For thou hast girded me with strength unto the
battle: thou hast subdued under me
those that rose up against me.*
PSALM 18:39

Utah's Saints were making ready for conflict. That's just what
Amasa Lyman's company found when they arrived: stockpiling, fear,
and preparation for war.

A bunch of Mormons hiked Echo Canyon to harass the coming
soldiers by loosening boulders which could crash down on horse and
rider and slow an army's progress just fine. They built ditches and
dams too, so they could flood the enemy's way if the boulders
weren't enough. Raiders rode out in hit-and-run style to set fire to
the government trains and stampede their animals. This was the
Utah version of the Nauvoo Legion, and its members could whoop
and cackle through the night if they had to, to keep the federal soldiers from sleep. Sylvester James, now grown beyond his teen years,
played his part in the mischief and quite enjoyed himself. Jane said
he didn't know trouble from turnips and warned him how easy
pranks can turn deadly.

Such caution made Syl more eager yet.

He and the other Mormon guerillas managed to torch some seventy-four wagons as well as all the buildings at Fort Bridger and Fort Supply. They captured fourteen hundred cattle too. General Albert Sidney Johnston, a right proper southern gentleman, was in command of the federal troops. He arrived with his Negro driver, his Negro cook, and two thousand soldiers, none of which was darker than the snows that had just started. Food would quick grow scarce for the troops. They had a few cattle for meat, but it looked like they'd soon have to settle for mule.

Brigham Young sent letters to Johnston, offering salt to flavor whatever eatings the soldiers could find. To which Johnston replied: "I can accept of nothing from him so long as he and his people maintain a hostile position to my Government."

What you had here was two powerful leaders, butting heads through their letters. President Young was certain the government would treat the Mormons just as polite as they had in Missouri days by hounding them out of their homes. He was not about to allow any such a thing. And General Johnston was certain the Mormons were ready to murder just about anybody and kidnap any woman in sight and force her into a "Mormon harem." He told the Saints if they came against him and his army, he would make more war than they'd yet seen in their history.

Johnston was ready to obey an order from President Buchanan to invade, and he kept his army drilled at Camp Scott. The snows arrived in Wyoming before Buchanan's order did, though, and the outside got cold and then colder. Sometimes it stormed so severe, the soldiers certainly thought they were bound for the grave. They had no firewood, and the snows were blowing wild and thick, wind whooshing and whistling, sucking every bit of heat out of every man's body, with no sign of a change.

Needless to say, the Saints saw this as the hand of God. Sylvester James derived particular delight in declaring that the good

Lord had opened up his portals to dump some reminders of real power onto the government forces. As for Jane, she didn't prize the notion of anyone getting frostbit, for she knew what it was to freeze. She felt sorry for the soldiers, Gentiles or not.

Johnston considered the cold nothing but nature, and he kept his post. His men might've felt different, but they didn't complain—at least not to him.

When the weather finally let up and the army got reinforced and supplied, they entered the Salt Lake Valley peaceably, displaying every ounce of discipline you'd expect from men who had wintered together and met the bugle's call each morning.

It was June now, and the army settled at a place they called Camp Floyd, halfway between Salt Lake and Provo but farther west in the desert. Johnston found Utah the most sterile country he could imagine. He would've been hard-pressed to explain why he should take on such a place, except he'd been told strong lies about the Mormons. Far as he knew, women were killing themselves right and left so they wouldn't have to marry their grandpa's uncle. He had heard that Brigham Young said the best favor you could do a non-Mormon was to just kill him straight off. Johnston had little doubt that the Mountain Meadows Massacre—wherein a number of travelers got killed by Mormons—was done on Brigham Young's order. Reports had it that Brigham could command such a thing time and again, just by crooking his little finger. Johnston's army felt it their patriotic duty to put down the "Mormon Rebellion," however worthless the land appeared.

It turned out there wasn't much to put down. A good many Mormons, including the Jameses, temporarily abandoned Salt Lake City so the army would have nothing to take over, and at least a few of Johnston's men deserted him and joined up with the Saints. A Prussian-born fellow named Charles Wilcken was one of these deserters. Of course, Porter Rockwell gave him the choice of doing that or dying, and conversion looked preferable to Wilcken at the moment.

Johnston's army—minus the deserters—quit the territory around 1860 with their soldiering days just beginning. They were on the verge of a true war, not just a staring contest. If the Saints had known what awaited these men, they might have wept from pity.

NOTES

The chapter title is from a traditional Negro spiritual cited in Higginson, "Negro Spirituals," 688.

Sylvester James was listed as a member of Utah's Nauvoo Legion (Wolfinger, "Test of Faith," in *Social Accommodation*, 132).

Details of the Johnston's army episode are from *Church History in the Fulness of Times*, 347–48.

Johnston's version of "the Mormon Rebellion" is from the biography written by his son William Preston Johnston, *The Life of General Albert Sidney Johnston* (201–47). That Johnston had a "Negro driver" (John) and a Negro cook is noted in that source on page 171. The general's response to Brigham Young's offer of salt is recorded on page 219: "So far as poison is concerned, I would freely partake of Brigham Young's hospitality, but I can accept of no present, nor interchange courtesies so long as he continues his present course. . . . Your salt you will take back with you; not, as I tell you, because I suspect its purity, but I will not accept a present from an enemy of my Government."

Letters to his family preserve details about the cold Johnston's army endured. The general mentions his habit of exercising daily and notes that his mustache "becomes an icicle" during these bouts. He also expresses his love for his family: "I do not repine, but in a great measure we make our own destiny, and ought to submit without murmuring; but I hope the future has many good gifts in store for us. I trust in God; in that consists the sum of my religion. No hour passes without my thoughts reverting to you and each one of my family" (Johnston, *Life of General Albert Sidney Johnston*, 243).

Charles Henry Wilcken was born in Holstein, Germany, on October 5, 1830. Seifrit writes that when Wilcken was en route to South America, he boarded the wrong ship and "found himself, several weeks later, in New York." Being short of cash, he joined an enlistment of men "to go to the western desert to put down a tribe of rebellious 'Indians' called Mormons." He deserted Johnston's army on October 7, 1857, and was captured by Mormon defender Jonathan Ellis Layne, who turned him over to Porter Rockwell ("Charles Henry Wilcken," 309–10). Ultimately, he became a bodyguard for Brigham Young and a close friend of George Q. Cannon.

Civil War

24

MY ARMY
CROSS OVER

Our lives passed away like as it were unto us a dream,
we being a lonesome and a solemn people, . . . hated of
our brethren, which caused wars and contentions.
JACOB 7:26

In the election of 1860, Abraham Lincoln got made the six-teenth president of these United States. But only a few weeks went by before these states were no longer united. On December 20th, South Carolina seceded from the Union. By the end of January, Florida, Mississippi, Alabama, Georgia, and Louisiana followed suit, and Texas was tending that direction.

The Rebels didn't waste no time. They attacked Fort Sumpter a month after Mister Lincoln took up his office. Strife swooshed into this country on a whirlwind and roused every man from his bed, whether it was a feather mattress or a pile of straw in the hayloft. The Civil War was on, and Jefferson Davis was declared president of the Confederate nation.

The war may have started in South Carolina, but it soon swept across the entire South and fired up the border states, including

217

Missouri. In Marshall, Mortimer Gaines's youngest son, Ben—ten years younger than Louis Gray—came out of the barn singing:

> Jeff Davis rode a big white hoss,
> Lincoln rode a mule;
> Jeff Davis is our President,
> Lincoln is a fool.

Through the grapevine telegraph, Louis already knew the war was heating up and getting bloody. He worried over Ben, whose skin and hair were so pale, seemed the slightest wound would drain him of color complete. He prayed the war stay far away.

But you already know how that prayer got answered.

Soon after shots were fired at Fort Sumpter, the very town that had locked up Joseph Smith—Liberty, Missouri—got singed: "Sesesh" troops captured its arsenal. Now, Liberty's arsenal wasn't near as big as the one in St. Louis (which got attacked some time later), but it contained several hundred muskets, a dozen cannons, and a good quantity of powder. Blood was spent in its defense and in its taking.

Come June, the residents around Marshall itself would feel the hot flurries of agitation.

On the 11th, Louis was traveling with Massa and Mizzus Gaines to Sedalia. They were set to buy farm tools and a bolt of satin. (The satin was for the Gaineses' twenty-year-old daughter, Betty, who was to be married shortly.) Louis was driving the double seater wagon, and Massa Mortimer was sitting next to the mizzus.

For miles, there were no hints of any scuffle ahead. The day was calm, and the horses trotted leisurely. But once in Sedalia, Louis had to halt. In the middle of the town square stood fifty men and a good number of animals. A Union soldier in starched blue, his buttons like gold coins, was making a speech.

"What be happenin' here?" Louis asked nobody in particular.

The mizzus breathed, "Will you look at this? It's the Yankee government trying to raise up an army in our own backyard! Oh, doesn't this look bad?"

Bad indeed. All these young men were forming a mob, some of them toting rifles.

The leader was a small fellow with a long, brown mustache. He was sitting proud on his bay. Louis guessed that without the horse under him, this man was a fairly inconsequential creature.

"I am Captain Parker of the Union." The captain's voice hadn't quite dropped into its manhood, but he was trying to sound lordly. "I have a commission to raise a company of men. All of you who want to enlist for three months, step two paces to the front."

Most of the young men did so and were sworn into service on the spot. They would be a mounted Union company. Each recruit had a horse—or would get one soon.

"Fools," muttered Massa Mortimer. "Things have come to a pretty pass when a free people can't choose their own way."

Louis murmured, "Ain't no gun in they backs. They seems to be signing up."

Massa glanced at Louis and raised his voice. "I suspect these fine young men would like to liberate you to your devices, boy. They'd like to release you from my protection. Now how would you enjoy that?"

Louis held the reins fast and kept quiet, though he later confided to the Lord, "Seem to me I been feedin' my own family *and* the massa's for many a year. My devices seems fine, Lord."

Before long, the new-formed troop had departed on their mounts to get armed. The visitors from Marshall could go about their business.

But things were not resolved so easy elsewhere. That same day, up in St. Louis, a small group of officers destined to be enemies were holding a conference, trying to find some way to keep Missouri out of the fray. Each man, looking sharp and polished, wore the color of his allegiance, either gray or blue.

At that meeting was Confederate lieutenant general Sterling Price, who had once stood guard over Joseph Smith and allowed his fellow guards to say vile things about the Mormons—that is, until Joseph rebuked them all. Price had led the Chariton militia in driving the Latter-day Saints out of Missouri. He had also refused to share his grub with any member of the Mormon Battalion. In short, the Mormons had some acquaintance with this man, who had already been Missouri's governor and would soon become famous in the war.

Of course, he had aged some since the years he made life miserable for the Saints. Now he was a white-haired, thick-whiskered, ruddy fellow, who seemed taller than he was because he kept his back so straight.

Union general Nathaniel Lyon strutted back and forth whenever he spoke, his spurs clattering. Lyon was more soldier than diplomat and announced, "Rather than concede to the state of Missouri, I would see you and every man, woman, and child in the State, dead and buried."

Well, such words didn't offer much hope. No surprise, Price took offence. He finally said the obvious: "This means war."

Lyon and Price would meet again, but it would be on the field of combat. And Louis Gray would witness one of the first full battles of the war when it touched down in Missouri. It would be at Boonville.

That town was the residence of the mizzus's aunt, who would be helping with Betty's wedding. This time, it wasn't just the massa and mizzus who made the journey but Ben too. He had missed out on a thrill when Louis had carted the folks to Sedalia, and he wasn't about to miss out now.

Coursewise, he got more than he bargained for. Boonville was exactly where the new Union recruits had journeyed to await their weapons, which would be coming upriver. Louis clucked his tongue at the horses, urging them down the trail, and caught his first sight of Rebs. A battle was about to bust Boonville open.

Ten horseback Rebs was half-hid in the forest. The Union recruits waited by the river. When the Rebs raised their guns, Louis whipped his horses to a gallop. He saw little Captain Parker and five other uniformed men bearing down from the west. Ben saw them too and shouted, "Damnation!"

"We ain't stoppin'!" Louis yelled. Ben scurried onto the buckboard, twisting his head so he could watch the ruckus.

The Rebs put spurs to their animals. The Union cavalry took their mounts and headed towards the Rebs. The only thing standing in their way was a farmhouse.

Louis reined the horses to a stop and tied them to the hitching post under a magnolia tree. Ben had already scrambled down to watch the glory of war unfold before his eyes.

"You better get your head down, Massa Ben," Louis called. "It might seem excitin', but it ain't worth dyin' for."

The Rebels could not get past that farmhouse, for it was bordered by high willows and two outback buildings, so they dismounted and opened fire with everything they had. To Ben's delight, the afternoon got broke up by shrieking miniballs and sudden explosions. There was so much blue smoke, you had to wonder how any of the soldiers knew where to aim.

When the haze cleared, there was one fatality: Captain Parker's bay. And there was Captain Parker, his leg caught under that dead horse.

The Union men pulled the horse off him, but Parker could not walk.

It was hard to tell who was fighting for which side, for only the few officers wore uniforms. As Parker was getting drug to safety, Ben saw his first gun-shot man. He knew this particular fellow, for he was kin. He was Uncle Jeb, and he had got shot through his upper arm.

Jeb's mizzus came running from the house, lifting her hoop skirt to her knees, screaming at first and then demanding of her husband why in tarnation he hadn't stayed safe in the house and why he had done such a fool thing as to fire buckshot at a Union horse.

Jeb was sitting up, as surprised as he was hurt. "Bad aim," was his only answer.

By then, Jeb's slaves—seven of them—had come from their quarters to see the doings.

"Fetch the camphor and some bandages," Jeb's wife demanded of the house servant.

Ben, in wonder and amazement, was watching his uncle's blood flow. "You just got to be part of the war, Uncle Jeb," he said. "By damn, you just got wounded for Jeff Davis!"

Uncle Jeb's pride was altered by the sight of his own blood and by the sting of the camphor, which his slave applied with some sly pleasure.

What none of them knew was that this was only a skirmish in a much bigger fray. And couldn't nobody imagine that Boonville was only a prelude and a mild one at that.

For a few weeks after that battle, the war resumed at a distance, but soon a mighty conflict was fought at Wilson's Creek, Missouri, headed up by none other than Sterling Price on the Confederate side and Nathaniel Lyon for the Union. After it was done, Betty's betrothed, who had been with Price, reported all the details, now that he was home safe.

Gracie Gray was serving the guests as the young soldier told all about the bloody happenings. He used grand gestures to describe the Confederate soldiers and showed disdain for "Billy Yank." He was clad in uniform, and Betty's eyes adored every seam and button.

Later, Gracie told Louis all about the soldier's account, though neither could fully imagine it, nor what it soon would mean for them. She repeated all she could remember: A white man named Price had sat proud on horseback, riding to the front whenever silence captured the field. Through the smell and haze of spent powder, he'd strain to see what his enemies were doing and then shout a command to his men, which they'd obey. They'd die for him, if he asked them to, and he near died for them at that place. He got struck twice by bullets and took a sizeable wound to his side.

Another man, General Lyon, got his horse shot out from under him and fell, bleeding from his leg. Somehow, he managed to mount another horse when a bullet caught him in the breast and he keeled over, dead as a hammer.

"The Price man," Gracie said, "he become a hero." Neither of them knew what to think of this war business, but it did make for a good story.

Well, the story took on real life soon enough—the day word reached Marshall that the hero himself was set to speechify, right there in the town center. Sterling Price would take the platform on November 16th. It was the news of the year. The general was set to flame the hearts of Marshall's farmers, trade their pitchforks for muskets, and make soldiers of them.

Price would come to Marshall straight from the war, tall and proud as a hero should be.

The Gaineses, with sons Ben and Wilbur, went dressed in their finest to hear General Price. Louis and Gracie Gray went too, and they took along their son James, now two years old. All the slaves, including Price's own attendant, waited behind the white folk. Word was that Sterling Price might someday be president of the Confederate nation. Nobody, black or white, wanted to miss hearing him now.

A stand elevated him so all could see and praise this famous man. Those in the back might've thought Price was eight foot high as he started speechifying, telling the farmers that their harvests were reaped, they were ready for winter, and now why couldn't they go to war?

"In the name of God and the attributes of manhood, let me

appeal to you by considerations infinitely higher than money!" Price shouted. His hands were clasped behind his back, and his chest was puffed out. It was a frosty day, and the general was dressed for it in his officer's coat. His breath made a plume. Seemed Sterling Price was burning Marshall's air.

"Are we a generation of driveling, sniveling, degraded slaves?" Price demanded.

Louis felt his face go numb, like it just got belted. The white folk were yelling, "No!" to that question. The coloreds were exchanging secret looks.

"Or are we men?" Price was hungry for a loud answer. "Are we men who dare assert and maintain the rights which cannot be sur-rendered?"

The farmers whooped again. The sound they made would some-day be referred to as the Rebel Yell, but for now, it was just a mess of hemp tillers getting excitement in their veins.

"Shall we defend those principles of everlasting rectitude—pure and high and sacred, like God, their author?" Somehow, Sterling Price was making his words echo in the frost. There were no walls or hills to send the sound back, but there sure was an echo. "Be yours the office to choose between the glory of a free country and a just government," he said, "and the bondage of your children!"

Louis glanced at James, who was fidgeting in Gracie's arms.

Price shouted, "I will never see the chains fastened upon my country! I will ask for six and one-half feet of Missouri soil in which to repose but will not live to see my people enslaved!"

At this, there was a shout so loud it started Baby James to sob-bing, which nobody noticed but Louis and Gracie.

"I hear your shouts!" Price thundered.

He was answered by louder noise yet.

"Is that your war cry which echoes through the land? Are you coming?"

The whoops, yells, throat-scraping hollers were constant, and so were a number of babies' cries—slave and free. Sterling Price's voice carried above them all. "Fifty thousand men! Missouri shall move to victory with the tread of a giant! Come on, my brave boys! Fifty-thousand heroic, gallant, unconquerable Southern men! We await your coming!"

"We're with you, general!" The same answer came from many mouths.

The shouting faces conjured a bad memory for Louis, and he stepped back. A mob much like this one had gathered two years ago, fever-pitched over another cause they considered just. Many of those who were here today had been there then when three slaves had got accused of various things. The white men of Marshall lynched two of them. They did worse to the third. Followed by mocking townsfolk, that sorry creature was escorted by two lawmen to the town outskirts. His hands were fettered to a saddle stirrup, and he was forced to walk barefoot over sharp rocks and burrs. But the worst was ahead.

In an open field, one of the lawmen stripped him to the waist. A hole had been dug and an old rail tie placed in it as a stake. The lawman dragged the Negro to that tie and chained him to it hand and foot. The purpose became clear. A good many onlookers now began piling tinder and wood around his bare, black feet. A boy-child, no more than five years old, was given the privilege of setting it afire.

Then commenced a scene to wring pity from the hardest heart. That doomed man tried to move his feet out of the red-hot chains. He grabbed the fetters with his hands, and the flesh of his palms burned to the bone. His face had been vacant while his accusers were leading him to this spot, but now he spread his lungs and screamed for mercy, for water, for death.

It took a long time for him to be burnt to nothing more than ashes and bone, and all the while the white folks were cheering. Just like they cheered now for Sterling Price. Women had set handkerchiefs to their noses, for the smell was something terrible. A few folks fainted, and some left in disgust. But most tarried to the bitter end and seemed to enjoy their entertainment.

Louis had watched it too—all from a distance, though there was no distance the stench didn't reach. He had known this man, just as he had known the two who got lynched, just as he had known a number of others who had gone to glory from a tree branch. Since their boyhood days, they had silently acknowledged each other on the street. He was certain those slaves were innocent, but he couldn't hold out a drop of hope that one white soul would believe him or them. So he had to be at their deaths to pray them comfort.

The war against the Negro had been going on for years. Now, as Sterling Price roused this crowd into a frenzy, Louis knew that the war would stretch out. It would wrench the hearts of every man, woman, and child, and God wouldn't notice the color of their wet cheeks.

"Will you join us?" Price was shouting.

The white crowd repeated, "We will! We will!"

Sure enough, these Missouri farmers were ready to sign their names to any list of unconquerable Southerners. Mortimer's sons, Ben and Wilbur Gaines, enlisted along with hundreds of others. No indeed, these white boys were not a generation of "driveling, sniveling, degraded slaves." They were members of a free race.

Louis whispered to his wife, "Let's go home." Then he locked eyes with Price's slave, who cut his quick away.

Both Ben and Wilbur wore regular clothes when they set off for the war. But when they came back to visit, they were decked out in Confederate gray.

NOTES

The chapter title is from a traditional Negro spiritual cited in Higginson, "Negro Spirituals," 686.

The song "Jeff Davis Rode a Big White Hoss" is from Berlin et al., *Remembering Slavery*, 213.

The taking of the Liberty, Missouri, arsenal is documented in a number of sources, including the introduction to volume 6 of Roberts, *Comprehensive History*, lxv. He saw the conflict in Liberty as a direct fulfillment of prophecy and a chastisement from God for the way Missouri had treated the Latter-day Saints.

According to Bigler (Diary, 24), Sterling Price refused to "haul grub" for members of the Mormon Battalion during the Mexican War when the Mormons asked for food. His refusal to share food may have been fortuitous for the Mormons, for Price contracted a form of dysentery while in Mexico, which never entirely left him. He missed the battle of Boonville during the Civil War because of the "illness [which] proved to be a recurrence of the Mexican dysentary or cholera, and he was confined to his bed when the first skirmish was fought between the Missouri militia and Lyon's forces" (Rea, *Sterling Price*, 44).

Sterling Price, eventually the governor of Missouri, had indeed led the Chariton militia against the Mormons, as documented in Phillips, *Missouri's Confederate*, 100. His participation in recounting "deeds of rapine, murder, robbery, etc., which they had committed among the Mormons while at Far West" is reported in the *Autobiography of Parley P. Pratt*, 179. Though his hatred of Mormons is clear, he was generally highly respected in Missouri (a statue honors him in Keytesville).

The beginnings of war in Sedalia and Boonville are extracted from Baker, *Soldier's Experience*, 10–12.

The terms "Johnny Reb" and "Billy Yank" are from Reid, "Black Experience in the Union Army," 249.

The St. Louis conference among Price, Lyon, and others is documented in Rea, *Sterling Price*, 43. Words ascribed herein to Price and Lyon are as Rea quotes them.

Particulars of the battle of Wilson Creek are extracted from Rea, *Sterling Price*, 52. The battles in which Sterling Price led his troops are listed in the same source on page 221. It is not surprising that Price won the battle of Wilson Creek: his forces were three times the size of Lyon's (McPherson, *Ordeal by Fire*, 156).

The speech by Price—delivered indeed at Marshall, Saline County, Missouri (the hometown of Louis and Gracie Gray)—is taken from McElroy, *Struggle for Missouri*, 287–88.

That Price was a slaveholder is a matter of record. His slave Adam Tucker served as his driver and accompanied him on his war campaigns. Another of his slaves, Henry (a household servant), was reportedly so devoted to the

Prices "that he remained with the family even after he received his freedom" (Rea, *Sterling Price*, 13).

The account of the lynchings and burning of three black men in Marshall, Missouri, on August 2, 1859, is taken from the *Staunton Spectator*, August 1859, page 2, column 5: "Negroes Hung—One Burnt at the Stake."

The
Emancipation
Proclamation
1863

25

MINE EYES HAVE
SEEN THE GLORY

*Because of the exceedingly great length of the
war . . . many had become hardened, . . . and
many were softened because of their afflictions.*
ALMA 62:41

The Civil War didn't affect Utah much, except in diverting the
Feds to causes other than peeking under Mormon blankets.

Sam Bankhead, slave to John and Nancy Bankhead, asked
Green Flake what it was the states were haggling over and got told
the reason. Sam answered, "My God, I hope the South gets licked."

The Salt Lake Theater Company did do a version of *Uncle
Tom's Cabin* in 1862, and Heber Jeddy Grant played one of the
"pickaninnies." But a staged performance about slavery was a far cry
from a war about it.

The telegraph had finally come to Utah by then, so news of the
conflict reached the Saints in short order. Truth told, many
Mormons figured the Civil War would end up being Armageddon
and Jesus would rapture the Saints into heaven the instant enough
blood was spilled. As far as most Mormons were concerned, they'd

just as well get the news from telegraph clicks and keep patient in their own place, letting God take his due.

Like a goodly portion of religious folk of the time, white Mormons believed slavery would not be resolved by the puny hand of any mortal. Black Mormons, as you might guess, were of a different mind. And when the Emancipation Proclamation arrived on the wires and thrummed through the grapevine on January 1, 1863, the colored folk—both freeborn and slave—had cause to celebrate.

To this day, most of us remember the Emancipation Proclamation with Watch Night. Youngsters nowadays don't always realize what it is they be watching for, and only a few of us remember its name is *Freedom*.

Back then, it was hard for a colored man to trust a white man's words, even if the white man was president of these United States. Many slaves stayed put on their massas' plantations after the proclamation, for they couldn't be sure it would stick. Maybe the white folks would let the Negroes tongue a taste of freedom and then snatch it right back. You can be sure there was more than one massa who neglected to mention what the president had done and figured coloreds wouldn't be able to read it anyway.

Elijah Abel could read—and did. He could not speak for a long time after he got the news. He took his wife in his arms and kissed her. With such happy tidings as these, she appeared an angel of God, magnificent as an April morning. She wore her hair in a back-knot, and only the unruly sprouts around her face had gone silver, shining like sprigs of lightning. The older she got, the more she looked like his mama, Delilah. On this day, he imagined his mama was right there with them, reminding him of what she had said on her death day: "Elijah, they is a God. They *is* a God."

Jane James wept when she heard the news from Annie Thomas and then ran all the way home—something she was generally too dignified to do. But didn't this occasion call for running and shouting and singing praises up to the Lord? The news and her tears jammed the words in her throat, and it took her a minute before she could tell Isaac, and testify: "Things has come to pass what Brother Joseph prophesied about the colored race being freed. The very things he said has come to pass. I did not hear him say so myself, but I knew of it."

Just about all us colored folks in this nation blessed the name of Abraham Lincoln. Some of us knelt at his feet when he passed by. We all thought of him as the Great Emancipator. The truth is, he hated slavery, but he still thought we was inferior beings—entitled to life, liberty, and the pursuit of happiness but not entitled to vote or hold office. He believed the differences between the races would forbid us all living together as equals. More than likely, he wouldn't have signed the Emancipation Proclamation at all, except he was persuaded that such would help the Union win. The Emancipation Proclamation, you see, is just one more evidence that God has no problem working through mortals—even odd-looking, strange-thinking ones like Abraham Lincoln.

Indeed, just as Lincoln knew it would, the proclamation raised the stakes of the Civil War. Most families got involved, no matter how much they tried not to. Sons and fathers chose sides and put on uniforms, knowing these clothes might be their shrouds. Mothers and daughters sent off husbands and brothers and tended the screaming, stinking bodies of the wounded.

Down Missouri, the war exploded in spurts. In Marshall, slaves kept on slaving, for the proclamation had not freed them. Louis Gray's life continued much as before—except that Massa Mortimer's sons were off fighting, and many a night the Grays and the Gaineses could hear cannon thunder. Gracie would weep, "They killin' everything."

Though Missouri had got taken by the North, many Rebels still abided there and made their presence known in rifle reports and barn burnings, usually late at night. Rumor had it that Reb soldiers would ask every Negro in sight if he wanted to be free. If that Negro said yes, they shot his face off. If he said no, they left him alone. Bushwacking Union men weren't much better. They went about doing pillage and plunder, and folks kept saying this was the most uncivilized war they could conceive.

Talk of secession still happened in Missouri, but it was hollow, gloomy talk, for so many families had spent their own blood, and nothing had come of it but more blood.

Talk of emancipation happened too, but a Missouri massa was like as not to tell his slaves that if they missed one lick of the scythe or one blast of the horn, they'd be holding conversation with the devil.

Such were the threats and torments of this time in our nation's history. Nowadays, we think on the Civil War as a massacre of men and their animals. We think on the thousands upon thousands of boys—from both sides—who died. We tend to forget that every soldier left family to grieve. That war was our nation's baptism in blood.

Wilbur Gaines saw the fall of General Sidney Albert Johnston, now a Confederate officer, fighting against the very United States he had served so proud in Utah. Johnston was felled at Shiloh.

Wilbur Gaines's own end came on that same field. He was scalped by a cannonball and dead before he could even cry out. One of his fellow soldiers reported all of this months after the battle, leaving out the more gruesome details when Mizzus Gaines was listening.

Ben's death was probably the saddest, for he was on his way home. In fact, he was nearly there and weary of this war he had been so eager to enter. His mama said later that if he had shouted loud enough, she could have heard his cries. She wondered if she had heard them, for they sure did visit her dreams.

General Price's army had pitched camp around Independence and then crossed over the Big Blue and down to Westport. Price told his men to "attack anything and everything wearing a blue coat." He told them they weren't fighting just white men now but their own Negroes. "You have never been compelled to sue for pro-tection against evils like these!" Price yelled on the morning Ben would die. "You are fighting armies composed largely of your own slaves."

It was so smoky, Ben surely couldn't see the color of the soldier whose bayonet found his breast. You have to wonder if he thought it might be Louis.

That was October 22, 1864, when the Missouri state militia came undone and Ben died. Oh, Missouri was a sorry sight that day. The slopes where the battles got fought were strewn with dead and wounded men, dead and dying horses, and useless weapons. There were many tree stumps pocking the battlefield. During the fight, four or five soldiers had cowered behind each one, resting for a moment, then running, crouched, for the next one to hide behind. By evening, near every stump made a shadow over a corpse or two, and most stumps held a limp body. From a distance, you'd think you were seeing blue and gray rocks, with rusty rivulets between. Up close, the stench told you exactly what this was. There was no glory now, no war cries or rifle fire. No enemies. Only silence like a hole in the air. And then the muffled sounds of gravediggers doing their job, and looters doing theirs.

NOTES

"Mine Eyes Have Seen the Glory" is the title of the famous Civil War song by Julia Ward Howe.

Sam Bankhead's comment, "My God, I hope the South gets licked," is quoted by Coleman, "History of Blacks in Utah," 55.

According to Hinckley, Heber J. Grant, 44, "In 1862 when the [Salt Lake] Theatre was opened, [Heber's] mother was engaged in the costuming depart-ment. About that time he appeared on the stage as one of the pickaninnies in Uncle Tom's Cabin."

Contrary to what many think, the Emancipation Proclamation applied only to the states then in rebellion against the Union and to the portions of Union states sympathizing with the Confederacy.

That the Mormons, for the most part, "did not anticipate the United States surviving the war" but that "the conflict was to spread until it had 'poured out upon all nations'" and "the Saints would shortly return to Jackson County and begin work on the New Jerusalem" is documented by Bush ("Mormonism's Negro Doctrine," 75). Eddins puts it this way: "As the War commenced the Mormons watched for the wicked to destroy the wicked and waited for the righteous to turn to the Mormon Kingdom as the only just government on the earth. They aligned themselves with neither North nor South but considered themselves the saviors of the Constitution and rulers of the world under divine direction" ("Mormons and the Civil War," iv).

Jane James's words about Joseph Smith's prophecy of emancipation ("Things came to pass what he prophesied about the colored race being freed. . . . I did not hear that, but I know of it") are from her interview with the *Young Women's Journal* (553; qtd. in Wolfinger, "Test of Faith," in *Social Accommodation*, 136).

Lincoln's writings show clearly that he did not believe in racial equality. He stated, "I am not, nor ever have been, in favor of bringing about in any way the social and political equality of the white and black races" (Donald, *Lincoln*, 221). His only goal was to preserve the Union. Responding to an editorial by Horace Greeley, Lincoln said: "If I could save the Union without freeing *any* slave I would do it, and if I could save it by freeing *all* the slaves I would do it; and if I could save it by freeing some and leaving others alone I would also do that. What I do about slavery, and the colored race, I do because I believe it helps to save the Union; and what I forbear, I forbear because I do *not* believe it would help to save the Union" (Donald, *Lincoln*, 368). Nonetheless, he was finally persuaded to sign the Emancipation Proclamation, announcing that on January 1, 1863, "'all persons held as slaves' within any state or part of a state still in rebellion would be 'then, thenceforeward, and forever free'" (Donald, *Lincoln*, 375).

Rebel forces in Missouri, though defeated early by the Union, were "in turmoil, and Missouri was the scene of a guerrilla war" (Donald, *Lincoln*, 408).

The report of Confederate soldiers killing blacks who claimed they wanted freedom is from a statement by former slave Sarah Debro in Berlin et al., *Remembering Slavery*, 311.

26

SLAVERY CHAIN DONE BROKE AT LAST

*Thousands did flock unto his standard, and did take up
their swords in the defence of their freedom,
that they might not come into bondage.*
ALMA 62:5

The same Yankee cavalry that beat Price's troops and killed Ben tramped through the Gaines farm two days after. A Union officer cantered his horse up to where Louis, on his knees, was tugging at weeds.

"What's your name, boy?" the soldier asked.

Louis looked up at the horse—a black stallion with its wet nostrils flaring and veins pulsing. The stallion danced a side-step when the soldier pulled the reins, then lifted its neck. The horse seemed more proud than compliant, but it obeyed.

The Yankee said, "Whoa, Liberty." It snorted, and the soldier stroked its neck. This animal and its rider seemed one creature, not two. Even the red-lined, blue cape draped the saddle like it belonged to the animal as much as to the man.

Louis stood, wiping his muddy hands on his pants. "Louis, sir."

"Are you a slave or a freeman?"

"I belongs to the Gaines family. That be their house yonder." He pointed to it.

"Is Gaines up there now, boy?"

"Yessir."

"I'll pay him a visit shortly. Right now, I want you to know that by the authority granted to me by Abraham Lincoln, president of these still United States, I declare you, Louis—what's your last name?"

"Gray, sir."

"I declare you, Louis Gray, released from the bonds any mortal man may pretend to hold over you. You understand?"

Louis looked into the officer's eyes. They were green sickles, squinting in the autumn sun. "No sir, I rightly don't."

"I'm declaring you free. You are no longer a slave."

Five other riders caught up with the officer in time to hear the declaration.

Louis moved his eyes from one soldier to the next. He swallowed. "I got family," he said. "They free too?"

"Name your family," the officer ordered.

"My wife be Gracie."

"I declare Gracie a free woman. Do you have children?"

"Two daughters—Elizabeth and Margaret. A son, James Louis. And my mama be here too. Her name Maria Gaines."

"Any other slaves besides your family here?"

"Yessir. They be a passel of us."

"I declare every Negro on this farm emancipated," the soldier announced. "I have the right to free any slave when a part of his state incites a rebellion, and I am exercising that right."

"The Yankees done won then? The war over?"

"Here in Missouri it is. And near over everywhere else, though we could use a few more soldiers. I invite you to consider celebrating your freedom by joining its cause. There are colored troops, you know. Whole cities of freed Negroes have put on blue caps and taken up arms. Black men and white men are dying for your free-dom. Give some thought to joining them."

"Yessir. I think on it all right."

"Now we'll inform Gaines of the realities of this nation."

Louis watched the horses gallop up to the house. He hurried along behind them but kept his distance.

Massa came to the door. Until this moment, Louis had never thought of Mortimer Gaines as a small man. But with that mounted officer towering over him, massa looked like a child, a dominated slave with no choice but to do what he was ordered.

Gracie was just behind the massa. She came out when the sol-dier called her by name, pronounced her free and told her to step outside the house, for she had no more duties there.

Mortimer Gaines stood aside to let her pass.

Gracie was tentative as she came down the porch stairs. She asked the officer, "Can't we stay here anymore? What we s'posed to do?"

"You can stay or go, but the choice is yours. If you stay, this man should pay you for your labor. Do you understand?"

"Yessir. I guess I do."

Mortimer Gaines summoned up a few words for the soldiers: "Haven't you taken enough already?"

The soldiers didn't bother answering, just watered themselves and their horses and then took their leave at a trot.

Louis and Gracie stared at the massa, who was no longer their massa.

All the while the Yankee officer had been speaking, Mortimer had been holding the small portrait of his youngest son, painted just before Ben went to battle. Louis knew the portrait. Ben looked so young in it, waxed hair parted down the middle, the fuzz on his upper lip trying to be a mustache, his expression hardly masking a giggle.

"Ben's dead," Mortimer sighed.

Louis could hardly find a response to such sad news. He

struggled for words. All he could manage was, "When you hear tale?"

"Messenger came this morning while you were slopping the hogs."

Louis thought he might topple over with all the changes his world had taken in the past few minutes. He was free and Ben was dead. "Poor Ben," was all he could say.

Gaines's voice was toneless. "My son fought for the life I've earned and inherited. He fought for a Southern man's right to choose how to manage his own affairs and property. Now the Yankees tell me I can't even vote unless I take a loyalty oath to them." He lifted his gold watch from his pocket and glanced at it. "Fifty hours ago, my son was alive."

Louis was thinking, *A minute ago, I was a slave.* What he said was, "I hope Ben didn't suffer."

Mortimer put the watch away as his wife joined him on the porch. The two couples stared at each other, not knowing what to say or what to expect.

"This war been hard on our family," Louis said. "Both your boys—they was all fired up, thinkin' battle would be grand. All they could see was speeches gettin' made and men gettin' fancy dressed. But war ain't never been good. Don' matter whose war. I worried 'bout both 'em, 'specially Ben. I guess maybe I had a feelin'."

"Everything has changed." Massa Mortimer's voice was dry. "But the war is not ended. I don't care what the Yankees said. They may have power to free you now, but I don't believe this would be the best time for any of y'all to go seeking your fortune."

Louis traded a glance with Gracie, and they nodded, understanding what they both were thinking. "Sir, you and the mizzus lost a lot this year. You'll be needin' help with the place. I believe we be stayin' on—for awhile."

"They'll be bringing Ben's body this evening. We'd appreciate it if you and some of the other boys would prepare his grave."

"It goin' pain us all to do it. We all done watch Ben grow up. Me and Jack can dig the grave. I'll get George to build the box."

The mizzus moaned a weak yes as she and Mortimer turned to go back inside.

It happened that quick and that simple. Louis and Gracie Gray and all their children, Maria Gaines and all her children, and all the other Negroes on the Gaines farm were free.

Not all elected to stay on the Gaines property, but the Grays did.

Come spring, freedom was official. Everyone—white and black—was still getting used to the word. White and black was getting weaned from slavery.

Notes

The chapter title is from a traditional Negro spiritual cited in Cone, *Spirituals and the Blues*, 41.

The victory of the Union in Missouri did not automatically liberate the slaves, and many feared that the Emancipation Proclamation "would undermine the loyalty of Maryland, Kentucky, and Missouri" to the Union, for these were yet considered slave states (Donald, *Lincoln*, 379). General John C. Fremont in Missouri had issued a proclamation emancipating slaves and permitting them to enlist after the Union forces took Missouri in 1862, but Fremont's superior officers revoked the order. In truth, Louis Gray would not have been legally emancipated until January 11, 1865, when a state constitutional convention liberated all slaves in Missouri (McPherson, *Ordeal by Fire*, 393). Nonetheless, it is not difficult to imagine an early emancipation in light of Price's efforts to retake Missouri, as some of the fighting happened quite close to Marshall. Areas of Union states still considered in rebellion were affected by the Emancipation Proclamation, and as late as June 1864 there were incidents of black men being punished for trying to enlist. According to Kynoch, a few "locals in Missouri caught a party of black men trying to enlist, whipped each of them, and returned them to their owners. One of the slaveholders was so furious with her bondsman for running off that she offered five dollars to anyone in the group who would shoot the slave on the spot; a partisan promptly obliged her" ("Terrible Dilemmas," 123).

Lincoln was initially reticent to form "colored troops," arguing that "half the army would lay down their arms and three other States would join the rebellion" if former slaves were armed to help the Union side. When he issued the Emancipation Proclamation, however, Lincoln announced that former slaves would be received into the armed forces and by spring "was urging a massive recruitment of Negro troops" (Donald, *Lincoln*, 367, 431).

The suggestion that "the arrival among us [the Union army] of hordes [of former or escaped slaves] was like the oncoming of cities" is from General Ulysses S. Grant's chaplain (qtd. in Oshinsky, *Worse than Slavery*, 15).

General Johnston did indeed die at Shiloh. His son describes his death as heroic, claiming that he likely would have survived his wounds had he not sent his surgeon to attend the Union's wounded soldiers, saying, "They were our enemies but they're our fellow sufferers now" (Johnston, *Life of General Albert Sidney Johnston*, 615).

Details of Price's attempt to recapture Missouri and his failure at Westport are from Rea, *Sterling Price*, 135–41. Price went to Mexico after the Civil War ended, but he returned to Missouri in 1867 and died September 29 (Rea, *Sterling Price*, 198).

According to McPherson, "Missouri suffered more than any other state from raids, skirmishes, and guerilla actions" (*Ordeal by Fire*, 158).

We know that the Gray family remained in Marshall. In fact, the home James Louis Gray eventually owned belonged to members of the Gray family until 1977.

27

BOUND TO GO

*He rent his coat; and he took a piece thereof,
and wrote upon it—In memory of our God,
our religion, and freedom, and our peace.*
ALMA 46:12

Gaines was right about the war not being over. And the Yankee officer was right about coloreds enlisting with the Union.

Black volunteers from South Carolina, Tennessee, and Massachusetts composed the first colored regiments. Eventually, recruits joined by the hoards, especially after Frederick Douglass said that if a black man could get an eagle on his button, a musket on his shoulder, and bullets in his pocket, couldn't no power on earth deny him citizenship.

Of course, a colored man was more at risk than a white if he was to get taken by the Confederacy. There was several Confederate generals who shot all Negro prisoners.

A blue-black fellow named Sam Joe Harvey survived a number of battles as a member of the 52d Regiment of the United States Colored Infantry. He swore to avenge each drop of Negro blood those Rebel generals spilled and relished every opportunity to do just that.

Sam was an escaped slave from Tennessee. He was no more than fifteen when he put on Union britches and lied about his age—which he could do easy, since he was tall. Even so young, he had enough anger in him to kill any man who might have been a slaveholder or the son of one. He didn't realize how angry he was, for he figured every Negro had to be that mad. Each lashing of Sam's back—and there had been many—had branded anger into his flesh and soul, and a battlefield was just the place to let that fury fly. He got satisfaction from killing Confederates. He wanted them to suffer like he had suffered. Every Reb he saw was a version of his own tormenter, and he was ready to give wound for wound. He valued the feel of a gun in his hands—short-arm or long. His muscles were trained by the cotton fields and could easy plunge a bayonet deep into a Reb's belly. Anger made Sam Joe feel alive. It was his liberation. In the war, he entered the forbidden world of white men and had power.

It's doubtful he served alongside Lew Manning, considering all the men in that war, but he might've, for Lew also soldiered in the colored infantry. Lew also saw streams running red with blood after a battle. He also saw bodies piled in unnatural hills. He didn't have the anger of a Sam Joe Harvey, for Lew had never been a slave. Like most soldiers, he just didn't want to get killed himself.

Battles were sporadic, but hunger was constant. Provisions arrived only rarely, and the troops were down to eating anything they could find, including dog. They called it "dog ham," and it filled a starving stomach good as anything else. Some of these men were so famished, they'd bite into a raw chicken, feathers and all.

Such hunger came with good reason, for they'd march days at a time to do battle. Then they'd bury the dead and march again to do more battle, often without feeding themselves, for they lacked provisions.

Each attack could cost thousands of lives and repeated the same scenes on different fields: men running, weapons roaring, and the stinking smoke making the whole place like hell. The trees would bend low and shake all over with the cannonballs' whoop, and men would fall down dead, their limbs tore off, their faces shocked at how quick and unexpected it come. The wounded would lie hollering for help. One black soldier said, "Killing hogs on the plantation didn't bother me none, but this am different."

Sam Joe Harvey preferred killing men to killing hogs, but Lew found man-killing a frightful thing. He thought he was witnessing the end of time. How could it not be, with folks so wicked? How could it get worse?

The commander would yell, "Tear cartridge!" Sam Joe and Lew both knew how to do that: They'd bite open the envelope that held a load of powder and ramrod it into the gun's mouth. The bullet acted as a stopper and held the powder in place. You had to be on the alert so you wouldn't load more than one charge at a time. Amidst all the noise, some wouldn't notice that their pieces hadn't discharged, and they'd ram another cartridge home before trying to fire. Then like as not the gun would explode in the poor soldier's face. You had to load, then fire, then bite another cartridge open. The fastest men (and that included Sam Joe Harvey, though not Lew Manning) could finish the process in less than a minute. Load again, fire again, until the haze wouldn't let you see beyond the muzzle of your musket. All around, chaos would shred any peace that might be brooding. Bullets would race so fast, the very air they ruptured could pierce a shirt like buckshot. The wind a cannonball moved could cut a man's neck.

Towards the end of the war, some of the white troops got a new style of ammunition: a metallic cartridge case. The soldiers said you could load these newfangled pieces on Sunday and fire all week long. White troops often had siege guns and mortars too. A screeching, eight-inch mortar fit right in with all the screams and yells of men warring or dying. This was noise could wake the dead—and it just might have. Could've been ghosts snaking out of guns, lurking around leaves, and coloring all the air blue and gray, like the uniforms themselves, so you couldn't see a thing and you smelled only powder and guts. Seemed indeed that devils had come to the party and brought all of perdition with them.

The Negroes' weapons weren't advanced, but they did their work.

Lew only occasionally knew where exactly he was making war. All he knew for certain was that he had never been so scared in his life. The fields he fought on reminded him of those he had crossed with his brothers and sisters when they journeyed barefoot from Wilton, Connecticut, to Nauvoo, Illinois. Back then, Janey could make them see the beauty in every little thing around them—even the frost that was freezing their toes. She could inspire them to sing praises to God no matter what difficulties they met. Janey could quote scriptures to the bluejays and say poetry to willows. He had to wonder what beauty she might find on a battlefield—except maybe the cause they were fighting for. Here these soldiers were, destroying God's creations, including a number of his children. They'd come upon a perfectly good field and tear it apart, explode dirt that might have nurtured corn stalks, make bloody ditches where there should've been groves of apricot trees. He hated this war and was glad Janey lived far from it. Surely she was someplace peaceful, growing pumpkins and poppies whilst the war was terrorizing every parcel of earth where God had set enough space for a fight. Lew loved thinking that when this war was done (if it ever was), he'd find out just where Janey was. He had married Lucinda by now, and he wanted to take her there and settle back down with the Mormons.

For now, though, he was a soldier and bound to the soldier's path, musket in his hand, cartridges in his pack.

When he finally got sick enough with the flux to get discharged and go home to Lucinda, he found St. Louis in a poorly condition. The war hadn't left it alone. Black-capped brutes with rags over their faces set fires and played at skullduggery all through the restless nights—and all nights were restless. Lucinda told him how ruffians had threatened her boss right as she was serving him supper. They demanded money off him and then beat him in the head for being a Union man. One after the other had stuck a pistol barrel in his mouth and said they'd delight in blowing his brains out. Four hours passed with such vile games. Lucinda was forced to serve the bullies all the food in that house, and she was forced to do other things too. Missouri had the devil in it.

Lew shook his head. He could feel badness in the air itself. He suggested the territory of Utah might be the place to settle and wondered why he'd waited so long.

But it would be awhile before they could set out for anywhere, for he was terrible sick, and with war hedging them in, this was no time to be traveling.

NOTES

The chapter title is from a traditional Negro spiritual cited in Higginson, "Negro Spirituals," 686.

Frederick Douglass declared, "Once let the black man get upon his person the brass letters U.S.; let him get an eagle on his button and a musket on his shoulder . . . and he has earned the right of citizenship" (qtd. by Kynoch, "Terrible Dilemmas," 126).

Some of the descriptions of the Civil War are drawn from the memories of former slave George Conrad as quoted in Berlin et al., *Remembering Slavery*, 261. The statement "killin' hawgs back on de plantation didn't bother me none, but dis am diff'rent" is from former slave Thomas Cole, quoted in Berlin et al., *Remembering Slavery*, 226.

Descriptions of weapons and ammunition used during the Civil War are from Hunt, "Ammunition Used in the War," 172–78.

We cannot be certain if the Sam Joe Harvey of our story (who has a more significant role later) served in the 52d Regiment of the Colored Infantry, but a Samuel Harvey is listed in that regiment. We do know Sam Joe Harvey was an ex-soldier.

Reports of Confederate officers killing captured blacks are authentic (Urwin, "'We Cannot Treat Negroes . . . as Prisoners of War,'" 247) and not uncommon. Many atrocities were committed against black soldiers at Poison Springs, Arkansas, where "the surprise of the enemy was complete—at least four hundred darkies were killed. No black prisoners were captured" (Lt. William Stafford, qtd. in Urwin, "'We Cannot Treat Negroes . . . as Prisoners of War,'" 236).

Disease was common among white and black soldiers in the Civil War. As Black puts it, "White troops were twice as likely to die for reasons of ill-health as in battle, while black troops were almost ten times as likely to do so," the biggest killer being "camp fever, which included the separate disorders 'diarrhea and dysentery'" ("In the Service of the United States," 132–33).

Other Wars
and Their Ends

28

HOLD YOUR LIGHT

I cried within my heart: O Jesus,
thou Son of God, have mercy on me,
who am in the gall of bitterness.
ALMA 36:18

During the years war was being waged east of Utah, Elijah Abel was waging his own war—this one against poverty. He and Mary Ann had managed the Farnham Hotel in Salt Lake, hoping it would bring steady income. But such was not to be. Back in Nauvoo, Brother Joseph had called and appointed Elijah the very first undertaker and made him one of the founding members of the Nauvoo Carpenters' Guild. But so many skilled woodsmiths had come into Utah now hardly anyone remembered Elijah's work, let alone hired him for it. And just when the money was most meager, the government asked for his earnings. He hadn't been able to pay his taxes a few years earlier, and again in 1864 he came up short.

That wasn't the worst of it, either. There was some shame to poverty, but most folks in these parts were living on scanty means. The most blistering shame was when Moroni Abel, sixteen years old, got accused of stealing a shaving knife.

Mary Ann was convinced her son was innocent, that some wicked child had planted the knife on him to make mischief. What was certain was that the firstborn son of Elijah Abel had been arrested by a policeman named Andrew Burt, then fined money the Abels didn't have, and finally sentenced to some days in a dank jail.

Mary Ann didn't see Moroni hauled off, but she heard about it soon enough. She packed him a basket of bread rolls while her husband watched.

Elijah was dead set against visiting his son in jail, and he didn't particularly like the idea of Mary Ann taking him a basket. This wasn't a time to reward that boy, he said, and hunger could do some good. "Might teach him right thinking."

Now, Mary Ann was used to letting Elijah do the talking for the family. This couple didn't fight. If Elijah seemed less than pleased over something she'd done, she'd generally apologize before he had a chance to say what it was upset him. In all their married days, they had had only two fights between them, and Mary Ann had been pregnant and jumpy both times.

But on this day, with Moroni in jail, Mary Ann was about to stand up to her man. She looked Elijah square in his face and said, "This be our baby. Your heart can't be so hard."

Elijah's brow sank. "What did you say?"

"You gotta take pity on him, 'Lijah."

His voice dropped to its full depth. All he needed now was a pulpit and the time to testify. "Mary Ann, this ain't about only us. He's chancin' everything. Can't you see that? A white boy can steal a cow and folks call it playful. A colored boy take a radish and folks say he come by thievin' natural."

She answered fast: "That's why somebody did this mischief on him. To make all us look bad."

He took a roll from the basket and bit into it. "We got us a position of at least some respect, and Moroni's squanderin' it. He's give them what they wanted—proof of what they already think.

Every single colored man or woman is shamed by what that boy done." He bit into his bread like it was somebody's fist.

"I don't believe Moroni stole that knife," she said in a steady voice, the strongest she had ever mustered before her husband.

"Why can't you face the truth? 'Course he took that knife. I been watchin' the devil work on that child for years, and I will not dote on the devil." Elijah flat-handed the wall like it was wicked. "Can't you see? Just when we was comin' close to gettin' our blessings, he's undid everything."

Mary Ann's gaze lingered on him. "We ain't close to gettin' nothin'," she said. "You the one needs facin' that truth." She covered the basket with a checkered cloth, set to leave out the door.

"Don't you be sassin' me, woman." He blocked her way. "I earned better than that. When you and that boy earn your due, then you can stand up on yo' hind legs."

"Mister Abel," she said, drawing herself up to her full stature, "I have respected you since before we was married. You been after me for years to speak my mind. Well, I am speakin' it now."

He stepped back and watched her, watched to see when her head would bow in submission and life would return to normal. "You got more to say?"

"Yes I do." Her voice was strong as she could make it, but it was still a little voice, suited to her frame. Such a fragile throat could hardly be expected to make big sounds. The onlyest time she ever yelled was when a child of hers was in danger, and even that was more yelp than yell. Back when they was on the trail, a time Enoch got too close to the Platte River, Mary Ann's yelling filched her voice for one entire day. That yell took all her effort, showed in her every blood vein, and served as a family joke for many months after.

But this ay, there was firm, womanly substance to her words: "You wrong on this, Elijah. And if I don't tell it, who will?"

His eyes narrowed like they could wilt her on the spot. "You sayin' I'm wrong in wantin' our boy to own up to his crime?"

"I'm sayin' you wrong in a good many things."

Elijah stared at her, looked away, and then stared at her again. "Wife, I don't enjoy you tellin' me what to do or how to be. I don't need no disrespect in my own household. There's enough of that outside the door."

"You think I don't know that? You think I don't see it? You think if you was misaccused and in jail, I wouldn't be takin' you bread rolls?"

He slapped his hips like he was his own horse. "I got to stand up for my position in this community."

"You worry about the community, then. I got to stand up for our child." Her voice got lower and stronger. "How many of us had to watch our babies get sold off the minute they stop suckin'? Ain't no woman goin' allow her child to get took away if she can stop it. Ain't no woman goin' let her child starve in jail if she got bread in her kitchen."

This was the first moment of his life when Elijah heard Delilah Abel's voice coming from Mary Ann Abel's mouth. He took another roll from the basket, eyeing his wife to see if she'd order him to desist. Delilah would've; he knew that for sure. "You finished?" he asked.

She met him eye to eye. "Finished."

"Good. Now, woman, far as I'm concerned, he can stew in there 'til his heart go soft as a potato on coals."

Once again, she gathered herself up and stood tall, set to pass this new test of her mettle. "That ain't no simmerin' pot. That jail is one big ice chamber."

"Then he can sit on ice and let his shame get so rigid, it'll take the Lord hisself to crack it."

At last her posture went limp. He thought she might kneel at his feet. "'Husband," she said, pleading now, "you willin' to abandon him same way these folks abandon you?"

He stayed quiet a long moment. When he spoke, his voice was tender. "This whole mess just got me lathered up."

Mary Ann let out a small gasp. She hadn't expected anything gentle from him.

He put his hands on her shoulders and drew his head close to hers. "Don't think I ain't worried. I got worry enough for all us."

"Moroni got snared in a trap of someone else's makin'," Mary Ann said. "And nobody believes him. Not even you."

"I've seen too much from that boy to believe anything easy."

"But, 'Lijah, when you choose to believe somethin', you believe it powerful. That's the man you be." She kissed his hand. "Now let me by, would you? I worry about that jail. So dark there. Mold in every corner. I heard they had rats."

Elijah held the door for his wife. He reminded her Moroni was a healthy boy and she shouldn't fuss over him too much.

Mary Ann took two steps and then stopped and faced her husband again. "I want you come with me."

"No. I can't do that."

"I say, I want you come. Our boy need to know you support him."

"No," Elijah repeated. "You go on and carry that child some bread if it calms your concern, but I can't come with you. You takin' the baby?"

This "baby" Elijah referred to was his namesake, now five years of age. Their family also included twelve-year-old Enoch, eleven-year-old Anna, and eight-year-old Delilah.

"I don' wanna be takin' a baby down to that jail," Mary Ann said. "The other chil'ren can look out for theyselves and him. Enoch might help you ready the Larsens' railing."

"I doubt the Larsens goin' want me doin' that railin' once they learn our disgrace."

She gave him a look suggesting he hadn't heard the last of her strong talk. "Then I can find a use for the railin' myself." She stepped outside the door, walking proud, not even glancing back.

After a long spell of pacing and thinking, Elijah let Enoch help him sand the railing, which was to be used in the Larsens' fancy house. He asked Enoch, "I ever tell you why I select yo' name?"

Enoch's voice was starting the change and squeaked between child and man tones when he answered, "A time or three, Daddy."

"I ever told you why I select the name of Moroni for your brother?"

"You named him for a angel."

"'Course, no angel goin' be stealin' no shavin' knife."

"Maybe if God tell him to." Enoch's hair was close-cropped, his clothes clean but old. How Elijah would have loved to dress his children in fine outfits like so many of the Saints, including the Larsens, could afford.

"You think God tell yo' brother steal that knife?"

"God might command 'most anything."

Of course, Elijah had taught his son that. Elijah had learned all the Bible stories, and now that he had become a full literate man, he loved reading his children Bible words. Every child in the Abel family knew the scriptures. "Like Jacob takin' his brother's blessing, you mean?" said Elijah.

"Is that the one put fur up his arms so's his blind daddy would think he was the other son?"

"That's him. Only what he done wasn't precisely stealin'. Remember, Esau straight-out sold him his birthright. Sold it one hungry night for a mess of pottage. You recollect that?"

"Yessir."

"One bad night, Esau threw all his most important blessin's away, jus' because he had a strong desire." He observed Enoch's work. "Son, you put more elbow grease into them strokes. These railings needs to be smooth as glass. If Sister Larsen should catch a sliver, our name will get dragged through the dirt even more."

"I think I need more drippin's on my flapjacks then, or else just butter. That way, my elbows might have more grease to spare."

Elijah chuckled, the first time he had made a happy sound all day. Enoch was something special, coming on his growth now and showing his grandmother's proud cheekbones. Jesus had been Enoch's age when he preached in the temple.

"You named for the man what made Zion." The story of Enoch and the City of God was Elijah's favorite from the pamphlet Brother Brigham had gifted him back in 1852.

Elijah ran his finger over his son's work. It was passable good. "Move on to the next rough spot," he said. "Yes indeed, Enoch was just a lad when God spoke to him, callin' him to preach the holy word to all the wicked folk of the wide world. Now, how do you suppose he felt?"

"I'd say pleased and proud."

"How would you feel if the Lord should speak to you in such a way?"

"I'd say, scared and fit to run."

Elijah chuckled again. "You one true-speakin' boy. I almost feel to give you the blessin' I had stored up for my firstborn, 'cept your mother would object and make it knowed every day for the rest of my life. Now, son, let me tell you, Enoch of old felt just the way you would: scared and fit to run. He say, 'Lord, Lord, I be a mere lad. Why should folks turn ear my direction? And how is it you sees fit to call me up as your servant, seein' I can't hardly get two words out without stutterin'?'"

"That's 'bout what I'd say."

"Oh, I felt such myself when I first got the call to preach. I felt that through every bone in my body. 'Now who'd listen to a colored?' says I. 'Who'm I to preach the word when I can't hardly read it?' Well, I took all such questions to the Lord, and he say to me, 'Elijah, where is your faith?' And I says, 'Lord, I still got faith. It jus' don't stand up too strong some days." Elijah stroked the wood and pronounced it fine. "'Course, my Savior took pleasure in sending trials my way. He still do. You know why?"

"Not for sure."

"That's how our rough edges gets rubbed smooth. Just like we makin' this wood smooth. The Lord took pleasure in givin' Enoch trials. Could be his name was set on handbills all over a forest, we don't know. But by and by, Enoch preached the word and folks paid him attention. They stopped thinkin' of him as a boy. They saw he was a man of God. Then faith rose up so strong in Enoch, he could see God's tears—plain as I'm seein' you. And he ask God a question. 'Lord, how is it you can weep, bein' as you almighty?' And the Lord say, 'The mighty *must* weep. The mighty got the power to put aside hate, and bring brother and sister together. I weep,' the Lord say, "'cause folks won't understand that easy truth, and they hate they own blood.' Well, in years to come, Enoch felt the pain too, and he wept 'longside the Lord." Elijah's own eyes teared up as he worked the wood with his son.

"Daddy, when's my brother comin' back?" Enoch asked.

Elijah sighed. "I don't know. Your mama seein' to him right now. He won't go hungry. Your mama's a good woman."

"No slivers in this railing."

"You done a fine job."

"Moroni ain't bad. Could be somebody stoled that knife and let him catch it."

"You soundin' like yo' mama. Well, maybe you both right. I hope so."

When Mary Ann returned that afternoon, Moroni was with her.

Elijah wanted to embrace his son but restrained himself. He asked simply, "Are you all right?"

Moroni stared at the floor. "Why we in Utah?"

"Where you think we ought to be?"

"I hate Utah."

"We're here because this is where we belongs," Elijah said.

Those words concluded the conversation, but shame still skulked around the household. Before a month had passed, it was so powerful, Elijah said they shouldn't stay in the area anymore—not with the way folks were talking behind them. Perhaps, when their business matters could get settled, the Abel family would try another place.

There was one more reason for such plans: Whether in dream or in truth, Elijah had sensed a presence he hadn't felt in years, a presence with so much hate, it rippled like heat. Black Tom Colbourn had been found with his throat slit and a sign around his neck saying, "Warning to all Niggers: Stay away from white women!" Elijah Abel was certain the presence that hated and killed Black Tom was something his own son could meet any day.

But he didn't want to move too far and not right away, so they were still in Salt Lake City when President Lincoln got elected a second time.

The inauguration speech was printed in the *Deseret News*. You may know the words yourself: "Fondly do we hope—fervently do we pray—that this mighty scourge of war may speedily pass away. Yet, if God wills that it continue, until all the wealth piled by the bondman's two hundred and fifty years of unrequited toil shall be sunk, and until every drop of blood drawn with the lash, shall be paid by another drawn with the sword, as was said three thousand years ago, so still it must be said 'the judgments of the Lord, are true and righteous altogether.'"

Elijah read those words to Mary Ann but could hardly get through them without weeping, for he had seen so many marks of the lash.

NOTES

The chapter title is from a traditional Negro spiritual cited in Higginson, "Negro Spirituals," 685.

The Abel family's financial difficulties are documented in Bringhurst, "Changing Status," 137, which states that "on at least two occasions, in 1855 and again in 1864, Abel was listed as delinquent in paying his taxes. Also in

1864, Abel's son M[o]roni 'was charged before Alderman Clinton with steal-ing a shaving knife from an emigrant on the Public square.'" The Abels were members of Salt Lake's Mill Creek Ward at this time.

The names and ages of the Abel children are as found in the 1860 cen-sus of the Thirteenth Ward (Salt Lake City).

The murder of Tom Colbourn is documented in Bringhurst, *Saints, Slaves, and Blacks*, 155.

The words of Lincoln's second inaugural speech are from Lincoln, *Abraham Lincoln*, 107.

29

MY LORD,
WHAT A MORNIN'!

*God has delivered me from prison, and from bonds,
and from death; yea, and I do put my trust in him,
and he will still deliver me.*

ALMA 36:27

It was April 10, 1865, when five hundred cannons let the United States capital know that General Lee had surrendered to General Grant. Then came the firing of guns and the ringing of bells. Union flags whipped the air in jubilation. President Lincoln asked a band to play "Dixie," declaring it a fine tune as well as a legal prize, for the North had captured it. The weary president proclaimed a day of thanksgiving.

Of course, Southerners didn't feel especially grateful. At least not white Southerners.

Us colored folk, on the other hand, we was dancing in our quarters and letting loose such songs as we'd never sung before, strutting joyful like we was dancing on gold clouds. It didn't matter what state the colored lived in, north or south—all us were emancipated with the surrender at Appomattox. There was no such thing as a slave in the United States now, and there never would be again.

Though the telegraph service was operating in Utah and the *Deseret News* reported the latest war news every Wednesday, the report of its end came by surprise. Like I said, the Saints thought the war would never cease until Jesus himself descended in glory.

The day the Civil War finished, the Latter-day Saints were holding general conference, Brigham Young and George Q. Cannon and other apostles speaking. So the *Deseret News* focused on the leaders' talks and didn't even mention Appomattox.

Folks found out soon enough, though.

When he heard the news, Elijah Abel climbed up Ensign Peak to talk to the Lord and the angels. He spoke his brothers' names, wondering if they had helped win that fight, and then other names as well. "Jeremiah Abel. Daniel Abel," he said. "You be free forever. Frederick Bailey Douglass, Sojourner Truth—God bless you for all you done. Amos Luther, you be free and never fettered again. Nancy. Nancy. Lord, watch over her if she's still alive and help her live happy. Dear and mighty Lord, you have spoke through the cannonball and the smoke of war. You opened the jail. I praise you, my Lord, for you destroyed the chains of the captive with your arm of power and opened the portals of the grave. I praise you, my Jesus. We are free!"

It seemed that the breeze around Elijah carried a multitude of other names—slaves who had died in the bonds and slaves who had found freedom; Africans who got stoled from their land and survived the seas; Africans who had drowned between home and heartbreak; black men and women who had cried out for God from the auction block and the whipping post and who found him in their own songs; heroes who had led the captive into Canaanland. Elijah could not distinguish any names, but they all seemed to be whispering the truth of their existence and the price of their legacy.

As for the James family, they were celebrating some other things besides the war being over. Sylvester had just got married, and the very woman he wed—Mizz Mary Ann Perkins—had once been part of a slave family belonging to Reuben Perkins, who had come to Utah from Tennessee.

She was a slim, tall girl, and Jane liked her. Both of these women were fussy about their clothes and the state of their houses. Neither one would set a foot outdoors without being dressed in their cleanest clothes, even if the fabric itself was shabby. It comforted Jane to think her son would not be living in squalor, for Mary Ann opposed dust as much as Jane did.

During the years when the North and the South were getting acquainted on the battlefield—soldiers of both sides being buried under the same dirt—Syl and Mary Ann had been getting acquainted in other fields: corn and wheat, to be specific. They had exchanged vows on January 31, 1865.

In Mississippi, Samuel Chambers, who had got baptized a Mormon when he was a boy and a slave, was now free. And he sure wasn't a boy now but a full-grown man, taller and larger than most, with kind eyes and features you wouldn't soon forget. He had already married once—in the slave sort of marriage, which you know didn't mean much. His wife was sold off from him, just as his mother had been. His wife got sent to Texas, and he never did see her again. So he married a second wife, Amanda Leggroan.

Amanda's brother, name of Ned Leggroan, took some interest in the gospel that seemed to guide Sam's life. Sam couldn't be sure he knew all the details of this religion, for it had been twenty-one years since Preston Thomas baptized him. He did remember that angels were visiting the earth. And wasn't freedom a sign of angels doing their job? He told his brother-in-law, "I must tell the truth. I ain't find the gospel; the gospel find me, and God done keep the seeds of life in me all these many years, so they bear fruit to this day. I cain't read. I cain't write, but I can feel what God be sayin' to me."

As a freedman, he worked four years doing sharecropping and

shoe cobbling, until he had enough money for himself and his family to make the trek to Utah, to gather with those who believed as he did—and maybe even see Preston Thomas.

The Leggroans decided to make the trek with them.

Down California, Biddy Smith Mason—a prominent midwife now, with some property to her name—was taking in poor folks of any race and feeding them from her own supply. She often worked with a Dr. Griffin in Los Angeles and visited prisoners in jail. Biddy knew enough about bondage to understand the many pains the inmates were feeling. They loved and honored her for her kindness.

Liz Flake Rowan lasted only three years after the Civil War ended. She died in 1868 but left a fine posterity. She and Charles had had children who would make the Rowan name a proud one.

In Missouri, Louis and Gracie Gray and their children were living on their own, though still working for Mortimer Gaines. Since being freed, they had been getting a share of what the farm produced.

Seemed now, most every Negro in this nation should be able to make a new and better life. At least, that's what we all thought.

NOTES

The chapter title is from a traditional Negro spiritual found in Burleigh, *Spirituals*, 30.

Lincoln's statements about "Dixie" being "fairly captured" and the descriptions of Northern celebrations are from Donald, *Lincoln*, 581–82.

That Latter-day Saints initially paid little attention to the end of the Civil War is supported by Eddins: "So little was made of the settlement of hostilities that it leads one to believe that the Mormons refused to acknowledge the termination of the war. They still looked for 1) the uprising of the Indians; 2) Their [the Mormons] return to Jackson County; 3) The spread of the war to many nations; 4) famine, plagues, and earthquakes to finish off the nations" ("Mormons and the Civil War," 123).

That Jane James was "very particular and fussy" in preparing for church or other public occasions is as stated by one of her descendants, Mrs. Henrietta Bankhead, in Carter, *Negro Pioneer*, 9.

The history of Samuel Chambers given in this chapter is recorded by

Hartley in "Samuel D. Chambers." Sam grew up an orphan, "slave traders [having taken] away his mother, Hester Gillespie, while Samuel was a small boy." According to Hartley, the records about the fate of Sam's first wife are contradictory, some indicating that she died and others that she was "sold into Texas." On May 4, 1858, Samuel Chambers married Amanda Leggroan, a slave of Green and Hattie Leggroan, in Noxumbra County, Mississippi (Hartley, "Samuel D. Chambers," 47). The words Sam speaks in this chapter are a liberal rendering of one of the testimonies the ward clerk recorded in the Eighth Ward, all of which are gathered in Hartley, "Saint without Priesthood."

Carter (*Negro Pioneer*, 28) says this of the Franklin Perkins family: "[Franklin was] born in North Carolina in the year 1813. This Negro family who belonged to Reuben Perkins came to Utah in the Andrew H. Perkins Company. Franklin's son by his first wife, a boy named *Ben*, came with them. . . . [Franklin's second wife was] *Fanny*, . . . an Indian girl born in Grundy County, Missouri. She married Franklin in 1835. After their arrival in Utah, they were taken to Bountiful, . . . where Reuben Perkins and his family settled. . . . [Franklin and Fanny's children included] *Sarah*, who was born in 1838, married Peter Livingston. . . . *Mary Ann*, was born April 6, 1840, in Grundy County, Missouri. She married *Sylvester James* January 31, 1865."

Biddy Smith Mason's philanthropic activities after her freedom was secured are substantiated in Hayden, "Biddy Mason's Los Angeles," 91, as well as in a multitude of other sources, for much has been written in her honor. She has been called California's "Mother of Civil Rights."

Hannah Smith married Toby Embers Crosby and became a well-known midwife. As Carter says in *Negro Pioneer*, 33: "Being an excellent horse-woman, [Hannah] responded to calls day or night."

Liz Flake Rowan's death in 1868 is documented in many sources, including Carter, *Negro Pioneer*, 19, which includes a picture of Liz's (and Charles's) gravestone. According to Mills, Liz Flake's descendants claimed she was baptized and a loyal member of The Church of Jesus Christ of Latter-day Saints, though perhaps eventually she affiliated with the Reorganized Church, which is mentioned in her obituary. Mills speculates that when the California Mormons were called back to Utah, Liz aligned herself with the Reorganized Church of Jesus Christ of Latter Day Saints, now known as the Community of Christ (personal interview). Skinner claims that Liz Flake "was a Mormon . . . and she remained in that faith all her life" (*Black Origins in the Inland Empire*, 5). His book includes a photo of her. We have been unable to locate any record of her baptism and so cannot document if or when it occurred, whether in her youth or adulthood.

Surviving and Letting Go

30

SWEET MUSIC

Even if ye can no more than desire to believe, let this
desire work in you, even until ye believe in a manner that
ye can give place for a portion of my words.
ALMA 32:27

Sad thing, isn't it, that Abe Lincoln didn't live long enough to help bring about the new and better life—especially sad for the South. Lincoln's death touched every heart in Utah and most especially the Negro hearts.

The day of Lincoln's funeral, Elder Amasa Lyman addressed a congregation in the Tabernacle with words suitable for grievers, and Utah draped itself in black. The Saints participated in mourning from a respectful distance. But Utah wouldn't be distant for long. She would get tied to the rest of the United States when the golden spike was driven into a railroad tie not too far from Ogden in 1869. The transcontinental railway turned the territory into a stopping point for all sorts of folk. Ogden in particular became a gathering place for coloreds, for jobs were there.

This was when the Abels moved to Ogden, chugging up the iron rails of hope.

But only days after settling into their new place, Moroni started coughing in a way Elijah recognized too well.

Some doctors said they could cure lung fever, but they would charge money Elijah didn't have. He couldn't sell his woodwork, couldn't find a hotel to manage, and the railroad jobs were uninviting. Oh, he prayed to the Lord for direction, but something seemed to be plugging up the heavens.

One evening, as Moroni was eating soup, Elijah and Mary Ann talked openly about the boy's condition. Elijah said, "If Joseph Smith was here, he would lay hands on our boy's head and take that fever away."

"Well, why can't you do that?" Mary Ann asked. Such was the faith this woman had in her husband.

She didn't know it, but Elijah had already blessed Moroni. No noticeable healing had come, leastways not at first. Elijah figured his faith was getting its tests and said as much to his wife.

"You doubtin' yo'self?" she asked.

"No," he answered fast.

"Doubtin' the Lord?"

"I ain't doubtin' the Lord. Jus' wonderin' for how long the gates stayin' closed."

"The Lord givin' you any idea on it?"

Elijah puckered his mouth. "We got to have money."

Moroni glanced up as his mama said, "That's what God reveal to you? I coulda saved you the trouble of askin' so high up."

Mary Ann had taken on new might of late, and her husband wasn't sure he liked it. "You gettin' awful sassy in your old age," he said. "The Lord expect us to do all we can, and he'll help with the rest."

Mary Ann observed Moroni, who had gone back to slurping his soup. "You know, I think he be doin' better. He ain't too bad sick, just some sick. He was worse yesterday."

"His color ain't good," Elijah said.

Moroni lifted his eyes. "You made me colored. Why fight it now?"

That made Elijah laugh, and it made him proud his boy had humor even when he was ill. And now that he looked Moroni over, it was plain some healing had come. Elijah scolded himself for doubting the Lord's power or his own priesthood. "You gonna be fine," he said, feeling sure of it and sure the heavens were open again—which certainly meant the idea he got the following week must've been inspired.

That idea was for the Abel family to do a minstrel act throughout the Ogden wards. White Mormons, like whites of all persuasions, had seen the staged version of Jim Crow or Zip Coon from the early days of the Utah settlement. Some of the white pioneers had even made up their own minstrel acts. Of course, Brigham Young hadn't exactly approved of such and came down pretty hard on them.

Well, Brother Brigham had power in many areas but not in this one. His rebuke didn't seem to halt a single minstrel act. Those shows were performed from the time there were Utah stages, and eventually Mormons clamored to have real Negroes singing the buffoonery. Salt Lake theaters had already hosted a number of shows with real blacks.

Elijah felt a minstrel act would give the family's pocketbook some breathing space and means to pay for Moroni's medicines.

When he announced his idea to Mary Ann, she walked slowly to their bed and sat. "You always been so concerned with maintainin' a righteous proud image. You said so many times how it hurt your heart to know how white folks see coloreds. Ain't you jus' goin' add fuel to their fire? We come to this?"

He sat beside her. "I've thought hard about it. Maybe that righteous pride ain't so righteous as you think. Maybe God jus' tryin' to show me I need to give whatever it takes to tend to my family. Now, Mary Ann, you shouldn't suppose this don' hurt me, 'cause it do. But we got us a sick boy and other children to think about. They more important than my pride."

Mary Ann was silent a moment, while Elijah watched and waited. Finally, she nodded and said, "All right."

It wasn't hard to make costumes. Most of the Abels' clothes were already so tattered, a few more slits made them just right for a Jim Crow act. The worst was when Elijah saw himself in the mirror, the paste of black cork on his fingers, ready to be spread over his face. For a split second, he remembered his own daddy in rags, heading for the auction block. He closed his eyes to black the memory and then opened them to black his face.

He instructed Mary Ann to put pillows at her hips and another at her chest. The public needed her to play the part of a fat old washerwoman who yelled at her children while lathering their wooly heads. She could not be beautiful. A beautiful Negress made white women nervous.

She cooperated, as she generally did, but you might have guessed the yelling part never did work for Mary Ann. Her shy nature wouldn't allow harshness, even if it was only playacting. Elijah finally just had her sing—which was one of his better ideas. By now, Mary Ann's singing had become a thing of beauty and could stop a body cold. Hers was a sweet, fluty voice. It could never fit the image white folks had of Loud Mammy, or of Jim Crow's sharp-mouthed woman. For the most part, she just stood behind the rest of the family singing and swaying her pillow-hips.

Moroni's sickness seemed nearly gone by the time they were making their act ready. His voice had dipped deep into a barrel of sound, and he knew how to make the most of it. He'd spread his lips to show the teeth he'd blacked out with tree gum and charcoal. Then, rolling his eyes up, he would render "Ol' Uncle Ned" or some other song like that.

Enoch's voice was finding its way to a baritone, though sometimes it seemed in need of oil.

The younger ones—Delilah, Anna, and little Elijah—weren't much louder than their mother, but they weren't near as shy about performing. When they acted the parts of uncombed pickaninnies getting chased by papier-mâché alligators, the audience would laugh hearty.

Minstrel acts often had a character named Bones (who struck rib bones together to make rhythm) and another named Tambo (who played the tamborine). The Abels knew all about the setup. Elijah played the part of Bones, and Moroni was Tambo.

So Elijah Abel, still a member of the Third Quorum of the Seventy, would call back his blackest talk, exaggerate a stupid smile, and say to the all-white audience: "Now that we got the railroad in Ogden, Tambo here started workin' the Jim Crow car." He'd point to Moroni. "Brother Tambo, he done tol' the colored folk he was the train's director, and sho' 'nuff, I seen him pointin' folks to the car—directin' 'em, just like he say." He paused for the audience to catch the humor. "And Brother Tambo," he went on, "he seem to take with them brown-skinned ladies! Yessir!"

Moroni came in then, jingling his tamborine and belting out the words: "Only with some of them, Brother Bones."

"Why not all of them? Who would you offend with your winsome ways and suave tones?" (White folks loved seeing Negroes try to use hard words and showing their ignorance in the process.)

"Oh, my windy ways and shave tones did it with me, Brother Bones. One of the ladies near got me fired off that train! When we arrive at the last stop, she ask me, 'Does I leave the car here?' I says to her, 'That's right, lady, 'less you prefers to take it with you.' She took such offence, she near got me bounced!"

"You know what I suggest then, Brother Tambo? You ought to get her a present to make her feel better towards you."

"I tried to. I thought I'd get her a prairie dog."

"A prairie dog?" Elijah exaggerated the sound.

"You know the prairie dog? I wanted to send it home to her for a curiosity, and after waitin' all day at the hole, out come a rattle-snake!"

The audience laughed and clapped. Seemed they thought there was no greater amusement than a Negro acting like a man.

Such was the entertainment many white Latter-day Saints appreciated and were willing to pay for. So the Abel family did a fine act for Ogden's wards and were better received as these mockeries than as themselves. Folks expected them to joke and sing and be a carefree bunch even after the show. Nobody considered the reality of the Abels' life or that tragedy could strike a family that told such funny stories.

But tragedy didn't care what show or what family it interrupted.

NOTES

The chapter title is from a traditional Negro spiritual cited in Higginson, "Negro Spirituals," 691.

Though Utahns may have ignored the initial signs of the Civil War's end, they paid appropriate respect to President Lincoln upon his death. The *Deseret News* (April 19, 1865) ran the headline: "Our Nation Mourning" and reported, "On Sunday, Wilford Woodruff, Stephen Richards, and George Q. Cannon delivered feeling and appropriate addresses upon the solemn occasion."

Later in Brigham Young's life, according to Hicks, he became "quite fond of such 'Negro melodies'" ("Ministering Minstrels," 52).

Minstrel acts (referring to blackfaced performers—initially whites caricaturing blacks but eventually blacks caricaturing themselves) had been popular throughout the United States from the 1830s on. Even in Nauvoo, according to Hicks, Mormons had heard minstrel entertainment "from the showboats on the Mississippi." In January 1853, a group called "The African Band" performed a minstrel act at the Salt Lake Social Hall; the next year, a blackface entertainer (called "genuine Ethiopian"), who did "a solo dance . . . in pseudo-black dialect" (Hicks, "Ministering Minstrels," 54). Hicks documents the performances of several minstrel acts in Salt Lake during the 1870s—these done by "authentic" Negroes, one of whom, a minstrel named Billy Wilson, was reviewed in the *Salt Lake Tribune* as having "the most expansive [food trap] of any nigger we ever saw." The *Deseret News* compared Wilson's mouth with that of a hippopotamus (Hicks, "Ministering Minstrels," 57, 59).

Bringhurst documents that the Abel family performed minstrel acts in the 1870s, during their stay in Ogden ("Changing Status," 137). In fact, Hicks notes, there were a number of "indigenous Mormon minstrelsy" acts during the 1870s, as well as outside minstrel acts. "Like most Americans," he says, "Utahns were impressed with the authenticity real blacks gave to their mannered performances" (Hicks, "Ministering Minstrels," 57). The jokes depicted in the Abels' minstrel act are largely extracted (with some modification) from Williams, *Black American Joker*. The structure of the act itself and the names of the common characters used in minstrel acts are accurate. According to Toll, *Blacking Up*, 54, the minstrel shows featured entertainers seated in a semicircle on stage with the tambourine player (Mr. Tambo) at one end and a "bones" or castanet player (Mr. Bones) at the other. They exchanged jokes and sang songs.

31

STAND YOUR TRIAL

Who shall separate us from the love of Christ?
shall tribulation, or distress, or persecution,
or famine, or nakedness, or peril, or sword?
ROMANS 8:35

The first hint that Moroni was sick again—and worse—happened one night when he tried to sing "Carry Me Back to Ol' Virginny." He couldn't finish the chorus for coughing. The audience thought this was part of the act and laughed. Moroni had to sit out the rest of the show.

Elijah asked afterwards how that cough had come into the song. Moroni said he didn't rightly know, but he had been coughing a lot. Elijah knew that already, since he had heard it, though he had tried not to. He wanted to persuade himself it was dust in the air aggravating his son's throat.

"Any blood with that cough?" Elijah asked.

The boy nodded yes.

Can you understand what that nod did to Elijah Abel? His memory knew every detail of his mama's death from consumption. His whole self turned to gooseflesh.

"Black blood or red?" he asked.

"Well, since it come from me, must be black blood. But it look awful red."

"This ain't the time for jokin', boy. Let me hear you breathe." He put his ear to his son's chest and heard breaths like someone sawing lumber.

"I be all right, Daddy," Moroni said.

But just as Moroni's voice had slid into man tones, his body soon slid into that disease—and the slide didn't take much time at all. Before long, he was hacking so much, he could barely bring in air. Sometimes it wasn't just a little blood that trickled from his lungs but a red stream. The Abels would be doing no more minstrel shows in Ogden or anywhere else.

Elijah grew certain this was a test like Abraham's. He, Elijah, would show as much faith as that old prophet. It was time to head up Ensign Peak again, with Moroni by his side. This would be their Mount Moriah, and Elijah would tell God to do his holy will, knowing there must be a ram in the bush.

Elijah took his son by stage to Salt Lake. Mary Ann wasn't happy about Moroni climbing up a mountain in his condition, but she understood the need and didn't voice more than a concerned plea to wrap the boy's neck in a good wool scarf.

As father and son traveled, Elijah explained why it mattered to be on that sanctified peak. They needed to show God they accepted his test and would do whatsoever he commanded. Likely, this would be the finest, roughest test the Lord would give before pouring out his blessings.

So they climbed the grassy, pebbly hill, stopping every so often so the boy could take his ease.

"You aimin' to sacrifice me?" Moroni asked with a half-smile.

"You jus' keep your mind on God providin' us a ram in the thicket," Elijah said and waited until Moroni felt ready for more climb.

At the summit, they knelt. Moroni asked if maybe he should be tied up for this offering, and Elijah counseled him not to mock the Lord but simply to listen. Then Elijah prayed: "I know we must be willin' to give up everything in this world, and Lord, I be willin', if such be your choice. I know you offered your Son on the cross, and I know you understand the pain of a father losin' what matter most. Now, if you require this boy's life, I accept it."

Moroni's eyes popped open. He peered over at his daddy.

"God, I can't believe you plans to visit death on us. I stayed faithful through trials only you and me knows about. I seen what the consumption can do. Seen it in my own mama, and I don't need no more of it. Now sure, Lord, you love us too much to bring such a trial on this family again."

Elijah turned, placed his hands on Moroni's head, and blessed him. He commanded the disease to leave off this child. Weeping, Elijah ordered the lung fever to abandon this young body.

Then they waited a moment, letting the breezes swell around them and hoping God's force was blowing through the clouds and straight into Moroni's breathers. Moroni looked down the hill they were about to descend. He said that he hoped healing was the good Lord's will, as he could use some help.

"You got enough faith?" Elijah asked.

Moroni hesitated. "I ain't certain in it."

Elijah's hands embraced his son's face and fingered every feature of that beautiful dark skin. "Son," he whispered, "you gots to have faith in the Lord. That be the way he work his miracle. That be the only way."

"You got full faith, ain't you, Daddy? Likely enough for the both of us."

Elijah pondered that. "I can't say it be full faith I got, but it be mostly full. And I'm willin' to wait on the Lord to answer my need. He may take me to the limit. He done so before. But he will hear my prayer. I feel that to the marrow of my bones. I seen many things in my years, and I ain't no young man. These hairs testify to that. I seen good men get beat and bad men get honor. I seen things make me want to give up on this Church. But my faith never been on the arms of flesh, only in my God."

Moroni lowered his eyes. He noticed sego lilies blooming between rocks and commented on how pretty they were. Then he said, "I stoled that knife, Daddy."

Elijah let the words idle in the air. "Why you tellin' me that?"

"Mama thought sure someone plant it on me to make mischief, and I never said different, but I stoled it. My eyes seen it and my fingers went after it before I could take a thought."

Elijah remembered his own mild thieving during his slave years and recalled the feeling it gave him. Doing something forbidden, taking something however small from the white world and possessing it, had made him feel strong, alive, and free. In reaching beyond the limits and taking something from the world he was not allowed to inhabit except as a slave, he had felt like a man who could act on his own. Of course, it made no sense to him that stealing a hat or a piece of wood could have made him feel liberated, and he wondered why God hadn't struck him down.

He did not choose to voice all this to his son. He said only, "Andrew Burt was hard on you—and that knife hardly worth a thing. He punish you more than you deserve, settin' you in that dank jail. I think that jail brought this sickness on you."

"I'm guilty for the knife, but he punish me worse than he would others. I think he punish me for my color."

"I know," Elijah said. "We all gettin' punished for bein' black. But I'm glad you man enough to confess to takin' the knife. Are you also man enough to see the result? You opened the door for that policeman to think bad of you. If you hadn't stole that knife in the first place, he'd had no call to haul you in. You understand that?"

"I do, and I'm sorry, 'cause I know it was ugly for you and Mama.

I wonder if this sickness came on me for my thieving and my lying. I wonder if God sent it."

Elijah shook his head. "That ain't the God I know. My God let us suffer blindness and disease so his works can get manifest. He punish us for our sins, but he don't expect a life for a knife."

"Daddy, you forgive me?"

Elijah embraced him. "I can't do nothin' but. I loves you, son."

A bad cough took Moroni, and there was blood in it. "My insides," he said when his breath came back, "they painin' me bad."

Elijah raised both his arms, just as he had seen Brother Joseph do. "Lord," he prayed, "ease this child's sufferin' while you be healin' him. Put it on me, if you wants. I offer myself in his place. Soothe my son."

After a moment, Moroni said the pain was tolerable, and they could start down the slope.

They spent the night at Jane and Isaac James's home and then returned to Ogden the next day.

Elijah knew the sickness would stop, just as it had stopped before. He kept telling himself that, even as Moroni's coughs got worse.

In the most troubling times, Mary Ann stayed with her firstborn without much sleep for herself. She worked on his fever with cold compresses and sang him sweet songs that were nothing like what they'd performed at the Ogden ward houses. Her songs now were hymns from her childhood, about Jesus calming tempests and watching out for his every creation. Moroni's favorite went like this:

> *We'll run and never tire*
> *Jesus set poor sinners free.*
> *Way down in de valley,*
> *Who will rise and go with me?*
> *You've heern talk of Jesus,*
> *Who set poor sinners free.*

Besides singing, she prayed out loud most of her waking hours. She just talked to the Lord while she did her daily work. By this time in her life, she was talking more than she ever had before.

As for Elijah, he struggled up Ogden's mountains or Ensign Peak many a day, to get closer to angels and hope for a ram. He lifted his arms, trying to snatch healing power from the skies. He willed his hands to be lightning rods for God to strike and fill with strength. But the more he prayed, the less hopeful and more angry his words became, until one day, Elijah Abel found himself railing at the Lord: "Have I not done everything you asked of me? I have waited in the jails of oppression just as Joseph of the Rainbow Coat—and my wait been longer than his was. I served in Potiphar's house, and I been faithful. Why is it you will not grant this blessin' to me? Have I done somethin' wrong? If it's me needs rightin', Lord, don't take it out on my boy! He be my firstborn and my hope for the future. Surely you don't need to take his life. Lord, you know I always been willin' to do whatever you require, and I still am! So why ain't you honorin' my priesthood? You honored it before. Why ain't you healin' my boy, lettin' him be whole and havin' a life to carry on? I ain't done nothin' but honor this priesthood. You know that, Lord. So let it bless my boy. I got the faith, and you got the power. Hear my prayer, I beg you, in Jesus' name. Make my boy better!"

But better never came. Before long, Moroni didn't even have the strength to stumble out of bed and hardly the strength to swallow the soft foods his mama fed him. Mary Ann was like a mother bird, dropping nourishment into the open mouth of her chick. But Moroni couldn't find energy to do more than loose his jaw and let the food go in. Sometimes when it got part way down his throat, a cough would fling it back out with blood. His body was fighting itself, and Mary Ann knew how the fight would end, even if Elijah didn't.

One night late, while Moroni was sleeping, she and Elijah sat on the floor watching him. Just after his birth, nineteen years ago, they had gazed at him in wonder. And here they were again, watching their baby. But sorrow had swallowed wonder this night.

After what seemed hours, Mary Ann told Elijah what had been on her mind for days: that he was keeping Moroni past his time. "I never imagine I be losin' this boy," she murmured. "But what he goin' through is worse. I can't bear seein' my baby suffer. Husband, you got to release your hold on him. Let God have his way."

Elijah pulled his wife in close. "In everything else, I accept the will of the Lord," he whispered. "I can't accept this, though. It ain't right."

She commenced crying into Elijah's chest. "If you always been acceptin' the Lord's will, stop tellin' the Lord what he need to do. Honey, you hurtin' Moroni more than he be hurtin' already. You puttin' it on him to have faith to get healed, and he feelin' like a disappointment for stayin' sick." Her body was shivering, and her words trembled. "I know it's painin' you. It's painin' me. I be the one what laid down and birth that boy. But it's me askin' you to let him go."

Elijah held her tighter and then wept harder than she was weeping. Neither noticed that Moroni had awakened and was gazing at them. Finally, Elijah closed his eyes and said, "Lord, I thank you for this good woman. You know what I want for my boy. You know what I beg you for. Nevertheless, I say it now, with my wife in my embrace: Not my will but yours be done. Amen."

"Amen," Moroni whispered.

A week later came the last night of Moroni's life. Elijah filled the watch time by telling stories about Moroni of old, just as he had done so often on the trek west. He told how Ancient Moroni had wandered this earth, avoiding enemies and trying to keep safe. "That was one lonesome man," said Elijah. "Hated by everybody around him. Hated most 'specially by the Lamanites, who was in the majority at the time. Moroni was a Nephite, and the races wasn't fond of each other."

With hard-won breath, Moroni managed, "Some things don't change." He was weak, and his voice showed it. "I think I can sleep some, Daddy," he said.

"Then you do it. You feel free to sleep long as you needs."

Moroni closed his eyes. He never opened them again.

Yet even when that last rattling breath came, Elijah wasn't ready to surrender his son. He spent his last hope on a miracle. It took a full day before he set about gathering materials for the coffin.

As for Mary Ann, she wept in private, waiting, knowing Elijah would make peace with this. When the time came, she brought him nails. Elijah stared straight ahead, jaw slack, eyes unseeing. He took the nails from his wife, and together they fashioned the box.

NOTES

The chapter title is from a traditional Negro spiritual cited in Cone, *Spirituals and the Blues*, 94.

Moroni Abel died of consumption on October 20, 1871, as recorded in the Ogden City Cemetery records, GS 979,228/01, vol. 220, pt. 1 (Bringhurst, "Changing Status," 147).

The hymn Mary Ann sings is "Down in the Valley," a traditional Negro spiritual (Higginson, "Negro Spirituals," 688).

32

WHEN I'M GONE

O ye fair ones, how could ye have rejected that Jesus,
who stood with open arms to receive you!
MORMON 6:17

Needless to say, the Abels weren't the only ones facing hardship
and sorrow. All these years, Isaac James had kept on dreaming more
and more about California. Events in Utah made those dreams
enticing, for with every new hope he had in Salt Lake, seemed the
ground would collapse around him. He and Jane had long been
fighting over their future: where they'd spend it, and if they'd even
be together to meet it. Their fights weren't frequent, but they cut
deep. They slashed each other with spiteful words and accusa-
tions—but none bears repeating. All you need to know is that five
years after the war ended, Isaac had decided to uproot.

Much time had passed since he had been an eager suitor hand-
feeding berries to Jane Manning and teasing her with stories. Such
distant memories of himself were covered by a sludge of disappointment now. Jane's faith had always been stronger than his, and he
could not endure the afflictions she accepted as "God's refinement."

By now, grim lines framed his mouth, and gray hairs met his temples. Jane hadn't grayed yet, though her face showed all the frowns she had ever made. They certainly showed when Isaac announced, "Jane, I need to talk serious with you. We've talked and fought about it, and we ain't one step closer to being at peace. Fact is, I can't keep on here."

She was making soap at that moment and stirred the fixings without even a hiccough in her motion. "You're right. We've talked about this before, so why do we need to talk about it now? Can't you see I'm busy? I got some big washin' on my hands today."

"I hope I'm more important than your chores."

"If we gotta go down that tired old road again, can't you at least wait until I'm done makin' this soap? You know it's gotta be in the right order and at the right time."

"We can talk while you toil."

She made a resigned, one-hand wave. "Go on then. Say what you got to say and get it off your mind. Ain't goin' be nothin' you ain't said before."

"I'm leavin'," he said straight and easy. "That's it. And I want you and the family come with me to California."

Jane answered with an overly unconcerned "Umhmmm."

"The war's done. Black folks is free, and Utah is connected to the whole nation now. The wide world's openin' for us, and all we got to do is walk through the door. That gold rush growed California. Lots of black folks settled there." He gestured wide, trying to catch her eye. "We got daughters, Janey. There ain't hardly no one for them to pick from here. Don't you want better for them? Utah is a wilderness."

He got her attention all right. She could have slung some of the lye concoction right into his face, she was so mad. "Sometimes you act the biggest fool I ever saw. I thought you was a man of faith. If our daughters needs husbands, what makes you think the Lord can't bring them husbands? If you had any manhood in you—"

"Stop it, Jane." He held his peace for a moment, seeing she was braced to get hit. Then he spoke calm. "I told you about my plan. And I meant it."

Her jaw was still tight, but her words were loose: "Ain't the first time you meant it."

"If I'd meant it before, we'd already be in California, livin' a better life than we livin' here. I'd be wearin' gold rings instead of dirt around my fingers. Our children would be associating with coloreds of consequence instead of gettin' disrespect everywhere they turn."

Yes indeed, they had traveled this fight's path before, but this time, Jane heard something different in her husband. She lifted her head and knew this time wasn't like all the others. All she could gasp out was, "Isaac, don't."

"Don't what? Don't go and be somethin' better? I thought you believe in all Brother Joseph say about eternal progression and such. Don't progression include us?"

"You think California goin' make you a man of position?" She set her fists on her hips.

"I won't fight with you, woman, and I won' repeat myself."

Jane's hands dropped. There was no doubt: If she didn't go with him, he was quitting her. All of him—neck, mouth, chin, and every joint—was fixed on this goal. There was a hard glint in his eyes. Everything but his body was already in California.

"After all these years, you doin' me dirt?" she whispered.

"I said I won' fight with you. I don' recommend you use fightin' words with me."

She waited to see what else he would say. He was staring her down and not about to back off. "You aim to come back anytime soon?" she asked.

"Can't say for sure. You might watch for me."

Her eyes filled. She wiped them with her sleeve and then commenced stirring the soap mush again. "You know I can't go with you," she said in a softer voice than she had used in any argument before. "Isaac, don't quit me. I'm your wife."

"Then come where I'm goin'."

She closed her eyes. "I can't. That's the only answer I can give."

"And you just heard the only answer I can give you." His lips squeezed together. "Jane, it's you makin' this choice."

She was weeping now, with her eyes still shut. "Isaac, my choice isn't just about where to live; it's about who I serve. I'm not after fancy makin's, honey. They're nice, but that's not my goal. I'm after my God, and I'm after doin' what he wants me to do." Her voice reclaimed its strength, and she spoke a quiet, certain witness. "When I went under the waters, I meant it. When I prayed over this gospel, I meant it. When I come across the plain and prairie with you, I meant it. And I was under the impression you meant it too. I will not unmean my life."

If it had been a colored congregation Jane was addressing, that speech would've been hailed with many amens. Isaac, however, was just one tired man, and her words made him tireder yet. His expression was blank when he answered, "I give you a prophecy: You will find life gettin' hard and harder. That's the direction I see here."

Jane waited a long moment before opening her mouth again. She asked him one question: "Was I wrong in thinkin' you'd be man enough to tarry with me?"

Now it was Isaac's turn to witness. He stepped back and pointed at her. "Jane, I've listened to you question my manhood three times in this conversation. You question my faith as a man. You question my courage as a man. You question my loyalty as a man. We been married twenty-four years, and I ain't never question your womanhood. Every trial you faced, I faced. Every hurt you got, I got. And I've respected you. But you showin' nothin' like respect for me. Not if you doubtin' my manhood. So you stay here and do as you see fit. Me and my manhood is goin' to California."

With that, he went inside the house.

This would not be a simple separation but a full divorce. They worked out their settlement. He deeded the family's property to her for five hundred dollars. Neither expected they'd be seeing the other again. If you'd asked them, they both would have said they didn't care. And for a while, they truly thought they didn't.

Of course, all these doings was hard on the children. Divorce unravels the whole universe for the young ones born to that undone pair, even if the young ones ain't young. Most often, they survive, and the James children did, bitterly.

As for Isaac, he headed out of Salt Lake with little more than a bag of clothes wrapped around a pile of high hopes.

NOTES

The chapter title is from a traditional Negro spiritual cited in Cone, *Spirituals and the Blues*, 71.

That "in late 1869 or early 1870, Isaac James left the household and sold most of the family's realty, consisting of a one-and-a-quarter acre lot and improvements, to his wife for $500 . . . indicat[ing] that Isaac intended his departure to be permanent and that he and his wife had not separated on friendly terms" is documented in Wolfinger, "Test of Faith," in *Social Accommodation*, 133.

As Hartley points out, the transcontinental railway made "easy access" to other parts of the country: "This linking by rails prompted hundreds of Saints who had been in Utah for years to go back to their home towns and see their relatives again. Certainly any blacks in Utah now had opportunity to go any place in the nation where they might think their lot would be better" (personal communication, August 1, 2001).

33

GET ON BOARD

He that hath received his testimony hath set
to his seal that God is true.
JOHN 3:33

Jane tried to keep up her house in the First Ward for a time, but with Isaac gone, she couldn't maintain such a fine place, humble though it was. There was no choice. The James family would have to take one more step down poverty lane. They would relocate in the Eighth Ward, where most other coloreds in Utah lived.

This may have seemed a sad move, but it had its rewards.

Their new place was plain but cozy: a two-story frame house set back from the street and surrounded by a white picket fence. It had a nice yard, too, suitable for Sunday picnics.

By the time Jane moved, the Chambers and Leggroan families had arrived in Utah. They also moved to the Eighth Ward, where they were all neighbors.

Jane put her yard to good use, inviting these families over for many a Sunday supper—downhome cooking. As a divorced woman whose only income was what her wash work and soap making brought, Jane could not afford to be fancy. But with everyone help-ing, they all enjoyed many a feast.

These picnics included Jane's children: sons Silas and Jessie, daughters Ellen and Vilate, Mary Ann and her husband, and Miriam and hers. Sylvester and his family never missed a single pic-nic—or any other offer of food, for that matter. Usually, the entire Chambers and Leggroan families were present too.

Jane loved to show off her garden. Sam and Amanda Chambers found inspiration for the fruit farming they would eventually do as Jane boasted up her collard greens and carrots. Nothing Jane showed would match the currants and berries the Chambers family would grow—and which would win many a state fair competition—but her garden was good enough to inspire any hard-working farmer.

By this time, Sylvester's daughters were just under six years of age, but they knew how to flirt with the Leggroan boys of like age. Same then as now: Children flirt by scampering after each other and pretending to be afraid of getting caught. That's exactly what these babies did, darting all around the adult conversation like happy puppies.

Though Amanda Chambers was a short woman, only about five feet tall and 130 pounds, she carried herself with dignity. She often told about life in Mississippi—how Judge Lynch was spreading his influence over the whole state like a swelling shadow. Besides the lynchings, black folks were getting arrested right and left if they weren't employed. The new jails were like slave quarters without any comforts, Amanda said. And Mississippi wasn't much different from the rest of the South—or the North either. At least from what she had heard.

Such words made Jane sad for Isaac—but vindicated too.

"It was Sam removed us from that and directed us here," Ned Leggroan reminded everyone. He said about the same words every week, after which Sam would volunteer the story of his conversion, opening it up by announcing, "I got born in slavery."

"So'd my mama," Jane would say, like she'd never said it before. Every time she repeated those words, she was filled with longing to see her mama. Jane was in her fifties now, as old as Phyllis Manning Treadwell had been when they undertook to leave Connecticut for Nauvoo. All those years had passed, and still Jane missed her mama.

"I took the gospel in my slave condition," Sam would continue, "and I knowed I done right, for I feeled the spirit of God. I was only twelve or thirteen years of age and I never heard another word of the gospel." Sam was in his forties, tall and imposing, especially when he'd stand to tell of his conversion. Except for his color, he looked like a Church authority.

"Imagine that!" Jane would say (and she'd say it many times during the conversating). "And still, you keep true to your faith."

"Indeed I do. Every tub must stand on its own bottom."

If you'd been at one of those picnics, you'd likely have heard the children's laughter above Sam's voice. Jane reminded Syl more than once that his children should be seen but not heard. When Syl would answer, "Let 'em play, Ma," she'd scold him like he was still a child himself. "I taught you better than that," she'd say, "and I thought you'd teach your children."

These words generally had a quick effect, but it wouldn't last. The giggles and running would start up again. Close your eyes and let yourself hear the happy sounds of children. Those were good, sweet times.

I suspect Sam Chambers enjoyed the hubbub. He sure never let the babies' noise keep him from telling his tale. "Twenty-three, twenty-five years, and I never heard another gospel word."

"But you remembered," Jane would prompt.

Amanda liked to add, "Sam remember everything ever happen in his life. That's because he repeat it so often."

"Wasn't free until after the war," Sam's story would continue. "Then I work four years, make money, and we come out here. We come because I knowed this was where the Mormons be, and I knowed that what I receive many years past was from God."

"I had a like experience in my youth. I seen Joseph Smith in a vision," Jane said sometimes.

Often, Sylvester would be holding his little daughter, who was pretty as could be in her straw hat and spotless blue dress with its white buttons fastened up her neck. It wouldn't have been hard to predict that within a few short years, Syl's daughters would marry the two Leggroan boys they played with at these picnics. In fact, a good many of the colored Saints married each other—Perkinses with Jameses, Bankheads with Leggroans, Grices with Bankheads, and so on. Even Jane James married one of the Mormon Negroes, Mr. Frank Perkins—Sylvester's father-in-law—though it only lasted a short time. I'd guess she was not the easiest person in the world to share a household with, for she always knew what she wanted and wouldn't quit jawing till she got it.

Yes, there were ups and downs in Salt Lake's colored neighborhoods. All these folks who had been through so much could look at each other and get satisfaction just from knowing they were still here.

What with Elijah Abel in Ogden, Sam became the head spokesman for the blacks, not only at picnics but other events as well. He was respected. Though he didn't hold the priesthood, he was an unordained, acting deacon in the Eighth Ward, and his wife was a deaconess. Of course, in those days, being a deacon didn't have anything to do with serving the sacrament. Deacons cared for the meetinghouses. They washed windows, swept floors, polished benches, and kept the stoves hot during winter. Sam said he felt joy in whatever he was called to do. Once, when wards were asked to provide deacons to usher at the Salt Lake Tabernacle, Sam was the Eighth Ward's only volunteer—and a jubilant one at that. There was even a day when the entire Eighth Ward gave a unanimous vote

of thanks to Brother Chambers "for being so faithful in the dis-
charge of his duties."

He didn't take such things lightly. "Without a testimony of
God," Sam said, "we ain't nothin'. It's a high and holy callin', bein'
a member of this faith."

What nobody mentioned was that this high and holy calling
came with greater sacrifice than anyone could have suspected when
they took baptism. Even Sam and Amanda had struggled over the
issue of tithing when they first got to Utah. They didn't know how
they could pay it and live. Here they had come all this way, with
nothing but their ox team, their wagon, and their family. But the
Spirit whispered that all things are possible to God, and so they paid
their tithes.

Jane's trials were harder than money ones, though. She hadn't
been born a slave like Sam and Amanda, but the Lord would not
let her out of this life until grief had plumbed her soul.

If she had realized what still lay ahead, she might've taken more
time to value the picnic lunches and the children's laughter.

NOTES

The chapter title is from a traditional Negro spiritual cited in Cone,
Spirituals and the Blues, 85.

The description of Jane's house on the east side of Fifth East Street
between Fifth and Sixth South in Salt Lake City is from Wolfinger, "Test of
Faith," in *Social Accommodation*, 134.

That Sylvester and Mary Ann James's daughters, Nettie and Ester, married two of Ned Leggroan's sons is documented in Wolfinger, "Test of Faith,"
in *Social Accommodation*, 143.

Samuel Chambers's words about his conversion and testimony are drawn
from his testimony recorded in the Salt Lake Stake Deacons Quorum Minutes
(qtd. in Hartley, "Saint without Priesthood," 18).

In the Eighth Ward, Samuel Chambers served as an unordained, acting
deacon, and Amanda as a "deaconness." Their responsibilities included cleaning the meetinghouse. As Hartley explains, "Deacons of that day had no
part in the sacrament service." After 1878, "the Chambers family farmed in

southeast Salt Lake City. . . . Samuel became an authority on the culture of grapes and small fruits, especially currants. These won him first prizes in various state fairs." He and Amanda also received patriarchal blessings. Sam was promised that if he were faithful, he would live a long life and prosper materially, and his name would be held in remembrance among the Saints. Indeed, both Sam and Amanda lived long lives, celebrating their fiftieth wedding anniversary in Utah (Hartley, "Samuel D. Chambers," 48–49). Today, their portrait is beside that of Frederick Douglass on the cover of the *Freedman's Bank Records* CD, a genealogical disk published by The Church of Jesus Christ of Latter-day Saints that contains the family names of all depositors in the Freedman's Bank—a total of 486,484 names.

The description of Amanda's height and weight is from Hartley's interview with Minnie Lee Haynes, Samuel Chambers's granddaughter by marriage, who cared for him and Amanda in their old age (personal communication, July 31, 2001). Sam's statement, "Every tub must stand on its own bottom" is also from that conversation.

That Jane supported herself and her family by manufacturing "some household items such as soap" is documented in Wolfinger, "Test of Faith," in *Social Accommodation*, 134.

34

BE WITH ME, LORD

Who comforteth us in all our tribulation,
that we may be able to comfort them
which are in any trouble.
2 CORINTHIANS 1:4

Once tribulation took to visiting Jane James, it didn't let up. For whatever reason, the Lord let opposition squeeze her like grapes in a press.

Until Isaac left, the only child Jane had lost was that stillborn son, her husband's namesake. But the very year after Isaac's departure, Mary Ann, that precious girl who was the first black baby born in Utah, died in childbirth. She was only twenty-two years old and suffered so to bring forth her baby. Jane, at her side the whole time, could hardly bear it. For weeks afterwards, she could hear Mary Ann's wails and moans and the way she kept calling, "Mama! Don't leave me!" Many times, Jane thought that only a woman could suffer such pains as what God required in the price of posterity.

The very next year, Miriam, Jane's second daughter, died of that same affliction reserved only for women.

Finally Silas, the son born on the Mormon trail at the Nishnabotna River, took the consumption. He died in 1872.

Jane was more than grateful when the Abels moved back to Salt Lake. The Abels were in the Thirteenth Ward now, but at least they were not so far away as Ogden. Mary Ann Abel—who had also lost a child, you recall—came calling on Jane the day after they arrived. Other folks had brought her bread and soup. Mary Ann brought a knowing heart.

There was hardly a titch of shyness now in Elijah Abel's wife. It was she who took Jane in her arms and said, "I can weep with you and pray with you all week, Sister Jane. We got enough sufferin' between us two to get the angels theyselves a-sobbin'."

That was mostly what they did—weep and pray and talk about their children. There were days Jane felt that she was more doll than human, that life was happening around her, but she wasn't in it. Mary Ann helped her feel real again. Both had thought the trek over the mountains was the hardest thing they'd ever do—back when they was doing it. But this faith-trek over God's peaks and down God's valleys, when he took their children to his bosom, was so much worse. No flesh bled, no bloody footprints got left on the trail, but each woman felt her heart had burst, then collapsed on itself, and found its rhythm again for another day of beating. Each woman was amazed that life kept on and they were still expected to arise every morning and make breakfast.

By this time, several temples were under construction or were about to be. Within a few years, there would be temples in St. George, Logan, and Manti. And the Salt Lake Temple was progressing daily, though the work was slow—too slow to suit Brother Brigham who went so far as to close the Endowment House for a while so saints would feel the urgency of building the temple. Why, here it was the 1870s and the Mountain of the Lord showed only one foot of wall for every year it had been under construction! The walls were just over twenty feet high, barely above the level of the first floor. Jane herself had seen the groundbreaking ceremony back in 1853, when Brigham had jabbed a pick into the icy ground, after Heber Kimball offered the dedicatory prayer. Who would have guessed how long it would take to finish what was started that day?

Now that the railroad was accessible, construction was moving quicker. In earlier years, it was a common sight to see groups of ox-pulled wagons toting three tons of stone—and the journey to unload that burden took half a week by itself. But times were changing. Though the railroad had taken temple builders away and put them to work for its own use, it compensated now for every muscle it had borrowed. A railspur was set to pass close to Temple Quarry, where the rock was being dug. Railcars were loaded and sent downtown along streetcar tracks. Steam locomotives pulled the loaded cars to the south gate of Temple Block. Most of the Mormon men of the Valley, black and white, worked on digging in that quarry, loading and unloading those cars, and then cutting and mortaring the sparkling granite into the house of the Lord.

President Young had grown large and rheumatic by this time. He used a cane whenever he went out of doors or out of his carriage. But he was still the Lion of the Lord. He would have that temple worked on no matter what other trials the Saints were facing nor how frequently Mister Death came a-calling.

Elijah Abel was true to his word and to his God. He spent every moment he could splitting rock or carving wood for the temple.

NOTES

The chapter title is from a traditional Negro spiritual cited in Cone, *Spirituals and the Blues*, 46.

The deaths of Jane's children during the early 1870s are recorded by Henry Wolfinger, "Test of Faith," in *Social Accommodation*, 138.

That the Abels lived in Ogden only a short time and then returned to Salt Lake City by the mid-1870s is supported by Bringhurst, "Changing Status," 137. At that time, they resided in the Thirteenth Ward.

As Tingen points out ("Endowment House," 20–22), the Endowment House was closed for a variety of reasons, perhaps paramount among them to encourage the Saints to finish the Salt Lake Temple. Those who needed ordinance work were expected to travel to St. George. Two months after the death of Brigham Young, the Endowment House was reopened and returned to its regular schedule on October 23, 1879. It was torn down a decade later when temples were operating in St. George, Logan, and Manti, and the Salt Lake Temple was nearing completion.

The details of the Salt Lake Temple's construction in the 1870s are from Cowan, *Temples to Dot the Earth*, 101. The groundbreaking of the Salt Lake Temple on February 14, 1853, had been attended by several thousand people. Cowan writes, "Because the ground was frozen, it had to be broken with a pick. President Young then declared the ground officially broken for the temple" (*Temples to Dot the Earth*, 65).

Petitions

35

STAND STILL, JORDAN

*I soon go to rest in the paradise of God, until my spirit
and body shall again reunite, and I am brought forth
triumphant through the air, to meet you.*
MORONI 10:34

Death came calling often in the Valley, on the rich and the
poor, and in due time it called on the president of the Church
himself.

On the twenty-ninth of August, 1877, Brigham Young died. His
remains were carried from the Lion House (a far more elaborate
dwelling than the adobe one Elijah had visited years ago) to the
Tabernacle, flanked by a thousand bareheaded men. The coffin was
set in a case with a glass window, so mourners could look on their
leader one last time. Green Flake helped dig Brother Brigham's
grave, after the thousands (including Jane James and Elijah Abel)
passed by the coffin to pay their last respects.

Elijah did respect Brother Brigham. He knew the deceased
president had tried to purchase slaves out of their bondage—and he
respected that. Still, since Brigham wasn't blocking the door any
longer, he wondered if the way might be opened for him to get his

temple blessings and be sealed to his wife. While Brother Brigham had been a great leader, he was fairly set in his ways regarding Negroes. Now, the Quorum of the Twelve Apostles, with John Taylor as its president, would be taking over leadership of the Church. Might they have a more generous cast of mind towards people of color?

Elijah prepared his petition. He spoke first with his bishop, Edwin D. Woolley, a short, square-bodied man, with a good beard. Brother Woolley had been a Quaker before joining the Mormons and often fell into Quaker speech, using "thee" as often as "you." Elijah always appreciated it when the bishop did that, for the Quakers were dear to him.

With some apprehension, he went to the Woolley home, one of the richest in the Thirteenth Ward. After complimenting the house and its furnishings, he launched right into his purpose: "You and I both knew Brother Joseph and Father Smith too, isn't that right?"

The bishop invited Elijah to sit and then answered that he knew Father Smith before ever laying eyes on Joseph, and he loved that old man with all his heart.

"I got my patriarchal blessing from Father Smith." Elijah sank into the deep cushions of the chair. "It said to me I was like an orphan. Then Father Smith pretty much adopted me as if I was his own son."

"Isn't that a wonder?" answered Bishop Woolley. "My own parents died young, and my brother got a blessing from Father Smith that said near the same thing. You're in good company."

"I feel blessed, sir." Elijah fingered the velvet chair arms. "But I hope I won't sound greedy if I say I sure do want more blessin's."

"We can all use more blessings, Elijah."

"Yessir, that's the truth. And I been workin' on that temple there. Why, you know that. I been offerin' the best I have in way of muscle and skill. Even when Brother Brigham said we had to tear down the foundation and start over, I didn't complain. I jus' kept workin'—and I'm a fair carpenter. I hope that ain't braggin'.'"

"That is simply stating the facts, Brother Elijah. If thee said thee were not a fair carpenter, I should have to bring thee up to the councils for dishonesty."

Elijah nodded to acknowledge the humor, but his aim was set, and he would not be distracted. "Bishop, I want to finish what got started in Kirtland. That's where I received the first ordinances—the washin's and anointin's. I know other ordinances is gettin' done in the Endowment House, and I ask you—. Now you know like I know, Brother Brigham had some strong views about a good many things."

"Strong views indeed," the bishop chuckled. "I felt the brunt of them more than once. He said what he thought and didn't worry that someone might write it down for posterity. Who knows how long we'll be haunted by some of President Young's opinions?" Brother Woolley's words didn't surprise Elijah, for everyone knew the bishop to be a bold, stubborn, outspoken fellow. Folks said that if Edwin Woolley should drown someday, the searchers would find his body upstream.

"Now, I don't mean to say a thing against Brother Brigham," Elijah said. "What he did to settle this valley had the hand of God in it. I respect Brigham Young for being the prophet he was."

"Good for you, Elijah. I feel much the same. Not everyone does, though, and that's no secret."

"No sir. I'm afraid that's no secret at all."

"Some say Brigham's death means it's no longer immoral to disagree with church leadership. A man won't be cut off for a difference of opinion now."

"I can guess who said so, and I've heard others say it too. But if some of the colored folks in the Valley heard anyone say such a thing, they'd be set to fight. Sam Chambers won't tolerate anyone, Mormon or Gentile, speaking ill of the leaders."

Bishop Woolley spread his hands over his belly. "As a Church leader, I appreciate that. Myself, whenever I felt to criticize Brother Brigham, I've been reminded of Brother Foote's dream. You know Warren Foote?"

"I have some acquaintance with him, yessir."

"Do you know about his dream?"

"So many people dreamin' 'round here," Elijah sighed, "I can't keep track."

Again Bishop Woolley laughed. "There are good dreams and there are bad ones, aren't there? Brother Foote's was a good one. He saw the Savior. And Warren, being troubled by something President Young had said, asked the Lord himself about it and if Brigham was leading the people right. The Savior told him President Young was doing as well as could be expected of any person in the flesh, clothed in mortality. Like all mankind, Brigham Young was subject to passions and imperfections. Then the Lord said that at his second coming, all things would be made right. That story has comforted me on many occasions."

"I find it a comfort too, sir, and I thank you for tellin' me. Only I wonder, now with President Young gone, maybe times has changed in the Lord's season. You know race was one of the things Brother Brigham held strong views on. He said he couldn't give me further privileges in the temple, owing to my color. He told me that some-day my race would get everything the white man has, but as far as my endowments and getting sealed to my wife, he couldn't feel much hope, and he never changed his mind. But now he's dead. Civil War's over, and I think the atmosphere's changed somewhat."

"Oh yes. There is a different atmosphere in Zion. Can you imagine Brother Brigham standing on the corner talking with the Saints? Or taking a morning walk alone like John Taylor does?"

"If Brother Taylor is the next prophet—" Elijah began but was quickly interrupted.

"Brother Taylor—yes, I saw him recently." Now the bishop

whispered. "In a Gentile pharmacy. He was buying a copy of the *Salt Lake Tribune*."

Elijah squinted. "Brother Taylor buying that Gentile newspaper? You sure you seen it right?"

"I saw it right because I was there myself."

"In the Gentile store?"

"I was buying medicine, you understand. ZCMI doesn't carry it. 'The Mormon Elder's Damiana Waters'—most powerful invigorant ever produced." He walked to his desk and took a bottle from the top drawer. "There's an even stronger brand, though. Cures a sallow countenance, pain in the head, uneasiness about the loins, weakness of confidence, pimples, and insanity."

"Maybe I ought to buy that one." Elijah smiled.

"Sorry, it only works on Gentiles. That's why they sell it in the Gentile store. We should have had it when Johnston's army stopped by." He laughed and sat again.

Elijah bent forward. "Bishop Woolley, I appreciate bein' able to chuckle with you. You always make me feel at ease. Only my purpose here tonight . . . . It ain't just that I want my blessings. Sir, I need them. Mary Ann been feelin' poorly, and sometimes I get this fear in the core of my belly that I might lose her before we been sealed. You know, I been a member of the Third Quorum of the Seventy. Am I still?"

There was no joking now. Bishop Woolley took in some air and waited a moment before breathing it out again. "Have you ever been released?"

"Nobody told me I was released. Never."

The bishop went quiet, as if his thoughts were crawling a long ways to meet his mouth. At last he admitted, "I don't know the answer to your question. But I'll be pleased to make the inquiries on your behalf, Brother Elijah."

"If I could get my sealin's—"

"We'll take one step at a time."

"Yessir. You know, when Father Smith gave me my patriarchal blessin', he blessed me against the powers of the destroyer. I feel that blessin' near every day of my life."

"A worthy blessing indeed. Devils are ever on the alert, you know. They're right on hand, waiting on the least vacuum to be made. Then they enter in, and there's a great deal more trouble to put them out than it was to admit them."

"Oh, I know that. I seen many things in my life. In this valley, I seen folks leave the gospel over the tiniest things. You seen it too."

"In my own ward, in my own flock, as thee knows. Some folks preach themselves so far from earth that they can't get their feet back on the ground."

"I seen it many times. A fellow finds a little rip in the doctrines, and he keeps pickin' at it and pickin' at it, pulling at the threads until all he got is a mess of thread with no sense to it at all. I seen folks start believin' lies and repeatin' them so much they think they're quotin' scripture. Folks get ideas and can't leave off spoutin' them. It's like that first foundation we laid for the Salt Lake Temple. It always was the wrong stone, but we kept building on it. Nine years we built on it, if I recall."

"About nine years, yes."

"Until Brother Brigham made us take it down and put up something better, something right and lasting."

Bishop Woolley shook his head in pity. "It's a hard thing to tear down what you've put so much time and energy building. It was hard counsel Brigham gave that day, and I heard more complaints in an hour than I ever heard on the trail. But not a one of us regrets starting over now. The temple will last through the Millennium."

"I believe it will," said Elijah.

"Yes, folks choose a foundation of sand, and they won't quit building on it. I've seen some of those foundations. I've seen apostasy close up. And I worry we've become a rich people, forgetting the poor. Or we have beggars who won't work for a penny. I've thought we should have 'begging recommends' for the poor, just like we have temple recommends."

Elijah leaned in closer. "Sir, I hope I have never asked for more than my due."

"No, Brother Elijah, you have not." The bishop patted Elijah's hand. "You're one of the most devoted workers I know. There have been times I've longed to give thee more than I could. And if I had the power now, I would give thee every blessing thee seeks."

"I only want what the Lord sees fit to give me," Elijah answered. "I won't ask for more."

"I pray his will be made manifest," said the bishop.

One reply came back soon: Yes, Elijah Abel was still a member of the Third Quorum of the Seventy. But the question of whether he would be able to enter the temple with his wife was yet to be answered. That answer would be some time in coming.

NOTES

The chapter title is from a traditional Negro spiritual found in Burleigh, *Spirituals*, 34.

The details of Brigham Young's death and the ceremony surrounding it are from Holzapfel and Shupe, *Brigham Young, 299.*

Green Flake's helping dig Brigham Young's grave is from Fretwell's interviews with Green's descendants (Fretwell, Miscellaneous Family Papers, 11).

That Brigham Young had tried to purchase slaves from their bondage is supported by at least one letter, addressed to Duritha Trail Lewis, dated January 3, 1860: "Dear Sister Lewis: I understand that you are frequently importuned to sell your negro man Jerry, but that he is industrious and faithful, and desires to remain in this territory: Under these circumstances I should certainly deem it most advisable for you to keep him, but should you at any time conclude otherwise and determine to sell him, ordinary kindness would require that you should sell him to some kind faithful member of the church, that he may have a fair opportunity for doing all the good he desires to do or is capable of doing. I have been told that he is about forty years old, if so, it is not presumable that you will, in case of sale, ask so high a price as you might expect for a younger person. If the price is sufficiently moderate, I may conclude to purchase him and set him at liberty. Your brother in the gospel, Brigham Young" (Lewis, "Life Sketch of Duritha Trail Lewis").

The characterization of Edwin Woolley as so stubborn that "if he were to drown, the searchers should look for his body upstream" is from Kimball and Kimball, *Spencer W. Kimball*, 14. Brigham Young respected Woolley's forthrightness, though sometimes disagreeing with his opinions, according to Arrington (*From Quaker to Latter-day Saint*, 320.) Said Brigham Young: "I do wish that men, who are fond of telling what wonderful knowledge they have obtained from the Almighty, would be as plain as Brother Woolley has been, and tell it from this stand to the people. . . . Let us have more of it, from others, and suffer me to correct you when you stray from the correctness of truth with regard to language, doctrine, and government."

That Samuel Chambers was "unwilling to tolerate criticism of LDS leaders" and was "known to verbally defend them when necessary, in private as well as in Church meetings" is from Hartley, "Samuel D. Chambers," 50.

The dream of Warren Foote is quoted in Arrington, *From Quaker to Latter-day Saint*, 444.

The statement by Woolley about apostates (referring to Elias Harrison and William Godbe, both former members of the Thirteenth Ward) is from Arrington, *From Quaker to Latter-day Saint*, 439. The actual quotation states that Harrison in particular had "preached himself so far from earth . . . that he had never yet come back."

The Salt Lake Temple was initially built on a sandstone foundation. Roberts writes: "In the summer of 1862, the foundation of the Salt Lake Temple . . . was taken out and relaid. Considering the fact that the foundation was 16 feet deep and 16 feet broad, and that the building is 186½ feet by 99 feet—this was no small undertaking; and nine years had been occupied in laying it. President Young said he expected this temple to stand through the millennium, and the Brethren would go in and give the endowments to the people during that time. 'And this,' he added, 'is the reason why I am having the foundation of the temple taken up'" (*Comprehensive History*, 5:136).

Woolley's words that "devils are ever on the alert" and his idea that beggars should have "begging recommends" are both from Arrington, *From Quaker to Latter-day Saint*, 333.

The meeting of Edwin Woolley and John Taylor in a "gentile store" and the descriptions on the medicine bottles found therein are from Taylor, *Kingdom or Nothing*, 261–62.

36

You May Bury
Me in the East

*Precious in the sight of the Lord
is the death of his saints.*
PSALM 116:15

Elijah's remaining question became more urgent as Mary Ann grew sicker. In all her care for her family, Mary Ann forgot herself, as so many women do. Now pneumonia was gurgling down her chest. It was November, and she still wasn't getting better. Death seemed crouched in the bedroom corner, ready to pounce and claim her.

For days, Mary Ann had forced herself out of bed to make Elijah's breakfast and dinner. Sister Rachel Grant, Relief Society president of the Thirteenth Ward, put a stop to that. Her own husband, Jedediah, had died of pneumonia years ago, and she did all she could to keep anyone else from succumbing to that dread disease. She was devoted to her ward sisters and saw to it that the block teachers sought out the sick and the needy. The Grants themselves had known something of poverty and were eager to fill an empty plate. Often, Rachel Grant asked for cash donations to supply the penniless, and more than once, the Abels had received of her generosity and the Thirteenth Ward's.

Sister Grant was the mother of that same Heber Jeddy Grant who had once taken a ride on Brigham Young's sleigh when Isaac James was the driver. She was a prim woman, immaculate in dress and manner. At this time of year, she usually wore a wool cape and a pleated, face-shading bonnet. She looked like mercy herself the day she paid a call on "the sick," meaning Mary Ann.

Her visit to the Abel home was not unexpected, though Elijah never much enjoyed the way the "presidentess" ordered people around.

"Sister Mary, what on earth are you doing out of bed?" were the first words out of Rachel Grant's mouth, the moment she set foot inside.

"Oh, I had to get up. 'Lijah's breakfast . . . " Mary Ann gestured to the corn pone she was cooking.

Though Rachel was deaf by this time in her life, she seemed to understand exactly what Mary Ann was saying. "He can see to his own meals. You get back into bed. That's where you belong until this sickness is passed."

Nobody in Salt Lake countered Rachel Grant. Certainly Mary Ann Abel didn't.

Elijah found it a little difficult to carry on conversation with a strong, deaf woman. Maybe conversation wasn't important anyway. Surely, Sister Grant required no answer when she told him the specifics of how to care for his wife, reciting healing recipes for teas and compresses as though he knew every detail of cooking and medicine, both. Anyway, she couldn't hear, so it didn't much matter what he said back to her—though he knew for sure if he said something rude, her hearing would return long enough to catch it.

"Now you keep that woman resting in her bed, 'Lijah." She drew her cape around her shoulders and discreetly pressed some money into his palm. "You care for her every day of the week, and don't you rest from that labor, not even on Sunday. I recall back in Nauvoo, I objected to Brother Joseph's request that we sing a popular song on the Sabbath. I told him, 'Why, Joseph, it's Sunday!' and he answered, 'The better the day, the better the deed.' Brother Abel, you do your good deeds for Sister Mary every day of the week. The better the day, the better the deed. I don't want to lose her, and I don't want you to lose her. I know too well how that feels."

He answered that he didn't think he could abide such a loss, but she didn't hear. She said she'd be sure Sister Mary received more visitors soon to clean the place up. (It was no surprise she would find the Abels' dwelling in need of cleaning, because she was the most fastidious women this side of the Rockies. Rachel Grant could slick up a kitchen faster and better than a cat licks its paws.)

"I'll take care of her best I can," Elijah said.

Whether she had heard or not, it made no difference. "And if we don't see you at church on Sunday," she said, "we'll know you're doing good works, just as the Savior would. If the ox is in the mire—"

"Yes, ma'am. I understand."

"I told the sisters we need a hospital for the sick closer at hand. Surely we could not be better engaged than in caring for the poor and the sick."

"You're a kind woman, Sister Grant," Elijah said. "I do thank you for this visit."

Apparently, she heard those words, for she replied, "You are most welcome."

Well, the kindness and the money might have helped, if Mary Ann's pneumonia hadn't turned the dark corner already.

By late November, her vigor had been drained, fever was roaring through her, and her skin was wearing the sheen of death. Despite Sister Grant's orders, she kept insisting on making Elijah's breakfast, until he commanded her to stay in bed, saying she wasn't to get out except for the most necessary deeds. He threatened to fetch Rachel Grant, if she didn't pay him mind. "I want all your energy on prayin' and healin'," he said.

She did as he asked and made several fine prayers for healing, as did Elijah.

Many people have prayed for many things, but God chooses his answers for his own reasons. Rachel Grant had made many prayers for her deafness to be cured too, but healing didn't come for Rachel Grant, and it didn't come for Mary Ann Abel. Soon, Mary Ann couldn't even find the strength to sit up in bed and hardly the strength to speak.

It was November 27, 1877—the day before Thanksgiving—when Elijah understood his wife was dying. He sat on the bed beside her.

Talk had never been the mortar of this marriage, and the two didn't talk much now. They just held hands, touched their heads together, and remembered. Elijah sometimes ran a cool rag over his wife's forehead. She worried that what she had was catching, but he would not leave her side.

"Reverend Abel," said Mary Ann, "I want you to know I'm glad you stopped by."

Elijah shrugged. "No trouble."

They gazed on each other a long while. "Honey, put your arm 'round me, would you please?" Mary Ann asked. "Lift me to you. Warm me 'gainst your chest."

Elijah did, then suggested they get under the covers. Beneath a patchwork quilt, he held her close, her head nestled under his chin.

Time ceased to be. They were together with their memories—the journeys they had taken across plain and prairie, bondage and freedom, sorrow and gladness. They were the only two people in this world who knew the details of their children's births. They were the only ones who knew all about the meals they had shared—the paltry ones of chit'lins and greens, and the richer ones when life was kind to their palates and they had eaten high on the hog—ham steaks and pork chops instead of pickled feet and snouts. They knew each other's bodies as God's sweetest gifts. They had tasted each other's tears.

Maybe hours passed, or maybe minutes, before she asked, "You know who I dreamed on last night?"

"If it was another man, I suggest you don't tell me," he whispered.

"Old Joseph of the Rainbow Coat."

Elijah pulled back and raised a brow at her, asking without asking if she was inventing tales.

"No, this was a fine dream," she said with some effort. "I 'spect God sent it. Ol' Joseph say for me to give you a message."

Elijah kissed his wife's forehead. Her flesh was still fevered. He wanted to cool it with the cloth, but she asked him not to leave her just yet. He could blow the sweat on her forehead to bring the fever down, she said, since she liked the smell of his breath anyway.

So he did that, steady and slow, as she told him, "Joseph think you been forgettin' him. He been waitin' on you years, and he gettin' tired."

He blew across her forehead one long, last time. "Well, if you dream on Ol' Joe tonight, tell him I found me a better-lookin' companion, and I aims to keep her."

She slept a little then but awoke with a start. " 'Lijah," she said, "I beg your pardon for anything I done to make you less happy than you mighta been."

"Honey, why you spendin' strength talkin' foolishness? Don't you know you ain't been nothin' but glad tidin's from the day I met you? No need of you beggin' my pardon for one thing on God's earth."

"I tried to make you a tolerable wife."

"You been better than tolerable. You are— Mary Ann, you won't leave me, will you?"

She winnowed his hair with her weak fingers. "Not permanent."

"Time without you would be mighty empty."

She slid her finger to his lip and soon was deep in slumber again.

Elijah left the bed as carefully as he could and went to his knees. He prayed in his mind, not aloud, for he wanted her to stay sleeping: *Lord, I don't know where my first woman is, or our baby. My brothers be lost to me somewheres in Canada. My mama's gone. Moroni's gone. Dear Lord, don't make me drink of this bitter cup, for I've had my fill. I need my wife, Lord. I can't do this life alone. You've required many things of me, and I beg you not to require this.*

Mary Ann stirred and felt the bed for him. "Where'd you go?" she breathed.

"I'm here, honey."

"You prayin'?"

"You mind?"

She said she didn't ever mind his prayers, but she felt cold without him holding her. She moved her hand over his head as he crawled back under the covers. "Put your fears aside," she murmured. "It's all right."

"I ain't afraid." But he held her so close she had to protest, saying he was squeezing too hard. He eased up and kissed her nose, her cheeks, her chin, gentle as he could. "I ain't afraid," he whispered.

Some hours later, Mary Ann Adams Abel passed away in her sleep. Elijah awoke to find her lifeless, her eyes half-open. He pressed his lips on hers—not just to kiss her but to give her his air and to find any of hers that he might coax back. She would not breathe again. He held her to him, his mouth opened to howl, but no sound came. At that moment, he knew how helpless he was.

He stayed with his wife's body, until morning was bright in the window and Enoch was at the door.

Nobody but God knows what Mary Ann's dying did to Elijah—the emptiness that seized him, the hollow stomach no food or drink could fill. There was no relaxing, only tension aching through his sinews. His every muscle felt stretched past its possibilities. Nothing earthly could salve his loss. He could not even build the coffin; Enoch did that.

Bishop Woolley presided, and Rachel Grant led the good sisters of the Thirteenth Ward in organizing songs for the service, draping the chapel door and podium in black and arranging a cornucopia of gourds to remind them of their bounty in the midst of their trials.

A recently returned missionary spoke at Mary Ann's funeral. Elijah would hear only a sentence or two before his mind would meander into melancholy paths. For the rest of his life, he could never recall the speaker's name.

"Sister Mary Ann was of the African descendancy," said the man.

Elijah wondered why that should matter and if the speaker didn't think they all knew about Mary Ann's lineage.

"Stanley the traveler has furnished the world with a complete map of the course of that mighty river, the Congo, down in Africa."

Elijah heard the songs the Abels had sung at the Platte River. He remembered that uneasy, life-giving Platte.

The Platte is so steady, but it can foam in swirls and currents without warning. Or it can be so still you question if it's moving at all. You never know. You think you know, but you never know. I am at the river today. I am at the Red Sea, and it ain't partin'. It's stagnant, breeding mosquitos to prick my flesh and get under my skin and prick my organs too. The river is covered in muck. I'd have to swish and dig and swish some more before I'd even find water, let alone dry ground so's I could walk myself to Canaanland. Lord, I want to be with her forever. Wherever she is, Lord, that's my promise land. Why are they stopping me in all this sludge of tradition? Why can't you part this river the way you parted it for Moses?

"The Congo will no longer be called by that name," the speaker was saying. "A fresh field is opened to missionary labor. The benighted tribes of the wilds of Africa will not long be left without the knowledge of the world's Redeemer."

Mary Ann was beautiful as Moses' Ethiope wife. She was graceful as Joseph's Egyptian woman. She held all the promise and all the faith of the widow of Sidon or Rahab of Jericho. There was nothing like night in her. She knew me in ways I didn't even know myself. How can I endure without her?

"In this, as in all the events which transpire on the earth, we recognize the finger of Providence. The curse pronounced on Ham thousands of years ago has been heavy upon his posterity. But in these latter days, the signs of the times portend the coming of sweet Mercy."

Her skin was gold. Her eyes were amber. Her cheeks were bronze. Will they never call her beautiful? My child bride. Lord, she was the best answer to prayer you gave me in all my days, and I wasn't even prayin' when there she was. What is it keeps my prayers from finding your throne now, when my eyes is sore and burnin' from lookin' through the clouds? Lord, I am seekin' so hard. I am knockin' at the gates of wherever you dwell and wherever you've hid up my wife.

"The emancipation of the colored race in the United States and opening up of the long hidden regions of interior Africa are indications of the workings of the Almighty towards the lifting up and final redemption of this branch of the human family."

We all shall know the truth, and the truth shall make us be free. I want them to see my wife and to know her glory. I want them to realize who she was and is. Lord, is it too much to ask?

"The fulness of the gospel may not reach them for years. But the angel which restored it to earth proclaimed the glad tidings that it should be preached 'to every nation and kindred and tongue and people.'"

Say her name.

"This is the great and last dispensation in which all that is hidden shall be disclosed, and all nations and lands with their history and relationship to each other will be made manifest."

She is my wife, the beginning of my days and the comfort of my nights. She is all the anguish this world has known and all the joy it might find. Her eyes saw me so clear. She could see me despite the clownin', minstrel paint on my face, despite my need to buy a place in a world that won't take me as a man. Her nose smelled the rankness of our son's disease, and she held his pain. She ministered to him like the angel I kept waitin' for. Why didn't I see her then as full as I'm seein' her now: Her breasts that fed our babies and made my slumber soft. Her hands, her legs, her private self. All, all, all of her. Say her name. Acknowledge my wife: Mary Ann Adams Abel.

"Happy is he," the speaker concluded, "who has eyes to see and a soul to understand the purposes of the Almighty and their manifestations throughout the world from day to day."

There was one more talk, more directly about Mary Ann and her kind soul. Two hymns were sung before the funeral cortege made its slow way to the cemetery.

The Abels followed the horse-drawn hearse in their shabby buggy. Elijah watched as the coffin was lowered into the ground. He ate the after-funeral meal without tasting it. Late that night, he returned to the grave and spread his body over the new-dug dirt. He wanted to feel peace but found anger moving in, possessing him, just as it had when he buried his mama so long ago.

Over the next months, he had moments when he felt to curse God and die. Often, he'd awake from a shallow slumber with his fists in the air, like he'd been pummeling angels.

He became a quiet man—every bit as quiet as Mary Ann had once been. He'd only eat if one of his daughters brought him food and waited until he finished it. He'd always been lean, but he became rawboned within weeks. His hair grew white, from root to stem. All of a sudden, he was old.

NOTES

The chapter title is from a traditional Negro spiritual found in Burleigh, *Spirituals*, 137.

Rachel Ridgway Ivins Grant, mother of Heber J. Grant, was the Relief Society president in the Thirteenth Ward and got along very well with Bishop Woolley. Both had Quaker background or Quaker family, and both were committed to caring for the poor. According to Walker, "Notwithstanding 'often having to endure insults,' the Relief Society block teachers canvassed the congregation to discover the needy and to secure for their relief an occasional cash donation. . . . During Rachel's three-and-a-half decade ministry, a time of scarcity and deflated dollars, the Thirteenth Ward Relief Society's liberality in cash and goods exceeded $7,750" ("Rachel R. Grant," 33). Rachel Grant is described and pictured in Slaughter, *Life in Zion*, 63.

Rachel Grant's deafness was her "greatest trial," occurring when she was almost fifty. Though she was not healed in her frequent attempts to find a miracle through temple baptism, her deafness had its advantages. It "insulated her from the family's quarrels [among Heber's children primarily] and prompted occasional humor. The children 'had no idea . . . how funny it was to see their angry faces and hear none of their words'" (Walker, "Rachel R. Grant," 33, 35).

Although in our story Rachel Grant refers to Mary Ann as "Mary," we cannot be certain what name she was most commonly called. Her tombstone in the Salt Lake City Cemetery, which is quite small, says "Mary Able." "Mother" is carved into the top of the stone. The epitaph, barely legible, says "Only sleeping."

Not long before Mary Ann's death, Rachel Grant is quoted as telling the Relief Society sisters of "the need of a hospital for the sick in our midst" and "we could not be better engaged than in caring for the poor" (Thirteenth Ward Relief Society Minutes, October 23, 1877).

The death of Mary Ann Abel on November 27, 1877, of pneumonia is recorded in the *Deseret News* and the Salt Lake City Death Records, 1848–84, GS 8,099, page 203 (Bringhurst, "Changing Status," 137).

The material presented as a talk at Mary Ann's funeral is actually from an article in the December 5, 1877, issue of the *Deseret News* (weekly), which was published within a week of Mary Ann's death. At the time, the Congo River was to have been renamed the "Lualaba," which, according to the newspaper report, was the name Livingston had assigned it.

37

GIVE ME JESUS

Unless a man shall endure to the end,
in following the example of the Son of the
living God, he cannot be saved.
2 NEPHI 31:16

Some Mormons call John Taylor the Champion of the Right. He was a man of humble English beginnings whose personal motto was "the kingdom of God or nothing." He had survived the attack at Carthage that snatched the lives of Joseph and Hyrum Smith, and he preached the gospel to the ends of the earth. With Brother Brigham gone, John Taylor inherited the reins of Church leadership.

He wore a beard like Brigham's, framing jaws and chin. His hair was white, and his heavy eyebrows overhung deep-set eyes.

Elijah respected him just as he had respected President Young, though it was no secret that Brother John, like Brother Brigham and most of the Saints and most Americans, didn't view the races as equal. Still, Elijah knew President Taylor had not approved of slavery. He had heard him talk about Africa as a "meadow of black flowers used to beautify white gardens"; heard him say that "traffic in human flesh made America less than an asylum for the oppressed."

Elijah was hopeful of a good answer to the question he had put to Bishop Woolley. He asked that it be raised now to President Taylor. More than anything in the world, he desired to be sealed to his wife forever, even though she had crossed the veil into God's realm.

Well, whether over sympathy for Elijah's plight or out of consideration for his faithfulness, several meetings got held to discuss the issue—and the issue soon expanded. Before long, it wasn't just over whether Elijah could have further temple blessings but whether he was entitled to the priesthood at all or whether he even held it. All sorts of questions were getting asked, and seemed every trail with a possible answer led back to a local patriarch: Brother Zebedee Coltrin. That created a problem, because sometimes Coltrin's memory wasn't quite right and sometimes it was flat wrong.

John Taylor had heard that Zebedee claimed personal knowledge of Joseph Smith saying Negroes could indeed hold the priesthood. So President Taylor went direct to the Coltrin residence in Spanish Fork to hear the report firsthand. He asked straight out, "Did the Prophet Joseph ever make such a statement to you?"

What he heard in reply was just the opposite of what he'd expected. Old Zebedee, now a poor, aged man with white hair flowing past his ears, said, "No sir. He never said anything of the kind in his life to me."

"What did he say?"

Brother Coltrin smiled. He enjoyed having the Church president right there in his home, asking for his help. "Oh, this argument goes back many decades—all the way to Nauvoo," he said. "The spring we went up in Zion's Camp in 1834, Brother Joseph sent John Green and me out south to gather up means. On our return home, we got in conversation about the Negro having the right to the priesthood, and I took up the side he had no right. Brother Green argued that he had. The subject got so warm between us that he said he would report me to Brother Joseph when we got home.

'All right,' said I, 'I hope you will.' And when we got to Kirtland, we both went to Brother Joseph's office together. Brother Green was as good as his word and reported to Brother Joseph that I said the Negro could not hold the priesthood. Oh, yes, I remember it like yesterday. Joseph Smith sort of bowed his head. Then he looked up at me, and he said, 'Brother Zebedee is correct. The Spirit saith the Negro can have no priesthood.' Now, I know Elijah Abel had priesthood—once. I believe it might've been a reward for the work he did on the temple. And you know, President Taylor, I was one of the seven presidents of the seventies. I heard the prophet say that no person with the least particle of Negro blood could hold the priesthood, so the moment Brother Joseph realized Elijah had Negro blood in him, the order came to drop him."

Then John Taylor asked a question that must have stung Zebedee Coltrin. "Brother Zebedee," he said, "you are not one of the seven presidents now. What have you been doing?"

Zebedee stiffened. He admitted he had been "ordered back" from his leadership position into the quorum of high priests. He was ready to defend himself, of course, and reported how it came about: There had been some arguing among the presidents of the seventy about who held the higher priesthood, a seventy or a high priest. When Joseph Smith heard about such contention, he directed the presidents get put back with the quorum of high priests.

"Other men were ordained to the presidency of seventies, and three apostatized," he pointed out. Then he resumed that other subject: "President Taylor, I washed and anointed Elijah Abel myself in the Kirtland temple. But in doing so, while I had my hands upon his head, I never had such unpleasant feelings in my life, and I said I never would again anoint another person who had Negro blood in him unless I was commanded by the Prophet to do so."

Well, those was the facts according to Zebedee Coltrin. You might wonder what answer President Taylor might've got if he'd asked John Green or Joseph Smith. The onlyest one telling this story now was Brother Zebedee. And it may strike you as silly that anyone would claim Joseph Smith hadn't realized Elijah was black. His race was revealed by his face. Besides that, Church leaders in Cincinnati had asked that he keep his preaching to the Negro population only. Don't seem there should've been any doubt about what he was. Even a chicken knows another chicken.

Apparently, John Taylor wasn't full trusting of Coltrin's answer either. Maybe there was just one too many contradiction in it. So he called another meeting, this one at Abraham O. Smoot's house in Provo. With him were John Nuttal, Brigham Young Jr., and—once again—Zebedee Coltrin.

Coltrin had a good many details nobody else seemed to remember receiving. Brother Smoot did add that Joseph Smith had instructed him to not ordain any slave to the priesthood.

That seemed to be all President Taylor needed to hear. He was ready to tell the Quorum of the Twelve what he had discovered and maybe set up a policy regarding blacks and the priesthood. But when he addressed the Quorum of the Twelve and announced what he had learned, a lone voice contradicted Zebedee's memory. That was Apostle Joseph F. Smith's voice.

Brother Smith, now wearing wire-rimmed glasses and a full beard, said it was no secret that slaves weren't ordained to the priesthood. Why, everyone knew that! Before freedom came, Mormon missionaries were instructed not to even baptize slaves without their masters' consent. But that policy applied to slaves, not all Negroes. The question of whether Elijah yet held the priesthood or had been "dropped" was answered easy. Joseph F. himself had seen two certificates verifying Elijah's status as a seventy—one of them issued in Salt Lake City. No, that good colored brother had never been booted from the Third Quorum. The apostle was sure of it.

The debate continued and eventually wound up right at Elijah's doorstep.

The Church's messenger was a young, bare-faced, blue-eyed

fellow. Elijah invited him inside his home, and they sat opposite each other before the fireplace, Elijah leaning in to catch every word, for he knew what was at stake.

The messenger reported what Zebedee Coltrin had said.

It took only a moment for Elijah to understand the direction this conversation would go. He could see the end from the beginning. He wasn't going to get any more temple blessings. What he hadn't seen coming was an attack on his right to priesthood or the questioning of his place in the Church. How could anyone believe Brother Joseph had dropped him from the Third Quorum of Seventies?

"I see," he said, but his mind was making more words than his mouth would utter: *I've buried their dead. My wife has nursed their babies. We've helped in every way we know how. I live my life to the highest degree I can. I try to carry myself as a priesthood holder should. Will they shut me out? Will they leave me lonely for eternity?*

Elijah swallowed and breathed deep to calm his voice before speaking. "The Prophet Joseph said I was entitled to the priesthood."

"Perhaps," said the messenger, "you were ordained before the word of the Lord was fully understood. Brother Coltrin suggested maybe you were given the priesthood as a reward for all the work you did on the Nauvoo temple. I hear you were one of the best workers there."

"Reward?" Elijah shook his head, feeling a stinging cold spread through every inch of his skin. He felt to chastize this young man but knew better than to start. So he quietly gave witness that Brother Zebedee's memory was incorrect. Zebedee Coltrin had not washed and anointed him. Another man had done that. Brother Zebedee had ordained him a seventy, though. "Besides," Elijah added, soft as he could, "priesthood ain't—is not—a reward for doing good works. Priesthood is God's gift, to be used for blessin' others. Who say the Lord give his power to somebody because they run good errands for him? My Lord Jesus never work in any such way!"

Their hearing is empty, and if I answer what my heart knows, they say I'm goin' against God. I've traveled this road before. I keep thinkin' it'll lead me somewhere, but it don't. Most every man puts up his own roadmark signs, tellin' his own ideas and traditions. One side of the sign say, "Love the ones who look like you" and the other side say to all us what don't fit that mold, "Stop walkin'."

"That's interesting information," said the young man. "Of course the Brethren will have to verify it."

Elijah held the chair arms tight. "I never been released from my priesthood. Around the time my wife passed two years ago, Bishop Woolley told me I was still a member of the Third Quorum of the Seventy. Bishop Woolley asked and got the answer."

There were more words in his head which he didn't speak: *Book of Mormon talk about there should be no 'ites' among us. It talk about one man not havin' more than another. Talk about if we don't have com-passion—charity—we don't have nothin'.*

The messenger asked if he might see the certificates that proved Elijah was a seventy. With nervous hands, Elijah produced the papers and gave them up. He felt he was surrendering his freedom documents and might never see them again.

"You'll be informed as soon as the matter is decided," said the messenger.

"Decided?"

All my life, these folks been 'deciding' my fate, thinkin' they know me soon as they see my skin. What they got to decide? Whether I can keep the gift the Lord give me? These people know the scriptures so good, but they can treat a man so bad. That African Brother—Gobo Fango, up to Idaho—his feet got froze 'cause they kept him out in the shed with no heat, like he was a animal. And now they slappin' me down as if there's a stink on my soul.

He wanted to tell this young man—this child—that he, Elijah Abel, had known and loved Joseph Smith and Joseph had known and loved him. Joseph's father had given him a blessing.

"My patriarchal blessing," he said slow, "promise me I'd be the weldin' link between the black and white races. 'Thou shalt be made equal to thy brethren.' That's what it say."

Standing, the messenger replied, "I'll refer the issue back to President Taylor."

It took all of Elijah's effort to see this visitor to the door. He said "Thank you," but in his mind were other words: *I'm so weary. I got me two names from the Bible, but I think my mama gave me the wrong one. She should've give me 'Job.'*

Yet another meeting was held with the Quorum of the Twelve. This time, Elijah's patriarchal blessing got read out loud. The words "Thou hast been ordained an Elder and anointed to secure thee against the power of the destroyer" put to rest any question about his ordination. His two certificates, which Joseph F. Smith presented, put to rest any question about Elijah's having been "dropped" from the quorum. The only thing in question was Zebedee Coltrin's memory.

Still, Elijah wasn't surprised when the presiding body of the Church all sustained John Taylor's decision that he could have no further temple blessings. He and Mary Ann could not be sealed.

It was a scorching, dry spring and summer, with crops burning and grasshoppers clasping every shoot of harvest, whittling away at the grain. The following winter was the worst the Saints had endured since their arrival. Thousands of cows and sheep froze to death. For Elijah, it seemed the heavens were spreading his feelings over all of Utah. Could it even be a punishment? He did not want to think it, though the sting of his denial would fester for the remainder of his life. But it would not whip him from the Church. Elijah knew who he was, and he knew the Lord. The final word would belong to God, and God would not be thwarted.

In 1880, when the Church celebrated the jubilee of the gospel's restoration, Elijah cheered the wagon that carried many Latter-day Saint leaders—most of them his acquaintances from Kirtland and Nauvoo days: Wilford Woodruff, Orson Pratt, Charles Rich, Erastus Snow, Joseph Young, John Brown, Thomas Bullock, H. K. Whitney, Truman Angell, Thomas Grover, and Zebedee Coltrin. He knew what Brother Zebedee had said about him and knew that Charles Rich and John Brown had been slaveholders. But this was the year of jubilee. John Taylor had reminded all Latter-day Saints that ancient Israel used the jubilee year to cancel the debtor's debt, to set the captive free, to relieve the oppressed. It was a time of forgiveness.

Elijah remembered the great Sojourner Truth testifying that Jesus had seared her heart and lit up her life so much that she could love "even the white man." He yearned for enough solace in his soul to fully love and freely forgive. He could hear Sojourner's voice— or maybe it was his mother's, or maybe Mary Ann's. He couldn't be sure whose voice it was, for it was distant as a star, though the words were clear enough: "This is Jesus. *This is Jesus.*"

"Lord," Elijah prayed, "uncanker my soul. Unburden me of my anger. I am puttin' it on the altar. It's been takin' up much space inside me, and I ask you fill that space with somethin' better."

NOTES

The chapter title is from a traditional Negro spiritual found in Burleigh, *Spirituals*, 39.

The description of John Taylor's life history is from *Church History in the Fulness of Times*, 422–23. His characterization of Africa as "a meadow of black flowers used to beautify white gardens" and his statement on "traffic in human flesh" are quoted in Bringhurst, *Saints, Slaves, and Blacks*, 57.

Zebedee Coltrin's words are recorded in L. John Nuttal's journal. (Nuttal was an assistant to President Taylor, as well as his son-in-law.) Coltrin's report is as follows: "The spring that we went up in Zion's camp in 1834, Brother Joseph sent Bro. J. [John] P. Green and me out south to gather up means. . . . On our return home we got in conversation about the Negro having a right to the priesthood—and I took the side he had no right. Bro. Green argued that he had. . . . When we got home to Kirtland, we both went in Bro. Joseph's office together to make our returns. Bro. Green reported to Bro. Joseph that I had said that the Negro could not hold the priesthood. Brother Joseph kind of dropped his head and rested it on his hand for a minute. And then said Bro. Zebedee is right, for the Spirit of the Lord saith the Negro had no right nor cannot hold the priesthood" (qtd. in Stephens, "Life and Contributions of Zebedee Coltrin," 54; spelling and punctuation standardized).

The conversation (recorded by John Nuttal) between John Taylor and Zebedee Coltrin, including Taylor's question as to why Coltrin had been released from his former position, is from Berrett, "Church and the Negroid People," 9–11.

Coltrin, who was a popular speaker in Spanish Fork (his residence) on Pioneer Day during the 1870s and who frequently shared remarkable spiritual experiences with his high priests quorum (remembered from forty years past), gave many accounts of experiences with Joseph Smith or with divine beings, only a few of which we have been able to corroborate. What is very clear is that Coltrin was wrong that "when Joseph Smith learned of Elijah Abel's lineage, he was dropped from the third quorum of seventy" (Nuttal journal, 281, qtd. in Stephens, "Life and Contributions of Zebedee Coltrin," 55). That false memory also calls into question other things he said at the time, including that Joseph Smith had said "no person having the least particle of Negro blood can hold the priesthood" (qtd. in Stephens, "Life and Contributions of Zebedee Coltrin," 55). Coltrin died July 21, 1887 (Stephens, "Life and Contributions of Zebedee Coltrin," 90).

The record of those attending the May 31, 1879, meeting at Abraham O. Smoot's house is from Stephens, "Life and Contributions of Zebedee Coltrin," 54. Smoot, former mayor of Salt Lake City and (at the time of the meeting) mayor of Provo, had also been a slaveholder. A woman named Duritha Trail Lewis (1813–78) had "sold the [two] women slaves to Reed Smoot's father [Abraham O. Smoot] . . . and with what she received from them and what she had left from her inheritance, she bought a small house and ten acres of land where the City and County building [Salt Lake City] now stands" (Lewis, "Life Sketch of Duritha Trail Lewis"). Interestingly, the purchase of the property where Salt Lake's City and County Building now stands was financed by the sale of slaves.

Joseph F. Smith recollected that Abel had *not* been dropped from the Third Quorum of the Seventy—on account of lineage or any other issue—because Smith himself had seen his "certifications as a seventy issued in 1841 and again in Salt Lake City" (Bush, "Mormonism's Negro Doctrine," 76). The history of the Third Quorum of the Seventy (December 20, 1836) states that Abel was originally ordained by Coltrin on December 20, 1836 (qtd. in Stephens, "Life and Contributions of Zebedee Coltrin," 56). The 1841 certificate would have been a recertification, as would the certificate issued to Abel in Salt Lake City.

The portion of Abel's patriarchal blessing cited in this chapter (and indeed read at the last meeting to determine the outcome of Elijah's petition) is cited in Bringhurst, "Changing Status," 131.

Abel's claim that "the Prophet Joseph told him he was entitled to the priesthood" is noted in Bush, "Mormonism's Negro Doctrine," 76–77.

That Elijah Abel "continued to be accepted as a member of the Third Quorum of Seventies as late as 1883" is recorded in Bringhurst, "Changing Status," 138. John Taylor "tried to reconcile the conflicting views of Abel, Apostle Smith, and Coltrin by suggesting that Abel had 'been ordained before the word of the Lord was fully understood.' Abel's ordination, therefore, was allowed to stand" (Bringhurst, "Changing Status," 139).

Gobo Fango was a South African man who was smuggled onto an English ship under the skirts of a Mormon immigrant. As Carter (*Negro Pioneer*, 49) records the J. Austin Hunter account: "He lived in Kaysville with the Lewis Whitesides family who had secured him from a family named Talbot, Utah pioneers of 1861. After he reached puberty, he was asked to sleep outside in a shed in cold weather, and his feet were frozen. As a result, he limped all his life." Gobo moved to Oakley, Idaho, around 1880 as a hired man for the family of Mary Ann Whitesides Hunter (sister to Lewis Whitesides). Gobo was eventually murdered. Though the assailants were known, they were never convicted. Their first trial ended in a mistrial; their second in acquittal. The jury found that Gobo's killers had shot and killed Gobo in "self defense," though Gobo had been unarmed. Carter (*Negro Pioneer*, 49) cites the folklore that Gobo wrote his will in his own blood, deeding all his money to the Hunter family and the Grantsville Relief Society. In fact, he did not write his will in his own blood but did ask that much of his money be donated to the building of the Salt Lake Temple.

Details about Utah's Jubilee celebration during which "President Taylor resolved . . . 'that we ought to do something, as they did in former times, to relieve those that are oppressed with debt, to assist those that are needy, to break off the yoke of those that may feel themselves crowded upon and to make it a time of general rejoicing'" are from Roberts, *Life of John Taylor*, 333.

The names of the Church leaders in the lead wagon in the parade are from Stephens, "Life and Contributions of Zebedee Coltrin," 81.

The Judge
Arrives
1883

38

HANGMAN JOHNNY

For after this manner doth the devil work,
for he persuadeth no man to do good,
no, not one.
MORONI 7:17

Sam Joe Harvey was in his mid-thirties by the time he got to
Utah. We can't even guess all he'd seen during his soldiering years,
but anyone who knows war can scarce forget its reeking sights.

When the white soldiers went back to their lives, they were still
men. They hadn't lost any luster but gained it as veterans, whether
winners or losers. Negroes found something different. For them,
many things hadn't changed. They weren't slaves any longer, but
they still weren't men. They were yet expected to answer to the
name "boy." Even whites who had treated them with some respect
during the war disregarded them once life turned away from battle.
Slavery was no more—at least not on the books. But where was a
former slave to go?

Some, including Sam Joe, remained in the army and became
known as Buffalo Soldiers. The army paid them thirteen dollars a
month to fight other dark folks—the Indians: Cheyenne, Comanche,

331

Kiowa, Apache, Ute, and Sioux. It was a desolate life, but Sam Joe had nothing else to fall back on. His long association with the military even netted him the name "U.S. Harvey."

But after years of being in uniform, Sam wanted something besides sitting astride a horse or marching. He hadn't upped in rank, and his record was marked with visits to the stockade, all because he rubbed everybody the wrong way. Seemed there was a blister on his heart, and it made him want to fight everything. He provoked most of the scraps. If ever there was a man in need of repose, Sam Joe was that man. But nothing could soothe him, not even a loving woman.

He had tried marriage a time or two but couldn't keep anger from bursting out of him and spreading poison. He wanted the world a certain way, and if it was different, he was as like to pull a gun as smile. There was no warmth in this man other than the heat of rage. He had lost hope and stopped trusting anyone years ago. Maybe he was crazy. Or maybe he was just one of those restless souls who needed a place to set. But no place gave him comfort for long.

The year 1883 found him tired and yearning for a permanent settling place. He had tried Colorado, but nothing worked out, likely because he found trouble easy as babies find dirt.

He ventured to Ogden but found only a fight there, and someone robbed him besides. So, narrowing his eyes at the whole world lest it take him for a fool, Sam Joe moved to Salt Lake.

Sylvester James discovered him eating thistle roots and rummaging through the trash one August morning, looking half-crazed and half-starved. Even when Syl offered him some lunch at Jane's, Sam Joe glared at him: "What you want?"

"Jus' tryin' to help," Syl answered. "You must be hungry, scrounging for food like you are. And I don't want nothin' from you. From the looks of it, you ain't got nothin' to give."

"I got no money for food," Sam Joe said. (Now, it turned out this was a lie. He had quite a bit of money but wasn't about to place himself in position to get robbed again.)

"I'm makin' you a offer."

Sam Joe grunted and then followed Syl to Jane's house, checking behind him all the time just in case someone was sneaking up.

Of course, Syl's own wife would've been happy to feed this man, but Jane James was an expert at it and would've felt slighted if Syl hadn't brought this stranger to her first. Jane believed in welcoming the homeless, knowing she might be entertaining angels or even the Lord himself. It wasn't fancy food, but Sam Joe gulped it down like he might never eat again.

"My," said Jane. "You got a appetite, all right."

By this time, Jane was in her sixties. Her hair wore many silver threads, and her joints buckled whenever the sky stormed. But cooking was still a good part of her life, and she'd do it until those hands were folded across her chest in the coffin. She did love taking care of folks the world put aside—especially colored folks.

"You got family?" she asked.

He shook his head no.

Jane understood that slavery had likely stole his kin. He didn't seem eager to talk about that or anything else.

Sam Joe spent the night in the James home and the next morning was ready to find work.

These were the ugly hot, dog days of August. Not the best time to be out looking for work. Especially for someone like Sam Joe Harvey. This kind of heat not only affected the body but the mind.

Jane knew of some folks seeking laborers. Francis Grice, a fairly well-off, colored restaurant owner, might connect him with a job.

It all sounded good, so Sam Joe legged out to meet Mr. Grice.

Indeed, there was work available, and it paid two dollars a day, which was a sight more than army pay. Sam Joe said he'd take it, but everything came apart when Grice announced it was farm work, some twelve miles outside of town. Sam Joe had thought he'd be helping in the restaurant. He had no desire to be ploughing and weeding and pitching hay—not in this heat, or at any other time of year, for that matter.

"I ain't lookin' to be no farmer," he said. "Lookin' for better than that."

"I thought you wanted a job," Grice answered. "You the one seekin' work."

"You fixin' to put me back on the plantation. No, I won't take slave labor. I had my fill of that and more. What you got I can do here in the restaurant?"

"Boy, I ain't got no plantation, and I ain't got no job here in the restaurant. Now if you wants to work, I got work. But if you just wants to sit on your hind parts and wait for somethin' to fall in your pocket, you'd better keep steppin'. Negro like you wants everything give to him."

Sam narrowed his eyes till they were thin bands of white. "What you mean, 'Negro like me'?"

Grice turned away. "I don't need your foolishness. I was trying to help because Mizz Jane sent you, but you can just trot your black behind out of here."

"Don't you turn your back on me!" Sam yelled.

"I said for you to get out of here! I'll turn my back on you, or I'll turn my gun on you if you don't get out."

That was all Sam Joe needed. He pulled his pistol and cussed. "Don't you threaten me, old man. I've shot more men than you've fed, and it wouldn't bother me a nickel to shoot one more. You must be out of your natural mind to talk about a gun you ain't even got in your hand."

There's nothing like looking down a barrel to make you reconsider your options. Grice decided to be quiet. The two men stared each other down in that raw silence, as Sam Joe backed out the door, muttering at the threshold, "Old fool."

By this year, telephone lines were up in Utah. The moment

Sam was out of sight, Francis Grice went to the nearest telephone—at a fire station down the block.

Now, Sam may have been out of sight, but he hadn't gone far. He watched Grice leave his store and knew trouble was on its way. His military training kicked in. He wanted more fire power. Sam Joe Harvey headed to the hardware store he had spotted earlier and purchased a rifle and shells. Twenty dollars for the repeater and two boxes of cartridges. He spilled one box as soon as the store-keeper handed it over and then scooped the bullets into his pocket and bolted out the door.

The phone call Grice made was to the marshal, Andrew Burt—the same Andrew Burt who had once jailed Moroni Abel.

The marshal decided that before confronting this hot-headed black man, it might serve to bring Elijah, who'd likely know something of the newcomer, or have some sway should things turn nasty. So Burt galloped his horse to the Abels' place.

Elijah answered the door, and there stood the marshal.

Andrew Hill Burt was a red-headed Scotsman with three wives and a whole mess of children. And he was not merely a policeman now but captain of the entire police force. He was also bishop of the Twenty-first Ward of Salt Lake City. Right now, he wore the expression he'd grown accustomed to: devil-may-care authority. Of course, Burt had no idea that Elijah Abel ever blamed him for a thing. More than likely, Burt didn't even know Moroni had died.

"Abel, we've got a situation," the marshal said. "You know anything about this new fellow in town—Sam Harvey? He stayed last night over at Aunt Jane's."

"Don't know him at all," Elijah answered.

"He's one of your people."

Elijah already figured this "new fellow" had to be colored, otherwise the marshal wouldn't be at his door. One of your people.

"What's he done?" Elijah asked.

"Oh, I got a call from Francis. Said the man was over to the restaurant looking for a job. Seems he and Grice had words, and Harvey wound up pulling a gun. I'm heading there now, and I'd like you to come along."

Elijah had just returned from his son's place and had felt to leave Old Creamy saddled after the ride. Now he understood why. The Lord knew what was coming. Elijah was to be of some use.

They rode quick to Grice's, where a crowd had already gathered. One of the men called, "You looking for that Negro, marshal? I saw him head toward the hardware."

Another added, "I saw him head down the alley."

Charles Wilcken, that old German convert who had deserted Johnston's army years before and was now the water master, stepped forward. "He has a rifle."

Burt asked if Harvey had said anything about where he was going. Grice reported that all Harvey had said was "old fool."

Wilcken offered to join the chase. His horse was ready to go.

"Fine," said Burt. "I could use another set of eyes. Grice, you come too. Hop up behind Abel on his mount. I want you to identify this troublemaker, though he shouldn't be hard to spot."

Indeed, he wasn't. Sam was quick-stepping it down the alley, rifle in hand. His eyes were darting every which way, for he figured he must be under pursuit and hoped to see his hunters before they saw him. He also wanted to find the easiest road out of town.

When they caught up with him, Grice pointed and yelled, "Marshal Burt, that's the man," as though anyone needed to be told.

Sam picked up his pace and cut through the ground between two buildings. The posse—the number had grown by now to seven—moved their mounts through the alley and up the street to head him off.

In front of the pharmacy, Sam Joe found himself cornered like a cougar up a tree. Marshal Burt called, "Hold on there, boy. I want to talk to you."

Sam swivelled his head right and left, surveying every possible path out of this fix. Every possible path was blocked by a horseman. He set his eyes at last on Andrew Burt.

Whether he was acting or in earnest, the marshal gave off the air of a man in complete control. He dismounted, as did Wilcken, Grice, and Abel.

"Grice said you pulled a pistol on him. That true?" Burt asked.

Sam stood defiant. "And if I did?"

"I'd suggest you cooperate and keep that smart mouth to yourself. Now hand over the rifle." Burt reached out like he truly expected Harvey would tuck tail and deliver up his weapon.

Sam stiffened as though he had been called to attention. "You a officer?" His mouth hardly moved.

"I am. I'm the marshal. Now hand over that rifle or lay it down, one of the two."

Sam's lips split into a strange smile as he raised his rifle smooth and steady, showing all his war-gained experience.

Before Elijah's eyes was Andrew Burt's destiny. Sam was aiming his rifle at the very policeman who had placed Moroni in that disease-breeding jail. For the first time, Elijah saw naked fear in the Scotsman's face. Many years ago, Elijah might've wished for such a scene as this, but now he was genuinely concerned for the man's life. The marshal was trying to act like he was still in charge, but he was a fool for doing it. Burt maybe couldn't see the depth of Harvey's rage. Elijah could. Here was an ex-soldier, an ex-slave, a colored man in a white man's world. Here was a man who had reached his limit and was primed to go over the edge and take someone with him.

"Son, you don't want to do this," Elijah called. "Ain't no need for this." He took a step toward Harvey.

The moment passed so slow. Elijah saw his own hand lift like a ghost's, heard his own voice as though from far away, "Son, do as the marshal tellin' you."

He was answered by a flash of light, the ear-stopping crack of the muzzle, and a plume of smoke that quickly spread into thin haze.

Andrew Burt was lifted clean off his feet, sideways. Then he was on the ground, arms jerking. Charles Wilcken sprang to the rifle, grabbing the barrel with one hand and Harvey's neck with the other. Harvey used his free hand to pull his revolver and aim it at the water master's heart.

There stood Elijah Abel, an arm's length away from the pistol. As Sam struggled to cock the hammer, Elijah lunged. Old though he was, Elijah still had the strength of a plough horse. He grabbed that gun the moment it fired, diverting it enough that the ball met Wilcken's arm instead of his chest. Just above the old German's elbow, a bloody fountain splattered drops on Elijah's hand as he wrestled the gun away from Harvey. The ex-missionary tackled the ex-soldier and threw him down, shouting, "What have you done?" Other men at the scene grabbed Sam, who was thrashing under Elijah's weight and cursing. They held him tight. There was no chance Sam Harvey would escape now.

During the ruckus, Marshal Burt had managed to pull himself into the drugstore. That was where Elijah found him.

"Now you hold on, Brother Burt," Elijah begged. "Gather your faith, and you hold on!"

Burt was already frothing pink foam at the mouth. His white face was getting whiter. Despite anything in the past, Andrew Burt's suffering wrenched Elijah's heart. But even more wrenching was the certainty that the police captain would pass beyond them to his glory and the looming premonition of what would follow here below, in Utah.

"Don't die," Elijah pleaded. "Please—you must not die!"

The nearest doctor—Brother Benedict—was called in. By the time he got there, the store front and street were crowded with gawkers, asking each other for details nobody was sure of yet. They cleared a path for Doctor Benedict and then went silent.

Elijah held the marshal's head in his lap and heard the final breath of the man he had once hated, heard that terrible rattle that said all was lost.

The doctor stood and pronounced what nobody needed to be told: "Bishop Burt has been killed." He went outside and repeated the same words. Then he asked that someone call for a wagon.

The crowd let out a singular gasp as though they was all one person.

That was the very moment Judge Lynch landed in Utah.

One voice shouted, "Hang 'im!"

Another shouted, "Hangin's too quick! I say burn 'im!"

Outside, Elijah Abel lifted both his hands, red with Marshal Burt's blood. He cried, "People! Brothers and sisters! We can't want lynchin' in Zion!" No matter how loud his voice, he would not be heard.

Sam Harvey was hog-tied on the ground, five men standing guard. Elijah walked toward him, met his familiar, defeated eyes, and then turned away.

"We'll need you to make a report, Abel," someone said. "Get the James folks too."

"Why do you want them?"

"They were the ones sent him to Grice, weren't they?"

"Can I change my clothes first? The marshal's blood—"

"Change and then get to the city building."

Two wagons arrived: one for Bishop Burt's body and one for Sam Joe Harvey, who was taken to city hall and searched. The ropes got replaced by handcuffs and shackles. The officers found $165.80 on him—a good deal of it gold and silver. One of the policemen eyed him calmly and then swung him around and hit him hard in the kidney. Sam dropped, and another man kicked him in the groin. Another kicked his face, and then they all were slugging and kicking him. Every person was a friend of Andrew Burt's, and every insult they gave Harvey's body was in the marshal's memory. Each man wanted to crack a rib "for Andrew." When the beating ended, Harvey was near dead already, but folks outside were still calling for a rope.

Word spread fast. By the time Elijah had changed clothes and gone for Jane and Syl, the crowd outside city hall had become a restless mob, growing by the minute. Within an hour, more than a thousand stoked-up people were in the yard, screaming curses and clamoring for "justice." Elijah's voice would certainly not be heard now.

The mob was so thick, he knew he couldn't get to the building. When someone demanded "Were they part of it?" and pointed to him and the Jameses, he realized all the colored folk in Salt Lake City were at risk. They needed to stay quiet and inconspicuous. So he led Jane and Syl across the street to safety behind a cottonwood. He suggested they have a quick word of prayer that God would calm these folks, for the soul of every person here was in danger if they got what they were demanding.

"Don't let this scourge come upon this people," Elijah prayed. "None of this is godly. None of this is saintly."

An officer came to the jail door, jittery and fumbling. The mob had built to near two thousand folks by this time, all using different voices but mostly the same words: "Where's the rope? Hang the nigger!"

When the officer instructed the crowd to disperse, a gang of well-dressed men shoved him aside.

Then someone in the jail pushed Sam Joe Harvey out the door. Harness straps were cut off horse teams, to be used as whips. A long rope began floating above the crowd, a hundred hands thrusting it forward. Some of us think it was Judge Lynch himself guiding that rope, dragging it over the crowd so that many hands might touch it and get condemned.

The last set of hands to touch it belonged to Tom Thomas,

Annie's husband, who Jane James had known since Winter Quarters. It was Tom Thomas who noosed Sam Joe's neck.

Jane shrieked, "Brother Thomas—no!"

As soon as Sam's neck was noosed, a policeman freed him from the handcuffs. The mob wanted to watch this Negro flail. A gang threw the rope over the closest branch and hoisted him up. Then they tied the rope to a hitching post. Sam tried to get the rope off his neck, his legs kicking at air. Two boys climbed some nearby benches and hit his arms until he lost his grip. He struggled and then just swung there, his eyes stuck up in his head like he was looking for God. But still, the mob was not content.

"Cut him down and drag him!" someone yelled.

Others responded like mad echoes, "Drag him! Drag him!"

Three men cut him down and tied his feet to the back of a freight wagon. Part of the crowd clambered into the wagon to lead this parade. A driver whipped the two horses, and the mob watched Sam's body get dragged through the streets. They followed, cheering all the way.

Elijah and the Jameses were holding each other tight. They were maybe the only three people of the two thousand who were crying. Sylvester had retched at the sight of Sam Joe's struggle, and there was vomit on his lips. "Ain't no justice here," Syl said.

Now, I don't know what all Syl had suffered in his life, and I doubt we can imagine how often despair had snuffed out his hope. What I do know is that when Syl spoke those words, something inside him broke and was released. Sylvester James had shed his faith.

NOTES

The chapter title is from a traditional Negro spiritual cited in Higginson, "Negro Spirituals," 693.

The Buffalo Soldiers got their name from Indians who thought "their hair resembled the shaggy coats of the buffalo." They were paid thirteen dollars a month plus rations to fight various Indian tribes, according to Schlissel, *Black Frontiers*, 54–55.

Most of the details on the Sam Joe Harvey lynching—including the presence of Elijah Abel, who did indeed wrestle the pistol from Harvey's grip—are from Schindler, *In Another Time*, 166–69. Other details, including the specifics of the lynching, come from Ron Coleman's fine research, which he generously shared. Many of the particulars are from newspaper accounts, which, in the fashion typical of the time, spared no detail in describing the gore of violent events.

By the time of the August 23, 1883, incident, Charles Wilcken was Salt Lake City's water master and "special police officer" (Seifrit, "Charles Henry Wilcken," 314). Wilcken was a large man and had served as a bodyguard to Brigham Young and John Taylor and was a close friend of George Q. Cannon. Seifrit says of Wilcken's involvement: "Wilcken had been summoned to subdue and take into custody a violent man, drunk, who was causing a disturbance and threatening citizens with a gun. During the fray Burt was shot and killed and Wilcken suffered a serious gunshot wound but nevertheless managed to subdue the gunman. He was unable, however, to prevent a mob from taking the prisoner from jail and lynching him" ("Charles Henry Wilcken," 314).

We do not know what involvement, if any, the James family had with Sam Joe Harvey. We do know that the Grice family was involved as this chapter records.

The history of the Salt Lake Twenty-First Ward (of which Andrew Burt was the first bishop), as recorded in Jenson, *Latter-day Saint Biographical Encyclopedia* (754), says of "Bishop Burt" merely that he "was killed by a Negro."

39

AWAY OVER JORDAN

For behold, are we not all beggars? Do we not
all depend upon the same Being, even God,
for all the substance which we have?
MOSIAH 4:19

When Annie Thomas herself came to Jane's door to pick up the laundry, Jane knew exactly what would happen.

It was plain Annie had been crying. Jane would make this easy for her.

"Why, Mizz Annie! You come all this way to pick up the wash, when I was set to tote it to you my own self. I ain't so old I can't do my work. And don't you look fine in that green silk and parasol! How is it you never seems to age?"

One thing Jane never commented on was how Annie had kept her figure. It was a sore wound, for Annie would gladly have given up her waistline for a child. She was still good looking, even in her fifties. Her hair, worn up loose, had gone a pretty, shimmery silver. She always looked happy, because her face wrinkles curved up.

"And look at that bonnet!" Jane said. "I never will know how they make them red ribbons appear so much like roses. So real lookin', you'd think they'd send out perfume."

Annie touched her bonnet. Usually she was bubbling with things to say. Today she was restrained. "Mister Thomas bought this for me last time he was in St. George with Ruth—another of his wives. They have a silk farm in St. George."

"Is that a fact? And he bought you that bonnet?"

"The dress too. To celebrate another birth. Ruth was safely delivered of a baby girl three weeks ago."

"Praise the Lord for that. Ain't that a blessin'! And ain't that somethin' he'd include you in the celebration? Now won't you step inside, Mizz Annie, after you come all this ways on such a hot afternoon?"

"I'm sorry. I can't. Jane, because of what happened—"

Jane grew sober. "Ma'am, I know you had nothin' to do with that."

Annie spoke rapidly and looked around herself every now and again. "I don't want you to think my husband is a bad or a violent man. He's not bad, and I would never wish to criticize him. Only I wanted to say something and I didn't know where I could say it, so I came here. I suppose you know he was with that mob."

"Yes, ma'am, I do."

"I don't understand whatever induced him to behave so. He has always been a kind man. You know that."

In fact, Jane did *not* know that, for she had seen some bruises on Annie's arms that looked to come from a man's grip. But she knew better than to mention such a thing now.

"Myself," said Annie, "I think the mob was on par with the murderer. I cannot imagine Tom would have participated in any way except for the mob fever and the fact he loved Andrew. But it hasn't benefited Brother Burt or his family to do this thing, has it? And for it to happen in our city—in the shadow of the temple—it doesn't show a Christian feeling."

"I agree with you," Jane murmured.

Annie glanced around herself again and whispered, "I attended the funeral for Brother Burt. Joseph F. Smith—Hyrum's son—spoke. So did none other than President John Taylor."

"I seen the carriages on their way to the funeral. Must've been eighty or more. But I— Well, I wasn't acquainted with Brother Burt, so I didn't feel I should attend."

"Probably a thousand folks went to that funeral, whether they knew Bishop Burt or not. And I want you to know, Apostle Smith condemned the mob, Jane. So did President Taylor. Condemned it hard. They both said all men should have the recourse of the law." Annie fanned her face with her hand.

"Ma'am, it's awful hot outside. Won't you come in? I'd be honored to pour you a glass of water."

"I'm sorry, but I can't enter your home or partake of your hospitality. Forgive me. I do appreciate the offer. What I wanted to say is—and I mean no criticism of my husband—only I don't comprehend what happened to him that day. Sometimes menfolk get riled up and before you know it, somebody's dead. You must know that better than I do."

"Yes," murmured Jane. "I lived in Nauvoo."

"Now, I'm not suggesting the nigger didn't get what he deserved—but he had no trial! He should've had a trial. That's all I'm saying."

"I believe the same thing."

Annie stiffened. "And now, I need to pick up my laundry. I'm hoping you've had a chance to finish it."

Jane had been braced for those words from the moment she opened the door. "I was fixing to take it to you tomorrow, Mizz Annie. Thursday, like always."

Annie looked away. "That's the other thing. I can't accept your services as our laundress any longer. Mister Thomas won't allow it. Now, I haven't changed my mind about your talent, and I doubt I'll find your match anywhere in the Valley, but Mister Thomas will not permit a Negro woman—"

"No need to explain things, ma'am. I only wish I'da knowed you was comin'. I'da ironed everything. Ain't ironed none of it. Ain't had the chance."

Annie produced a tight smile. "I'll find somebody else to finish it. Tom's got someone in mind already. I have my buggy set to take it from you now. Maybe this will give you more time to do things you've been wanting to do. You won't have to worry about washing our clothes, so maybe you can write poetry. Wouldn't that be something if you could write poems? We'd have you and Sister Eliza Snow both. Two kinds of Mormon poets."

Jane matched Annie's smile as best she could. "I never got schoolin' in how to write," she said. "A lot of us coloreds missed out on some learnin'. I can read passable good, but I never learned writin'."

"Why, I could teach you!" Annie volunteered this before she could catch herself. She clapped her hand over her mouth as soon as the words were out. Her cheeks were blushing fierce. "Not just yet, of course. The mood must change some first. I know you understand that."

"Yes, ma'am. I certainly do."

"But times will get back to normal. I'd imagine you have tales from all over, and wouldn't that be something if you could write them down?" For the first time, Annie was smiling like she meant it.

"Yes, ma'am," Jane said. She excused herself to fetch the laundry and toted it to the buggy.

Annie had spread her parasol and was feeding the horse a handful of grass. She gave Jane some money—more than the usual. When Jane tried to return the extra, Annie refused to accept it. She assured Jane they were friends, and should they meet in the street someday, they would be friendly.

Jane answered the only words her mouth would make at this moment: "Yes, ma'am." She did not mention that all the money she had in this world came from washing white folks' clothes. Losing customers was inviting greater hardship. The bit of extra money Annie had left would tide them over for only a few days. The Relief Society provided her a Christmas basket every year, containing meat, sugar, dried fruits, and such, but Jane's supply was meager indeed. By now, she had not only Jessie to support (the only one of her surviving children still living at home) but grandchildren as well from the daughters she had lost. And she could not predict if Annie's action would be the first of many others.

As you might suspect, Jane was not the only one to feel the ripples from Harvey's lynching. It wasn't long before the Grices were accused of poisoning nine colts belonging to their neighbor. There was no real evidence that Grice was responsible, but evidence didn't seem to matter. Nobody would visit the restaurant, and the Grices heard muttered curses wherever they went. Though Francis and Martha Grice had been making a tolerable living, they couldn't do a thing now. There was no choice but to move.

They settled near Boise, Idaho, abandoning the fine house they had built together. It stayed vacant for years and was eventually torn down. Folks learned later and beyond any doubt that Grice was innocent of the poisoning, but it was too late. That Negro family was gone.

Just about every colored person in Salt Lake City felt the heat of mob fever, even after Sam Joe Harvey was cold in his grave.

NOTES

The chapter title is from a traditional Negro spiritual cited in Cone, *Spirituals and the Blues*, 59.

Though the lynching mob numbered nearly two thousand, many of them members of Bishop Burt's own ward, there were certainly many in Utah who deplored the action. Some of the words we have attributed to Annie Thomas are actually from statements of pioneers recorded in Carter, *Heart Throbs of the West*, 11:194. Said Rachel Emma Woolley Simmons, daughter of Elijah Abel's Thirteenth Ward bishop, Edwin D. Woolley: "A tragedy. One of the saddest events happened last Saturday, August 25, ending the life of . . . Andrew Burt, [who] was shot by a negro that he was called to arrest. As he came near, the Negro fired and killed him instantly. This enraged the bystanders to such frenzy that they lynched the murderer on the spot. Although he deserved to lose his life, I didn't think it was right to take such vengeance. I am thankful there were none of my family engaged in the affair. I think the mob were on a par with the murderer. The Lord will deal with them as He sees fit—it hasn't benefited Brother Burt or his family to do this thing as it was done. I am sorry it happened in our city, it don't show a Christian feeling. . . . I attended the funeral of our brother [Andrew Burt]. The exercises were conducted as usual on such occasions. Brother Joseph F. Smith preached the sermon. . . . Brother Taylor followed Brother Smith condemning the way in which the mob acted. He spoke my mind exactly; he wanted all men to have the benefit of the law. There were thousands at the funeral—near eighty carriages went to the cemetery."

In like manner, the *Salt Lake Tribune* editorialized that the lynching "was done under the noon day sun and in the shadow of the temple of the Saints. We do not believe there has been a parallel to the case in American history. Mobs have hung men repeatedly, but never before that we remember of have the policemen who had the prisoner in charge, first beaten him into half insensibility and then turned him over to the mob. This is not a question between Mormon and Gentile; it is one in which the good name of the city government is at stake" (qtd. in Schindler, *In Another Time*, 166).

That Jane James received a Christmas basket annually "in recognition of her service and limited income" is documented in Wolfinger, "Test of Faith," in *Social Accommodation*, 127.

The Grices' suffering from racism when accused of poisoning Charles Colbrook's nine colts and leaving Utah as a result are documented in Albright, "Special Destiny," and in Carter, *Negro Pioneer*, 32.

40

O Lord, I'm Hungry

*This spake he, signifying by what death he
should glorify God. And when he had spoken
this, he saith unto him, Follow me.*
JOHN 21:19

When Tom Thomas got acquitted for his part in Sam Joe's demise and nobody was held responsible, Sylvester could not stay silent. He tried talking to his mama, but she told him to keep his mouth quiet or she'd keep it for him. Syl knew there was only one person he could talk to: Elijah Abel. So he walked to the old man's place, knocked, and waited for an answer—which took some time, for Elijah's steps were getting slower by the day.

If you had seen Elijah Abel when he answered Syl's knock, you'd never have guessed he could've wrestled a pistol from a big man like Sam Joe Harvey. You'd hardly imagine he could pry a honeystick from a baby. That's how beat he looked.

Syl didn't feel up to exchanging pleasantries on this sad morning. Walking straight into the kitchen, he started in railing against everything and everyone around him. "Ain't nobody willin' to listen

349

to my voice," he muttered. "Ain't nobody hearin' me ask for justice. Right now, I hate everything I see 'ceptin' you."

Elijah gestured to the table. "I 'spect you mean me to take that as a honor. Boy, those are nice, pleasin' words. But that ain't what this is about. Syl, I'm concerned over you. Take a seat. Let's talk."

Sylvester was pacing exactly the way Elijah had done in his younger days. "I can't sit," Syl said. "Too much in me to sit. Brother, I am sick of all this mess. Make me sick to my stomach."

Elijah didn't have the strength to stay standing, so he took a seat himself. "I know," he said. "I feel the same way. But you can't let it get to you, boy. It'll eat you up if you do."

"Mama keep tellin' me I ain't seein' it right, but you got to be blind not to see what's happenin'."

"Syl, there ain't nothin' you can do about it. They done hung him. He's dead. Gettin' yourself all worked up ain't solvin' a thing. What's been done ain't right—I agree with you there. But we don't have the power to change what is. You're wearin' yourself out—and wearin' me out just watchin' you pace like you're doin'. Sit yourself down."

"My mama say—"

"Your mama understand. She's not blind to the fact. But she tryin' to keep you safe. As hot-headed as you actin', she's scared you goin' put yourself in Sam Joe's place."

Syl tried sitting for a moment but couldn't keep himself still. Banging his fist on the table, he stood up and burst out again: "Mama too scared. She too timid. Always tryin' to show her good side to these white folks. They don' care about her good side or her bad one. All they see is Black Jane."

Elijah drew a deep breath. "Don' you go diminishin' your mama, Syl. She got a life worth of experience. Can't nothin' come of fightin' 'cept more bad. All you be doin' is spittin' in the wind. Your mama understand that."

"She don't understand a damn thing in this world. All she knows is to please them."

Now it was Elijah banging his fist on the table. "Boy, don't you dare come in my place and talk that way. I'm tryin' to help you, and so is your mama. I won't stand for any disrespect. If you can't mind yourself, then you can get out of my kitchen and out of my house. Your mama and me been and done four times in our lives what you ain't done even once. You understand me?"

"Yessir. I'm sorry. I didn't mean no disrespect."

"Now you ain't lived as long as your mama and me, but you already know your options is limited. You could kick against the pricks all you want, but all you goin' get is pricks in the foot and sore toes. You can't win this battle."

Syl set his palms on the table and bowed his head.

"And what about your wife?" Elijah asked. "How she feel about this? She too young to be a widow. And you got children. That's somethin' my oldest boy will never have. I would give anything in this world to have Moroni back with me, married like you married. Raisin' a good crop of babies. Boy, you got to know that once Judge Lynch visit a place, he don't like to leave in a hurry. Now, I knowed you since you was startin' your teen years. You've growed to a fine man now. You got muscle to you, and you dark as dirt no matter who your daddy was. Ain't nothin' like a big, tall, dark Negro to fire a white man's fear and get his imagination workin'."

"God made me big, tall, dark, *and* Negro. I can't change none of that. White man needs to change the fear he got. And until he does—"

Elijah held up a hand to stop him. "Son, I know what you feelin'. I feel it myself. Don't you go thinkin' I ain't got anger, 'cause I do. It ain't right, but it's the truth. The Lord already know, so I won't pretend. Only difference between you and me is that I know rage ain't goin' get nothin' done." He reached across the table and grabbed Syl by the arm. "Did I ever tell you 'bout how, when I was a missionary, I got accused of killin' a white woman and her whole family?"

"What?"

"It ain't a story I trusted to many folks, and it ain't a memory I particularly treasure. You understand why. Some folks just hearin' it today would still wonder if I was guilty. Except for a miracle of God, I'd be buried somewhere's in New York. Sit and listen to me."

At last, Syl sat himself down.

"The woman's husband killed his whole family," Elijah said, "and then he claimed it was a black man done it. I was the nearest Negro at hand." He told not only the story of that accusation but how he had been brought up for Church reprimand for threatening to knock down Elder Christopher Merkley, his white companion.

Syl said, "My mama got stories like that too—gettin' stopped by the law just for being colored. How do you stand it, brother?"

Elijah shrugged his bony shoulders. "It ain't easy. But we can't reach into nobody's chest and change their heart. Only the good Lord can do that. Even still, they got to be willin' to accept it. You know, Syl, I don't think the Lord got angry over what they done to Sam Joe. I think he wept over them the moment hate smoked across their minds. What's it say about a man that he derive pleasure watchin' another man's body gettin' dragged through the streets? What's that say about him? Now, you can get mad at the Church. You can get mad at the Brethren. You can get mad at this whole state. But you can't force to change what God can't force to change. For the time bein', the devil goin' take his due."

"An' we just stand by and watch the devil collect?"

"That's right. And we try not to be part of what he collect. Now I tol' you the best I can. Think on it. I been to enough lynchin's for one lifetime. Understand?"

"Yessir."

"Son, wouldn't you care for a bite to eat?"

Syl let out a sigh so long, seemed he had been keeping it bottled inside for days. "I haven't had a morsel since yesterday. Yessir, I'd enjoy a slice of bread."

Elijah moved like all his joints ached, which in fact they did. "How about some strawberry jam to go with it? My daughter brought me too much jam for one man to eat in a month. Delilah make jam almost good as her mama." He sliced the bread and set it on a plate alongside the jam. "Don't you be shy about it. You have as much as you want. Sometimes the fruit of the field can remind us God's still sendin' light to this ol' earth, and we calm down."

Syl spooned a good dollop onto his bread. He hadn't realized how hungry he was till his mouth juices swelled up. Still, he ate slow, speaking between bites: "Brother Abel, I understand all you sayin'. And I know you got more wisdom than I got. Since my daddy left, you been the man I turn to in my need. I want you to know I respect you with all I have. If I do go against your counsel, it ain't out of disrespect."

Elijah shot him a knowing look. "Delilah be bringin' by fresh bread this afternoon. Why don't you drop over and share company with an old man tomorrow?"

"I'll give that some thought, sir. You pass along my regards to your family." Syl stood and twisted the doorknob. "Thank you for takin' time to hear to me." He opened the door and headed down the weed-tangled path.

Notes

The chapter title is from a traditional Negro spiritual cited in Cone, *Spirituals and the Blues*, 47.

A Tom Thomas was acquitted for his part in the lynching, though we have been unable to trace which Tom Thomas that was, because there were many of that name (Schindler, *In Another Time*, 168).

41

WRESTLING JACOB

Our fathers went down into Egypt,
and we have dwelt in Egypt a long time;
and the Egyptians vexed us.
NUMBERS 20:15

Sylvester paid mind to Elijah Abel for a few days, but he could not get shed of Sam Joe Harvey. Sam's ghost would not quit him.

Around midnight, when Sylvester could no longer endure his own silence, he walked to Tom Thomas's house. On the front porch, under a rock, he placed a page he had tore from a Book of Mormon. One verse was circled: "Wo unto the murderer who deliberately kills, for he shall die!"

It had taken him all day to find just the words he wanted.

The next night, he returned to the Thomas place with another page of scripture, the words "Thou shalt not kill" circled.

This time, Tom was waiting for him.

"Boy?" Tom said, coming from behind a bush.

Syl ran and Tom took chase, tackling him on the dirt road.

"Cuss fire to your black heart!" Tom hissed. "What do you think you're doing? Ripping pages from holy writ and leaving them on my doorstep? You wanting to threaten me, you burr-headed puke? Or you trying to preach? Because I can preach you plenty. I suspect the city would be better off if I preached you a message you'd never forget. You got my wife in there bawlin' like the end of the world, scared outta her wits. You are going to pay for that."

Still pinned, Sylvester fired back: "I may be black and I may be burr-headed, but I ain't no murderer."

"Boy, you can't correct me on a thing I've done, and I will never answer to you or any other colored." Tom pounded his fist into the small of Syl's back. "I know who you are, Sylvester James. You figured the night would mask your black face, but it won't. Now you listen to me: what that murderer Harvey did should teach you something about what lurks inside you and every other Hamite. I am bound to protect this city. I am bound to protect the virtue of our women and the peace of our streets. You keep up this kind of meddling, and you will find yourself in poor light and hot trouble." He lifted Sylvester by the back of his pants and stood him up. "Now don't you try runnin' or I'll give you worse than you've got already. Let's walk to your mama's now, and you listen to what I've got to say."

It was a twenty-minute walk, with Tom Thomas harping all the way and Syl hurting with every step. When he asked to relieve himself, Tom allowed a brief moment. In the moonlight, Syl could see there was blood in his urine.

At the James home, Tom called, "Aunt Jane! It's Mr. Thomas. I've brought you some laundry to tend to."

Jane opened the door, kerosene lamp in hand.

Tom said, "This boy of yours has been up to some mischief. I'm going to leave it for him to tell. But this is a fact: If he sets foot on my property again, he'll be coming home in the back of a wagon." He turned to Syl and swore under his breath, "I'll see you to a painful grave the next time."

Then he was gone.

Jane's hand was sprawled over her mouth. She set her lamp on the shelf and then put Syl's arm over her shoulder and her arm around his waist. "Sylvester, let Mama help you. Lawd, what's happened? Why can't you stand straight?"

"Thomas hit me in the back while I was down."

She helped him sit at the table. "What were you doin' at his place at all—and this time of night? You ain't got business over there. Oh, look at you! How bad you hurt?"

"I don't know, but I was pissin' blood on the way home."

"What you done, Sylvester?"

He sneered. "I left Thomas some words to choke on." Then he told her all of it.

Syl could have mouthed her answer with her. He had heard it often enough: "I raised you better than that. You can't be doin' such things. You got responsibilities. You're a father. A grown man and a father!"

"I done what I aimed to do. There won't be no more of it," he said.

"Syl, I'm scared for you." She wiped her eyes with her fists. "You're like your daddy. Pushin' and pushin' and never bein' satisfied. You keep on, and what's goin' happen to your wife and babies? Don't you care what happens to them or to yourself or to me? We have to live here, son. Now you stay clear of Brother Thomas."

"Mama, he sure ain't my brother. But I'll stay clear."

"You're grown, and you don't have to agree with me. You don't even have to love me. But you *will* respect my home and what I say. There ain't a thing I'd put past Tom Thomas or a number of others. Your wife know your whereabouts?"

"No."

"Did she know what you was doin' tonight?"

"No."

"And do you care how worried she must be?"

"Mama, stop preachin'. You said it. I'm a man. Treat me like a man. Just some things I can't let be."

"You'd better stay here the night and head back to your wife in the mornin'. Too many things happens in the dark, and you're in no condition to go home anyway."

He kissed her cheek and gave her a one-armed hug. His insides pained more than he had known they could.

Notes

The chapter title is from a traditional Negro spiritual cited in Higginson, "Negro Spirituals," 689.

The scripture referred to is 2 Nephi 9:35.

Calling
and Callings

42

I Stood on the River of Jordan

When ye are in the service of your fellow beings,
ye are only in the service of your God.
MOSIAH 2:17

Maybe it was an act of mercy. Maybe it was an attempt at a general apology. Or maybe it was just a way of giving an old Negro something of worth to do. Whatever the reason, President John Taylor called Elijah Abel to his third mission for the Church in October 1884. Elijah would serve in the northeast United States.

It didn't even occur to him to turn down this call. He was grateful for the opportunity. He remembered how strong he had felt God's presence during his other missions—the first to New York and Canada and the second to Cincinnati. A missionary's life meant climbing Jacob's ladder, relying on the Almighty from one rung to the next. His body may have been old, but his spirit was ready for a climb.

Apostle Joseph F. Smith set him apart. Many Mormons—black and white—came calling at his home the Sunday before his departure. Sylvester came too but chose not to tell him much of his own life. He didn't mention that a Salt Lake judge had fined him twenty dollars for disturbing the peace at Tom Thomas's house. He didn't mention that he had been called in to his bishop and would likely be excommunicated. No need to burden Elder Elijah with such news. But Syl did want to talk to him, so he waited until all the other guests had left. It was near midnight before they had chance for conversation. They sat on Elijah's old couch.

Syl said, "Everybody colored thinks of you like the best we got."

"That's sad news indeed," Elijah chuckled.

"No it ain't. I think you might be our best. I know you doin' this thing out of true desire. You ain't like some what wrestle with shadows just to prove themselves."

Elijah picked at his fingernails and seemed to be pondering some deep idea. "I don't need to prove myself to nobody. God goin' prove me. He been doin' that a long time."

"You believe in this Church. After everything—"

"I believe in the truth, Syl. The truth will set us free. The truth tells me who I am, and it don't much matter what anyone else say or think. Your mama believe the truth of this gospel too. She sacrificed much to follow our prophet."

"I come the same distance she did. I crossed the same trail."

"Aw, you was a child then. You didn't rightly have the choice. But you ain't no chil' now." Elijah paused before asking directly, "So what do you believe?"

Syl shook his head in a slow, rueful sweep. "I don't know what truth is, sir. Ain't even sure what's real. I still feel anger. That's real, and it's mine."

"You may think I'm about to tell you how bad anger is."

"No sir. I never could predict what you'd tell me."

Elijah pressed his fingers together, making his hands a loose cage. "Like I told you, I had anger in me hot as metal in the blacksmith's fire. Now you think on that, Syl. The smith get the metal so hot, he can shape it on the anvil, make it useful. Then he immerse it in cool water, or oil sometimes. I wonder if I'd be of much use to God if I'd never knowed the full heat of anger. God don't care for the lukewarm, you know. He spew the lukewarm out his mouth. But heat he can work with and cold he can thaw. And one day not long ago, I gave up all my boilin' anger to my Lord. I let him shape me, then baptize me over and over again, just like a smith baptize his workpiece. I gave myself to his refinin' fire and told him to temper me, to mold me into something he could use to good purpose. At least I try to give myself over to God. You see, a fire can burn and destroy most anything if it ain't controlled. But the right kind of fire, in the right place—that's what can make us into swords or wagon wheel rims." Elijah stopped talking and contemplated the room. "You know, I will miss this place," he said.

Syl shook his head again. "Maybe if I spent every day with you, I could feel the way you do. For me, if I had the chance to leave, I'd take it quick as a buzzard take a bite off a dead coyote. I wouldn't miss these people here for a second."

"I ain't here for *them*, son. And I didn't have to come here. Deep in my soul, I wanted to join with the Saints. Now, I knew they'd be less than I hoped. Ain't we all less than God wants us to be? I've wore disappointment like a frock coat many a cold winter. And sometimes it was a cold winter in the heat of August. But I can't never quit believin'. No matter what I see, no matter what happens to me or them I love, I can't quit this faith. I ain't leavin' to get outta Utah. I'm leavin' to preach the gospel that brought me here."

"Yessir."

"Now you look after your mama, won't you?"

"I always have."

"Don't you be breakin' her heart."

Syl glanced away. He knew he would indeed be breaking Jane James's heart and soon. The process to excommunicate him had already begun, but he didn't want to talk about it. He said, "I will pray for you, brother. I will pray that the good Lord bless you every step of the way."

"I will pray God's blessin's on you too, son. And on your household and on your mama's."

A week later, all the Negroes in Salt Lake—Mormon and non—saw Elder Elijah Abel off at the train station. Those who knew the words sang to him "Praise to the Man" and "Come, Come Ye Saints." Then Jane James stepped forward.

At first, it seemed she was just making a speech. Then her words took on rhythm. In her quavering, mournful voice, she sang a song only she and Elijah knew, because they were older than the others. To the rest, it seemed she was just making it up as she went along, picking it out of her soul's great store of music:

> O, good news! O, good news!
> De angels brought de tidings down,
> Just comin' from de trone.
>
> As grief from out my soul shall fly,
> Just comin' from de trone;
> I'll shout salvation when I die,
> Good news! O, good news!
> Just comin' from de trone!

So Elder Elijah Abel was taking "good news" to folks in the northeast. Now he would preach the gospel to all sorts of colored folks, many of them former slaves. He hoped to find them ready for even greater freedom.

NOTES

The chapter title is from a traditional Negro spiritual found in Burleigh, *Spirituals*, 95.

Elijah Abel was called to serve his third mission by John Taylor (Bush, "Mormonism's Negro Doctrine," 76) and was set apart for this mission by Joseph F. Smith (Bringhurst, "Changing Status," 138).

We do not know the particulars of Sylvester James's excommunication from the Church, only that he "remained a member of the Church until 1885, when he was excommunicated for 'unchristianlike conduct,' a vague charge that could cover a multitude of greater and lesser offenses. He never returned to the Church thereafter" (First Ward records, cited in Wolfinger, "Test of Faith," in *Social Accommodation*, 168, n. 73). Although it seems significant that Sylvester's excommunication happened so soon after the Sam Joe Harvey lynching, we cannot be certain the two are related.

The song Jane sings is "Good News," a traditional Negro spiritual cited in Higginson, "Negro Spirituals," 691.

43

Blow Your Trumpet, Gabriel

The Lord giveth no commandments unto the children of men, save he shall prepare a way for them that they may accomplish the thing which he commandeth them.

1 NEPHI 3:7

By the time of his third mission, Elijah was in his seventies, though every creaking joint in his body felt much older, especially after that long train ride. He knew from his weakness that there wasn't much life in him. Despite whatever questions he had for the Almighty, he still wanted to finish his mortal time with the name of Jesus on his lips. All his days, he had had to choose what he would forget and what he would remember. Whatever he chose to forget, he would not forget his Lord. He did not understand why God would permit the Negro people to languish as some were, but he knew sure God was a God of love. It was humans who kept finding new ways to divide themselves, exalt themselves, enslave themselves or others. The Lord had nothing to do with such badness. One of Elijah's goals on this mission was to tell his people how God saw them.

He found many of them thriving, doing well in business, building up churches and their own homes, running their own farms and opening their own shops.

Of course, poverty hadn't quit the nation, and the conditions some of our people were living in near broke his heart. Still, there was many a family ready to hear the words he preached, and he baptized a good number. Baptizing was a joyful deed. He could almost hear his mama sing:

> You may talk of my name as much as you please,
> And carry my name abroad,
> But I really do believe I'm a child of God
> As I walk in de heavenly road.

Yes, Lord, yes. Elijah was walking that heavenly road. He knew there was freedom greater than what man could invent with his money-minting machines. There was freedom that kept you alive and hopeful even while you waited in the pit. There was freedom that promised you not just a glad heaven after a sad life but a right-now knowledge of who you were, which no one could strip away unless you let them. You could rise beyond what anyone did to you and get to know Jesus because it was Jesus whispering your name and wiping your tears and touching your wounds with his sweet balm.

Elijah was not assigned a missionary companion and sometimes felt all alone in the world. Not more than a week passed, though, when his old companion returned.

At first, it looked like a shadow coming slow over a bright hill and then floating across the brittle grass. Elijah thought it might be an angel woman and prayed God for the miracle of Mary Ann to join him or to call him home, he wouldn't care which. He squinted as the shadow neared and the robes spread, and then he saw the face. It was Joseph of the Rainbow Coat.

Elijah nodded once to acknowledge his old friend, and the two of them meandered down a cart trail and later to many a house in Ohio.

Joe hadn't aged near as much as Elijah had, though he was showing some wrinkles around the eyes. His Egyptian headwrap covered his hair, but Elijah suspected it had turned just as white as his had.

By this time, Elijah's hair had receded all around his scalp, away from his ears and forehead. His headskin shone like new where the hair had abandoned it, but most of his face was furrowed, like God was setting up to plant seeds between the eyebrows and around the mouth.

Ol' Joe didn't look near so worn and didn't act it either. Joe never had to sit down to rest, but Elijah ran out of breath often. The Lord worked through him anyway. Whenever he found someone to talk to, the Lord put power under his words. Elijah took that to be another miracle and gave thanks. He loved preaching to anyone who'd listen but most especially to folks who were mired in despair. It wasn't hard to find them.

Some Negroes who'd moved North were not faring as well as others, though it was the rare former slave who would choose the bonds over what he had now, however paltry it was. Elijah met one old woman who wasn't wearing freedom well at all, though. She thought she might prefer slavery to the uncertain times she was suffering and said so straight out. She was a widow of two weeks, feeling her aloneness as a lively hurt. "We got lickin's back then, but we got food when we was hungry. No slave knowed how it was to lack food."

Elijah answered, "Many of the Israelites wanted to go back to Egypt too."

"Oh, I hear that story a thousand times." Her voice was thin as paper.

"Myself, I think whatever freedom God made for us be worth the journey."

The woman sat on her porch and beckoned Elijah to sit beside her. That porch was so rickety, he feared it'd give way under him, skinny though he was.

The woman was skinny too and such an ancient thing—so many wrinkles, Elijah thought she resembled the mummies Brother Joseph once displayed in Nauvoo. Surely she was past one hundred years and had never known a day of freedom until 1865. Her neck was the hue and texture of a raisin and so short it looked like someone had squashed her.

"When my husband been with me, he hunt," she said. "Us et what he shoot. Squirrels, rabbits, you name the critter and we et it. You know what I eats now? Soup. They's a smokehouse down the road. Leastways, it been a smokehouse for some while, till the folks of the big house abandon everythin' and move west. I takes the boards off that smokehouse, where the pig grease spilt, and I cooks them boards in a pot of water with some greens. That's how I flavors my soup. With boards."

"I calls that clever," Elijah said. "I believe I'd like to sample such soup."

"I calls that starvin'," the woman answered, but she served him a warm bowl of it, cackling and showing off her toothless, pink gums.

Elijah's gums were just as toothless and pink as hers, and he laughed just as loud. Then he testified strong: "Sister, despite all we suffered, I know my Redeemer lives. Now I want you to listen to me and let the Spirit move you. Sister, though worms destroy this body and this house and everything my eyes can see, I still plannin' on seein' my Lord with these same eyes. I still plannin' on receivin' his embrace and everything I ever dreamed of havin', and everything I ever lost, includin' my wife, my mama, and my son. And, sister, I think this soup taste fine. It renews my strength like the word of God renews my soul."

Again, she cackled. It was clear she derived pleasure watching him eat. She was willing enough to be baptized, until she learned it would mean getting dunked in a pool of water. She never had learned to swim and couldn't trust Elijah's old arms to pull her out once he dipped her under. When he suggested she trust the Lord's strength, she said she'd have to meet the Lord first to judge his muscle. She cackled once more, then thought for a moment, and decided she should trust the Almighty better. After all, if the Lord could pull us colored folks out of the fetters of slavery, surely he could bring her out of some water. So she submitted and became the last woman Elijah baptized in his life.

He thought of her often as he continued his mission. He would soon remember starvation better too, for he traveled days with hardly a bite to eat. Even when he found a farmhouse, it was often abandoned. There were nights he had no shelter but the bare trees, and the ground was frosty.

One day, he asked out loud why it was that colored folks got such a hard life. It wasn't that he had lost his faith, but he was curious of the answer. Brother Brigham and many others had talked about a curse. Elijah had to ask why it was that black folks seemed cursed in some ways. He offered the question while he was walking through a thicket.

"What if it ain't a curse?" Joseph of the Rainbow Coat answered out of the blue. Though Ol' Joe was either a vision or a figment of imagination, Elijah still had to scour the forest with his eyes to discover where the ancient ruler was. He found him up a tree, wearing all his fancy Egyptian garb. Joe wasn't holding onto so much as a twig but sat secure, not even swinging his legs. He sat like the branch was a throne.

"Say that again," Elijah said.

"I say, What if it ain't a curse? What if it be a callin'?"

Elijah scratched his head. "Now what you meanin' by that?"

"You think I knowed the good to come from my gettin' sold into slavery? You think, when my brothers was sellin' me to the

Ishmaelites, I was sayin', 'Oh, this must be right and jus' what God wants. Someday, I be in position to save my brothers. Don't you worry none. I aims to have me a adventure.' You thinks that's what I was sayin'?"

"No. I suppose you went kickin' and screamin'."

"I was too scared and too shocked for such carryin' on's. I kept thinkin' at least one of them would tell me this was a bad joke and call me back. Wasn't until we was on the road, I knew my brothers meant it."

"Some things takes a body by surprise. Ain't that the truth!" Elijah said. "But I guess you teached them a lesson."

"Not till they was ready to learn it. Couldn't teach them till they was ready. You know what they says 'bout leadin' horses to water. No, when the famines come and they needed what I could give them and they approach me on my throne, I kept watching they eyes. 'Course, they didn't recognize me, being I was decked out in my Egyptian attire."

"Just like now."

"That's right, just like now. I was lookin' wealthy and blessed. I was wearin' gold 'round my wrists and gold 'round my neck, and my face was painted like one of the 'Gyptian gods. And there they was. Judah. Reuben. Oh, I had no problem recognizin' them, even though they didn't know me from Adam."

"Or from Cain."

"That's right. Or from Cain either. There was Zebulon. Issachar."

"I knows the names. Been studying the Bible half my life."

"They'd growed up. Judah's hair'd got gray."

"Happens. Myself, I could do with a few more hairs—gray or black. Wou... n't matter. 'Course, it don't matter much anyhow, since my good looks departed years ago and left me hangin'. So there was your brothers. Oh, I wish I could see my brothers again."

"I talked Egyptian, so they wouldn't know I was their relation."

"Quite a joke you was playin' on 'em!"

"Weren't no joke. It was part of a test. I needed to see if they was ready to get delivered. Wasn't until Judah said he'd sooner go to jail than let my baby brother go that I knowed they was ready. Then I couldn't keep myself from cryin' out loud."

"And you says, 'Brothers, I am Joseph.'"

"'Brothers, I am Joseph.' Had to repeat it time and again. Seemed they'd forgot the name as well as me. 'I am Joseph. Your brother!'"

"I am Elijah," he whispered.

"As you might guess, they figured I'd kill them straightway. But I told them how everything they intended for meanness, God turned to good. ''Lijah, it wasn't no curse of God that I landed in the pit. It was God's way to take care of all us." Joseph of the Rainbow Coat was no longer in the tree but right beside him, looking so real, Elijah was sure he could reach out and feel the softness of that silk robe. And Joseph's voice was rich and certain: "I thinks you took a big assignment from God hisself when you agreed to get borned under the conditions you accepted. Imagine agreein' to get born a slave!"

Elijah snorted. "I agreed to gettin' born in the bonds 'bout as much as you agreed to gettin' sold off by your brothers."

"You can't remember it, but I believe you did agree. It come as your assignment. Your mission. So's you could test your brothers and save them when they was starvin'. Jus' like you been doin' for years, and just like you doin' now."

"I ain't no slave now."

"You a survivor now, 'Lijah. You a survivor! God's done put you through his fires. I know they was hot. You was burnin' for a long while before he could shape you. But he did shape you, brother. Just like you tol' Sylvester James. And here you be, spreadin' the gospel of peace, even though you felt more like a warrior than anything else your whole life. Look at me and you seein' yourself. Ain't we somethin'? And we both know what it is to be waitin' on God."

"Prayin' and pleadin'."

"And servin'. And doin' his biddin'. Waitin' on him. You understands things like you never understood before. Here you be, a missionary once again! 'Cept can't nothin' take you by surprise this time. Not even handbills on every tree. After all you been sufferin', here you be! You servin' the Lord and preachin' his word. Why, that's as good as givin' out grain, 'Lijah! And you gots the power to do it."

"To be truthful, I feels a little hungry myself, Joe."

"You goin' be filled, 'Lijah."

"My body doin' poorly. Feelin' sick."

"Don't nothin' surprise me in that news. You a old man. Maybe you'd best go back to Utah, if you feelin' that bad."

"To die there, you mean?"

"Naw, I can't say."

"But you knows it."

"You got friends in Utah. Remember all them folks seein' you off at the railway station? They can take care of you now."

"Carry my bones?"

"Whatever the Lord decide."

They started walking a slow walk, for Elijah had lost near all his strength. "I miss my wife somethin' awful," he said.

"She doin' fine, 'Lijah. Lookin' after you in moments you don't 'spect."

"I never got sealed up to her for eternity. I can't imagine heaven bein' heaven without her."

"Now don't you go distrustin' the Lord, 'Lijah. He always make a way. You ain't goin' miss out on a single one of your blessin's."

"I believe that. But I still miss her from here. I miss my mama. Miss my son. Dyin' don't seem so bad if it's me dyin'."

"You go on back to Utah, Elder Abel. I think that'd be the best idea."

Then Ol' Joe disappeared.

What surprised Elijah was how smart a figment of his imagination could get over the years. And how stubborn.

NOTES

The chapter title is a traditional Negro spiritual, cited by Cone, *Spirituals and the Blues*, 95.

The song Elijah remembers hearing his mother sing is "The Heavenly Road," a traditional Negro spiritual cited in Higginson, "Negro Spirituals," 691.

The statement "We got our lickings, but just the same we get our fill of biscuits every time the white folks had 'em. . . . Nobody knew how it was to lack food" is from former slave George Conrad, quoted in Berlin et al., *Remembering Slavery*, 265.

44

BEHOLD THAT STAR

And this shall be a sign unto you;
Ye shall find the babe wrapped in swaddling clothes,
lying in a manger.
LUKE 2:12

Elder Elijah Abel stayed with his mission another week but then knew it was time to go home. One bright Wednesday, he used his last dollars to pay for a ride to Utah. He barely managed to step into a buggy, which carted him to the train. He rode that train to Salt Lake City.

Jane James came calling at Enoch's house, where Elder Abel was staying. They had a good many conversations, and he told her all about his mission and how things looked back east with slavery gone. For her part, she read him scriptures about Christmas, since it was December. She read him all about the Son of God getting born in a stable and worshiped by the humblest of folks and then by the wisest. She read him about Jesus' swaddling clothes and how Mary had to set him in a manger, since there was no room for his people in the inn. She sang him about the star:

Behold that star
Behold that star out yonder
Behold that star—
It is the star of Bethlehem.

Enoch kept a bedside vigil as Elijah lapsed in and out of deep sleeps.

On the afternoon of Christmas day, Elijah sat full up in bed and started speaking. Seemed he was going to recover after all, for he sure had plenty to say. His voice was somewhat breathy and somewhat frail, but he managed to keep talking.

Jane James had been rubbing consecrated oil into his forehead. He thanked her for that kindness. It reminded him of the woman in the Bible anointing Jesus' feet, and when a disciple suggested that woman was wasting valuable perfumes and oils, Jesus said to leave her be and let her minister to him. Elijah asked Jane if she recollected that scripture, which she surely did.

"Sister Jane," he said then, "do you understand your position?"

"What you mean, 'my position'?"

"You and me, Jane James, we the only colored folk in this whole city who knowed Brother Joseph Smith. We the only colored folk here who got us patriarchal blessin's from the Smiths themselves. Father Smith blessed me and said I was like his own son."

"Hyrum Smith blessed me."

"Jane, you and me the only colored folk here with such memories and such position. We got a voice. Can't many of us say that. Now, you know better than anyone, I've asked time and again for my blessin's in that temple. I doubt I'll be alive to see the temple when it's finished, but you likely will be. You ask for your blessin's, Sister Jane. You the only one with any chance. Don't you let the petitions stop just because I ain't here. You go visit President Taylor. Go your own self. Keep askin'."

"You want me to walk on up to the Church president's house my own self and make my request? Well, you must think me a pretty bold woman."

"No, I don' think you a bold woman, Jane. I knows it."

She smiled. "Thought I was keepin' it secret."

"No ma'am. You bold in every motion of your hands and every glimmer of your eyes. Not a bad bold. You bold like a diamond, and jus' that bright too."

"Comin' from you, Elder Abel, I don't know as I've had a sweeter compliment."

"I says what I sees. Sister Jane, I been prayin' for you since all your troubles began."

"Brother Elijah, my troubles began before you ever met me."

"But the worst ones, they come late in life, ain't that so? I prayed many a prayer for you."

Jane's eyes filled. "It may surprise you to know it, sir, but I always been aware of your prayers. The white folk maybe don't understand about your priesthood. But I do. There was days I felt your prayers right in my house. There was days I heard your voice, the very words you was speakin', though you was miles away. I never told you about it. Never told no one. There was days when I was most alone that the angels carried your blessin's to me. And I thank you. The Lord never gave me all I wanted, but he comforted my heart. And I know you was a part of that. I believe in your priesthood."

"Then let me bless you now," Elijah breathed. "I'll let my children stay to hear this, because it's important. Kneel here at my bedside, Jane, and lean your head to where my hands can cover it."

She did as he asked.

"Give me your full name, sister."

"I am Jane Elizabeth Manning James."

He nodded slowly. "I like that name. Do you like it?"

"Comes with some unpleasant history. Slave name from my daddy. And my ex-husband's name still holdin' on. But besides all that, yes, I do like it. It's mine."

"I'm glad you feel that way, because I want the angels recordin' this blessin', and I want them writin' down that full name."

He placed his hands on her head, and spoke in a stronger voice than he thought he had: "Sister Jane Elizabeth Manning James, by the authority of the holy priesthood which I got under Brother Joseph's hands, I bless you. You know who you are and how much the good Lord cherish you. I bless you with the strength you need to finish your work on earth. Sister Jane, you're a example of good. Those in the other world who knew you here, they so proud of you. And in years to come, many folks will learn of you, and they goin' be proud too. Jesus loves you. He seen you from his cross and from his throne. You will understand how many people you've touched. Be bold, sister, and walk where you need to go. God will guide your feet, and He will never let go your hand. You already know that, don't you, for you have experience. Remember what you already know. In the name of our Lord Jesus Christ, amen."

"Amen," said Jane and kissed both his hands as they dropped from her head. Seemed some of his own strength got spent in strengthening her.

Elijah's sons and daughters were weeping, for the Spirit was full in that room. He reminded his daughters to live up to their mother's example. He told his sons to keep faithful in all things. Then he stopped his eyes on Enoch, saying, "I apologize for not being here in the future. Now, I want you take care of your family. Watch out for your sisters and for my namesake. You keep this gospel, son, and you spread it whenever and however you can, just like the man you was named for. Endure what God give you. Promise me that."

Enoch promised.

"And now, I'd be obliged if you'd acknowledge your grandmother."

Enoch roved his eyes around the room. "My grandmother?"

"I say for you to acknowledge her. You know better than to ignore a guest in this house."

Enoch exchanged glances with the others. "Where is she, Daddy?"

"What happened to your eyes, boy? Why, she's standin' right next to you, by your left shoulder. Acknowledge her the way I taught you."

Enoch looked tentatively to his left. "Hello, Mizz Delilah."

"Thank you," Elijah said. Then he addressed his long-gone mama: "Good to see you again. I can't even say how good. Been such a long time, and I missed you powerful. And my, my! Them robes is glitterin' indeed! Even prettier than I thought!"

"Is he outside his mind, Sister Jane?" Enoch whispered.

"No. He's jus' goin' in and out of this world. Let him close his eyes and slumber. Give him permission for that, Enoch, so he won't feel to tarry past his time."

"He woke up so strong, talkin' like he was still on his mission."

"The Lord gave him a little extra at the end. Right now, he's seein' beyond what we can see. You tell him to rest."

"Daddy," said Enoch, "why don't you let yourself take a nap?"

"That does sound pleasant," Elijah answered, though it wasn't clear who he was talking to. Then he said his last words: "Mary Ann."

He closed his eyes and slept soon after, and it didn't take long for that sleep to become his last. Those present laid his body out with reverence. They all knew that this was a great man.

True to her word, Jane went to President Taylor's house that very evening. He had moved from the simple adobe structures known as Taylor Row and was now living in the Gardo House, which the Church had made his official residence. Jane had never been there and was stunned by the sight. This place was four stories high, topped with a cupola. The windows were arched and framed in fancy swirls and flowery designs. There were balconies, porches with colonnades, cornices, and bay windows. It was nothing less than a palace, and she wiped her hands before even knocking.

One of President Taylor's wives showed her inside. Jane waited on a soft carpet, gazing at the rich furniture and the oil paintings on the walls.

President Taylor, wearing a fine suit, came down the stairs to greet her. He limped a bit, since he still held a slug in his leg from the Carthage massacre, but he didn't let on that he felt any pain. He insisted she sit in the parlor and partake of some water, but she told him the news before sitting or accepting any drink: Elijah Abel had passed on.

President Taylor paused a reverent moment. "He was a credit to all you people," he said.

Jane wanted to ask him right that moment if she might enter the temple. She'd even be willing to travel to St. George to do it. But there was clearly much on John Taylor's mind, so she did not pursue the matter but left quickly, hearing the words behind her, "Thank you for bringing the news. Brother Abel's death is a loss to all of us and certainly to you people."

Elijah's obituary was printed on December 26, 1884, in the *Deseret News*. Jane asked Sylvester to read it to her, as the print was too small for her eyes.

"Died, Elijah Abel: In the Thirteenth Ward, December 25th, 1884, of old age and debility, consequent upon exposure while laboring in the ministry in Ohio. Deceased was born in Washington County, Maryland, July 25th, 1810. He joined the Church and was ordained an Elder as appears by certificate dated March 3rd, 1836. He was subsequently ordained a Seventy, as appears by certificate dated April 4th, 1841. He labored successfully in Canada and also performed a mission in the United States, from which he returned about two weeks ago. He died in full faith in the Gospel."

Notes

The chapter title, which is also the title of the song Jane sings, is from a traditional Negro spiritual found in Burleigh, *Spirituals*, 123.

Bringhurst states: "Abel's missionary activities . . . were cut short by ill health, and he returned to Utah in early December 1884. Two weeks later he died of 'old age and debility.' His motives for going on a mission at such an advanced age is a mystery, especially at a time when his status as well as that of blacks in general had deteriorated. Perhaps he was motivated by a desire to demonstrate his 'full faith in the Gospel' and thereby obtain long-sought temple endowments and sealings before his death" ("Changing Status," 138). Note 74 (on page 147) in "Changing Status" records the *Deseret News* report of Elijah Abel's death. The report is dated December 26; Abel died on December 25, 1884 (Bush, "Mormonism's Negro Doctrine," 77).

Elijah Abel's obituary cited in this chapter is as it appears in both the *Deseret News* (weekly), December 31, 1884, and the *Deseret Evening News*, December 26, 1884, though the punctuation has been standardized. The mention of Elijah's priesthood ordinations would not have been included in a white man's obituary. Whoever wrote the obituary thought it important to emphasize that Elijah Abel did indeed hold the Melchizedek Priesthood.

Elijah Abel's tombstone, next to his wife's in the Salt Lake City Cemetery, spells his last name Able, though there are various spellings of his name in the Church records. Just as MaryAnn's tombstone has the word "*Mother*" carved on its top, so Elijah's has the word *Father*. His epitaph reads simply "At Rest."

That Jane James called on John Taylor at his home on Christmas day, 1884, is in her own letter to President Taylor, dated December 27, 1884. She says, "I called at your house last Thursday to have conversation with you" (qtd. in Wolfinger, "Test of Faith," in *Social Accommodation*, 148; spelling standardized). The Thursday before December 27, 1884, was Christmas day, the day of Elijah Abel's death.

The description of John Taylor's house (the Gardo House) is from Roberts, *Life of John Taylor*, 331.

By 1884, Bishop Edwin Woolley had also died. The bishop of the Thirteenth Ward at the time of Elijah's death was Millen Atwood (Jenson, *Encyclopedic History*, 749). He likely would have officiated at Elijah Abel's funeral.

45

BOUND FOR THE PROMISED LAND

*Awake, and arise from the dust, . . . and put on
thy beautiful garments, O daughter of Zion.*
MORONI 10:31

Elijah's funeral was held at 10 o'clock on Saturday morning, December 27, followed by his burial in the Salt Lake City Cemetery and a simple luncheon. After these rituals, Jane was ready to pursue her request to President Taylor—by letter, this time. There was only one problem: She still couldn't write. She would need a scribe. Of course, the first person to come to mind for that job was Annie Thomas.

She had not seen Annie in many months and hoped the mood had changed enough that they'd be able to talk. Maybe Tom would be gone. A lot of the Mormon men were headed to diverse places and trapdoors to avoid federal prosecution, for new laws made it a crime to cohabit with more than one wife. Any man doing plural marriage out in the open was liable to be thrown in jail and have all his property confiscated.

This was the first time Jane had ventured to the Thomas house with no laundry business in hand.

It was early evening, and Annie herself answered the knock, gasping, "Jane!" when she opened the door and embracing her like they were not only friends but sisters. It was the first time Annie had ever hugged her.

"Good to see you, Mizz Annie," said Jane. "May I come in?"

Annie did not hesitate, so Jane knew Tom was not at home.

It didn't take long to explain her need of a scribe, and it didn't take long for Annie to write the words Jane dictated:

December 27, 1884
President John Taylor

Dear Brother:

I called at your house last Thursday to have conversation with you concerning my future salvation. I did not explain my feelings or wishes to you. I realize my race and color and can't expect my endowments as others who are white. My race was handed down through the flood, and God promised Abraham that in his seed all the nations of the earth should be blessed. As this is the fullness of all dispensations, is there no blessing for me?

I, with my father's family, came from Connecticut forty-two years ago the fourteenth of last October. I am the only one of my father's family that kept the faith.

You know my history, and according to the best of my ability, I have lived to all the requirements of the gospel. When we reached Nauvoo, we were nine in the family and had traveled eight hundred miles on foot. Brother Joseph Smith took us in and we stayed with him until a few days of his death.

Sister Emma came to me and asked me how I would like to be adopted to them as a child. I did not comprehend her, and she came again. I was so green, I did not give her a decided

answer and Joseph died, and I remain as I am. If I could be
adopted to him as a child, my soul would be satisfied. I had
been in the Church one year when we left the East. That was
forty-two years the fourteenth of last October.

Brother Taylor, I hope you will pardon me for intruding on
your time so much, and hope and pray you will be able to lay
my case before Brother Cannon and Brother Joseph F. Smith,
and God will in mercy grant my request in being adopted to
Brother Joseph as a child.

I remain your Sister in the Gospel of Christ.
Jane E. James

When they were finished, Annie said, "I don't pretend to understand why things are the way they are. I know I've been blessed by
the Lord, and I will not deny that. But sometimes I wonder if God
doesn't have greater mansions stored up for your family than for
mine. I shouldn't say this, but maybe I'll be doing your wash in
heaven, Jane, and you'll be the one in charge."

"Ma'am, I don't think you should say that," Jane answered. "I
don't think we'll be washin' clothes in heaven anyway. And the
Lord has his reasons for the way things are here. I trust him."

"I think you trust him more than I do." said Annie.

"Now you mustn't say that either, Mizz Annie. We live our own
lives, and we do the best we can. All us do."

Jane herself took the letter to President Taylor's house, walking
all the way. Her knees testified to her age, and every step pained.
She had walked many miles for this Church and wanted God to see
she was willing to walk miles more.

She would not get a response to her request for a while, because
the Church leaders soon went underground themselves to avoid
prosecution for bigamy. When the answer came at last, it came from
Angus Cannon, Jane's stake president. Inside the letter was a

recommend for her to do baptisms for her deceased family, and these words:

> Mrs. Jane James:
> I enclose you your recommend properly signed, which will entitle you to enter the temple to be baptized and confirmed for your dead kindred. You must be content with this privilege, awaiting further instructions from the Lord to his servants. I am your servant and brother in the gospel.

Jane was so excited over the prospect of entering the near-finished temple to do the baptisms, she hardly noticed she wasn't getting all she asked for.

Notes

The chapter title is from a traditional Negro spiritual cited in Cone, *Spirituals and the Blues*, 80.

The spelling and punctuation of the original dictation from Jane James to John Taylor has been standardized in this text. Her letter was dated December 27, 1884 (Wolfinger, "Test of Faith," in *Social Accommodation*, 148).

According to Wolfinger, "Although [Jane] learned to read in later life, she probably never learned to write. An examination of her legal transactions reveals that she often signed her name by a mark and that she dictated her correspondence through friends" ("Test of Faith," in *Social Accommodation*, 127).

The Edmunds Act was passed by the United States Congress in 1882. "It defined 'unlawful cohabitation' as supporting and caring for more than one woman. . . . The law also disenfranchised polygamists and declared them ineligible for public office. Not only those who practiced but also those who believed in plural marriage were disqualified from jury service. All registration and election officers in Utah Territory were dismissed, and a board of five commissioners was appointed by the president of the United States to administer elections." The Edmunds Tucker Act was passed in March 1887, four months before John Taylor's death. It required wives to testify against husbands and for all marriages to be "publicly recorded. Women's suffrage was abolished in Utah, the Perpetual Emigrating Fund was dissolved, as was the Nauvoo Legion. . . . The Church was disincorporated, and authority was given to the United States attorney general to [confiscate] all Church property and holdings valued over fifty thousand dollars" (*Church History in the Fulness of Times*, 427, 433–34). John Taylor and other Church leaders went into hiding in February 1885.

Jane was not the only person of African descent petitioning John Taylor for temple blessings. Wolfinger writes of a letter sent by stake president Joseph E. Taylor to the Church president on September 5, 1885, which reports Joseph Taylor's "personal knowledge" of several specific cases in which blacks or mulattos had received their endowments ("Test of Faith," in *Social Accommodation*, 164, n. 43). The letter, cited in part in Taylor, *Kingdom or Nothing*, 350, contains a request for a girl "in the Eighteenth Ward" who wanted a temple marriage but who was "a very light mulatto." Joseph Taylor states: "She now desires to press her claim to privileges that others who are tainted with that blood have received. For example, the Meads family in the Eleventh Ward. . . . I am cognizant of all these having received their endowments here. Brother Meads is a white man. He married his wife many years ago; she was a quadroon and died some three years ago. . . .

"The question I desire to ask is: Can you give this girl any privileges of a like character? The girl is very pretty and quite white, and would not be suspected as having tainted blood in her veins unless her parentage was known." The question was delicate because of the precedents Joseph Taylor cited and because of Brigham Young's adamant statements about one drop of Negro blood tainting the lineage (1852 speech to the territorial legislature) and Zebedee Coltrin's belated claim that Joseph Smith had said "no person having the least particle of Negro blood can hold the priesthood" (qtd. in Stephens, "Life and Contributions of Zebedee Coltrin," 55). Perhaps a more definitive policy might have been set had the Church not been in such turmoil over the Edmunds Tucker Act and all its implications.

The response to Jane from Angus Cannon, president of the Salt Lake Stake, was written on June 16, 1888 (Wolfinger, "Test of Faith," in *Social Accommodation*, 148).

O Pioneer!

46

OH WASN'T THAT A
WIDE RIVER!

But if a man live many years, and rejoice in
them all; yet let him remember the days of
darkness; for they shall be many.
ECCLESIASTES 11:8

During this time when Utah was beset with trouble, Green
Flake was getting tried in more personal ways. His wife, Martha,
passed away on January 20, 1885. Bless him, he could hardly bear to
be in the little house that still held so much of her, to see the sights
that had been part of their together life, now that she wasn't at his
side. He decided to move to Gray's Lake, Idaho, to live near his son,
Abraham. To be truthful, it wasn't just loneliness that prompted
him. He had heard Abe wasn't living the gospel. Abe had become
friendly with moonshine. Green couldn't let that continue and
aimed to call his son to repentance. So he headed up to Idaho.

Now, it's not every day a member of the vanguard company of
the Mormon pioneers moves into your community. Green may have
been colored, but he became a respected citizen of Gray's Lake—
which was not the norm for Negro folks in Idaho at that time.
Unfortunately, colored Mormons were not always welcomed to the

Church. It got so bad that a fellow named Oz Call was assigned to visit black Mormons in the area, since some folks—who *called* themselves Latter-day Saints—said they wouldn't be attending meeting should a Negro happen to be there.

Green didn't pay mind to these attitudes. He visited Latter-day Saint churches in Iona and Milo, Idaho. Sometimes he sang, sometimes participated in gospel discussion, and often told his life story and bore his testimony. He could and did speak something powerful, and Oz Call said Green was "the best damn missionary" he ever knew.

Well, however good a missionary Green was to others, he didn't succeed overly much with his own son. That was a sorrowful thing, but it didn't stop Green from missionarying all over the Idaho valley—though his work was usually with one or two people at a time.

When he was invited to be a guest and speaker at a Pioneer Appreciation Day in Willow Creek, Idaho, he was shy about accepting. He wasn't accustomed to addressing crowds and felt nervous about being an honored guest. He never considered himself anything special. But Ned Leggroan happened to be living in Idaho at the time and assured Green nobody was fixing to mock him. They wanted to pay proper tribute to what he'd done as a pioneer.

Needless to say, it required some persuading, for Green was not one to strut or shout his own praises. But he finally did agree. He would be right there with a survivor of the Martin handcart company, as well as an Indian fighter, a woman who had walked to Utah in 1848, veterans of the Mormon Battalion, and a fellow who'd been part of Johnston's army but who (like others you've heard about) wound up joining the Church instead of fighting it.

Of course, all these pioneers were aged by now. Green wore a bowler hat and a nice suit on this Pioneer Appreciation Day, but his hair was white and fluffy and his face lines deep. He sat on the platform next to a white man old as him, who had been in the Martin Handcart Company.

Green didn't tell this man his memories—about seeing tears in Brother Brigham's eyes when news of that company's troubles reached Utah. Green had been in the congregation when Brigham announced the plight of the waylaid, snowbound Saints. That would've been the year 1856. He remembered precisely, for it was the same year he and Martha had conceived Abe.

That important year, Church leaders had learned that a thousand Saints were still on the plains. Their handcarts hadn't been ready for them after their long ride across the ocean, so they had waited to begin their journey until late in the season—and it proved to be a merciless season. All the talks of the 1856 October conference took up the subject of rescue.

Green was a freed man by that time and helped rescue those suffering pioneers. He saw the bloodied, frozen feet of the survivors and the mournful eyes of those who had lost family to the pitiless snow and sleet. He wondered now if he had taken the hand of the very man who was sitting beside him on this platform of honor. He wondered if he had helped that man into a wagon that would save his life. The man didn't seem to remember him, but Green was hit with a slew of recollections.

After the rescue, Brother Brigham had wept aloud, Green remembered—the hardest tears he had ever seen the prophet shed. "Prayer is good, but when baked potatoes and pudding and milk are needed, prayer will not supply their place," President Young had said. The new arrivals were starving, and all of the Saints needed to pitch in and help. Green could almost smell the corn pudding Martha had made for those poor, half-froze folks.

He missed her so much.

"I was in that company," said the old pioneer survivor, who was the first speaker. "And we suffered beyond anything you can imagine. Many died of exposure and starvation. I pulled my handcart when

I was so weak and weary from illness and lack of food that I could hardly put one foot ahead of the other. I looked ahead and saw a patch of sand or a hill slope and said, 'I can go only that far and there I must give up for I cannot pull a load through it.' I went on to that sand and when I reached it, the cart began pushing me. I looked back many times to see who was pushing my cart, but my eyes saw no one. I knew that the angels of God were there. Was I sorry that I chose to come by handcart? No. Neither then nor any minute of my life since. The price we paid to become acquainted with God was a privilege to pay, and I am thankful that I was privileged to come."

Green let his mind dwell on those words. He thought about the price he himself had paid to become acquainted with God and knew in his every fiber that it all was worth it. Green wasn't much, at least not in his own opinion, but he sure would be less if the Lord hadn't been his friend. And with the Lord as his friend, maybe Green was more than he supposed.

Bishop Simmons introduced him, and Green took the pulpit. He started slow but then got going and told his tale—what it was like to dig and hack out the trail the later pioneers would follow; what it was like to drive Brigham Young's wagon and to know Brother Brigham on a personal basis; what it was like to see a grizzly bear lying dead at his feet and to see tears of pity in his Martha's eyes. The more he talked, the more he remembered, until it seemed his whole life was painted in the sky around him. It was a lovely life, he thought. It wasn't easy, but it was lovely. He was pleased to bear witness of the gospel and of the Lord.

When he finished, he asked if anyone had questions for him. One little girl in a fancy straw bonnet stood and shouted so the crowd could hear: "Mister Flake, what was it like being a slave?"

Bishop Simmons leapt to his feet. The whole audience seemed embarrassed, as though such a subject were indelicate for this festive occasion.

"Brother Flake, you don't have to answer that question," said the bishop. He appeared eager to spare the Negro any shame or else to keep the party happy and not remind folks of how things used to be.

Green wanted to answer, though. "Bein' a slave is all right," he said, and a rumble went through the crowd. "If you jus want to be a slave, that is." His voice got louder. "But many of us colored folk wanted a better life, if we could find one. I was raised a slave and had a massa to tell me what to do. He gave me a place to sleep, fed and clothed me, worked me, and told me what to do each day. Sometimes I got whupped, when I needed it, and my massa would give me a big kick in the pants if I sluffed off or made a mistake or if I was lazy."

As he spoke the words, he remembered Massa Madison clearer than he had in years. Madison never had the chance to get old, Green reflected. Neither had Mizz Agnes. And Liz, dear Lizzy, had died before she crossed her fortieth year. It had near broke his heart to learn Liz was gone. That news had found him years ago, and he still got a twinge of sadness when he remembered her. She wasn't someone you'd forget easy. He recollected Liz Flake from the day of their first meeting. He could picture her as a little bitty thing, all decked out in that yellow frock, holding a bouquet of yellow roses with most the petals gone. He recalled her happy, almost grown-up face telling him a crop of colored women—including someone named Martha Crosby—had arrrived at Winter Quarters. Seemed unnatural that someone so good and so perky as Liz would pass away young.

Of course, there was some advantage to taking an early death, but not near the advantage to living a long, full life. As Green was seeing it now, his time on this earth had been full indeed. He found himself grateful.

"Now, slavery been around a long time," Green continued. "And the colored folks got sold like they was a horse, a cow, or some other animal. They become the owner's property, and they work long and hard for the massa. Most everyone don't want to be a slave and be in bondage to another, because you cain't have even your own thoughts and dreams. You cain't plan for the future when all decisions gets made by someone else," he concluded.

As he took his seat, his thoughts returned to Martha. They had both been slaves when they married. If their massas had been mean enough to care more about money than love, Green and Martha could've got sold off from each other and their babies sold away too. Thank the Lord, Green said to himself, that he and his woman had had the privilege of growing old together. Thank the Lord they had been delivered.

"There are many kinds of slavery," Bishop Simmons said as he introduced the former soldier of Johnston's army.

Green's mind drifted. He thought that the worst kind of slavery must be bondage of the heart, where a white man can't see a colored man's face as one of God's creations—or where a colored man can't see a white man's face the same way. The worst kind of slavery was where you couldn't get delivered, because you had shackled yourself tight and given the keys to the devil.

After the meeting, the fellow from the Martin Handcart Company extended his hand to Green and said, "You did just fine."

Green wondered if years ago he had extended his own hand to that man, in harder, younger times. He hoped he had.

NOTES

The chapter title is from a traditional Negro spiritual found in Burleigh, *Spirituals*, 141.

Flake reports that "according to historian John Fretwell, Oz Call was 'assigned' to the African-American members of the LDS Church in and around Idaho Falls, Idaho. Call was assigned to them because the African-American members were supposedly not welcome to attend regular LDS church meetings in Idaho Falls, and many of the white LDS members refused to attend religious services when African-Americans were present. Green

[Flake] did however visit and attend other LDS Churches in Iona and Milo, Idaho, where he was cordially received. In some of these LDS Churches he sang, took part in Sunday school discussions, told his life story, and bore his testimony from the chapel pulpit. He also went to some of the local schools and spoke to the children" ("Green Flake," 25, n. 117).

Information about Abraham Flake's drinking problem, which was one reason Green chose to settle in Idaho, is from Fretwell (personal interview, December 8, 2000).

The Pioneer Appreciation Day happened as we have described it, and the speakers were the ones mentioned (Fretwell, Miscellaneous Family Papers, 9.)

Brigham Young's words about prayer not supplying the place of needed food is from *Deseret News*, December 10, 1856, 320 (qtd. in "Remembering the Rescue," *Ensign*, August 1997, 47).

Allen and Leonard record: "[Brigham Young] and other leaders devoted their conference addresses [October 1856] to the task of delivering the handcart pioneers. . . . On October 7, an advance group of twenty-seven men with sixteen mule teams was on its way eastward with provisions, and more were to follow. Both companies [Martin and Willey] were rescued, though only after more than two hundred had frozen to death. The last group struggled into Salt Lake City at the end of November" (*Story of the Latter-day Saints*, 285).

The statement from the survivor of the Martin Handcart Company is from Hanks, *Blossom*, 35, citing the *Relief Society Magazine*, January 1948, 8.

Green's description of slave life is from Fretwell's interview with Udell (Miscellaneous Family Papers, 9), which begins as follows: "This question [about what it was like to be a slave] came from a young person at the Pioneer Appreciation Day. There was a gasp from the audience who thought the question was too personal. Bishop Simmons spoke out and said, 'Brother Flake, you don't have to answer that question.' He said he would be proud to answer that question."

1891

47

A City
Called Heaven

*The Lord God shall commence his work among all
nations, kindreds, tongues, and people, to bring about the
restoration of his people upon the earth.*

2 NEPHI 30:8

Now, in the Mormon life, there was often talk of the restoration
of all things. Some figured that meant that regardless of what the
federal government said or did, God would restore whatever his
people needed. Jane believed in the law of restoration and was
grateful for it, for she had lost many things she hoped would be
restored to her—such as good looks, unwrinkled skin, and most of
all, those dear children of hers who had passed on. What she never
did anticipate being restored to her in this life was Isaac James. She
figured Isaac was out somewhere gambling and drinking and
undoing all his Mormon habits, reversing his life.

Such was not the case. Isaac James was making his way back to
her and doing it with a sick body. He came by train now, no handcart, no wagon, and no ticket. He was hobo-ing back to the Salt
Lake Valley like a no-account drifter.

Some folks talk about "high yellow" complexion. Isaac had

always been a nice hazelnut brown. Maybe drink had damaged his liver, but his eyewhites had gone high yellow as if his heart pumped bile instead of blood. His lips were crusted, and his skin was like parchment. For two weeks, he had sat hunched up and freezing in a train car, wondering if he would die there. He shared the car with two other black men, who planned on continuing to Denver.

Isaac didn't say much. He was in pain, and one of his fellow-travelers asked him—respectful as he could, for Isaac was considerably older than either of them—what they should do if he were to die. Isaac said he would be grateful for some kind of burial, even a shallow one, that he would prefer such to being thrown out onto the track hill when the train stopped. He understood their concerns, for the car was smelly enough, given they had all had to relieve themselves in the corner, and a dead body would contribute to the stink. But he did not enjoy the idea of rotting out in the open air. It was cold enough, being late October, that his decay wouldn't be immediate. He did not wish to be the bones someone discovered come spring.

His companions didn't have to bury him, though, for he was still alive when they reached Salt Lake in the middle of a shivery night. Waving a quick goodbye to the other hobos, who seemed happy to have him gone, he tried to straighten his back. He had been curled up in the corner for so long, he could not straighten himself much at all. Still half balled-up, he made his way to the old house. He didn't even get to the porch but collapsed and slept on the ground.

In the morning, a disgruntled white fellow found him there. When Isaac asked for Jane James, the man said she had moved some time back. He helped Isaac stand and directed him to Jane's new house. Isaac found a good walking stick and started towards his ex-wife.

Her new place was on Fifth East Street. It was not a bad residence, though it could've used a new coat of paint.

He stood as tall as he could and knocked.

Jane herself answered. She had aged too, but he could see her young self just beneath the wrinkles.

She said, "Yes?" then, "Oh, Lawd Awmighty. Isaac, is that you?" The last time Jane had seen her ex-husband, he was a fairly handsome man, with dark, fleecy hair and wispy burnsides.

"I'm pretty sure it is." His words whistled, since most all his teeth were gone.

She brought both her hands to her mouth and spoke through them. "You look a fright. Where did you sleep last night?"

"Outside. At the old place."

"On a cold night like that? Come inside. You need to warm up and clean up. Let me draw you some hot water for a bath and fix you up some oatmeal. Stove's already burnin'. It's a good stove. Has a water bin."

"I'm glad you got you a good stove," he said, then added quietly, "I know I don't deserve a thing."

She didn't answer but moved her arm to his back to help him over the threshold. His steps were slow shuffles, but they got him inside.

After he was cleaned up and wearing a suit of clothes that had belonged to Silas, he sat with Jane at the table.

"How's the children?" he asked. It seemed the logical question after a twenty-year absence.

She told him which of their children had died and how. Each name brought him back a full spread of memories. So Silas, the baby they began their journey with, got stole away by consumption. If Isaac had been one step closer to death, that news would've taken him over the edge. All these years, he had imagined Silas as living, breathing, and raising babies of his own. Mary Ann and Miriam were dead too. How could that be?

"I been wanderin' in the wilderness," he said finally. "I sure never intended this—endin' up this way. Thought I was strong enough to be somebody. Now, God's took all my strength and showed me how weak I am."

"Why, that's good knowledge, Isaac," she answered. "Can't nobody escape such knowledge."

He raised his eyes. There she was, across from him, as though they had never parted. There was oatmeal on the table, and no accusation in her face.

"I am sorry," he said.

"I know you are. But I guess you know, sorry don't touch it."

He ate two bites of cereal, but his stomach wouldn't tolerate much food. "Jane," he said, "I don't feel worthy to be here. Maybe I was wrong to come. Some things I done with my life is so wicked. If you knowed—"

"I ain't askin' 'bout your business. You have to work that out with the Lord."

Over the next hours, they conversed off and on, both of them remembering all the good and bad they had suffered, all the ways they had hurt or healed each other in the past.

He slept on the couch that night. It wasn't until his second day in the house that he told her over breakfast, "You all I got, Jane. I been travelin' towards you—seem like years. Come a day long ago when I knowed I can't never be my full self without you at my side."

She rubbed her forehead then sat herself down in her rocker. "Isaac, we don't even need to begin this conversation. We can't go back. Too much happened. It's been too long. The good times was too far back, and the hard times was too recent."

"Can't you forgive me enough to find love in your heart for me? I have love for you."

She answered softly, rocking her chair. "I am a Christian. I do forgive you. And I do love you—as my brother and as the father of our children. But that other love died when you walked out on me. I don't mean you any harm—I mean you only good. But we can't go back to being what we once was."

He pondered. "If you won't take me back, can I at least have a place to rest my head? I don' know as how I'm goin' last much longer."

"I wouldn't turn away anyone in need, and I won't turn you away."

Isaac wiped his tears. His knuckles were so swollen and scaly, the fingers looked like stubs. "How have you survived, Jane?"

She kept rocking and gave an answer like it was a lullabye: "I don't know. I just keep puttin' one foot in front of the other, and God take care of the rest."

Isaac didn't live but a year after his return to Salt Lake. In the last months of his life, he and Jane renewed their friendship so strong that Jane decided the next time she asked to get adopted into Brother Joseph's family, she would ask if Isaac might also get that privilege.

His funeral was held at her house, November 15, 1891.

The same year Isaac died, Biddy Smith Mason passed to her reward as well—and it must've been a fine reward, for she had spent her life after slavery taking care of poor folks and visiting prisoners in jail. She knew all about bondage and could give a kindly word and often a few dollars. She became a wealthy property owner and a charitable woman, active in the first A.M.E. church in California. Whoever would have guessed, seeing her a slave, what all Biddy would accomplish in her days? What might Robert Smith have thought that day he tried hauling her off for Texas, if he'd been privy to her future?

And Biddy wasn't the only colored woman the Mormons had brought out west who was setting precedents in California. Liz and Charles Rowan had had three children before Liz passed. Their daughter, Alice, grew up to be a schoolteacher. She taught white children in Riverside for several years—the first time in the nation's history where a colored woman taught in a white school.

In Missouri, Louis and Gracie had raised a fine family. Their son

James Louis Gray had already found himself a wife and put down roots in Marshall.

Back in Utah, there were yet surprises awaiting Jane, even in her old age. Happy surprises and sad ones. The Salt Lake Temple was two years from completion, and her brother, Isaac Lewis Manning, a widower by now, was thinking of Utah once again. He was thinking, wouldn't it be a fine thing to be with his sister?

He knew she was living. Somebody as mulishly stubborn as Jane Manning James wouldn't go easy from this life. He made his preparations to join her in Zion. He would become the unexpected companion of her twilight years.

This all goes to show that God never stops delivering surprises. You just open your eyes each day and wonder what's coming. You hope, like all us do, that today's surprise will be a good one. And you remind yourself, like all us should, that you can't always tell for sure.

NOTES

The chapter title is from a traditional Negro spiritual cited in Cone, *Spirituals and the Blues*, 82–83.

The deaths of Jane and Isaac James's children are recorded in Wolfinger, "Test of Faith," in *Social Accommodation*, 138: "Two daughters, Mary Ann and Miriam, died in childbirth. A third daughter, Vilate, died in 1897 at age thirty-eight. One son, Silas, died at age twenty-five in 1872 of 'consumption.' Another son, Jessie, died in 1894 at age thirty-seven."

That Isaac James's funeral was held in Jane's home is verified in Wolfinger, "Test of Faith," in *Social Accommodation*, 133.

At the time of her death, Biddy Smith Mason was described as "the richest woman in Los Angeles" (Hayden, "Biddy Mason's Los Angeles," 99). In 1988, the First African Methodist Episcopal (A.M.E.) Church "erected a headstone for her . . . as a founding member of the first Black church in [Los Angeles], a church which is still one of its largest and most influential, especially in the area of social activism in the community" (Hayden, "Biddy Mason's Los Angeles," 98). Mayor Tom Bradley dedicated a plaque to Biddy's honor in a Los Angeles park, and in 1989, "The Power of Place" installed "a major new public art project: 'Biddy Mason's Place: A Passage in Time'—on the site of her old Spring Street Homestead" (Hayden, "Biddy Mason's Los Angeles," 86).

Alice Rowan's precedent-setting time as a schoolteacher in a white school is documented in Carter, *Negro Pioneer*, 20, and in Arrington, "Mississippi Mormons," 51, which says: "One black woman, Alice Rowan . . . became a schoolteacher and taught white children at Riverside. She may very well have been the first black to teach at a white school in the United States."

James Louis Gray, Darius Gray's grandfather, married a biracial woman named Annie Collier.

BIBLIOGRAPHY

Albright, Nathleen. "A Special Destiny." Unpublished reader's theater production.

Allen, James B., and Glen M. Leonard. *The Story of the Latter-day Saints*. Salt Lake City: Deseret Book, 1976.

Arrington, Chris Rigby. "Pioneer Midwives." In *Mormon Sisters: Women in Early Utah*. Edited by Claudia L. Bushman. Cambridge, Mass.: Emmeline Press, 1976. 43–65.

Arrington, Leonard. *From Quaker to Latter-day Saint: Bishop Edwin D. Woolley*. Salt Lake City: Deseret Book, 1976.

———. *Great Basin Kingdom: Economic History of the Latter-day Saints, 1830–1900*. Lincoln, Neb.: University of Nebraska Press, 1966.

———. "Mississippi Mormons." *Ensign*, June 1977, 46–51.

Arrington, Leonard, and Davis Bitton. *The Mormon Experience*. New York: Knopf, 1979.

Baker, Daniel. *A Soldier's Experience in the Civil War*. Long Beach, Calif.: Graves and Hersey, 1914.

Bankhead, Mary Lucile. Interview by Allen Cherry, 11 April 1985. Interview 824, transcript. LDS Afro-American Oral History Project, Harold B. Lee Library, Brigham Young University, Provo, Utah.

Beasley, Delilah. *The Negro Trail Blazers of California*. New York: Negro Universities Press, 1919.

Berlin, Ira, Marc Favbeau, and Steven F. Miller, eds. *Remembering Slavery*. New York: New Press, 1998.

Berrett, William E. "The Church and the Negroid People: Historical Information

Concerning the Doctrine of the Church toward the Negroid People." In John J. Stewart and William E. Berrett, *Mormonism and the Negro*. Orem, Utah: Book Mark, 1960.

Bigler, Henry. Diary, 1846–1850. Special Collections, Harold B. Lee Library, Brigham Young University, Provo, Utah.

Bitton, Davis. *George Q. Cannon: A Biography*. Salt Lake City: Deseret Book, 1999.

Black, Andrew K. "In the Service of the United States: Comparative Mortality among African-American and White Troops in the Union Army." In *The Price of Freedom: Slavery and the Civil War*. Edited by Martin H. Greenberg and Charles G. Waugh. Nashville, Tenn.: Cumberland Press, 2000. 131–44.

"Blacks." *Encyclopedia of Mormonism*. Edited by Daniel H. Ludlow. 4 vols. New York: Macmillan, 1992. 1:125–27.

Blum, Ida. "History Explodes 'Negro Myth.'" *Nauvoo Independent,* December 30, 1965, 1.

Book of Mormon. Salt Lake City: The Church of Jesus Christ of Latter-day Saints, 1981.

Bringhurst, Newell G. "Charles B. Thompson and the Issues of Slavery and Race." *Journal of Mormon History* 8 (1981): 37–47.

———. "Elijah Abel and the Changing Status of Blacks within Mormonism." In *Neither White Nor Black*. Edited by Lester E. Bush Jr. and Armand L. Mauss. Midvale, Utah: Signature, 1984. 130–48.

———. *Saints, Slaves, and Blacks: The Changing Place of Black People within Mormonism*. Westport, Conn.: Greenwood Press, 1981.

Brown, James S. *Life of a Pioneer*. Salt Lake City: George Q. Cannon and Sons Co., 1900.

Brown, John. *Autobiography of Pioneer John Brown*. Edited by John Zimmerman Brown. Salt Lake City: Daughters of Utah Pioneers, 1941.

Burleigh, Harry T. *The Spirituals of Harry T. Burleigh*. Miami: Belwin Mills Publishing, 1984.

Bush, Lester. "Mormonism's Negro Doctrine: An Historical Overview." In *Neither White Nor Black*. Edited by Lester E. Bush Jr. and Armand L. Mauss. Midvale, Utah: Signature, 1984. 53–129.

———. "Whence the Negro Doctrine? A Review of Ten Years of Answers." In *Neither White Nor Black*. Edited by Lester E. Bush Jr. and Armand L. Mauss. Midvale, Utah: Signature, 1984. 193–220.

Byrne, Henry. "James Marshall: Discoverer of Gold." *Society of California Pioneers Quarterly* 1, no. 3 (1924–26): 1–97.

Cannon, Donald Q., and David J. Whittaker. *Supporting Saints: Life Stories of Nineteenth-Century Mormons*. Provo, Utah: Religious Studies Center, BYU, 1985.

Carter, R. Kelso. "Standing on the Promises." In *Amazing Grace: 366 Inspiring Hymn Stories for Daily Devotions*, by Kenneth W. Osbeck. Grand Rapids, Mich.: Kregel Publications, 1990.

Carter, Kate B., comp. *Heart Throbs of the West*. 12 vols. Salt Lake City: Daughters of Utah Pioneers, 1939–51.

———. *Negro Pioneer*. Salt Lake City: Daughters of Utah Pioneers, 1964.

———, comp. *Our Pioneer Heritage*. 20 vols. Salt Lake City: Daughters of Utah Pioneers, 1958–77.

———, comp. *Treasures of Pioneer History*. 6 vols. Salt Lake City: Daughters of Utah Pioneers, 1952–57.

Castel, Albert. *General Sterling Price and the Civil War in the West*. Baton Rouge, La.: Louisiana Press, 1968.

Church History in the Fulness of Times: The History of the Church of Jesus Christ of Latter-day Saints. Rev. ed. Prepared by the Church Educational System. Salt Lake City: The Church of Jesus Christ of Latter-day Saints, 1993.

Coleman, Ronald. "A History of Blacks in Utah, 1825–1910." Ph.D. dissertation, University of Utah, 1980.

Cone, James H. *The Spirituals and the Blues*. New York: Orbis Books, 1991.

Cowan, Richard. *Temples to Dot the Earth*. Salt Lake City: Bookcraft, 1989.

Cowan, Richard, and William E. Homer. *California Saints: A 150-Year Legacy in the Golden State*. Provo, Utah: Brigham Young University, Religious Studies Center, 1996.

Davies, J. Kenneth. *Mormon Gold: The Story of California's Mormon Argonauts*. Salt Lake City: Olympus Publishing, 1984.

Deseret Evening News. Salt Lake City, Utah.

Deseret News (weekly). Salt Lake City, Utah.

Doctrine and Covenants of The Church of Jesus Christ of Latter-day Saints. Salt Lake City: The Church of Jesus Christ of Latter-day Saints, 1981.

Donald, David Herbert. *Lincoln*. London: Random House, 1995.

Eddins, Boyd L. "The Mormons and the Civil War." Master's thesis. Utah State University, 1966.

Family Search File. Utah Valley Regional Family History Center, Harold B. Lee Library, Brigham Young University, Provo, Utah.

First Ward Census. Historical Department, The Church of Jesus Christ of Latter-day Saints, Salt Lake City.

Flake, Carol Read. *Of Pioneers and Prophets*. Privately published, 1974.

Flake, Joel A. Jr. "Green Flake: His Life and Legacy." Unpublished paper for History 490, Brigham Young University, August 11, 1999.

Flake, Osmer. *William J. Flake: Pioneer-Colonizer*. Privately published, 1948.

Freedman's Bank Records. CD-ROM. Salt Lake City: The Church of Jesus Christ of Latter-day Saints, 2001.

Fretwell, Joe. Personal interview with Margaret Young and Darius Gray. December 8, 2000, Fresno, California.

———. Miscellaneous Family Papers on Green Flake. Supplied by Joel A. Flake Jr., Payson, Utah.

Gray, Darius A. Personal genealogical records.

Gudde, Erwin G. *Bigler's Chronicle of the West*. Berkeley and Los Angeles: University of California Press, 1962.

Hanks, Ted L. *Blossom: The Enoch Train and the Edmund Ellsworth Handcart Company of 1856*. Salem, Utah: Ted L. Hanks, 1998.

Hartley, William G. "Saint without Priesthood: The Collected Testimonies of Ex-Slave Samuel D. Chambers." *Dialogue* 12 (summer 1979): 13–21.

———. "Samuel D. Chambers." *New Era*, June 1974, 46–50.

———. Personal communication, 31 July 2001.

———. Personal communication, 1 August 2001.

Hayden, Dolores. "Biddy Mason's Los Angeles, 1856–1891." *Journal of California History* 68 (fall 1989): 91–100.

Hicks, Michael. "Ministering Minstrels: Black Face Entertainment in Pioneer Utah." *Utah Historical Quarterly* 58 (winter 1990): 49–63.

Higginson, Thomas Wentworth. "Negro Spirituals." *Atlantic Monthly* 19 (June 1867): 685–94.

Hinckley, Bryant S. *Heber J. Grant: Highlights in the Life of a Great Leader*. Salt Lake City: Deseret Book, 1951.

Holzapfel, Richard Neitzel, and R. Q. Shupe. *Brigham Young: Images of a Mormon Prophet*. Salt Lake City: Eagle Gate, 2000.

Hull, LeAnne von Neumeyer. *A Story of Bridget "Biddy" Smith Mason: Her Legacy among the Mormons*. Online. Available at <http://ww.ldssocal.org/history/biddymason.htm>. Retrieved July 10, 2000.

Hunt, O. E. "The Ammunition Used in the War." In *The Photographic History of the Civil War*. Edited by Francis Trevelyan Millar. 10 vols. New York: T. Yoseloff, 1957. 5:172–78.

Jenson, Andrew. *Encyclopedic History of The Church of Jesus Christ of Latter-day Saints*. Salt Lake City: Deseret News Publishing, 1941.

———. *Latter-day Saint Biographical Encyclopedia*. 4 vols. Salt Lake City: A. Jenson History Co., 1901–36.

Johnson, Charles, Patricia Smith, and the WGBH Series Research Team. *Africans in America: America's Journey through Slavery*. New York: Harvest-Harcourt Brace & Company, 1998.

Johnson, Jeffery O. "Utah's Negro Pioneers of 1847." Research paper, 1969. Young University, Provo, Utah.

Johnson, Walter. *Soul by Soul: Life Inside the Antebellum Slave Market*. Cambridge, Mass.: Harvard University Press, 1999.

Journal of Discourses. 26 vols. London: Latter-day Saints' Book Depot, 1854–86.

Journal History of the Church. Archives, The Church of Jesus Christ of Latter-day Saints, Salt Lake City.

Johnston, William Preston. *The Life of General Albert Sidney Johnston: Embracing His Services in the Armies of the United States, the Republic of Texas, and the Confederate States*. 1879. Reprint, New York: Da Capo Press, 1997.

Katz, William Loren. *The Black West*. Seattle: Open Hand Publishing, 1987.

Kimball, Edward L., and Andrew E. Kimball Jr. *Spencer W. Kimball*. Salt Lake City: Bookcraft, 1977.

Kohler, Charmain Lay. *Southern Grace: A Story of the Mississippi Saints*. Boise, Idaho: Beagle Creek Press, 1995.

Kynoch, Gary. "Terrible Dilemmas: Black Enlistment in the Union Army during the American Civil War." In *The Price of Freedom: Slavery and the Civil War*. Edited by Martin H. Greenberg and Charles G. Waugh. Nashville, Tenn.: Cumberland Press, 2000. 107–27.

Laugel, Auguste. *The United States During the Civil War*. Bloomington, Indiana: Indiana University Press, 1961.

Layne, J. Gregg. "Annals of Los Angeles." *California Historical Quarterly* 13 (1934): 302–54.

Lewis, Crystal P. "Life Sketch of Duritha Trail Lewis, 1813–1878." Unpublished typescript. In possession of Carol Harless, Los Altos, California.

Lincoln, Abraham. *Abraham Lincoln: Great Speeches*. New York: Dover Publications, 1991.

Lyman, Albert R. *Amasa Mason Lyman: Trailblazer and Pioneer from the Atlantic to the Pacific*. Delta, Utah: Melvin A. Lyman, 1957.

———. *Francis Marion Lyman: Apostle*. Delta, Utah: Melvin A. Lyman, Publisher, 1958.

Lyman, Edward Leo. *San Bernardino: The Rise and Fall of a California Community*. Salt Lake City: Signature Books, 1996.

Lyman, Eliza Maria Partridge. Holographic journal. In Special Collections, Harold B. Lee Library, Brigham Young University. Reprinted in Carter, *Treasures of Pioneer History*, 2:213–85.

McElroy, James. *The Struggle for Missouri*. Washington, D.C.: National Tribune Co., 1909.

McPherson, James M. *Ordeal by Fire: The Civil War and Reconstruction*. New York: Knopf, 1982.

Mills, Marilyn W. Personal interview with Margaret Young. July 19, 2001.

Nauvoo Seventies List: Selections. (Biographical and Genealogical data) from Seventies Records. "Seventies Called or Ordained 1835–1850" (page 1). Historical Department, The Church of Jesus Christ of Latter-day Saints. Salt Lake City, Utah.

Neasham, Aubrey. "Sutter's Sawmill." *California Historical Quarterly* 27 (1948): 109–33.

"Negroes Hung; One Burnt at the Stake." *Staunton Missouri Spectator*, August 2, 1859. Newspaper Transcriptions.

Oshinsky, David M. *Worse Than Slavery: Parchman Farm and the Ordeal of Jim Crow Justice*. New York: Free Press, 1996.

Painter, Nell Irwin. Introduction. *Narrative of Sojourner Truth: A Life, a Symbol*. Edited by Nell Irwin Painter. New York: Penguin Books, 1998.

Phillips, Christopher. *Missouri's Confederate: Claiborne Fox Jackson*. Columbia, Mo.: University of Missouri Press, 2000.

Pratt, Parley P. *Autobiography of Parley P. Pratt*. Edited by Parley P. Pratt Jr. Salt Lake City: Deseret Book, 1938, 1985.

Rea, Ralph R. *Sterling Price: The Lee of the West*. Little Rock, Ark.: Pioneer Press, 1959.

Reid, Richard. "Black Experience in the Union Army: The Other Civil War." In *The Price of Freedom: Slavery and the Civil War*. Edited by Martin H. Greenberg and Charles G. Waugh. Nashville, Tenn.: Cumberland Press, 2000. 79–106.

Relief Society Magazine, January 1948, 8.

"Remembering the Rescue." *Ensign*, August 1997, 38–47.

Roberts, B. H. *A Comprehensive History of the Church of Jesus Christ of Latter-day Saints, Century One*. 6 vols. Salt Lake City: The Church of Jesus Christ of Latter-day Saints, 1930. Reprint, Provo, Utah: Brigham Young University Press, 1965.

———. *The Life of John Taylor: Third President of the Church of Jesus Christ of Latter-day Saints*. Salt Lake City: Bookcraft, 1963.

Savage, W. Sherman. *Blacks in the West*. Westport, Conn.: Greenwood Press, 1976.

Schindler, Harold. *In Another Time: Sketches of Utah History*. [A collection of articles first published in the *Salt Lake Tribune*.] Logan, Utah: Utah State University Press, 1998.

Schlissel, Lillian. *Black Frontiers: A History of African-American Heroes in the Old West*. New York: Aladdin Paperbacks, 2000.

Seifrit, William C. "Charles Henry Wilcken, an Undervalued Saint." *Utah Historical Quarterly* 55 (fall 1987): 308–21.

Skinner, Byron R. *Black Origins in the Inland Empire*. San Bernardino, Calif.: Book Attic Press, 1983.

Slaughter, William W. *Life in Zion: An Intimate Look at the Latter-day Saints, 1820–1995*. Salt Lake City: Deseret Book, 1995.

Smith, Joseph. *History of The Church of Jesus Christ of Latter-day Saints*. Edited by B. H. Roberts. 2d ed. rev. 7 vols. Salt Lake City: The Church of Jesus Christ of Latter-day Saints, 1932–51.

Smith, Lucy Meserve. Journal excerpts in *Women's Voices: An Untold History of the Latter-day Saints, 1830–1900*. Edited by Kenneth W. Godfrey, Audrey M. Godfrey, and Jill Mulvay Derr. Salt Lake City: Deseret Book, 1982. Paperbound ed., 1991. 261–71.

Stegner, Wallace. *The Gathering of Zion: The Story of the Mormon Trail*. Lincoln, Neb.: University of Nebraska Press, 1964.

Stephens, Calvin R. "The Life and Contributions of Zebedee Coltrin." Master's thesis, Brigham Young University, 1974.

Stowe, Harriet Beecher. "Sojourner Truth: The Libyan Sibyl." In *Narrative of Sojourner Truth*. 1850. Reprint, edited by Nell Irvin Painter. New York City: Penguin Books, 1998. 102–17.

Taylor, Margery. Personal interview with Darius Gray. April 12, 2001.

Taylor, Samuel W. *The Kingdom or Nothing: The Life of John Taylor, Militant Mormon*. New York: Macmillan, 1976.

Thirteenth Ward [Ensign Stake] Relief Society Minutes, Oct. 23, 1877. LR 6133 no. 1. Historical Department, The Church of Jesus Christ of Latter-day Saints. Salt Lake City, Utah.

Tingen, James Dwight. "The Endowment House." Paper for History 490, Brigham Young University, December 1974.

Toll, Robert C. *Blacking Up: The Minstrel Show in Nineteenth-Century America*. New York: Oxford University Press, 1974.

Udell, Bertha (a descendant of Green Flake). Personal interview with Joe Fretwell, including accounts of Green Flake's words delivered at Pioneer Appreciation

Day and other events. Contained in Miscellaneous Family Papers supplied by Joel A. Flake Jr., Payson, Utah.

Urwin, Gregory J. "'We Cannot Treat Negroes . . . as Prisoners of War': Racial Atrocities and Reprisals in Civil War Arkansas." In *The Price of Freedom: Slavery and the Civil War*. Edited by Martin H. Greenberg and Charles G. Waugh. Nashville, Tenn.: Cumberland Press, 2000. 233–48.

Van Wagoner, Richard, and Steven C. Walker. *A Book of Mormons*. Salt Lake City: Signature, 1982.

Walker, Ronald W. "Rachel R. Grant: The Continuing Legacy of the Feminine Ideal." In *Supporting Saints: Life Stories of Nineteenth-Century Mormons*. Edited by Donald Q. Cannon and David J. Whittaker. Provo, Utah: Religious Studies Center, BYU, 1985. 17–42.

Whittaker, David. "Polygamy." *Journal of Mormon History* 11 (1984): 43–54.

Williams, Henry L., ed. *Black American Joker: An Inexhaustible Collection of Minstrels' and End-men's Amusing Answers—Bluffs and Bouncers—Comic Catches . . . etc.* Denison's Series, vol. 7, no. 48. Chicago: T. S. Denison, 1897. In *From Slavery to Freedom: The African American Pamphlet Collection, 1824–1909*. Rare Book and Special Collections Division, Library of Congress. Online. Available at <http://frontiers.loc.gov/ammem/aapchtml/aapchome.html>. Retrieved July 17, 2001.

Wolfinger, Henry J. "Jane Manning James: A Test of Faith." In *Worth Their Salt: Notable but Often Unnoted Women of Utah*. Edited by Colleen Whitley. Logan: Utah State University Press, 1996. 14–30.

———. "A Test of Faith: Jane Elizabeth James and the Origins of the Utah Black Community." In *Social Accommodation in Utah*. Edited by Clark S. Knowlton. Salt Lake City: American West Occasional Papers, 1975. 126–72.

Young, Brigham. "Speech by Gov. Young in Joint Session of the Legislature. Feby. 5th 1852 giving his views on slavery." Brigham Young addresses, Ms d 1234, box 48, folder 3. Historical Department, The Church of Jesus Christ of Latter-day Saints. Salt Lake City, Utah.

Young Woman's Journal 16 (1905): 551–53. Also in *LDS Collectors Library* CD-ROM. Salt Lake City: Infobases, 1997.